Agnes Aubert's Mystical Cat Shelter

By Heather Fawcett

The Emily Wilde Series
Emily Wilde's Encyclopaedia of Faeries
Emily Wilde's Map of the Otherlands
Emily Wilde's Compendium of Lost Tales

Agnes Aubert's Mystical Cat Shelter

HEATHER FAWCETT

Agnes Aubert's Mystical Cat Shelter

orbit-books.co.uk

ORBIT

First published in Great Britain in 2026 by Orbit

1 3 5 7 9 10 8 6 4 2

Copyright © 2026 by Heather Fawcett

The moral right of the author has been asserted.

All characters and events in this publication, other than those clearly in the public domain, are fictitious and any resemblance to real persons, living or dead, is purely coincidental.

All rights reserved.
No part of this publication may be reproduced, stored in a retrieval system, or transmitted, in any form or by any means, without the prior permission in writing of the publisher, nor be otherwise circulated in any form of binding or cover other than that in which it is published and without a similar condition including this condition being imposed on the subsequent purchaser.

A CIP catalogue record for this book
is available from the British Library.

HB ISBN 978-0-356-52578-5
C format ISBN 978-0-356-52577-8

Printed and bound in Great Britain by Clays Ltd, Elcograf, S.p.A.

Papers used by Orbit are from well-managed forests
and other responsible sources.

Orbit
An imprint of
Little, Brown Book Group
Carmelite House
50 Victoria Embankment
London, EC4Y 0DZ

The authorised representative
in the EEA is
Hachette Ireland
8 Castlecourt Centre,
Dublin 15, D15 XTP3, Ireland
(email: info@hbgi.ie)

An Hachette UK Company
www.hachette.co.uk

orbit-books.co.uk

For Artemis, of course

CHAPTER 1

I paused on the threshold of the shop to stamp the frost from my boots. It settled on the sills and cobblestones at night now, a fine white fur, as if winter were a great beast who skulked through the city while we slept, leaving bits of pelt behind. At least the snows hadn't arrived yet, which was some relief.

I removed my gloves, surreptitiously checking my sleeves for cat hair. The landlord, an older, narrow man, watched me with an expression of gravity disproportionate to the situation.

"It's a good size," I said, finally giving up the attempt at honesty. The shop was not as bad as some of the others, but even if it were, I was desperate to find something to compliment. I noticed only a little mould in the corners, and no evidence of mice, though it was perhaps half the square footage claimed by the newspaper advertisement.

M. Levasseur smiled, not quite hiding his relief. "It is that," he said. "You will not find anything larger in this neighbourhood, mademoiselle, where folks work hard and learn to make do."

He gave me a pugnacious look, as if readying himself for an

argument. I only smiled, feeling a stab of relief—this suggested that I was not the first to enquire about the place. And now that I had seen it, I could guess which side—landlord or tenant—had been rejected.

"Good location for a charity," he went on. "The Sisters of Salvation have their shop across the square. And Saint-Jean gives free meals almost every day."

"Oh?" I said nervously, pretending to be surprised. On my walk there, I had passed Saint-Jean, a pretty but worn-looking stone church at least a century old, and the Sisters of Salvation, which provided free clothing to those who could not afford any. I had, in fact, made use of both during especially lean years.

A foghorn sounded, and I heard the rumble of ships being unloaded at the river wharves, smelled the mingled algae and soot. I could not help thinking that an isolated location such as this, tucked in amongst warehouses and far from the bustle of the city, was not ideal for my particular needs.

You'll make do, a little voice lectured me. It added in its pessimistic way, *You've been turned down eight times. Stand up straight.*

I adjusted my posture and smoothed the tension in my face, aiming to project the confidence of a seasoned businesswoman. It was more difficult after a long day; my back ached, and on the whole I would have preferred to be at home in a hot bath.

"Why are you moving?" M. Levasseur said bluntly, as if already anticipating an unfavourable reply. He struck me as a frowning sort of man, with the perpetually lowered eyebrows of one who makes a study of disapproval, but nevertheless he seemed to be warming to my presence, and especially to my approval of his property, those abundant eyebrows levitating higher on his pale face.

"I was renting a shop on Rue Sainte-Roseline," I said simply.

"On—" His expression changed. "You weren't *there*? Where it happened?"

I did not want to discuss this. And yet I very much wanted him to feel sorry for me, so I made myself say, "You read about it in the papers, then?"

"Of course. They said a dozen shops were blasted."

"Yes—I'm afraid mine was among the hardest hit. It is, at present, barely habitable. My landlord, Mme. Richard, will verify the particulars."

I opened my folder and removed a piece of paper. On it were a half-dozen references, their names and addresses neatly typed.

"I know her—a good woman." His face, I realized, had reddened a little on my behalf. "Goddamn magicians! Duelling in broad daylight, in the middle of a street full of decent, hardworking folk. But isn't it just like them?"

"Indeed," I said, my throat tightening. "So you understand my haste to move."

"Goddamn magicians!" he said again. Abruptly, he seized my hand and pressed it. "You have my condolences."

Embarrassingly, his concern brought tears to my eyes; I cry as easily as I blush—namely, at the drop of a hat. At the same time, I felt the uncoiling of a familiar resentment, which had long been apt to emerge at the mention of magicians. I didn't like this side of myself, and endeavoured to push the anger down. Anger had always struck me as an impractical emotion, anger at magicians even more so—not that the inequity of their power, and the poor use so many put it to, did not warrant it. And yet if one were to be angry about *that*, one might as well be angry at the whole world.

M. Levasseur took me on a tour of the upstairs apartment,

his manners notably improved. It was as dismal as the downstairs shop, poorly insulated and rather dirty, and the hot water in the bathroom sink barely trickled. But the upstairs was just for me, so I didn't worry over it too much. The bedroom window afforded a view of the St. Lawrence and had a ledge wide enough to accommodate even His Majesty's ample behind. He had a fondness for window ledges, and I could easily picture him there, lazily sunning himself.

"I can see you'll be no trouble," M. Levasseur said as we made our way back downstairs. "I never like arguing with my tenants. Ruins the relationship. Just last week I evicted a woman from an apartment not far from here. She had two children, but did she tell me when she signed the lease? I don't like renting to children—you never know what they'll do to a place. When she fell behind on the rent, it was almost a relief."

"*Ça alors*," I murmured.

He was at least good enough to seem chastened by the look on my face, for he added quickly, "It's a matter of upkeep—maintenance doesn't come cheap. I take my responsibilities seriously, unlike some. You wouldn't believe the stories I hear."

"Any in particular?" I said, because I was beginning to wonder if M. Levasseur's poor opinion of his colleagues might not be taken as a recommendation. And yet the human heart is an eclectic thing, an assemblage of prejudices and affections, and I'd known the man for only ten minutes—how was I to know how the ledger was weighted in his case?

He eyed me, seeming to take my measure. My face is round and frequently red, for reasons sometimes related to emotion and other times to no factor I can identify, which together with my wide-set eyes makes me appear younger than my thirty-five years, as well as earnest and overeager. Élise likes to joke that I look as if I am forever on a mission to sell cookies.

I am unexceptional in every other respect, from my hair—naturally curly, but rather unruly and more pale than it is any specific colour—to my mundane height and figure, but I've found this to be an advantage in dealing with the sort of individuals who resent those who stand out.

"If I had a daughter," he said at last, "I'd warn her away from the place on Rue des Hirondelles, for one. Can't keep a tenant, and no surprise. Something not quite right about the owner. You hear odd stories... Then there's that restaurant in Montgomery Square—the basement floods at least twice a year."

"I appreciate the advice," I said, though I was disappointed it was not more relevant. I wasn't looking to rent a restaurant, and I didn't need to enquire further to know I'd never be able to afford a shop on Rue des Hirondelles. It was odd, though—this was at least the third time in a week I'd heard mention of that particular street. First Élise had suggested we canvass the shops there for donations, then a man handing out flyers had tried to convince me to attend a musical performance at one of the cafés.

I shook my head. A coincidence, no more.

"Let's get started on the application," he said, politely pulling out a chair for me at the rickety table. He drew a wrinkled bundle of papers and a pencil from his vest pocket. "What sort of charity do you run? I don't need specifics, just a general idea. I've got it—you knit sweaters for orphans, *hein*?"

Here was the moment. I steeled myself and said, "It's an—animal charity."

"Ah!" he said. "You raise money for the elephants or some such? I've heard elephants are having a time of it these days."

I had the sense that he had not given much thought to elephants before now. "Not elephants, no. Cats."

"Cats?" he repeated, and never have I seen a look more blank. "What about them?"

Despite the cold, I felt a prickle of sweat along my hairline. I'd practiced the conversation in my head, and yet still I felt it drifting off course and towards the same conclusion the others had. "The city has a large cat population—"

"That it does," he said, frowning. "I had a colony set up shop behind a building of mine. Unsanitary little things. So you take care of them, do you? It's not a bad idea, though they do keep the rats down."

"Ah," I said with a forced laugh. "We—yes, we take care of them. Though not in that way. My organization takes them in, cleans them up, ensures they're adoptable, then tries to find them a comfortable home."

"You take them in?" His blank expression seemed to be slowly transforming into one of horror. "Where?"

I suppose I should have known at this point that the situation was beyond repair, but desperation propelled me to continue, and also I have a tendency to babble when under stress. "Cats are extremely clean creatures. And as companion animals, particularly for the elderly, as well as the ill and infirm—well, their value to society cannot be overstated. Indeed, I once visited a hospital with a resident cat who—"

"You take these animals in," he repeated, more slowly this time. "And you want to house them *here*?"

I swallowed. My silence was answer enough.

"Oh, no," he said. "No, no, no. That will not do."

He stood abruptly, taking the papers and pencil back and tucking them into his pocket, his eyebrows descending to their former latitude.

"Mine is only a small organization—" I began.

"Very good, mademoiselle," he said, giving me a tight smile as he moved towards me, one arm politely extended as he shooed me from the shop with an efficiency that suggested extensive practice. "Best of luck getting your charity off the ground."

"We've been in business for over five years," I said, even as I was swept ever closer to the exit. "My current landlord can—"

"Mind the step," he said, opening the door. And then, with an abruptness that left me breathless, I was standing on the landing, and the door had closed in my face.

CHAPTER 2

I wandered for a time after that, my feet choosing the direction, paying little attention to my surroundings. I believe it was the cold that shocked me out of my daze; the sun had set, and the sky was a wash of navy and violet, the street lanterns flickering to life. I looked up, startled to find myself in the heart of the old city, standing outside a café just beginning to bustle with the evening crowds, men and women in their good hats and coats. Somehow, I was approaching an intersection with Rue des Hirondelles, where there was the shop for rent that M. Levasseur had unnecessarily warned me away from.

At the thought of M. Levasseur—not to mention impossibly out-of-reach rents—I felt my vision grey. I gazed into the café window, which was lightly steamed, many of its confections arrayed in little baskets in easy view of passersby. I must have stared at an egg tart for a solid minute, stomach rumbling, before I reminded myself of my budget—there would be no egg tarts until I found a place to live and work, and perhaps for some time after that, depending on the cost of my new accommodations.

I then spent another period of time staring at a chocolate brioche.

The bells of the basilica began to sound, though it wasn't until the narrow street was filled with their ghostly echoes that I realized the time. I turned from the café and hurried home, avoiding a knot of young people who seemed half drunk already, two of the girls clasping hands and spinning in a circle, laughing, their skirts and coats fanning about them.

It wasn't a long walk from the bustle of the restaurant district, but it felt it. The cobblestones grew more uneven, forcing me to mind my step, and the buildings leaned towards each other. My neighbourhood was mostly working-class apartments made from the customary grey limestone, with the odd grocer or café thrown in; about half were out of business, partly because the tram lines didn't come this far. I stopped outside what should have been an unexceptional little place with dingy stonework and a rusty iron door, but was now quite an eye-catcher, given that two of the windows were shattered, their shutters blackened as if by fire. Between them was what looked a little like a lunar crater, about ten feet wide and imperfectly boarded up—I'd had a terrible time of that because the hole was so jagged and uneven, the scorched stones peeling back on either side as if they'd melted and re-formed. On the door was a sign that read:

Les Amis des Chats—Refuge Animalier
Cat Friends—Animal Shelter

I had not been the worst affected—*that* honour went to the sandwich shop across the street, which had seen all its windows shattered, its foundation cracked, and its door blown backwards into the shop. The owner—an elderly man named Hamad who, despite his gruff and unsmiling demeanour, had routinely brought leftover deli slices for the cats—had been unable to afford the repairs. Now it sat abandoned, empty windows yawning like dark mouths.

I could hear His Majesty yowling at me before I even put my hand on the doorknob. How the beast sensed when I came within fifty feet of the building was a mystery I'd never solved; either he did it by smell or—more likely, knowing His Majesty—some unholy sixth sense.

I unlocked the door, locked it firmly behind me, then pushed through the wooden gate I'd installed beyond the antechamber. His Majesty was coiled about my legs in an instant, loudly protesting the delay in his supper. Banshee, somewhat less intemperate, stood and goggled at me from the middle of the room with her perpetually confounded expression. The shelter cats, who occupied an array of cages in the next room, also began to register their protests, though I knew Élise had been attending to them for most of the afternoon.

"I know," I said, pausing to disentangle His Majesty from my ankles. "I'm sorry—I was distracted by pastry. You wouldn't understand, of course. If it doesn't bleed, it isn't food."

I wiped my feet on the welcome mat, which was embroidered with the shelter's motto, *A cat is the soul of a home,* in French and English, which we also had on our stationery. Then I fed the two of them—His Majesty first, of course; he would accept nothing less.

The black cat had come into my life a year after Banshee had. Despite having essentially wandered into the shelter—I'd opened the back door one morning and found him perched coolly on the step as if waiting for an appointment—he was not even slightly tame, but seemed to have adopted the appearance of being so out of self-interest. An enormous beast with a single white boot, His Majesty ruled the shelter with an iron paw. He disdained the fellowship of other felines but delighted in the role of tyrant, stalking about the shelter cats as if they were little more than furniture and stealing food with impunity, except on the occasions when he decided to make an example of some foolish upstart. He had never been challenged twice.

Naturally, I had never dared attempt to adopt out His Majesty, and as he showed no signs of wishing to move on, I had officially declared him my responsibility, although his entrance into my life had been more akin to a hostile takeover. He was not an affectionate cat, demonstrating a cunning tolerance of petting but little enjoyment, though he had a great fondness for laps, and would stake his claim to mine whenever I took some time for myself with a book, growling low in his throat when I considered putting the book aside. More than once had I been forced to stay up past midnight before the beast deemed his considerable square footage adequately warmed.

Banshee, a nearly round tabby, was perhaps the only cat able to dwell alongside the likes of His Majesty without being terrorized, for Banshee was unterrorizable, not from strength of character but from a complete lack of sense. I doubted Banshee would survive a day if left to her own devices, for she would routinely get herself into impossible danger, clambering up to the rafters or into claustrophobic crawl spaces, whereupon she would become stuck. She demonstrated no awareness that fire was hot, and had made multiple attempts at getting inside the woodstove while it was alight, until Robin had finally built a screen around it. Banshee's most habitual occupation was sitting in the middle of a room and staring fixedly at a single point for no discernible reason. His Majesty, having made a few attempts to frighten her after he moved in—on one occasion pinning her to the floor with his jaws around her neck—seemed to have decided such efforts were beneath him when it came to creatures as pathetic and inexplicable as Banshee. I'd occasionally had the impression that he even pitied her, for he would sometimes deign to allow her to curl up against him, which was not a liberty he allowed any of the shelter cats.

Banshee's name came from her curious voicelessness; never had I heard her make a sound, purring excepted, though she often seemed to be trying, sometimes even wandering about the place opening and closing her mouth in my direction, as if desperate to warn me of some impending doom. Robin and I used to joke that she was, in fact, creating an appalling racket, but that it was a sound that could be heard only by the inhabitants of some unhallowed supernatural realm.

I fed the shelter cats next—we had forty-eight, which was an all-time high and a great strain on our budget, but what could I do? Turn them out, with winter on the horizon?

I paused at Thoreau's cage to give him extra attention. I knew I shouldn't play favourites, but Thoreau, a genteel senior whom Élise had found shivering in a box behind the central train station, had been at the shelter six months, the longest of our charges.

The cat leaned into my hand. Thoreau was a beautiful, gothic grey, and the least demanding of the brood. Given the pitiable state in which we'd found him, from mites to broken ribs to an infected eye, I often had the sense he was still attempting to comprehend how dramatically his existence had been altered.

Clowder was pawing at the bars of her cage with increasing desperation, so I opened the door for her to hop down to the floor. Her four kittens—only about a month old—followed, which I could tell Clowder did not appreciate. She gave me a harried look.

"You're right, I'm sorry," I told her. "You deserve a little holiday, don't you?" I checked that each of the kittens was well, then lifted the lot—two orange tabbies, a tuxedo, and a small calico, like her mother—into the cage and closed the door.

I spent a few moments tidying, shadowed by Clowder and Banshee. Clowder kept a nervous eye on His Majesty, but he was not in the mood to exercise his authority, and was sleeping off his dinner in his favourite chair, tail twitching.

The shelter layout was simple; it had been a tailor's before, which had proven ideal for my purposes—the large back room where the coats and dresses had been worked on was big enough for the cat cages, while the smaller space at the front was all we needed for interviewing prospective adopters. Off the back room was a tiny kitchen. It was as dilapidated as the rest of the shelter, and one could only get it so clean before one's efforts were thwarted by ancient and immovable stains.

The wind picked up, whistling through the hole in the front room. I endeavoured to ignore it.

I had been planning on a meager repast of cheese and tinned soup—between us, Robin had been the chef—but I found that Élise had been to the café on the next street and left me a mushroom pie wrapped in paper. It was still slightly warm.

I stared at it with a mixture of annoyance and despair—how many times had I told Élise I didn't need her to mother me? It wasn't as if she and her husband could support a third person on his meagre city councillor's salary. Élise and I had only what little remained of our parents' inheritance to our names, and I wanted her to keep every penny of her half, not feel the need to support her widowed sister.

My annoyance lasted no more than a moment, though; my stomach was rumbling too insistently. I hadn't eaten since breakfast, and devoured the entire pie standing up. It was buttery and filled with porcini in a warm, spiced cream sauce. Heaven, in other words.

Somewhat rejuvenated, I finished up the evening chores, consulting the clipboard to see what Élise had already taken care of—she made fun of my checklists at every opportunity, but didn't go so far as ignoring them. I freshened the blankets and litter boxes, then added wood to the stove, trying to be as sparing as I could.

Mme. Richard had told me I could take as long as I liked to move out, but we'd both known this to be a hollow kindness with winter on the horizon. Not only was the shelter essentially open to the elements, but our oil heater had been damaged beyond repair, and wood was expensive. My landlady had said she could not afford the substantial—and necessary— repairs any more than Hamad could. So this would become another silent space within the noise and movement of the city, an architectural ellipsis.

I drew a slow breath, trying to push against another wave of anger. Naturally, the police hadn't caught the magicians who'd thought it reasonable to duel in the middle of a city street. Magicians rarely *were* caught when they broke the law, which was not an infrequent occurrence. My impression was that the only thing preventing them from tearing the world apart by the seams was their rarity. Scholars of magic estimated that fewer than one in a million were born with any degree of magical gift, and within this was a great deal of variation. Most could manage only the simplest of charms.

And thank God for that.

"Come, Banshee," I said once the shelter cats were all attended to and shut away again. The tabby, who had been staring at an empty bit of wall in consternation, gave one of her silent yowls and followed me upstairs.

Here there was only one small room below the sloped roof; it had been used as storage before Robin and I moved in five years ago. We'd scavenged two narrow beds from a thrift store, hauling them awkwardly up the old stairs and then pushing them together, giggling all the while. We'd not been married long in those days—not newlyweds anymore, yet often it felt that way.

I'd considered removing the second bed after Robin died, but in the end could not bring myself to part with it. Now the bed was, essentially, the property of His Majesty.

Perhaps I should not have implied that His Majesty disliked all human company. For in truth, he had made an exception for one person in his life, and that was Robin.

I'd never been able to work out what it was about Robin. He loved the cats, but so did I, and he was a noisier person than me, for Robin liked to talk, turning almost every anecdote into a story, and often growing so animated he waved his hands about. Maybe it was his unfailing politeness and good humour, which he extended to the cats, asking Banshee if he could please trim her claws and excusing himself whenever he had to step over someone.

The night after Robin died, His Majesty had refused to sleep, wandering about the shelter and frequently parking himself by the front door, scratching obsessively at it and yowling at me, as if he thought Robin were on the other side, waiting to be let in. Towards dawn, he'd finally curled up on Robin's pillow.

The cat glanced up at me when I entered the bedroom, and I wondered, as I often did, if he had been hoping to see Robin. I sensed a disappointment in his inscrutable feline gaze as he put his head back down, but I may have been imagining it. Perhaps I simply wanted company of sorts.

Now Robin had been gone two years, and even with my penchant for tears I no longer wept over him every night. But it had been a long and lonesome day, and so I allowed myself a bit of a cry. His Majesty stayed curled up on the pillow, by all appearances ignoring me—nevertheless, he was there. Banshee was sympathetic, though this was more distracting than anything else. She kept trying to bat the tears from my face no matter how often I pushed her away, seeming to assume, as she generally did, that the tears were the cause of my distress rather than a product of it, and thus an enemy to be vanquished.

Eventually, I dried my face, wound the alarm on the little brass clock by my bed, and turned out the light. Banshee settled herself between me and His Majesty, and together we slept.

CHAPTER 3

"What sort of shop is it again?" Mathieu asked. "I'm sorry to forget—I have five showings this morning."

"Typing," Élise answered with a breezy smile. "We average around two dozen customers per day. Most come in for letters, but we had an author in last week, didn't we, Agnes? The poor dear—I've never seen handwriting that bad. We're also hoping to start a rental service as soon as we can find a good wholesale price on ink ribbons. There's been such a shortage recently—surely you've heard?"

She chattered on while I did my best not to scowl at her. Since we were children, Élise had taken a disturbing pride in her ability to lie, and went about it with all the commitment and native flair of a songbird announcing the arrival of morning—we'd talked through our story beforehand, but she was inventing most of the details as she went. It was one of her worst qualities, I thought, as my stomach gave an anxious burble.

Though undeniably useful.

The landlord stopped listening halfway through her speech, I estimated, glancing down at his notebook and nodding absently. We stood by the counter of the empty shop—most recently occupied by an accountant—with the autumn light spilling through the window and highlighting the tidy contours of the space, one long rectangle tucked between a cobbler's and a laundering service. It would be cramped for my needs, but I ached for it nonetheless.

Mathieu scribbled a note, then adjusted the unwieldy stack of loose papers tucked into the notebook's binding, a hodgepodge of invoices and building plans. I stifled an urge to reach out and straighten them. How did a person get anything done amidst that sort of disorder?

"When can you move in?" he said once Élise had completed an amusing anecdote about a baker with such an atrocious hand her assistants were forever replacing baking soda with baking salt and applesauce with apple cider.

"As soon as possible," I said, grateful for the opportunity to provide an honest answer. I was not happy with this fabrication of Élise's, which I'd only come round to after days of relentless harping on her part. It was not fair to the landlord, who had the right to know that I would be filling his property with cats.

"You will not survive the winter," Élise had finally said bluntly. "Or *they* won't."

This I could not argue with. Winter did not envelop Montréal so much as attack it. Last year the drifts had covered every square and piled all the way up to the second stories of the stone apartments, so that their inhabitants had donned snowshoes and exited out the windows, sometimes pulling children behind them in sleds.

It was not always like that. Perhaps this winter would be mild.

Perhaps.

"Is there a problem with your present situation?" Mathieu enquired, knitting his eyebrows.

"My shop is on Rue Sainte-Roseline," I said. "The damage was substantial. We cannot remain there."

He frowned. "I didn't know there was a typist's on Rue Sainte-Roseline. My aunt lives by the park on the corner."

"Ah, but that's no surprise," Élise said in a rueful voice while shooting me a brief, murderous glare. Élise looked a great deal like me, only prettier, with an elven delicacy about her features that most found universally charming, and she generally took the lead in any negotiations we undertook—when we were little, this had included arguing for larger desserts—because she had more success than I did. I did not resent her for this, nor did she lord it over me; we'd simply accepted that this was the way it was for us.

"I'm afraid we're dreadful at marketing," she continued with a self-deprecating grimace. "We don't even have a sign on the door! Our clients know us by word of mouth."

The landlord smiled politely. "Well, I'll send word by Friday at the latest—do you have a telephone?"

We assured him that we did—in fact, it was Gabriel's office number on the application, but he would do nothing but grumble about being made to play secretary again until Élise appeased him with a kiss, at which point the grumbling would cease.

We exited the building, and Élise and I waited while the landlord locked up. The rent on any shop off Charlotte Square was above my budget—far above—but there was nothing for it. I would just have to find a way to increase our donations. If I didn't, well—I was going to be evicted anyway. Ruthlessly, Élise had calculated that even if Mathieu discovered our deception after I moved in—highly likely—it would take six months or more to actually evict me: the present backlog for hearings at the tenancy tribunal.

Mathieu turned to shake our hands as my stomach gave another lurch, rumbling away in an embarrassingly loud manner. All this deception! I was not made for it, and Élise knew it. She gave me another steely look as I took Mathieu's hand, as if preparing herself to interject should my conscience tear a last-minute confession from me.

The man must have heard my stomach going off, or perhaps it was something else about me that softened his expression as he released my hand. "I'm sorry you've been forced to move," he said. "That must have been something, though. To be so close to such a powerful enchantment! Did you get a look at the magician who cast it?"

This remark—or rather, the enthusiasm with which he said it—rendered me temporarily speechless. Élise came to my rescue. "Fortunately not. Have you an interest in magic?"

He gave an embarrassed huff of laughter. "I'm afraid so," he said. "I'm sorry—I've been a bit obsessed with magicians since I was a boy. Can't enchant anything myself," he added ruefully. "Not for lack of trying. But I follow their doings in the papers. Including the Witch King—I wondered if he might have been behind the explosion in Rue Sainte-Roseline. Something of that scale, you know—and they say he's in New York now." Mathieu looked both disturbed and excited at the prospect. "New York isn't far, is it? Only a few hours by train."

"Not far at all," I agreed. Havelock Renard, first called the Witch King by those who wished to insult him—the epithet had over the years acquired a darker and almost mythic resonance, like Baba Yaga or Bluebeard—was thought to be the unofficial leader of the worst class of magician: namely, those who romanticized apocalyptic displays of magic. "And nowhere near far enough."

"I'm sorry," he said, a flush reddening his dark skin. "Please understand; I'm not one of those ghoulish hero-worshippers. His power is extraordinary—in an appalling way, of course."

I opened my mouth to argue that *appalling* was, if anything, an understatement, but Élise calmly cut in. "Yes, and the rest of us can only hope none of the others are inspired to bring about the end of the world. Goodness! Just because Renard failed three years ago doesn't mean he will the next time he tries—him or the next power-mad lunatic."

"Well, we don't know for certain that was his plan," Mathieu said with the air of someone about to launch into a familiar line of argument. "One can't believe everything in the nursery rhymes."

"'Hair full of spiders, / Eyes like twin fires'?" Élise said. "Is that not one of the songs children sing about him? I'd believe worse about Havelock Renard."

Mathieu fiddled with his pen. "I'd like to offer you the place. I'll have a chat with Hamad. I'm sure he—"

"With who?" Élise said sharply.

"Hamad El-Koury. Surely you've met him? He ran that sandwich shop on Rue Sainte-Roseline, and he's an all-round excellent fellow. If he can vouch for you, then you needn't look any further. I'll even waive the deposit—it's only fair. You've not done anything to deserve this—unfortunate turn of events."

"That's awfully kind," Élise murmured, even as I saw her brow knit slightly as she scrambled to think our way out of this. Oh, Hamad would vouch for me, certainly—as the responsible, highly organized, and neighbourly owner of a well-run cat shelter. My head began to ache, and I was abruptly aware of how little I had been sleeping.

"Good, good," Mathieu said, smiling. "Then I can—"

"Thank you," I interrupted. "But you needn't trouble Hamad. I've thought it over, and it seems the place is too small for our needs. I appreciate your time."

I walked away, leaving Élise and Mathieu staring after me.

CHAPTER 4

My sister caught up to me at the fountain in Charlotte Square, where I had collapsed upon the stone seat, wiping tears from my eyes. I was trying to do so circumspectly, so as not to cause a scene, but nevertheless a couple seated a few feet away were eyeing me with concern.

"None of that," Élise said irritably, pulling me into her arms. I knew she was not irritated with me, of course, but with the general situation. Despite being two years younger, Élise had often acted as the older sister when we were children, likely because she had the advantage of height. This had commonly taken the form of her holding my hand and marching me through the streets whenever we went out, bossily instructing me to stay close to her at all times, as if her additional inches came with a protective magic that I lacked.

"Listen," she said, drawing back to look me in the eye. "After you stormed off, Mathieu told me about a place by the port that will be vacant next month. I'll go and make enquiries."

"You'll only have to lie again," I said, wiping at my eyes and willing myself to stop blubbering.

"Yes, and it will be easier without you standing there looking at me like I've insulted our mother," she said. "If we strike out again, I'm going to ask Gabriel for help."

"He doesn't have time," I argued, which wasn't the real problem, and we both knew it. Gabriel was up for reelection in the spring, and the race was far too close for comfort. If any whiff of scandal made it into the papers—and arm-twisting landlords to help his sister-in-law's charity would certainly qualify—it could be the end of his career.

Élise didn't bother to argue. "If only your Mme. Richard weren't such an insufferable miser," she said. "She could afford the repairs, but she's happy for the excuse to sell the place for redevelopment."

"You don't know that," I protested. My landlady was a cantankerous sort, but beneath it was a kind heart. "She's allowing me to stay as long as I need, at half the rent."

"Oh, Agnes," Élise said, gazing at me with fond exasperation. "Your shop has a wall missing! Of course she's allowing you to stay—who else would want the place? She shouldn't be charging any rent at all, the villain. Have you forgotten the leak in the roof, which she refuses to fix?"

"She's getting on, Élise," I pointed out. "It can't be easy, keeping up these old buildings."

Élise groaned. "If you say one more sympathetic word about that woman, I'll push you into the fountain," she said. "Look, I'll stop by yours this evening. Will you promise to take the day off? You've been working flat out for weeks."

"I can't," I said. *There's only me*, I thought, but didn't say. I didn't want Élise to feel guilty that she could not be of more help. We'd had this argument—about my overworking myself—too many times for anything productive to come of it.

She sighed, gave me another quick embrace, then bustled off. Élise seemed to be always bustling off somewhere these days—as Gabriel's campaign manager, she was needed at his side as often as I needed her at the shelter.

I wandered away from the fountain, thinking that I might take the tram to the library—I could check the rental listings yet again. But I was so lost in thought that I must have taken a wrong turn, which I didn't notice until I found myself in Rue des Hirondelles.

"You again," I muttered. Why on earth did I keep ending up here? Was some higher power determined to torment me?

A sort of reckless spite filled me—it had no particular object, unless it was myself—and I decided I might as well take a look at the place M. Levasseur had warned me against, though I'd be unable to afford it, no matter how disreputable the owner. What else did I have to do?

Nothing at all, apart from return to the shelter and stare at the hole in the wall, I thought. I let out a strangled chuckle, and a man walking in the other direction started and gave me a wider berth.

Rue des Hirondelles was a narrow street flanked by walls of greystone buildings with tall windows, each made up of several dozen small panes, the uppermost of which shone gently in the afternoon light. Only a narrow strip of sky was visible between the French mansard roofs, but despite the cramped proportions, I'd always found the street's character charming, on the rare occasions I chanced this way; there was something tucked-away about it, like a jewel box that unfolds to reveal layers of hidden pockets and drawers. The cobblestones rambled up a small hill, at the top of which was an old stone church with glowering gargoyles and glittering stained glass. The overhanging greenery from the window boxes seemed well tended. Near the midway point was a little square, too small for an official name. This had a pretty row of silver maples along one side with benches underneath, and a rather noisy café—La Fin, which kept late hours—whose tables took up half the square.

It was not a wealthy neighbourhood, though the larger-than-average proportions of its shops and the rarity with which they went up for rent put it beyond what I could afford. Most of La Fin's customers, I noted, were sailors, factory workers, and other hardy folk; I saw only sensible hats and well-worn shoes among the passersby, and there were some—perhaps heading for the soup kitchen just past the square—who seemed to have fallen on hard times. But the street and its inhabitants had the air of being well cared for, somehow, in a way that went beyond its basic tidiness, but which I could not fully articulate.

I walked up the street and then down again, pausing before another bakery selling—to my dismay—chocolate brioche. A few of the shops were closed that day, but I noticed none that seemed vacant, nor any advertising a vacancy. Either M. Levasseur had been mistaken or the place had been snapped up already.

I paused just above the square to squint through the window of a store that seemed devoted solely to scarves and had its sign turned to *Fermé*. The curtains were drawn, so I could only peer through the square of greenish glass in the door. Something about it piqued my curiosity—perhaps it was only that this end of the street was older, but the shadows seemed to have more weight, which gave the shop a haunted air.

Next door was an unkempt little bookshop. Despite the disorderly display window and teetering book-towers upon the table out front, there was something inviting about it.

I ducked inside, setting the bell jangling. The noise, however, did little to disturb the shop's only occupant, an older woman napping in a chair behind the counter. The shop was narrow and stuffed with crowded shelves illuminated by warm lamplight.

"Madame?" I said.

The woman's eyes twitched open, and she blinked at me for a moment. "I'm sorry, miss," she said in English. She was a small person neatly encased in colourful homemade knitwear, from her sweater to her hat to the blanket over her knees. "I can barely pay my own salary here. You might try La Fin."

It took me a moment to realize what she meant. Glancing down at my briefcase and the notebook tucked under my arm, which was neatly divided by cardboard tabs, I quickly added, "Oh, no—I'm not looking for work. I was wondering about the place next door."

The kindness in her eyes was abruptly replaced by wariness. "Well, what are you doing here, then? They're not closed. *That* place never closes. Do you not know the way?"

I could make no sense of this. "I heard there was a shop for rent in the neighbourhood," I said slowly, noting that her knuckles had gone white against the arm of her chair.

"And where did you hear that?" she said. "From one of *them*?"

"Ah," I said inarticulately. Though I am fluent in English, it is not my first language, and when a conversation does not follow the expected pattern, I tend to flounder. I was beginning to wonder if the woman was entirely well.

She leaned forward and fixed me with a sharp look. "If you don't know what I mean," she said, each syllable clipped and precise, "then turn around, and look elsewhere. There are plenty of places for rent in this city. Wholesome places. If you *do* understand me, then I must kindly ask you to leave. I don't want trouble—can't afford it."

She lifted herself to her feet with the aid of a cane and carefully navigated her way through the shelves, then disappeared into what I assumed was a back room.

I gazed after her, sifting through what she had said. Only one thing was clear: the shop next door was indeed the one I sought. I wondered if she had some conflict with the landlord—disputes between neighbours could be bitter indeed.

It was a mundane explanation, and I wished I could believe it. The truth was, though, that even if the woman had informed me that bloodcurdling screams could be heard emanating from the shop in the dead of night, I still would have made my enquiries. This likely sounds absurd, akin to the follies of silly fairy-tale heroines who cannot stop themselves unlocking doors they have been expressly told not to open, but the fact those stories often leave out is that paying heed to vague warnings is the prerogative of those comfortably situated in life.

I went to the scarf shop and rapped upon the door. Whatever the woman thought, the place was definitely closed. I half expected the door to creak open and some ghostly hand to beckon me in, but there was only a little silence, followed by the sound of perfectly ordinary footsteps approaching, and then the door was pulled back to reveal a young man.

He was in his early twenties, perhaps, with longish dark hair, olive skin, and a rather worried expression. He smiled at me with a warmth that implied I was a much pleasanter alternative to whatever visitor he had been anticipating.

"How are you?" he said. "I don't believe we've met—Yannick Abrams, hello. Were you looking for anything in particular? Do come in—rather blustery, isn't it? You don't need to knock, you know; just walk right in."

This was all said in a single breath, and, thoroughly perplexed, I murmured my thanks and allowed him to usher me into the shop.

I was confronted by a large echoing space with walls of brick and floors of fog-coloured flagstones. I saw instantly that it was a historic building, the floors nearly medieval in appearance, like those dating to the city's founding, whilst the windows were arched in the late-eighteenth-century style and the brickwork was perhaps half a century old. It was a layered sort of antiquity, like an archaeological site, and I wondered how many shops the place had held over the generations. It was mostly empty, but in a way that suggested it had been ransacked rather than tidily packed away. A few chairs and delicately carved tables were scattered haphazardly along the walls, one piled with brightly coloured scarves, another with wooden hangers. The counter by the front windows held an old cash register with the sort of oversized keys that clacked alarmingly when pressed. The helter-skelter appearance of the place was emphasized by the uneven light—the heavy curtains were drawn, and only an oil lantern burned on one of the tables, which threw strange shadows.

I frowned. What had Yannick been doing before I knocked—sitting alone in the dark?

At the rear of the shop, near a door that must have led to a back room, was a large and inexplicable oven built into the stone wall, which made me wish I had not just been thinking of fairy tales.

Yannick was adjusting the neat suit he wore in a fidgety sort of way, as if he were not much used to wearing one. "What were you hoping to find?" he said.

An oddly phrased question. "I'm sorry," I said. "Perhaps I was misinformed, but I understood this place was for rent."

His face went through a remarkable series of transformations at that—startled, then comprehending, then dubious, and then, abruptly, delighted. I almost wanted to laugh, wrong-footed as I felt, for I'd never met a person who better exemplified the phrase *like an open book* than this Yannick Abrams.

"Ah!" he said. "You have a shop! Yes, we do have a vacancy—we *are* vacant, I mean. Yes. What sort of things do you sell?"

This was asked with an air of desperation, as if to distract from his odd reaction. I said, too discomfited to be anything but blunt, "Well—cats, in a sense. I run a charitable organization that rescues and rehabilitates street cats, then offers them up for adoption. Our goal is to eventually put an end to the unhoused population living in the city, if we can drum up the resources. We have a small staff—it's mostly my sister and me, as well as the odd volunteer."

"How lovely," he said, and I watched as the thoughts churned in his head before my very eyes. Oddly, he'd had no discernible reaction to *cats*, but *charitable organization* had elicited a definite spark of excitement. "Have you been in business long?"

I gave him an overview of the history of Les Amis des Chats, making sure to mention my many positive references as well as the docile dispositions of our current wards, all the while waiting for the other shoe to drop. He listened with a pleasant smile, clearly occupied with some internal conversation.

"You are the landlord, yes?" I enquired when I'd come to my conclusion.

"The landlord?" he repeated. "Oh, no. I'm his—his representative."

This was said with such transparent delight at having come up with a suitable response that I almost felt sorry for him, even as my unease ballooned. Had no one ever told the man that his thoughts were as obvious as a smudge of food at the corner of his mouth?

"Would you care for a tour?" he said eagerly.

"I—" *No, thank you,* said a wise little voice, which I ignored. "Might I ask the rent first?"

"Of course!" And he named a sum less than half that of M. Levasseur's rate.

I blinked at him. "Per week?"

"Per month." He looked suddenly worried—or, rather, more worried, for there was an ambient anxiety about him. "It's on the low side, I know—but you see, we've had difficulty keeping tenants. The last one—an importer of scarves from around the world—left without notice. The one before that was a baker who couldn't even be bothered to take his pies with him. We found them still in the window display one morning, and no trace of the man himself."

"I see," I said again. Well, at least the bakery explained the oven. I hoped.

"Come, come," he said, all smiles again. I trailed after him as he led the way to the back of the shop, waving his hand at the scarves and informing me that they would all be packed away before I moved in. The flagstones were so uneven that I felt as if I were attempting to keep my balance on a ship at sea. I could not help goggling at the amount of floor space—we could comfortably house at least ten more cages and still have space enough for volunteers and visitors to circulate without tripping over one another.

I paused by the witch-like oven, starting as a waft of some buttery scent reached my nose. Croissants, perhaps, or shortbread? Hadn't Yannick said the baker had been *before* the scarf merchant?

"Do you still use that?" I enquired.

Yannick blinked at the oven, then gave it an odd, irritable frown. "No. We should have it bricked up, actually. It's just in the way."

Through the door at the back was a little sitting room with a couch, writing desk, and bookcase. The windows overlooked a narrow alley, beyond which was Parc Saint-Aimé, a square of gardens and trees, its single path lined with lanterns. A large portion of the room was taken up by a gaudy Persian rug.

"The trapdoor is under there," Yannick informed me, smoothing the edge of the rug, which was folded over, with his foot. "I wouldn't try it—the basement hasn't been maintained, and it's quite unsafe. Mould everywhere—rats too. Massive rats! You know how these old buildings can be."

From this I immediately understood that if indeed the place was haunted by ghosts or worse, the basement was their domain.

"Don't worry," I said with absolute sincerity, for I was not quite so foolish as a fairy-tale heroine. "I have no interest in exploring."

He beamed at me.

We went up the spiral staircase, another relic of a bygone era, but not of the charming variety: it had no railing and was so narrow as to create a forbidding darkness. The upstairs apartment, however, was cozy and welcoming. The floor was a scuffed parquet and the place smelled of must and cobwebs, but there was nothing wrong with it that a good airing wouldn't fix. A narrow hall divided two bedrooms—both spacious and clean—from a large reception room with intimidating ceilings and elegant wainscot, casement windows so tall I counted at least two dozen panes in each before I stopped counting, and a little balcony overlooking the park. The crimson armchairs looked ancient, but in an expensive way, the sort I could picture long-dead aristocrats lounging upon.

"It's rather dusty," Yannick said, frowning critically. "I'll ensure it's cleaned before you move in."

He showed me the kitchen, which was small, and the bathroom, which contained exposed pipes that clanked and shuddered alarmingly when I turned on the water, and there was no electricity up here, only oil heaters and candlesticks, but it was otherwise night and day compared to M. Levasseur's property—as well as thoroughly, ridiculously opulent. I could not help gaping at everything.

"I apologize for that," Yannick said as the pipes continued to clank. He grasped one and gave it a slight shake. "I may have an en—I mean, I may be able to fix this. Or, rather, a plumber will. Yes, I'll have a plumber take a look before you move in."

I made no reply. I'd grown quiet as we moved from room to room, my unease deepening to something closer to panic. I'd been hoping all along that I would find an explanation—any explanation, even a terrible one. Perhaps the shop had been inhabited by a successful murderer, one who made furniture out of his victims' bones. Perhaps it was infested with foot-long cockroaches immune to all traps and poisons devised by mankind. But as the moments passed, and neither repurposed skeletons nor monstrous insects showed signs of materializing, my anxiety grew and grew.

"There you have it!" Yannick said when we returned to the main floor, where the fall sunlight streamed invitingly through the antique windows, and outside, a cart laden with flowers for the florist's trundled over the cobblestones like something out of a postcard. I remembered quite clearly that the curtains had been closed when we'd gone upstairs, and also that I'd heard no one come in the door.

"What do you think?" he said.

He watched me, his gaze full of suppressed but perfectly transparent eagerness, and I gazed back, at a loss. The place was perfect, yes—terribly, ominously perfect, and my every instinct told me to thank Yannick politely, walk out of the shop, and never return. I felt as if I were being drawn towards something dark and inexorable, like a leaf nearing a cataract. I could do it, of course—simply turn and walk out the door. Return to the shelter in Rue Sainte-Roseline and attend to the cats and my checklists. Resolve to pick up the search again tomorrow, to find another shop where the landlord would close the door in my face, or apologize with a regretful sigh. And then repeat the process the following day, and the day after that, until winter arrived and there were no doors left to try.

I turned back to Yannick. "When can I move in?"

CHAPTER 5

It took perhaps ten minutes for me to decide I'd made a calamitous error.

No, that isn't quite correct—I'd known all along I'd made a calamitous error, but had chosen to see this as a lesser calamity than homelessness. But was it? As I made my way through the gathering twilight, I stopped a half-dozen times, on the threshold of going back to tell Yannick that, in fact, the place would not do for a cat shelter.

My main concern was magic.

It was the curtains that had made me think of it, as well as Yannick's clear desperation to find someone—anyone—to rent the place. I strongly suspected that the shop had been home to a magical tenant before—perhaps it had even been the baker, who had pressed his spells into his tarts and loaves. I didn't know if this was possible—like most, I understood little of magic, as magicians were not exactly forthcoming about their trade—but everyone knew that spells were attached to physical objects. Magicians did not wield magic so much as summon it from some mysterious otherworld and bind it to our own, via vessels they called Artefacts. Anyone could *cast* a spell, which merely involved speaking a word to release the magic from its vessel, be that a pendant or ring, book or decanter. Doing so was dangerous, though, because spells cast by mere mortals were far more likely to go awry than those cast by magicians, sometimes even causing the death of the spellcaster.

That didn't stop people from wanting Artefacts, of course. And it was for this reason that the trade of such Artefacts was illegal in Montréal and most other civilized places. It was said that a small number of shops still operated in secret, though no doubt some were run by charlatans eager to prey upon the foolish or desperate.

I found myself increasingly convinced that I'd hit upon the most likely explanation. The place had been a magic shop at some time or other, and the magician had left behind some curse, or curses perhaps, so terrible that nobody would remain there long. Perhaps the banister transformed into a hungry snake at the stroke of midnight. Perhaps the cash register put warts on your fingers. It was also possible that nothing was actually wrong with the place, but that its reputation alone was enough to keep most sensible tenants away.

I had come to a stop for probably the tenth time, just outside a restaurant, its windows steamed and glowing as the lilt of a violin drifted through the door, certain that I would turn around. Naturally, that was when I saw him.

He was only an insignificant shape to my eye at first, small and pale, a discarded sheaf of paper, possibly, crumpled by the wind. But then the shape moved, and the light caught in his eyes.

He was three months old, I guessed, not yet full-grown but lacking the bumbling locomotion of early kittenhood. He was slender as a shadow, and quite afraid of me, but despite his fear he came to me immediately when I crouched down, which told me all I needed to know.

I looked around, wondering if there would be siblings, and eventually I found one—black, in contrast to her grey-and-white brother, tucked into a crevice in the back stairs of the restaurant. Someone had been feeding them, but sporadically. I waited for maybe an hour by the steps to see if the mother would return, though I already knew she would not. These two were not the first cats I'd found in such a situation.

Finally, my hands thoroughly chilled and my stomach rumbling insistently—the smells emanating from the restaurant were torturous—I gathered up the pair as best I could, tucking them into the large pockets I'd sewn inside my coat for this very purpose—pockets that, when occupied, led all those who crossed my path to assume I was at least slightly mad, or perhaps a magician myself, the storybook kind who used familiars to do their bidding. She struggled a little, but he did not, curling himself into a warm lump against my chest.

My coat emitted only a few growls on the way home, during which I gave no further thought to the shop in Rue des Hirondelles, nor did I continue my agonized internal debate. There was no longer any point.

CHAPTER 6

The key Yannick had given me fit neatly into the lock, which made me start. It seemed that it should have snapped off in my hand, or simply refused to turn, and I realized that I still hadn't come to believe I'd been offered the shop, or perhaps that I'd accepted it. I pushed the door open and then simply stood there, squinting into the shadows. It was an hour before sunrise, but much of the city was awake, and several passersby eyed us as they hastened to their destinations, their collars turned up against the autumn chill.

Élise did not share my hesitation and stepped past me as I dawdled on the threshold, her heels clicking smartly. Within, we found the shop much as I'd seen it the previous week, its weary opulence and echoey proportions, the scarves scattered about like discarded magic tricks. The place still had the smell of baking, something with nutmeg and cardamom this time.

I turned to find Élise pivoting slowly around on her heel with her lips parted, blinking as if she'd just awoken from sleep.

"Well!" she said, and then seemed unable to say any more.

"Well," I agreed.

"It seems haunted, doesn't it?" she continued, after another moment had passed, during which we simply stared about us like two field mice who'd taken a wrong turn and found themselves in a king's garden. "Though I can't say why."

I knew what she meant. It wasn't just the age of the shop, the centuries visible in the grooved flagstones—the city had plenty of old buildings. There was a palpable presence that seemed especially pronounced in the darker corners, as if the shadows were *aware,* and watchful. Something creaked below—likely nothing, merely the arthritic restiveness of an old building, and yet it was difficult not to shiver.

"The cats," Élise said, a question in her voice.

"Won't notice the difference between this and a hovel," I finished. "So long as they're warm and fed."

This seemed to steady her, and she nodded. "We'd best get to work, then."

And so we did.

Our first day in the former bakery passed in such a blur that I could scarcely remember it afterwards. We spent most of it elsewhere, packing up the last few boxes at the old shelter and hauling everything across the city. Mina, currently our sole volunteer, arrived after lunch to assist with all the bustling and turmoil that accompanied moving into any place.

Mina was a hard worker but difficult to get to know; she spoke little and rarely about herself. As a child she'd been in foster care, living in more homes than she'd had birthdays before ending up on the streets and then in custody after a string of petty thefts. She'd come to us initially for her community service, but hadn't stopped returning once she'd worked it off. I was proud of her now, for she had a small place of her own and a spot at the local university, where she was studying to be a historian. Élise and I overlooked the rare occasions when we noticed the donation money was a little short; I had seen the building where Mina lived, and anyway we would have paid her if we could have afforded it.

I awoke the following morning to a sensation akin to being stretched in multiple directions at once. As it turned out, transporting fifty-two disgruntled cats and their various accoutrements from one neighbourhood to another was not the easiest of tasks. We'd been able to hire a horse and wagon for an hour to move the heaviest items, but the three of us had still needed to make a half-dozen trips each, navigating narrow lanes and uneven cobblestones while laden with boxes and suitcases, and I suspected my back would be sore for another day or two. To make matters worse, it had been raining, and the cats had spent the rest of the day sulking in their cages as their fur dried into uneven waves. One item that was always in short supply at the shelter was blankets, a problem compounded by the rain—they had gotten as wet as the cats during transit.

His Majesty sat at the foot of the bed, glaring at me. He had additional cause to resent me, for we'd had to leave most of our furniture behind. I'd placed Robin's pillow next to mine in the new bed, a creaky four-poster that had come with the apartment, but the cat was unappeased.

"I'm sorry," I said. I was not entirely certain I was speaking to His Majesty. I lay there for a while, gazing at the ceiling.

But cats were at liberty to wallow in their misfortunes; I had to go to work. Determinedly shoving aside the image of Robin's bed sitting in the dark back at the old place, I made myself get up and prepare for the day, pulling on my favourite periwinkle blouse and wool skirt, and even taking the time to wrestle my hair into a tidy braid.

I exited my bedroom cautiously, starting a little when

the floorboards creaked underfoot, feeling like a burglar who must disguise my movements. The bedroom across the hall contained a dressed bed and wardrobe, but it was full of shadows, the heavy curtains drawn. I wondered who had lived there—had the baker had an assistant?

The basilica was announcing half seven as I made my way carefully down the stygian staircase and into the shop, where the autumn light streamed reassuringly through the mullioned windows and Élise and Yannick were already bustling about the echoing space, which was now crowded with boxes.

"Breakfast is on the counter," Élise called from the cages we'd stacked against the south wall, where she was tipping food into Thoreau's bowl. Yannick was dangling a bit of string for Marmalade, one of Clowder's kittens. He gave a delighted laugh when the cat missed the string and pounced on his hand instead, kicking impotently with his tiny back legs.

"Ah," I said, staring at him. "Did you need something?"

He rose, looking flustered. "Yes—I mean, no. My apologies if I'm interfering. I only thought I'd drop by to lend a hand. If you need it."

"We certainly do," Élise said, giving Yannick a smile that made the young man blush. I went to the counter to apply myself to the breakfast Élise had purchased, wood-fired bagels wrapped in paper, which I guessed she'd obtained from the bakery down the street. When I returned, Yannick was on his hands and knees with a basin of water beside him, scrubbing one of the cages.

I gave Élise a look. "You shouldn't smile at him like that," I muttered. "He isn't used to you."

Élise only shrugged and replied, "If ever I have the chance to trade a few smiles for clean cages, I'll take it," with her usual ruthless pragmatism.

I was unsettled for most of the morning, feeling both too busy and at loose ends. I suppose that's to be expected in a new environment, but also I was still waiting for some curse to fall upon me.

I quieted my anxiety as I always did: by putting things in order.

There is no better balm for the cares and tribulations of life, I've found, than throwing oneself into the organization of one's environment. I went through the boxes; sorted the file folders of receipts from the last quarter, which had become horribly jumbled in transit; directed Élise in the unpacking of food and supplies; swept the floor and wiped dust from the sills and sconces; and generally put our new shelter to rights. And if none of this did anything to solve our larger problems—the ominous mystery that the shop presented, the constant precarity of our finances—nor lighten my lingering melancholy, still I felt, looking about the place, which now contained only a single stack of boxes and crates, as if I'd created a little harbour for myself in which I might take shelter from any storm.

"Is your former tenant returning for her scarves?" I asked Yannick. I was running my hand over one, unable to help myself. They were the finest garments I'd ever touched, the cashmere as soft as new-fallen snow. Many were woven with threads of actual silver or gold, which lent them a weight that was pure wealth. A few were trimmed with cream-coloured pearls.

"Ah—no," Yannick said. "I was planning to donate them to charity. But you're welcome to wear them, if you like."

I glanced back at the scarves. Banshee had hopped onto the table and was kneading one patterned with some sort of aristocratic hunting scene, dogs baying at a fox in a tree. "Charity," I repeated.

And with that, our blanket shortage was solved.

Absolutely nothing strange or magical happened that morning. As expected, we struggled to find the supplies we needed, for they were still packed away or stored in unfamiliar places. As we cleaned and organized, though, the shop seemed to brighten, as if it were waking up. The uncanny shadows weren't banished, but they retreated farther into the corners. Banshee followed me from room to room, yowling as if another apocalypse were nigh, though I knew she was merely protesting the size of her breakfast.

"You're on a diet," I scolded her. Banshee, despite my careful rationing of her food, gained a pound with each passing year, and her white stomach had reached a queenly circumference. I suspected His Majesty was abetting her somehow, perhaps by allowing her his leftover mice. The black-and-white cat killed for sport, not sustenance.

We hung the sign upon the door and decided we might as well open for the day. Though I hadn't yet worked out how to use the cash register, I doubted our new neighbours would be beating down the door with donations.

It wasn't long before we had our first visitors, a young couple with a child who fell instantly and irrevocably in love with a pair of Clowder's kittens. Delighted by this unexpected success, I waived the fee, which was more of a suggested donation anyhow, and they left the shelter with a delighted child and two additions to their family, while Clowder seemed only too pleased to have her burden lightened.

"Back down to forty-eight," I muttered to myself with a smile. I wasn't just happy that the kittens had found a good home; two fewer cats meant two fewer mouths to feed. Given the state of our finances, it would come as a great relief if we could reduce our charges to a more manageable number.

The sky cleared after lunch and golden light streamed through the windows. The rumble of horse-drawn carts and the occasional automobile outside formed a pleasant backdrop—this part of the city was much more bustling than Rue Sainte-Roseline. Banshee claimed a patch of floor lit by a sunbeam, rolling onto her back and generally behaving as if she'd forgotten she'd changed locations, which was entirely possible. The shelter cats had nestled into their new blankets with pleasure, and looked entirely ridiculous set against the gold thread and costly wool, though naturally they displayed only self-entitlement and had already put rents in more than one scarf. The only exception was Thoreau, who had sniffed the glittering scarf I offered him with suspicion before returning to his well-worn flannel bed.

I began, for the first time, to feel optimistic about our prospects. Had all my anxieties been nothing more than an overactive imagination, fuelled by my recent brush with destructive magic? Perhaps my mysterious landlord was simply an inept businessman.

Unfortunately, my success that morning was proven an anomaly rather than the start of a run of luck; the few visitors we had after lunch were more curious about us than interested in bringing home a pet. I spoke to an elderly couple who lived above the library, then a young waitress at La Fin. While we exchanged pleasantries, I noticed Yannick speaking to a small, elegant woman by the counter, who wore a cloak lined with luxuriant fur. Her hair and eyes were dark against a pale face, and there was something about her that drew my eye, though I couldn't put a name to it.

Banshee, meanwhile, had worked herself into one of her panics. She paced about, howling silently at me, her spine stiff with tension.

"Hush," I told her, a ridiculous admonishment from my perspective, but certainly Banshee seemed to think she was clearly communicating her feelings. "Go find His Majesty, if you're in that much of a state." The large cat often had a calming influence on Banshee, even if he did sometimes respond to her panic by repeatedly swatting her on the head.

The waitress left and the woman in the fur approached me. "Cats, *hein*?" she said, smirking at them, then at me, as if I were in on some joke. "That's a new one. What happened to that uptight woman? The one with the scarves?"

"She—decided to change locations," I said. Something about the stranger made me uncomfortable. "Without notice, I was told."

The woman nodded, seeming unsurprised. I couldn't guess her age, nor could I tell which animal her coat had been made from. Without another word, she turned and strode to our back room, closing the door firmly behind her.

This was odd, but because I'd seen her talking to Yannick, I assumed she was some associate of his, who must have therefore felt she had special dispensation to wander about as she chose. This annoyed me, but when I went to see what the woman was up to, I found the little sitting room empty. So she had gone out the back door, then, choosing to use the shelter as a shortcut between Rue des Hirondelles and Parc Saint-Aimé. I tripped over the Persian rug as I turned to go— the corner had a habit of folding over on itself.

Élise and I turned our attention to my afternoon checklist,

which primarily consisted of grooming tasks—nail trimming and checking the cats for matting. Thoreau required regular bathing due to his age, and one of the other adults had an allergic rash I was attempting to treat with a lotion I'd purchased from a sheep breeder.

"How many checklists do you have?" enquired Yannick, who for some reason was still hanging about.

"Don't ask questions you don't want the answers to," Élise muttered as she expertly manhandled Fantôme, a pale Siamese who disdained nail trimming more than most.

I rolled my eyes. "Morning, afternoon, and evening," I replied. "Hardly a vast number. And it prevents us from overlooking any chores."

"You're forgetting the weekly checklists," Élise said. "One for the shelter, the other for the accounting."

"Well, yes, but—"

"And the monthly checklists," she went on. "And the monthly inventory. And all those diagrams of our donations and expenses you keep in the filing cabinet."

"Those are charts, not checklists."

"Ah, charts." Élise gave Yannick a knowing look—he was beginning to smile. "Agnes's second-favourite occupation."

I threw a comb at her.

"It must be hard," Yannick said slowly. He was sitting at one of the wooden tables, which still had several scarves scattered across it, petting little Marmalade, who'd fallen asleep in his lap. Yannick had initially reacted to the cats with polite puzzlement, but he had warmed to them quickly, which had improved my opinion of him.

"Running this type of charity, I mean," he elaborated. "Most folks don't see much value in the creatures, do they?"

He looked immediately stricken by his own bluntness,

seeming to assume I'd take offense. I merely replied, "We've had our ups and downs. Our income has always been small—we've survived this long because we're organized. We don't have the funds to be wasteful or sloppy."

"And have you always had so many?" Yannick said, glancing at the rows of cages, stacked two high.

"Last spring was a bad one for kittens," I said with a sigh. "But the number of stray cats has been going up every year—which means the number of cats freezing to death on the streets has *also* been increasing. We've estimated that around a thousand cats survive each winter, though most aren't adoptable. To put a dent in the population, we'd need to start neutering the ferals, but we don't get nearly enough donations to afford that. We do what we can for the tame ones, but I fear the situation is only getting worse."

"My," Yannick said, blinking. "I had no idea it was such a complicated problem."

Élise released Fantôme, who gave a parting hiss and stalked back to his bed to sulk. "We could use more donations," she said. "More volunteers. What charity couldn't? But we've gotten by, and who knows what the future holds? It's helpful to have a reasonable landlord."

She gave Yannick a grateful look, allowing her long lashes to droop a little. But the look also had a question in it, and after a moment, Yannick said, "It was in our interest to have the place rented out as quickly as possible."

He looked nervous then, as if he'd said too much. Muttering something about inspecting the plumbing, he excused himself.

Élise and I exchanged meaningful looks. Élise didn't share my concern about the shop, and had lectured me for even thinking of turning down Yannick's offer.

"So much the better if the place is haunted or cursed" had been her position. "The only good landlord is one starved for rent and desperate to please. Warts and snakes are easily dealt with, and the most ghosts can manage is making a nuisance of themselves, which makes them no worse neighbours than the living."

I turned to find Mina at my elbow, fiddling with her fingertips. "What's wrong?" I said. "Is it His Majesty again?" For His Majesty liked to terrorize Mina, hiding in corners and lunging at her ankles as she passed. The feral creature sensed weaknesses in people as well as in other cats, and took as much delight in exploiting them.

"Officer," she said. "Just there. What does he want, do you think?"

I turned to look in the direction she indicated. A man with reddish hair and a pale, freckled complexion stood before the cage containing the two kittens I'd recently rescued, holding his hand up to the bars. The sister, whom I'd christened Lynx for her temperament more than anything else (her brother was Monk), was attacking his fingers with gusto. The man did not look like law enforcement to me, but I didn't question Mina's assessment. I squeezed her arm and went to stand beside him.

"Would you like to hold that one?" I said politely. "She's a bit feisty, so if you're new to cats, I might recommend her brother."

He turned, smiling at me. I sensed something then, a certain piercing quality in his gaze, which I felt take my measure in a single glance. His smile, though, was amiable enough. He was around my age, and uncommonly handsome, with sharp features and dark eyes framed by long lashes.

"I'm only browsing," he said.

"Ah." I nodded towards the cats with mock gravity. "And were you looking for a specific size or colour? We have a broad selection, as you can see."

He smiled again, more genuinely this time. "I actually dropped by to welcome you to the neighbourhood."

"That's kind of you." Lynx was now sticking her front paw through the bars, slashing impotently at the air by the man's shoulder. I clicked open the lock on the cage door and lifted the cat free, then plunked her into the man's arms.

"I'm sorry," I said, "but she seemed to want a proper introduction."

He gave a surprised laugh. The black cat froze briefly, on her back in the man's arms, before delightedly attacking the lapel on his wool coat.

"Little beast!" he said warmly. "Well, I grew up on a farm, so I'm used to the ways of cats. I think I know what will appease her—here we are."

He lifted the cat off his coat and placed her on his shoulder. Lynx froze again, her mouth still comically hanging open. Then, to my astonishment, she butted her head against his ear and settled herself on his shoulder, seeming eminently pleased with her new vantage.

"I'm afraid you've no excuse not to take her home now," I said. "You're far too comfortable with each other."

"I wish I could," he replied, looking away with a wince, as if embarrassed to disappoint me. "But I would make a poor companion—my work is demanding, and I'm rarely at home."

"Do you have a shop nearby?"

"No, but I often work in this part of the city," he said. "Detective Rouzet. Please call me Laurent."

"I see," I said, noting that he held my gaze a little longer than necessary, as if to gauge my reaction. I had none—I could think of no reason why the police would have an interest in the shelter, apart from the banal one he'd already given. Even if my theory was correct and the place had once housed an illegal magic shop, this had nothing to do with me.

I gave him my name and held out my hand. He had warm eyes that narrowed considerably when he smiled, which made me wish to trust him automatically. At the same time, there was a guardedness about him that made me feel slightly wrong-footed, but I put this down to his profession.

He asked to see my rental contract, which I had no qualms about showing him. He frowned at the place where I had signed my name.

"Agnes?" he said, pronouncing it in the English way, with a hard G. "Not *Agnès*?"

"I'm named for my grandmother," I said, smiling. "She was Scottish, and particular about the spelling of her name. You may pronounce it either way."

As I spoke, I wondered if I could somehow convince him to leave without making him suspect me of something. I didn't like that he made Mina uncomfortable.

"Have you met the landlord?" he said.

"Only the caretaker, Yannick. Do you know him?"

"Yes," he said, and the word was like a wall, stopping me from enquiring further. I was startled and a little alarmed—I thought of Yannick, with his puppyish enthusiasm and transparent expressions, and wondered what on earth he could have to do with anything under Laurent's remit.

"I'm not surprised the owner didn't interview you himself," Laurent continued. "I understand he's abroad at present, and that he spends little time in the city. Did you have any qualms about renting a place from a person you'd never met?"

It was clear he felt there was only one correct answer to this, and meant to make me flustered. I replied politely, "Not particularly, for I was in no position to be choosy."

I gave him a summary of my situation and the state of the place on Rue Sainte-Roseline, which he digested with a thoughtful expression. As I saw no reason to beat around the bush, I added, "The rent was surprisingly affordable. I wonder if you know the reason—I guessed the place might have acquired a reputation from some prior tenant's misbehaviour. Is the owner perhaps not as discerning as one might hope?"

Unfortunately, Laurent seemed well practiced in deflecting curiosity, and the noise he made in response to this could have meant anything. "I wouldn't mind speaking with him, should he turn up," he said. "My aim isn't specific; I like to be acquainted with the local business owners, and I've found him—difficult to pin down. Would you mind telling me if you see him? I'll stop by again."

"Ah," I hedged, thinking of Mina. "Perhaps we could meet elsewhere? There's a café down the street. I'd be happy to buy you a coffee."

He blinked at me, and his ears reddened. Only then did I wonder if there was an additional significance to the warmth in his eyes, and, short on the heels of this, I heard my own words again. This, coupled with his evident embarrassment, made me turn pink. "I meant—well—"

"Yes," he said, running a hand through his hair, which only made him look more inconveniently handsome. "That would— Only I'm not supposed to— Well, I should be off. Thank you for—the cat. I'll think about it."

"Wonderful," I said, now thoroughly desperate for him to be gone. I'd always been dreadful when it came to flirtation—it had been lucky for me that Robin, alone among men, found my awkwardness charming. Now it seemed I'd found a way to deploy my awkwardness at men I wasn't even interested in.

Well, if nothing else, I'd landed on an effective strategy for dampening police interest in my affairs. Laurent was out the door within seconds.

"Did you just invite a man to coffee?" Élise demanded. She'd edged closer during the tail end of our conversation, and stood looking equally astonished and delighted. "An attractive man at that?"

"No," I said. "Don't look at me like that. He won't be back."

Élise regarded me with a considering smile, and her gaze followed Laurent across the street. "I wouldn't be so certain."

CHAPTER 7

Time passed quickly at first, a haze of long days spent cleaning, sorting and resorting, and rushing off to purchase some accessory that we hadn't needed at the old place but was suddenly critical at the new one. I grew used to my bed, to the clank of the hot water pipes, the smell of the old oak parquet, and the way the sun poured through the west-facing windows in the afternoon. I doubted I would ever feel at home in the warm luxury of the upstairs apartment and tried to spend as little time there as possible—I never used the sitting room, and crept from the bedroom to the bathroom in the morning like a mouse navigating a clearing. Not once did the curtains open of their own accord, though some mornings I could have sworn I saw them twitch, as if they wished to. Overall, the shop continued to present itself as lacking in both ghosts and magic.

This lasted one week.

The oven was the first dark omen, as I could have guessed it would be. I had noted on my first visit that it smelled of baking, and I came to realize, once the scent of our floor polish had faded a little, that it still did—but only in the mornings;

the smell dissipated after a few hours. It often varied: sometimes citrus, others chocolate, and sometimes it was clearly sourdough or otherwise savoury. Was someone breaking into the shop and making use of the oven in the night? It was the only explanation I could think of, and yet it was impossible. Not only did I lock up carefully, but the stones of the oven were cold in the morning, the decaying ashes within undisturbed.

Of course, I soon realized that there was no need for someone to break into the shop at night. Someone was already there.

It was only in growing used to the shop that I realized it. As I came to recognize the clanking of the pipes, which would sound even when no one had touched the taps, and the groaning of the lightless well that was the staircase, I also came to know which sounds did not fit the old building's pattern. Namely, the intermittent bangs and creaks from the basement.

A particularly loud thump sounded one morning when Élise was assisting a couple interested in one of our tabbies.

"Ghosts acting up again," Élise said, the barest hint of a smile in her eyes. The couple tittered. When the noise came again an hour later, Élise stamped on the floor.

"What do you think that will accomplish?" I said despairingly.

Élise shrugged. "Whatever it is, it will have to learn to keep it down when I'm with a client."

She spoke dismissively enough, but I saw, and pretended not to see, how her shoulders stiffened when the noises came again.

The woman in the unidentifiable fur did not return, but others like her did. I could not work out why they reminded me of her, for they all looked different; perhaps it was only in the way they drew my eye, as most were finely dressed and took up space in the way of wealthy people, but I didn't think so. The closest I could come to describing it was to say to Élise, nonsensically, that they reminded me of paintings.

First there was a man with an ivory cane and an immaculately tailored black cloak lined with emerald silk. He spoke not a word to me, merely gave me a nod when I welcomed him to the shelter and swept past, making for the back room as if he were late for a meeting. I was on my own then, and the shop was quiet, and so I heard the distinct creak followed by—as if I had not guessed already—a thump and a slight tremor in the floorboards that could only be the trapdoor to the basement falling shut.

He emerged perhaps an hour later, giving me that same polite nod, and went out the front door. Most of them exited through the door to the alley—or I assumed they did. I supposed it was possible that some fell monster made a meal of them down in the basement, and they never left.

After him came a pair of men, muttering to each other, more subtly but also more expensively attired, their hats worn low enough to shade their eyes. They didn't acknowledge me in any way, though the shorter one frowned at the cats, as if they offended his eyes. He returned the next day alone, once again striding through the place as if he owned it. Happily, His Majesty was in a foul mood that day, crouched glowering by the back door like a gargoyle, and slashed at the man's ankles as he passed. The man made a movement as if to kick him—deeply unwise where His Majesty was concerned—and ended up with two clawed ankles and a long tear in the hem of his cloak, the latter inflicted by a grey tabby named Céline. His Majesty had no interest in either friends or minions, but some of the younger cats paid fealty to him anyway, and would take it upon themselves to harass anyone His Majesty took a dislike to.

Another day, a nervous young woman slunk into the shop as if expecting an attack, her hair in disarray. She was the only one who spoke to me.

"I don't have much time," she said, after running her gaze over the shop several times, as if we might be hiding someone.

I could have pretended I had no idea what she was after. But I wanted her gone, her and all the others, so I simply pointed towards the back room. She nodded once and hurried away, not bothering to close the door behind her. Thus I saw her fold the rug back and lift the trapdoor, a simple rectangle cut out of the floor with a brass chain attached. I did not see what was below it, because the trapdoor blocked my view, but I could tell she descended a flight of stairs, slowly lowering the door behind her.

I could have followed them into the back room, of course, and peered into the space below the trapdoor. I could have waited for them when they came out again, or asked what they were doing down there. But I never did.

Élise and I were in agreement on this point. "Is any of this worse than a nuisance?" she said. "And is tolerating a nuisance worse than returning to an unheated ruin? It's a small price to pay."

While the mystery gnawed at me, I agreed with her. I was additionally motivated to avoid the basement due to my unwillingness to admit that my theory had shifted. I no longer thought the place had once housed an illegal magic shop. I now wondered if the owner of the shop had never left.

At the end of that week, I paid a visit to the bookstore next door. Oksana, the owner, was not napping this time, but busy with a customer. I was pleased to see that her shop was not always quiet; several people waited in line, each with a stack of books. The weather was moody that day, the wind rambling up the narrow street, woven with leaves from the maples in the square. The wooden sign above the bookshop creaked back and forth.

I waited until the customers had paid and gone, then approached the counter. The woman glanced up at me, narrowing her eyes. This did not seem a promising start, but I reminded myself that a face might have a natural tendency towards mildness or severity, as a clock has towards haste or tardiness, and was thus not always a reliable measure of mood.

"You again!" she said.

So much for that, I thought ruefully. I decided to change my approach, for this was a person who seemed to value bluntness.

"I despise magicians," I said. "I have never had anything to do with them, and hope I never will."

She blinked at me for a moment. "Seems a bit late for that."

I felt the breath leave me. So—there was my confirmation, of a sort. "You know who my landlord is."

"I've been in this neighbourhood for decades," she said. "I know *all* my neighbours. Including those who don't wish to be known."

I waited for her to elaborate. She didn't. "I would be grateful for anything you could tell me," I said. "But only if it won't put you at risk."

"What did the police want?"

I hesitated, taken aback by her tone. "They—you mean Laurent?"

"I mean Laurent. He's more cunning than he looks, that one, and more determined than the others ever were. He's been poking around that shop for nearly a year. I saw him through the window speaking to you. What did you tell him?"

This was baffling. I'd expected her to sigh at me for ignoring her warnings, or perhaps to suspect I was in league with whatever mysterious entity inhabited the basement, and distrust me. Instead she seemed to distrust me for an entirely different reason.

"You warned me to stay away from the shop," I said slowly. "You implied there was something terrible about it."

"Did I say that?" Oksana countered. "I warned you off because you seem like the wrong type for the place. I could see it a mile off—you're just the sort that would make a report to the police and cause all kinds of trouble for the neighbourhood."

"I don't—"

"It's your face," she went on. "You look like the woman on the cookie tin."

I flushed. I knew which cookie tin she meant—it was sold in shops around the holidays and featured a beaming hearty-looking woman with red cheeks brandishing a tray of shortbread. It was partly why Élise teased me as she did, though she also liked to say that I had a face for organizing bake sales.

"I'm not surprised you operate some silly charity," Oksana added in a mutter.

"You believe charity is silly?"

"That one is. Do you not realize there are *people* in this city who need help?"

I decided to assume the woman didn't mean to be rude, despite the evidence. A self-interested assumption—I cannot tolerate it when people dislike me. I never stop thinking about it, to the point where it is as though I am wearing their dislike wherever I go, which chafes like wet shoes.

"The city seems to have room for more than one form of charity," I said.

She gave a disdainful grunt. "What are you so worried about?" she said. "Magicians like cats. The stories say Havelock Renard can turn himself into a black one."

"The stories also say he collects the screams of his victims in jars," I pointed out. "And takes his enemies apart just so he can sew them together to make new enemies. When it comes to magicians, I prefer to trust in what they *do* with their power, not the stories people tell about it. You clearly know more than you are saying—is there no way we might come to trust each other?"

The woman only regarded me with folded arms, forefinger tapping against her elbow. "What about the others?" I said in frustration. "The baker and the importer? The police never took an interest in them?"

"They kept quiet. You should do the same."

I felt my composure slip. "Even if the shelter is being used to trade in spells that could harm someone?"

"A neighbour is a neighbour." She looked about to say more, but changed her mind. The bell jingled behind us, and Oksana hurried over to offer assistance to the man who entered. I waited to see if she would speak to me again, but she seemed to be pretending I was not there. I left.

CHAPTER 8

Something woke me late that night. At first I thought it was the wind, which tapped at the window insistently. I lifted my head and saw that winter had come to the city.

Beyond the window was a tumult of flakes, puffy as popped corn, which heaped themselves upon the stone sill. I rose and gazed out at Rue des Hirondelles, its quaint and rambling character, which had grown so familiar to me, and which was now made foreign by the drifts growing steadily deeper. The newspaper box on the corner had vanished, and the gargoyles on the church up the street wore white nightcaps.

I wrapped myself in my robe to watch the snowfall, feeling a twinge of childlike excitement. I was warm, with a roof over my head and four solid walls, not three. Winter was no worse than a monster in a storybook: it could frighten but not harm me. For the first time, the shop felt snug rather than haunted—it helped, I supposed, that there were two floors between me and whoever lurked in the basement. If they were still there—surely they left sometimes?

I decided to congratulate myself on my decision to accept Yannick's offer. It had been a risk, but one had to take risks to get anywhere, I philosophized. Hadn't Robin and I taken a risk in opening the shelter, investing his savings and most of my inheritance? We'd rescued dozens of cats from miserable states, and we hadn't folded yet.

I trailed my fingertip absently through the condensation on the window, feeling the familiar ache of longing for Robin, like a second heartbeat. Philosophy was always a meagre comfort, especially in the small hours of the morning. In the past, I'd told myself that as long as the shelter flourished, I'd always have a piece of Robin. Now I found myself wondering why I'd taken comfort in this, because what good was a piece? Was an echo any better than silence if it brought to mind the absence over and over again?

Lost in my ruminations, I leaned my forehead against the cold glass, watching the snow swirl in the wind.

I became aware, slowly, of a scraping sound downstairs.

I turned, then started so violently I hit my shoulder on the window frame. Banshee sat in the doorway, her mouth open in a silent, unending howl, her fur standing on end and her eyes fiendishly lit by the streetlamp. When she saw that I was finally giving her my attention after so callously ignoring her desperate cries, she turned and darted into the hall, glancing back at me.

My hands shook and my heart beat rabbit-fast in my ears, but still I paused to pull on some clothes, because the idea of facing whatever was downstairs in my bathrobe felt absurdly inappropriate. I contemplated remaining in my bedroom, but that seemed worse, somehow. While I was reasonably certain now that it was a person and not a ghost lurking in the basement, it was a ghost that filled my imagination, gliding upstairs and cornering me in my room, rattling the doorknob and moaning.

I went downstairs.

When I emerged from the dark stairwell into the lesser darkness of the shop, I saw nothing unusual—which was, of course, worse than immediately happening upon some monster. The front door was closed, the curtains too. The air, though, had a hint of frost in it, as if it had recently tasted the night outside. Then I noticed a figure standing by the cages.

Hand trembling, I reached towards the light switch and pushed the button.

It was a woman, her dark hair still speckled with snow. She wore a red cloak that trailed on the ground, and she had removed one fur-lined glove to pet Thoreau, whom she held in her arms. The scraping sound must have been the cage door opening. The woman had sharp features that lent her an impish, mischievous look, further emphasized by the dark sweep of her eyeliner and the single mole she had pencilled onto the side of her chin. I knew instantly that she was like the strange visitors who frequented the basement.

His Majesty perched upon the counter, watching her, the tip of his tail twitching. Banshee, meanwhile, paced by the front door, howling impotently.

"Who are you?" I demanded. "I—we're closed."

"Are you," she said, not looking up from Thoreau as she scratched his chin. The rings she wore flashed in the light. She clucked her tongue at the cat, and his ears perked up. "Much as I'm charmed by your shop—an unusual commodity to trade in, cats—I am not here for you."

Something told me I did not want to know the answer to my next question. I asked it anyway. "What are you here for?"

"Lock, of course." Her voice was smoky, her accent Parisian. "I know he's here. And I know he has his Artefacts with him. Everyone said he was in New York, which delayed me, as did the wards he placed upon this shop to prevent me from finding it. But he couldn't throw me off the trail forever."

"Lock," I murmured. It was not possible. I told myself that I didn't understand her.

"Havelock Renard, the Witch King," she continued mercilessly. "Also called the Shadow-walker, as well as the First Dark Mage—another exaggeration. Magicians have no lords, and all our power is born from darkness. He is not first in anything, except perhaps his ability to make a nuisance of himself."

We stared at each other in silence for a long moment. Thoreau began to squirm.

I gave a burble of laughter. I couldn't help it—it was so absurd. The Witch King, in my cat shelter. Where was he, lurking in the litter cupboard? Hiding in the basement?

"Oh," I murmured, cold dread blanketing me once more. Yes—if he was anywhere, he was in the basement.

"You're mistaken," I said.

The woman made no reply. She touched one of the rings on her hand—she wore a great many, heavy bands of silver and pale jewels the colour of dawn, and one of gold on her thumb—and murmured a word. A light appeared in midair, barely the size of a honeybee, and bobbed lightly up and down. It fell towards the floor and went out. The woman nodded as if the thing had spoken.

At the sight of the enchantment, I went as still as a deer at the snap of a twig. All I could see was the hole in the wall of the old shelter. A small, detached part of me noted that I was almost certainly in shock, and also that I should probably make for the door with all haste. But the woman was still holding Thoreau, and there were the other cats, only a few of whom were paying us any attention—the bulk slept or groomed themselves, characteristically disdainful of all but their own concerns, even and including an impending magical cataclysm. Clowder was licking her rear end.

"You won't summon him?" the woman said. "Very well—I'll do it myself. He does love to complain that I'm too dramatic."

And she began to tear the place apart.

Thoreau, thankfully, leapt free of her arms, disappearing up the stairs, followed closely by Banshee and His Majesty. The entire building began to shake, the tables lurching about violently, and several of the cat cages fell to the ground, their occupants yowling. The windows shattered, taking the warmth with them, and the storm spat a mouthful of snow into the shop. A tremendous crack formed in the ceiling, raining plaster upon us, and the filing cabinets I had spent a full day reorganizing toppled onto their sides, spilling papers everywhere.

I fell to my knees and began to crawl towards the cats—it was pure instinct; any rational thought had been swallowed by a roiling panic. If I'd been thinking clearly, I would have launched myself at her, for if I hadn't guessed it before, I knew now that she was a magician, and clearly bent on shaking the place with her magic until it collapsed to its foundations. She stood with her palms uplifted and her eyes half-shut, smiling as she murmured something I couldn't hear, like a saint overcome by religious ecstasy.

I managed to wrench open the door of Clowder's cage, which had fallen to the floor, and she and the kittens raced for the second story. I didn't know that they would be much safer up there, but perhaps the windows had smashed upstairs too, and they could clamber along the rooftops if the place began to cave in. I got another cage open, and Fantôme, more sensibly, made for the empty windows and the snowy street beyond, as did Lynx. I tried to open the next cage, which housed an enormous orange cat named Choux, but my fingers were trembling so that I could barely grasp the latch. Choux, as helpful as cats generally are in emergencies, swatted at my hand.

The trapdoor banged open so violently that even above the creaking and trembling of the shop, I jumped. The door to the back room had come off its hinges and hung leaning against the wall, so I saw it when my mysterious downstairs neighbour made his appearance—though I wished I had not.

It was not a man at all. In fact, it was much closer to the ghost of my nightmares. What emerged from the trapdoor was more absence than presence, a shift in the shadows that had the rough outline of a figure, and that figure was only somewhat human. It was too tall, for one thing, all teeth and claws, and it moved with the grace of a panther, trailing shadow that swirled with burning embers. Never have I seen a thing more otherworldly or horrible. I would have screamed if shock hadn't stolen my voice.

The woman had taken no notice of the trapdoor opening—probably she had thought she'd caused the noise, given that she was actively trying to bring down the roof. The crack was lengthening, and a chunk of ceiling fell to the floor and shattered. The shadow-thing collided with the woman, sending her sprawling across the floor. And then, abruptly, the creature vanished, and I became aware that a man stood by the broken back door, as if he'd come up behind the monster.

He was dark-haired and graceful, with glasses that sat askew on his nose. And he was dreadfully handsome, but in an almost jarring way; his face had a mismatched, pieced-together quality, as if painted by a portraitist whose model was changed out before each session. I sensed the same strangeness in him that I had seen in the mysterious visitors, who put me in mind of figures from a Renaissance painting by an old master, only in him, this effect was more concentrated and startling. He was the sort of person one couldn't help staring at, an optical illusion my eyes needed to solve.

The shock of his appearance was lessened, however, by his undignified attire. He had clearly been abed, and was barefoot and dressed in what looked like navy blue pyjamas. He wore as many rings and earrings as the woman did, as well as a strange pendant with a gold coin dangling from it, but they didn't create the same effect on him; with the oversized pyjamas, he looked more like a boy playacting as a pirate. His dark hair was in tangles where it wasn't sticking straight up.

"Hello, Lock," the woman said, with an uneven sort of laugh—she had struck the ground hard and was sprawled in an elegant heap against the counter, half propped on one elbow. "Did I wake you?"

"I think you woke every inhabitant of this street since the Middle Ages," he said, grabbing at the doorframe as the building gave another shudder. It was only an aftershock, though; the terrible earthquake had stopped. "Did you not think, Valérie, that you might bring the building down on your own head as well as mine?"

Even through my shock, a part of me registered the strangeness of this, that he would show any concern at all for this woman. He came towards her as if to help her to her feet, but she touched one of her earrings and he flew backwards and struck the wall. I *thought* she did something more than that, for the air rippled oddly around him for a moment, until he made a sharp gesture, then it cleared.

"What was that?" the woman said, looking uncertain for the first time since her arrival. "I've never felt a counterspell like that before."

"Haven't you?" His tone was still sardonic, but something in it had hardened. "Perhaps it wasn't any counterspell of mine, Ri, only a stirring of empathy that bungled your incantation. Don't worry, I'm sure the sensation will wear off quickly."

"Still that childish attitude," she snapped. "Still slipping and weaving your way out of the simplest of questions. You even *look* like a boy."

"Yes, I apologize for not being more presentable. I didn't know you would be ransacking my shop. Give me notice next time; I'll put on a suit."

As he spoke, he removed a leather pouch from his pocket, then excavated a small golden coin. He lifted the coin and spoke a single word that made the thoughts rattle about in my head as if they'd turned to coins themselves, and which I forgot as soon as I tried to remember it.

The woman—*magician*, I made myself think, even as my mind shrank back from the word—rose into the air in the most horrible and uncanny fashion, as if there were a hook in her chest drawing her up. At the same time, the air seemed to solidify into ghostly ropes binding her arms to her sides. Not quickly enough—she managed to wrench one hand free, and grasped the ring she wore on her thumb.

She spoke another unintelligible word, and a bolt of lightning—lightning!—arched from the ring towards the other magician. I found my voice then and screamed like a child, but he only lifted a hand and *caught it* somehow, holding the light pooled in his palm like liquid gold. He held his hand up and closed his fingers into a fist, and as the light went out, a thunderclap shook the shop.

"Predictable," he said, sounding disappointed. He brushed

his hands together, which sent little sparks skittering over the floor. "The thunder was a novel touch, though. Give up, Ri—you've made it past the wards, but you will go no farther."

"If I were predictable," the woman said, her voice strained by the ghostly rope now snaking along her throat, "you would not be in your nightclothes."

Somehow, she managed to twist her arm just enough to shove her hand into her pocket, from which she drew a piece of paper folded into something that resembled a bird. She rasped a different word—that is all I can say, that it was different from the others—and then something enormous and weighty was descending from the ceiling.

I saw it immediately, crouched on the floor as I was, looking up at the magicians as they fought. But Havelock Renard—if it truly was him—was still watching the woman, perhaps anticipating another bolt of lightning.

If I had to put a name to it, I would have said it was a dragon. Its head was shaped like some deep-sea behemoth's, yawning open to reveal glittering and jagged shards of crystalline teeth, and it was covered in scales of emerald and obsidian. Its eyes were pure flame, a fire that bloomed also at the back of its throat, as if the creature had been shaped from some hellish subterranean cavern.

When at last the magician sensed the doom descending towards him, his ringed hand whipped up, and his mouth opened to shout something. But it was too late, and his rings were devoured along with the rest of him. The creature's mouth closed over him with an oddly gentle snap, a small morsel for such an immensity.

There was a moment when the only sound in the shop was the low growling of the remaining cats. Then the monster burst apart in a shower of jewels and knife-sharp crystals.

I screamed again, shielding myself with my arms, but instead of being impaled by gemstones, I felt myself struck by many small rustling things, as if I'd angered a horde of moths. I opened my eyes and found myself surrounded by paper birds, lightly singed and smoking. They'd been made from receipts, I realized dimly—there was a typewritten list on the wing of the closest one. *Panais* was the only word I could make out.

"Eight cents," I murmured. They'd been overcharged.

Part of me noted that my fixation on the price of parsnips was perhaps a sign of some internal collapse, but anything was preferable to thinking about what I'd just seen. I had never actually witnessed magic before, only its aftereffects, and I felt a sharp pang of grief for the person I'd been ten minutes ago. I sensed a vast chasm between us.

The magician stood in the same place where the dragon had eaten him, brushing bits of paper from his clothes. "That one needed more magic," he said. He looked pale, and I could tell the creature had given him a genuine fright, but there was also a gleam of childish delight in his eye, as if a part of him had *enjoyed* it.

"Oh, Lock," the woman murmured. I was thrown by the sorrow in her voice. "You've spent too much time in the shadows. Did I not warn you against it when we were young? How much of you is left?"

"Enough," he said, seeming untroubled by her nonsensical question. He wasn't watching her as she rotated slowly in midair, but sifting through the jingling contents of the leather pouch.

"You know what I want," she said. "Why not simply give it to me and put an end to our feud? Do you not have enough treasures to content yourself with? Give it to me, and I'll be on my way, and you can go on with your experiments without me bothering you for anything more than dinner and some shared reminiscences now and then."

"There you are," he muttered, digging a coin out and tossing the pouch over his shoulder. It hit the floor with a thunk, and one of the cats hissed. At that he stilled and then turned, blinking, towards where I crouched by the cages.

"You've—" The surprise was giving way to a kind of baffled indignation. "Valérie. You filled my shop with *cats*?"

The woman gave a breath of laughter. I was a little surprised she had not passed out or been sick yet, though the faint sheen of sweat on her forehead suggested that she was not quite as collected as she seemed. "The cats were here when I came in. When is the last time you left that workshop of yours?"

He continued to stare at the cats with dismay, as if they were a graver threat than the magician who'd almost brought the building down on our heads. He removed his glasses, rubbed his eyes, and put the glasses back on, as if that might alter anything. It was at this moment that I found my voice.

"What is the matter with you?" I cried hoarsely. "She's getting free!"

He looked at me with a start, then whipped around again, for indeed, the woman had managed to pull her knee to her chest, allowing her to wrench one of the buckles from her shoe. She drew in a deep breath.

I would never know what terrible spell she would have unleashed—perhaps the room would have filled with monsters the size of the dragon. But the man was quicker, and when he unleashed the enchantment in his coin, winter swirled into the shop, coils of snowy wind that suggested many-jointed skeletal hands, which wrapped around Valérie's body and dragged her, screaming, into the night.

I blinked at the window she'd vanished through. How far would the enchantment take her? Would it lift her into the storm and drop her again with the next blanket of snow? What sort of range did a magician's power have? One mile? Two?

I pondered the matter with the same blank absorption with which I'd considered the price of parsnips.

The magician came towards me then, moving with an impossible grace that put me in mind of the shadow-monster—where had the thing gone? Clearly it was his creature, to be summoned at his whim. I scrabbled backwards on my hands, but I only collided with the cages.

He stopped a pace or two away, though, staring at me. "Agnes," he said. "You're here."

I hadn't any idea how to respond to this odd remark, because where else would I be? Still, it was such a contrast to what I had been expecting—namely, being levitated into the air or perhaps fed to another shadow-monster—and spoken in such an ordinary tone that I went numb with relief, and even allowed him to help me to my feet. His palm was warm, and embers of lightning still clung to it, which popped against my skin. When I drew my hand back, one was sticking to me, and I hurriedly shook it off.

"How did you know my name?" was the first question that rose to my lips. An inane one—I answered it myself. "Of course—Yannick."

"Yannick," he agreed, still staring at me with a furrowed brow, as if *I* were the renowned dark magician who had just defeated her enemy in a whirlwind of magic.

"Is she gone?" I said. Really I wanted the two of them gone together, and a part of me hoped the woman would reappear and drag him off with her, so that I could lock the door and board the windows behind them. But I wasn't foolish enough to think it would be so simple, nor to assume that I—and the cats—would survive another battle of magic unscathed. She had tried to tear the shelter apart and he had stopped her, so that made him the lesser of two monsters, cold comfort as that was.

"For the moment." Like Valérie, he spoke with a Parisian accent. "Knowing my magnificently quarrelsome sister, we've maybe ten minutes before she frees herself and starts shaking the building again like a child with a new toy."

"*Sister?*" I repeated. "Sister! She tried to kill you!"

"She knows I'm more capable than she is," he said, seeming lost in thought.

"But—" Perhaps I was misunderstanding, and throwing lightning bolts at each other was the equivalent of friendly horseplay for magicians, but it had certainly looked like attempted murder to me, or at best a careless sort of malevolence.

I shook my head, trying to clear my mind. Even through the veil of shock, I found myself seizing upon the problem and grasping for practical solutions to throw at it. "Can you use these?" I poked at the leather pouch on the floor with my toe, not wanting to touch it.

"What?" he said. He was rubbing a hand through his hair absently, only making it into more of a bird's nest than it already was. "Oh—those are just hexes. It was all I had time to grab. They won't be enough."

"They—" My throat was dry, and the word broke at the end.

I became aware, in a way I somehow hadn't been before, that I was talking to a *magician*. "They made her levitate."

He waved a hand, as if this were nothing. "Ah! I have it."

He darted to the trapdoor, and then, too quickly—far too quickly—he was back, and he was wearing a cloak. It was a fine thing, charcoal grey with theatrical flourishes, like nothing I'd ever seen in a shop, but the effect was ruined somewhat by the pyjamas underneath, as well as his bare feet, which combined to give an impression closer to an escaped hospital patient than the most feared magician in a century.

I was shivering, which meant that the shock was either wearing off or worsening, I couldn't tell. "What is that supposed to do?"

"I've woven several spells into this cloak," he said. He approached one of the windows, murmured a word, and it was filled with glass again. "Each of the pockets has one, as does the lining. And—" He paused, glancing down at himself. "Three of the buttons. I haven't got to the others yet."

He began to detail the spells in an enthusiastic tone, oblivious to my complete lack of interest, and I heard not one word he said. Finally I gave voice to the only clear thought in my head at that moment. "You are *not* Havelock Renard."

"Who am I, then?" He looked amused. "Alveric of Erl? Well, I suppose in one sense you're right. People tell all sorts of silly stories about me, so I doubt I'm the person you're imagining."

I let my breath out. "The apocalypse. Three years ago. That wasn't you, then."

He made no reply, only murmured to another of the windows, which repaired itself in a heartbeat. Maybe he didn't like the word *apocalypse*. After all, the world hadn't truly ended, it had only looked like it was going to, in the way that it can look like rain.

"It *was*," I murmured. "You almost ended the world. You, standing right there."

"It's a bit more complicated than that," he said, looking oddly flustered. "Who on earth are you, anyway? I thought Yannick rented the shop to a charity."

"He did!" I gesticulated at the cages, where the poor cats hunched in various states of fury and terror. We had forty-five now; a surge in adoptions had dropped the number briefly to forty-one before we'd taken in a frostbitten mother with kittens.

"*Cats?*" He gave me an appalled look, as if he had never heard of anything more ludicrous. "It would be a charitable act to do away with the vermin, and you've filled my shop with them? Has Yannick lost his mind? Oh, I suppose it's no concern of his if the place is infested with fleas—he doesn't live here." He made an exasperated sound and went back to rubbing his hair.

Vermin was such an insult, and so unexpected in that moment, that I could only splutter in response. And though I knew it was not what I should have been giving my attention to, still I found myself snapping, "I'll have you know that every one of these cats has regular flea treatments."

He wasn't listening to me. "What have you done to the place?" he said, frowning as he turned to take it all in.

I couldn't see what he was so offended about. We'd moved the tables, which had been scattered haphazardly about the shop, to form an L-shape against the south wall. The cat cages were stacked neatly atop them. The scarves had been given to the cats or folded neatly and put away. Besides that and the addition of several filing cabinets, we'd changed only the light, replacing broken fixtures and adding several standing lamps to give the place a warm glow.

"Apart from sweeping up an inch of dust?" I said. "Very little. We've made it look less like a haunted house, I suppose."

He shook his head. "We'll move it," he muttered to himself. "Yes—that's the only way."

"Move it?" To my dismay, I could think of only one way to interpret this, and it involved more magic. "Move the *shelter*?"

He grimaced, seeming to dislike the reminder that I'd sullied his shop with cats. "It will take a good deal of magic, but it's nothing I haven't prepared for. I suspected she'd track me down eventually."

I could have asked any of the dozen questions that flitted through my mind at that: How had Valérie tracked him down in the first place? What did she want from him, and why didn't he simply give it to her? But one thought rose above the others.

"Fantôme," I murmured. "He ran outside, and Lynx after him—I can't leave them."

I sprang towards the door, which had been blasted open. But he was suddenly before me, having moved with the inhuman grace of a gust of wind, as if, just for a moment, he'd become shadow himself.

"Are you mad?" he demanded as I fell back from him in terror. "I've no idea how far I blasted Valérie. What do you think she will do to you if she comes upon you wandering the streets? She will suspect you know where I've gone, and never let you go until you tell her. As magicians go, Valérie is less charitable than I."

"She—" My voice faltered. I couldn't stop picturing his monster, all claws and shadow. "You almost ended the world."

"Yes," he said.

I took a step backwards, away from the door and the winter night beyond.

"Wise choice," he said.

He went back to the windows, rooting around in the pockets of his cloak and drawing out more coins, tiny silver ones this time. He placed one on each sill.

"These hold magic from the Third Fathom of the Rivenwood," he said, sounding pleased with himself. "And I've left the weaving of conveyance unfinished—I should be able to stretch it to encompass the entire shop, and thread the *other* shop into the pattern."

He kept babbling this sort of nonsense at me as he paced around the shelter, laying his talismans along the walls and in the corners. Once I was certain his back was turned, I darted through the door.

"Agnes," he cried after me, which made me stumble in surprise—I still wasn't used to the fact that a magician knew my name.

Not "a magician"—Havelock Renard, I made myself think, because it was not possible to doubt it any longer. *That is Havelock Renard, in his pyjamas or not, and if you had any sense, you would keep running and not look back.*

On my feet I wore only the socks I'd been sleeping in, and within seconds the snow was sending splinters of cold up my legs. Fortunately, Fantôme had not gone far—he was sitting on the window ledge of the next shop, and began mewling piteously as soon as he saw me. I scooped him up, calling for Lynx. I floundered about in the snow, which was past my knees, for an indeterminate amount of time—likely no more than five minutes, but that feels much longer when one is expecting to be blasted apart by a malevolent magician at any moment. At last I found the black cat crouched beneath a staircase in the alley three doors over.

She yowled at me, her fur so fluffed she was almost round. I could tell she would require extensive coaxing to emerge of her own accord, and I had no time. So, regretting that I could not be more gentle, I grabbed her by the scruff and hauled her out. She raked me with her claws for that, but I grimly maintained my grip and sprinted back to the shelter.

I became afraid, suddenly, that I'd find some other shop there instead. And then a wave of hysteria threatened to overwhelm me again, as I realized I was worrying that Havelock Renard would *not* be waiting for me.

But when I crossed the threshold, the shelter was still there, cats and all, and Havelock stood drumming his fingers on the counter, though it was clear he'd finished preparing his spell some time ago. He was watching me with an odd look that seemed half reproachful and half assessing, but there was also something perplexed about it, as if he hadn't the slightest idea what to make of me. This was more than a little unnerving: Why should Havelock Renard bother to make anything of me at all?

Then he spoke a word, and the world split in two.

CHAPTER 9

It was the most curious sensation I have ever experienced. Curious, and thoroughly *horrid*. There was a monumental tearing sound, and then on the heels of this a rather unpleasant sort of squelch, as of a boulder-sized boot being pressed into mud. At the same time, I felt as if *I* were being ripped apart—or, rather, ripped free of some sticky substance I somehow hadn't noticed before, then hurled, not gently, neither up, down, nor sideways but somehow *between* all the earthly directions, and into another stickiness that enveloped me like a monstrous cobweb. The sensation faded almost immediately—which is to say, nowhere near soon enough—and I fell to the floor, my head spinning and my stomach seeming to hover somewhere above me.

"My apologies," Havelock said. He was leaning against the counter, looking slightly more dishevelled than before, but otherwise unaffected. "I didn't think I had time to smooth the intention behind the spell, and most spatial magic falls into the Wayward order; it's best to leash it to a compass spell, which I don't have on hand."

This was all completely unintelligible, not to mention unhelpful. "Where are we?" I demanded, trying to stand. My head gave another lurch and I abandoned the attempt, bowing my head over my knees. At least two of the cats were throwing up.

"Rue Sainte-Sophie," he said, sounding pleased with himself. He straightened and began pacing in front of the windows, which were in a long row, not separate like those in the shelter, but oddly seemed to be covered by the same green curtains. He lifted the edge of one and squinted through the glass, admitting the grey light of dawn.

I swallowed and looked around. He hadn't moved the entire shelter, just ourselves, the cats, and the counter with the cash register. Even as my head spun and my thoughts tangled together in a useless attempt to comprehend what had happened, a small part of me couldn't help noticing the proportions of the shop—easily fifty percent larger than the place on Rue des Hirondelles—and picturing the additional cats we could house.

I froze. At the rear of the shop was a monstrous stone oven. And there was the back door, a little farther away from the oven than it had been in the other shop, but still hanging off its hinges. Even the flagstone floor had come with us, though the individual flagstones seemed wider.

"This *is* the shelter," I murmured. "Isn't it?"

"For the most part," he said absently. He'd excavated a handful of what looked like river pebbles from a pocket and was placing them on the windowsills and along the walls. He continued in an absurdly reasonable tone, "Oh, but I didn't bring the exterior walls. The neighbours would have noticed. But everything *between* them is here, only stretched a bit."

"What on earth does that mean?"

He made no reply, still pacing from window to window and pausing to mutter to himself, or perhaps to the pebbles. In the same moment, my mind cleared enough for me to remember the poor cats, who were more important than interrogating him anyway, and I hurried to attend to them.

They were unharmed, though clearly terrified, cowering at the backs of their cages. I doubted I would improve their mood by setting them loose, as most cats are alarmed by unfamiliar environments, and indeed they only shrank into themselves when I reached in to pet them. Clowder, though, was out the door as soon as I swung it open and sticking to the front of my sweater like a burr. I wrapped my arms around her and only barely managed to catch one of her kittens, an undersized ball of fluff named Ron Ron, as he leapt after his mother. I placed the kitten on my shoulder for want of anywhere else to put him.

I turned to find Havelock watching me, his dark eyebrows knitted. "What is the point of your charity?" he said. "Do you provide shelter for other city pests? Will I find raccoons stuffed in the upstairs closets?"

His voice held more genuine confusion than it did disdain. There was a ringing in my ears, and for a moment I was so angry that I could barely see. It wasn't a sentiment I liked to indulge; I've always preferred to make amends with people rather than carry around resentments. Perhaps this was why giving in to my anger was so satisfying, and also I had long wished for the chance to tell a magician just what I felt about him.

"What is the matter with you?" I demanded. "You've endangered my life—not to mention my business and reputation—as well as my *cats* by deceiving me about your identity. Lynx and Fantôme might have been killed! And who knows how long we've escaped from your sister—what if she returns? What is your plan to keep her away from here? What am I supposed to do now that you've moved the shelter to a new location? Surely the police will notice such a ridiculous display of magic and think we're in league now—I could be shut down! And what will happen to the cats then? Did you think of *any* of this, or are you incapable of considering anyone besides yourself, like all other magicians?"

Now, it's unlikely that I cut a particularly intimidating figure in that moment, with a cat stuck to my sweater and a kitten on my shoulder—Ron Ron seemed to take offense to my raised voice and was biting my ear. But I recoiled from my own boldness almost as soon as the last word left me, and cowered back, certain that he would blast me into the storm as he'd done with Valérie.

But to my astonishment, Havelock had also fallen back a step and was gazing at me with trepidation. "What a sermon!" he said. "Do you think I'm happy about this? I don't want anything to do with your charity, if you can call it that. For one thing, it's so silly that it stands out, which defeats the purpose—my shop requires a cover that is nondescript. And, two, I'm allergic to cats. I don't know what Yannick was thinking."

He returned to whatever he was doing with the pebbles. Several coins lay scattered about the floor from his battle with Valérie—did they have magic still in them? I had no idea, but as soon as the thought occurred, an uncharacteristically violent urge overtook me, and I snatched the coins up and began hurling them at him, one by one, in the hopes that he might end up magically strung up like Valérie, or, even better, transformed into something unpleasant.

"Ah!" he cried as one connected with his nose, and he shielded his face with his arm. Another coin bounced off, narrowly missing his glasses. "Now I'm convinced—Yannick has lost his senses, renting my shop to such an obstreperous person. Can't you see I'm working?" He gave me a considering frown. "I should fetch a sleep spell."

"You—" I stumbled to my feet, dislodging Clowder and Ron Ron, and raised my hands. "Don't you *dare*. Don't you dare do magic on me."

"It would be for your own good," he said, but he was already turning away again. "But I can see you'd only be more insufferable after you came to. Stop pestering me. Valérie could have learnt of this place too, you know. I have to make sure the wards are secure."

"From what I saw at the other shop, your *wards* are as good as useless," I snapped. "Will you at least do me the courtesy of telling me why she attacked us in the first place? Or is it beneath the dignity of the great Witch King to speak in anything other than nonsensical gibberish?"

He paused, toying with the pebbles in his hand. "She thinks I have a particular Artefact. A book that allows a person to travel to the past, there and back. It is the only enchantment of its kind ever created. But it doesn't exist—it's a rumour, and I've no idea why she's so convinced I have it. According to magical lore, it was created by Alice Vortigern, the greatest magician who ever lived, in the seventeenth century."

I was so relieved that he had finally answered me with something approaching clarity that a sliver of my anger dissolved. "Then—she wants to change the past?" I said. "But no—that's impossible. Even for magicians." I felt another surge of terror, thinking of such a spell in the hands of someone as violent as Valérie. "Isn't it?"

"I suppose so," Havelock said in a flippant tone that did little to reassure me. "I'm not a scientist. Most magicians fantasize about getting their hands on the spell because it would lead them to *other* powerful spells—namely, those housed in Vortigern's library. She put all her spells in books, and her library burned to the ground in the 1680s, around the time of her death. A magician who could retrieve even a dozen of Vortigern's spells in the moments before they burned could become the most powerful person in existence. That would not change the past, would it? The library was reduced to ash, and what would be altered if a handful of ashes went missing? But as for the present—well, that's another matter."

A shudder went through me. "Her spells are dangerous, then?"

His gaze grew distant. "One is rumoured to grant immortality. What is more dangerous than that? More people than you think would commit murder for such a spell." He shrugged, and placed another pebble against the wainscotting. "Though Vortigern is dead, so it seems unlikely that it ever existed. Why wouldn't she have used it on herself?"

"What about fathoms?" I said, trying to settle my whirling thoughts. "You used that word before. Magic, it—it comes from these fathoms?"

"It comes from a world called the Rivenwood, which we magicians have divided into fathoms, each darker than the last. They are imaginary borders, like lines on a map; the Rivenwood is contiguous."

"How many fathoms are there?"

"Five that we know of." He paused. "But from a practical standpoint, four."

He was truly the most infuriating man I'd ever encountered. "It's one or the other."

"No one has ever ventured to the Fifth Fathom," he said. "No one has dared. Likely it would tear a magician apart, even the most powerful among us. I don't mean physically. We wouldn't return as ourselves, but as something"—he seemed to search for words—"*else.*"

"I haven't the faintest idea what that means," I said despairingly. My dizziness seemed to be worsening. "What *is* the Rivenwood?"

"A world that lies behind this one like a shadow," he said. "It is entirely forest, strange and dark as all our oceans put together, and it grows stranger and darker the deeper one goes. It's a beautiful place. Too beautiful."

He paused, and I assumed he was ruminating, but he only turned his head and sneezed into his elbow. "The forest is the source of all magic," he went on stuffily. "Mortals have stumbled into it from time to time, through doors left open out of carelessness, but only magicians can travel freely between worlds."

"Why didn't you all just stay there, then?" I cut in bluntly. "If that's where you get your power from."

His expression became unreadable. "Magic is a dangerous thing."

"Dangerous to *you*?" I said. "How? Or do you mean you have enemies in the Rivenwood?"

But he had reached his limit of helpfulness, it seemed, and only replied caustically, "I have enemies of all descriptions, few worse than your ten-pound flea collectors." As if to underscore his point, he sneezed again.

I regarded him with disbelief as he murmured at his pebbles and fiddled with the curtains and lintels—I assumed he was doing magic, even if its effects were invisible to my eyes. Finally I said, "I have never heard anything so selfish in my entire life."

That brought him up short. I could see it was not remotely what he'd expected me to say, if he'd expected anything at all; at times he seemed to be speaking more to himself than to me. "Selfish," he repeated.

"Of *course* it's selfish!" I exclaimed. "This place, this—*otherworld* where magic lives—you could simply stay away from it, but instead you bring its magic into our world, where it doesn't belong, and inflict it upon ordinary people simply trying to go about their lives. *People,* not minor characters in a book titled *The Life of Havelock Renard.*"

I thought he wouldn't reply at first. He was gazing at me now in a confused sort of way, and I had the impression that nobody had ever spoken to him as I was doing.

I felt a prickle of terror. Now that the mingled fury and panic were wearing off, I was hit by the full realization of what I was doing. *Naturally no one has become angry at him before,* I thought. *This is Havelock Renard, and if anyone annoys him, he need only speak a word and transform them into a paper clip.*

But he didn't turn me into a paper clip, only turned away and said, as if it were an answer, "Magic is who I am." There was something oddly youthful in his voice.

I gave a breath of laughter. "And do you ever think of anyone besides yourself?"

"You *do* enjoy judging people, don't you." The awkwardness vanished, replaced by irritation and a cold sort of amusement. "We've been acquainted all of ten minutes, during which I've saved your life *and* your hapless menagerie, and all you've done is lecture me. I've never met a more self-righteous moralizer in my life. So you don't think I use my talents wisely, do you? Well, I wonder what you would be doing with yourself if you didn't have all these moggies to fuss over. Rounding up pigeons?"

My face flushed. "We would not have needed saving in the first place if you had been honest about who you were, because obviously I would not have taken the rental!"

I felt the lie as soon as I said it, and tried to tell myself it did not exist. Of course it would have been madness to rent the place had I known the Witch King dwelled down in the basement like some mythical monster.

And yet I couldn't help thinking, *If he'd only* stayed *down there. If only his enemies had never found him.* Élise and I could have remained in our state of blissful ignorance, and the cats would have been safe and warm in a more expansive home than they'd ever had before.

A home funded by illegal magic! my conscience protested weakly, and I grew even angrier at Havelock, but now only partly because he was wicked; it is impossible not to despise a person who calls to mind uncomfortable truths about oneself.

Havelock paused in the act of placing a pebble in a tiny crevice in the stone wall. He raised his arm, and I fell back, convinced he was about to unleash another horrible spell, but he only sneezed into his elbow again, and then again.

"Damn these cats!" he cried in a congested voice. "What did I tell you?"

"Would you like a tissue?" I said, maliciously polite.

He glanced over his shoulder and gave a start. "That one's loose!"

I turned and found that His Majesty had joined us silently, blinking his golden eyes at Havelock in a considering sort of way.

"Come, Your Majesty," I called, holding out my hand. "Here, boy."

But His Majesty, uniquely attuned to human discomfort, stalked towards Havelock, who fell back another step.

"What is it doing?" he demanded. He covered his mouth again and gave another violent sneeze. "And why is it so *large*? Can you not control it?"

"Your Majesty!" I hastened after the cat, but he only darted closer to Havelock, tail curled in a playful question mark. I made a dive for him and missed, the cat snaking aside and giving me the kind of growl that suggested he was eminently contented with this new game. Meanwhile, Havelock ducked behind the counter.

"Don't think I won't enchant you," Havelock threatened, seemingly to me, but it was possible he was talking to the cat. We might have continued in this ludicrous manner, me chasing His Majesty and His Majesty chasing Havelock, but there came an abrupt pounding on the door, and it was loud enough to jolt even His Majesty to attention.

CHAPTER 10

Both Havelock and I froze at the interruption, but he recovered more quickly than I.

"Valérie has never knocked in her life," he said, moving towards the door. His Majesty hopped onto the counter, all the better to keep Havelock in his line of sight. "And anyway, I've established that the wards are functioning, so even if it *is* her, she could only posture and act menacing, which is a regular hobby of hers—"

"Wait!" I cried. "That awful noise, when you relocated the shop—could someone outside the building have heard it?"

He opened his mouth, then paused. "Ordinarily, no," he said finally. "But as I said, I didn't have time to smooth the spell's intention, which made the journey rougher than it should have been. It's possible that—"

The pounding came again. "Hello?" came a voice. "Police."

"Yes," I said faintly, "I think someone heard it."

A second voice—an unfortunately familiar voice—said, more quietly, "What do you think?" which was followed by a murmured conversation.

"Laurent," I said, and it came out as half a groan. "Detective Rouzet—he came by last week, asking questions about you. He'll recognize the shelter. What do we do?"

Havelock, far from offering up any helpful solutions, made an irritated sound and scowled at the door. "Yannick is the one who deals with the police. I haven't the patience for it."

"At least they don't know we're here," I said, then added in a hoarse whisper, "Wait a moment. *Why* don't they know we're here?"

"The shop looks vacant from the outside," he said. "And they can't hear us, even if we shout." He gave me a dirty look. "Fortunately."

I gritted my teeth. We both stared at the door, Havelock rubbing at his hair again. The officers spent another moment murmuring together, then there came the unmistakable sound of shuffling feet, which slowly died away.

"They're gone," I said, overcome with relief.

"For now," Havelock said grimly. "Likely they've left to get a warrant. They'll kick the door in if we don't open it then. I suppose I could weld it shut with an enchantment, but that would rather raise their suspicions, wouldn't it?"

My relief was swallowed by panic. "What do we do? How much time do we have? Can you move the shop back to Rue des Hirondelles?"

"Not quickly enough," he said. "I only had the one transposition spell, and *that* magic is of the Third Fathom; I can't just make another on short notice. I'd guess we have an hour or two, at most."

I didn't bother enquiring how he'd come to be such an expert in police warrants. "You'll have to—to enchant them, then. Make them forget all about us."

"There is no such thing as memory magic," Havelock said.

"Don't you think that if there were, nobody would have learned of magicians in the first place? We'll just—" He looked around, frowning. "Hide the cats, I suppose."

I gave a disbelieving laugh. "Have you ever tried to *hide* a cat before? They aren't exactly cooperative beasts. And we have nearly fifty! You'd have less difficulty hiding a gorilla."

Havelock drummed his fingers on the windowsill. "If only I could summon Yannick—he'd know how to deal with this. But I sent him to Gaspé to barter with an Artefact smuggler."

"Yannick," I repeated. "Who *is* Yannick, anyhow?"

"Yannick is Yannick. He has no secret identity. You think that man could have kept it to himself?"

I almost laughed, picturing Yannick's animated expressions. I stopped myself and scowled at him. "Then he *is* your representative?"

"He's my apprentice. He's been with me two years now."

"What!" I couldn't believe it. Yannick Abrams, a magician. "But he isn't—" I frowned, squinting at Havelock, who seemed both *more* and *less* real than a regular person. "He doesn't *look* like a magician," I finished, unable to articulate what it was they looked like. "Like the rest of you."

Havelock shrugged. "He hasn't been practicing magic long, thus the change is less visible in him." He added in a mutter, sweeping his gaze around the shop, "We can put the scarves away, and I've a spell that can disguise the oven. That's only a minor charm; I've plenty of *them*. But that still leaves..."

"A disguise," I murmured. An idea had crept unpleasantly into my thoughts. I say *unpleasantly,* because I had just then been wondering if it might not be easiest to simply turn Havelock in when Laurent returned. I could plead ignorance regarding the magic shop and its owner's identity.

But would Laurent believe me? I had no idea. How plausible was it that I'd had no inkling my shelter was being used to hide such an unsavoury operation? And even *if* Laurent believed me, what would happen to the shelter if Havelock's shop was shut down?

I already knew what would happen. Winter was here, and we had nowhere else to go. Like it or not, I was stuck with Havelock Renard—absurdly, horribly—at least until Élise and I could work out what to do about the situation.

Grimly, I said, "I have an idea."

CHAPTER 11

When the knock came again, I was ready. We'd finished ten minutes before—Havelock had been right in his estimate, and the police had returned after barely an hour. I'd spent the time pacing so energetically I half expected to see a groove in the floor.

Havelock, for his part, had changed into strange but expensive-looking clothes, which had the same air of the theatrical as his cloak: dark slacks and an oversized sweater made from a fabric I didn't recognize, as well as pointed leather boots. Then he seated himself moodily on the counter as we waited, one leg drawn up, looking the very image of the volatile Witch King of his reputation. He seemed to veer back and forth between a kind of social awkwardness, imperfectly concealed by sarcastic commentary, and a cold, unnerving confidence. This was almost worse than the abeyant danger of his magic, as it made me nervous and off-balance, unsure which aspect of his personality my questions would be met with. I was remembering to be afraid of him again, and I both avoided his gaze and felt my attention irresistibly drawn to him, as a prey animal would eye a predator. I hated it.

He'd unleashed some sort of orb that reminded me a little

of the one Valérie had used, though his was larger, with the suggestion of wings. He opened his hand to send it darting from one end of the shop to another, or crooked a finger to make it turn lazy spirals over the floor. His Majesty had regarded it with wary disdain, but Banshee—who had emerged from her hiding place upstairs—had naturally made several ill-advised attempts at catching it, yowling silently at me whenever I stopped her.

"Well?" I said, straightening my skirt. "Are you not going to hide yourself? It would defeat our efforts to have you sitting there, glowering. You might as well have *wicked magician* tattooed on your forehead."

He removed a coin from his pocket. "Let them in."

"Fine," I said, too fed up with him to argue. I was still sweating, and I had several new scratches on the backs of my hands. If he wanted to sit there and watch himself get arrested, let him.

I plastered a smile on my face and unlocked the door. "We're not open till nine," I began, blinking against the light of the bustling street. "But if you—oh! Detective Rouzet."

"Agnes?" He goggled at me. His face was red from the cold, almost a match for his hair, and he wore a plaid scarf over his wool coat. Beside him was another officer, this one in uniform, a woman with a severe look and intimidatingly broad shoulders. Their breath rose around them in clouds, and a dusting of snow clung to their coats, though the sun was beginning to break through the storm.

"Is everything all right?" I said, not bothering to hide my worry.

"I—that's what we're trying to determine," he said. "The neighbours reported an explosion."

I wasn't sure I'd describe the colossal squelching sound as

an explosion, but what else could you call it? I nodded, thinking desperately of Élise. How would she manage this? No doubt she'd have a tidy lie already on the tip of her tongue.

"Yes," I agreed, and my tone was so natural it surprised me. "In the alley behind the shop, it sounded like. I assumed some kids got hold of a firecracker from the stores for the winter festival."

Laurent made no reply, only kept blinking at me, but his companion said brusquely, "Do you mind?" and motioned to the shop.

"Not at all." I stepped aside for them. They stamped their boots free of snow on the landing and looked about them. I gave a little start, for Havelock had vanished like—well, a magician.

"Nice place," the other officer said, giving me a gruff smile. "Been here long?"

"First day," I said, returning the smile. I pictured Élise, her easy confidence, which somehow seemed to increase whenever she launched into one of her elaborate fabrications. "Our main branch is on Rue des Hirondelles. We've been doing so well that we decided to open a second location."

Some of the confusion left Laurent's face, replaced by skepticism. "A second location? You've enough demand for *two* cat shelters?"

"We hope to open a third within a year or two," I said breezily—I was beginning to enjoy myself. I had always fantasized about expanding the charity, and even if I knew it wasn't real, I couldn't help but lean into the act. "We're planning to use this one for the more difficult cases, and for veterinary appointments, given the space—checkups, treatments, spaying and neutering, that sort of thing. Rue des Hirondelles will remain our primary location. But we'll offer adoption services at both branches."

"And what will your neighbours think about that?" the second officer said, looking amused for some reason. I wondered where on earth we were—Rue Sainte-Sophie was several miles long, bisecting the business district and several eclectic immigrant neighbourhoods.

"We've not yet introduced ourselves," I said with a regretful shake of my head. "It's been a busy time. We've had to do most of the moving-in at night, after we close the other shelter."

Laurent was staring at the cat cages, which now lined the rear wall, blocking access to the invisible oven—it was still *there*, for Havelock had merely created the illusion of solid brickwork, and I had even put my hand in it, to watch my arm disappear into the wall. I'd opened the windows to dissipate the infernal bakery aroma. Apple and cinnamon this time.

"Is that Lynx?" Laurent said.

"Hmm?" I affected confusion while my heart gave a nervous skitter.

Laurent paced to the back of the shop and peered through the bars of the third cage from the left. We'd rearranged the cats within them, as well as the cages, and had moved three of the orphaned kittens into the cage with Clowder and her remaining brood to give the illusion of a different litter. The poor calico—now enchanted to look like a tortoiseshell—sat glaring at me, none too pleased to have her charges expanded in number. One of her foster children was teething on her tail.

"I thought—" Laurent's voice trailed off. He gazed past the bars at the grey cat peering back at him, who stuck her paw through, slashing it in his direction. "This one looks a great deal like Lynx."

I forced a laugh. "Oh, don't you remember? Lynx is black. She's at the other shelter, of course. She took quite a liking to you, didn't she? She's still available, if you're interested."

I began to babble about our adoption process while Laurent frowned and Lynx continued to claw unhelpfully at the air, in no doubt of Laurent's identity nor her desire to get to the man who'd been so taken with her, and she, it seemed, with him.

"You've quite a few orange ones," the other officer noted, having come to stand at Laurent's side. "And look! They've all got a white eye patch."

"It's a common pattern," I said while silently cursing Havelock. I'd made this exact point to him, but he'd only argued that it was faster for him to replicate one illusion multiple times than create a new one for every cat. We'd only changed their colour—everything else remained the same.

They're cats, Havelock had said, infuriatingly oblivious to my concern. *The police are not going to examine them closely.*

"And look at the coat on this one," the woman went on. She crouched down and squinted at Thoreau. "Why, he's practically red! I've never seen a red cat before. Who knew?"

"That's a rare breed," I said weakly. "The—the Danish foxcoat."

The officer elbowed Laurent. "You could be related!"

"Offer them tea," an accented voice murmured in my ear. "It will make them remember how busy they are."

I gave a yelp that I managed to bite back, resulting in an odd sound, half gasp and half snort.

Laurent turned to me. "Agnes?"

I smiled, or tried to. "I thought I saw a mouse."

"You've a ready solution for that," the woman said. She was

still examining Thoreau. "You know, I quite like this one. He's getting on in years, isn't he, but look at that face."

I realized I was shivering lightly. I could sense Havelock standing very close behind me, like a phantom, his chest only an inch or so from my back—I'd felt his breath in the hollow of my ear. The problem was that he was completely invisible, which made everything in me cry out at the wrongness of it. Perhaps magicians were used to this sort of thing, but I wasn't.

He placed his hand lightly on my shoulder, and I watched in horror as four little creases formed in the fabric of my blouse. "It's only me," he murmured, and I almost laughed—as if I should take comfort from this. He was close enough that a lock of his hair touched my temple when he leaned in, sending a shiver through me like the brush of a ghost's fingertip. He smelled smoky and slightly sweet—a mixture of incense and cigars, most people would have guessed, yet I knew that was not it.

It was the smell of magic. The smell that had filled the old shelter when I came home to find a hole blasted in the wall. This was stronger than that, without anything human woven into it.

"Would you care for some tea?" I managed, still shivering. Havelock had taken a step back—how I knew that, I don't know, I only knew that his presence had a gravitational pull, or maybe it was fear sharpening my senses.

"Thank you, but we should be off," the woman said, straightening. "We still need to see if anyone else in the neighbourhood heard anything. But perhaps I'll return later."

"Absolutely," I said. I wasn't certain if she meant to return to see Thoreau or to interrogate me further, but once again I began babbling about adoption fees and paperwork, which seemed to be the right response. A little smile played on her face, and she cast a longing, almost childlike look over her shoulder at the cats. Laurent, at her side, remained silent.

"Thank you, Agnes," he said, giving me a look that I couldn't interpret. "No doubt I'll see you again back at Rue des Hirondelles. I'm often in that neighbourhood."

And with that, they departed.

I closed the door behind them and leaned against it, just in time to see Havelock reappear.

It was as if he'd come out from behind a curtain, its fabric made from the light and colours of the shop itself. There was a faint ripple, and he stepped sideways, brushing at his clothes as if removing dust.

I felt a wave of nausea, and there came a ringing in my ears. I slumped to the floor before I passed out, though I think I *did* pass out, just for a moment. When I opened my eyes, he was crouched at my side. I didn't like the way he was always darting about or appearing in unexpected places. It put me in mind of a spider.

"Hair full of spiders, eyes like twin fires," I murmured.

"What?" he said.

"You need to help me with the cats," I informed him—my voice was a little fuzzy, and felt as if it were coming from somewhere else. "Their breakfast is late, and I have to get on with the checklist."

He wrinkled his nose. "Oh, of course—I'll get right to it. You heat the water for their baths and I'll pour the milk, and then you can send for an ambulance while I pass out on the floor, wheezing."

"Cats don't need baths," I mumbled. My head was swimming dreadfully.

Havelock took no notice. "I must travel to the Rivenwood to gather the magic necessary for putting the shop back where it was," he said, and frowned. "I was not planning to venture there so soon after my last visit, but needs must."

"Why?" I said. "Will—will something happen to you?"

"I'm touched by your concern for my well-being," he replied, a little too glibly. He pressed something small into my hand. Another coin. "Or I would be, if you hadn't just sicced your Lilliputian panther on me. Stay here until I get back. If Valérie returns, you can alert me by speaking the incantation I've inscribed in the metal—"

I dropped the coin as if it were a hot coal. "I'm not doing magic."

He leaned back on his heels, adjusting his glasses at me. "It's a simple first-order spell. I would have thought you'd want some way to protect these miserable beasts." His words seemed to trigger a memory, and he cast a spooked look over his shoulder, but His Majesty was nowhere to be seen. The slippery creature had hidden himself somewhere when he'd seen what we were doing to the other cats, likely viewing such alterations as an insult to his dignity.

"I have no intention of staying here until you return," I said, and a sudden fear seized me. "You had better not lock me in."

Perhaps if he were a little less distracted, and not so evidently preoccupied with whatever wickedness he was plotting next, he might have noticed that I was teetering on the edge of my sanity, but he only looked at me as if I were being deliberately ornery. His expression hardened and something flickered in his eyes. Something else, or possibly some*one* else—that's the best I could describe it. "I don't have time to argue with you. If you care so little about your life, by all means go strolling about the city while Valérie is hunting you."

"Do *not* lock me in," I repeated, because I wasn't listening to him at this point. My terrified mind had fixated on this, for some reason—that he would disappear and leave me trapped there like a maiden in a dragon's cave, kept in store until its appetite returned. Élise would have no idea where I'd gone. All I wanted in that moment, overwhelmingly, was Élise.

He left me on the floor and strode to the middle of the room. He started sideways, for Banshee had emerged from some corner and came towards him with her tail raised, mouth opening and closing. This didn't surprise me: given the cat's unhinged nature and general witlessness where her personal safety was concerned, it was natural that she should mistake Havelock Renard for a friend.

"What a racket," he said, or I thought he did; I must have misheard, for Banshee was making no more noise than she generally did—which is to say, none at all. "Out of the way, you ridiculous creature."

The way of what? I had time to wonder, before his meaning became suddenly, horrifically clear.

A door appeared in the middle of the shop—I say *door* only for want of a better word. Though roughly door-shaped, it was more like a gash in the fabric of the world, jagged and flickering. Beyond the door was an ancient forest at night, colossal trees clothed in layers of moss and ivy. I realized a heartbeat later that it wasn't night, only the trees were so large and their canopies so lush that little light could slip through. The air was cool and scented with rain and green leaves, and the forest floor was carpeted in flowers, mostly white, like scraps of lace, but there were wild roses, too, clambering up an oak tree, and a line of blue in the distance where the white flowers became something else.

I was drawn forward almost against my will. There was something about that forest that made me wish to wade into it like a summer sea. Through a gap in the trees I saw a glimpse of mountains, towering and snowbound. Atop the nearest one was a stone ruin, too ancient and decayed for its purpose to be guessed at. I realized another ruin lay only a few feet beyond the door—a pile of stones nearly consumed by moss, and what might have been a mosaic floor, broken and leaf-strewn.

I was shivering again, and the clean smell of rain and wildflowers no longer felt welcoming, but wild and inhospitable. What *was* this place, and why had it been abandoned? The longer I gazed at it, the more uncanny it seemed. The boughs swayed too elegantly, as if the trees were composed of something more soft and slippery than wood, and the flowers were improbable in so shadowy a place, as if they were fed by the darkness. Something—someone?—howled in the distance.

"Havelock," I cried in sudden warning, because something was *there*, in the forest. I saw it darting behind one tree, and then another, as if it was trying to conceal itself. It had only the vaguest shape of a man, and seemed made from billowing shadow. Another shade lurked in a copse in the distance, or perhaps more than one—it was difficult to discern where the tree-shadow ended and the creatures began.

"It's all right," Havelock said. He was gazing into the forest world with a strange expression on his face: warily, but with a smile hovering around his eyes that suggested the place was not only familiar to him, but congenial. "Those are only spectres—weak ones. They won't trouble me."

He stepped through the door, and as he did, his human

likeness was gone. It did not seem to change into something else, but rather *dissolved,* as if it had been little more than mist or something equally insubstantial, which the wind could scatter. In his place was the monster of shadow and flame I had glimpsed before, formless and terrible, and then he vanished into the forest.

Perhaps he closed the door behind him, or maybe it drifted shut. I didn't see, for I had fainted dead away again.

CHAPTER 12

When I came to, Banshee was licking my hand. She placed her paws on my arm when she saw my eyes open, then butted her head against my chin.

My head spun. The shelter smelled of magic, and where Havelock had disappeared into that dark forest, the floor was stained black, as if from spilled ink. I rolled onto my side, dislodging the cat, and threw up. This had the useful effect of both settling my stomach and giving me something to do. Once I was certain I could stand, I cleaned the floor, then picked up Banshee, who'd been shadowing me the entire time, a worried look on her small face.

"It's all right," I whispered. "I'm all right."

I don't think I convinced her any more than I convinced myself, but she nestled into me as I shivered, her claws pricking my arm.

I desperately needed fresh air, so naturally I decided to ignore everything Havelock had said. Why he thought I'd listen to him after what I'd seen, I had no idea, but the overriding thought in my head was to put as much distance between myself and Havelock Renard as possible. And anyway, I didn't share his belief that Valérie would bother abducting me—why would she? Havelock cared nothing for me, and therefore I was useless to her as a bargaining chip.

Before I could do anything, though, including get my head on straight, I had to attend to the cats, who were chirruping at me in the way they always did when they wanted food. Either they were unaffected by what they had seen or they simply deemed cohabitation with a monster of lesser concern than getting their breakfast on time.

Never have I been so thankful for my checklists! I went through the morning one, luxuriating in its familiarity and orderliness, how it took a project of overwhelming complexity—the care and maintenance of several dozen demanding beasts of varying temperaments and health—and reduced it to the size of a sheet of paper. If only every problem in life could be dealt with thus.

I looked around for His Majesty, but I couldn't find him anywhere—not unusual, that; the creature liked to skulk about, perhaps to cultivate an air of mystery. I left his breakfast on the floor in the kitchen and went to the nearest telegram office to send a semi-coherent message to Élise. Then I went to a bakery, bought a chocolate brioche the size of my head, and ate the entire thing with my bare hands while sitting on a bench, barely noticing the stares of passersby.

The pastry was warm from the oven, the chocolate like ribbons of silk, and it calmed me a little. I hadn't taken note of a single thing I'd seen on my walk along Rue Sainte-Sophie. I knew the street well enough, though I didn't usually come as far as this block; it was busy here, unlike the gentle bustle of Rue des Hirondelles, with a tram that ran every four minutes during the height of the day. Colourful awnings advertised restaurants and cafés, all packed, but there were also a number of office buildings. The headquarters of *The Daily Gazette*, the city's largest English newspaper, was on the next block. Despite the snowstorm, the street was crowded, the shop owners having already cleared the snow from their sidewalks. A snowplow drawn by blanketed horses rumbled slowly down the street.

When I reached our newly relocated shelter, I stopped and began to laugh.

The stone shop front was conventional enough. It had no awning or signage, and the windows were covered by the same green curtains from the Rue des Hirondelles shop. What was curious about it was its location.

To the left sat Les Trois Soeurs, one of Montréal's most expensive restaurants, which naturally I'd never set foot in. It wasn't open yet, but I could make out several waitstaff circulating within, adjusting the mahogany furniture and setting elegant lanterns atop each table.

To the right of my new cat shelter, even more ludicrously, loomed the imperious façade of the city's main bank, with its towering columns, grand portico, and gleam of chandeliers visible through the glass doors. Impeccably dressed men and women, most carrying briefcases, marched up the wide flight of stairs, their expensive coats billowing behind them. A pair of women hurried past me, shoes clicking on the sidewalks, and I abruptly became aware of how shabbily I was dressed. The bank's staircase merged with the sidewalk outside the cat shelter, so that if you exited and took three paces in that direction, you would find yourself mounting the immaculate stone steps towards the towering grandeur that was the heart of the city's business realm and home to more wealth than I could conceive of.

I stopped laughing once I realized I was attracting stares and ducked back inside the shelter, locking the door behind me and then leaning against it.

I was going to kill Havelock.

I repeated this to myself because it was fortifying; in truth I knew I'd do no worse than scowl at him and try desperately not to cower—and that was the best-case scenario. Now that I knew what the Witch King truly *was*, I was inclined to think his reputation had painted a rosier picture than the reality.

CHAPTER 13

Élise arrived less than an hour after I sent the telegram. Gabriel was with her, dressed in a smart charcoal suit, but he informed me almost as soon as we'd exchanged hugs that he wouldn't be staying.

"I've a meeting in the Latin Quarter," he said. "I hope you two have a productive day—if there's anything you need, let me know."

"Of course," I said, noting his total lack of curiosity with regards to our new location, and the glance he exchanged with Élise. My sister had warned him about our mysterious and likely unsavoury landlord, and now, I guessed, she'd instructed him that he was to have as little to do with the shelter as possible in order to safeguard his reputation.

"Away with you," Élise said to him playfully as he paused at the door, looking as if he might change his mind. Gabriel was a solid, handsome man an inch or two shorter than Élise, with brown skin and wavy hair just beginning to grey at the temples. In his youth, he'd been a professional weightlifter who kept trim running marathons, and while the last decade had added a certain bulk to his midsection, still he gave off an impression of strength and sturdiness that had served him well in his political career, and which he was happy to play up for the papers, ensuring he was photographed helping to build housing for the poor and shovelling sidewalks after especially bad storms. In this he was a practical man, and yet he hadn't lost his enthusiasm for the job nor his skill at translating his principles into progress, even if he first had to compromise them a little—he'd been the reason several of those housing initiatives had passed in the first place.

"I mean it," he murmured to her. "If there's anything—"

"There isn't," she cut in. "Especially not with the election coming up. Your sister-in-law runs an animal shelter, and I help sometimes, and that's the extent of your knowledge on the subject. You're far too busy to worry about a bunch of alley cats."

"Not if these *cats* are dangerous," he said.

"The only person you have to worry about today is Michel Clement. He was your third-largest donor, yet he's not given you a penny this year. Go find out why, but first make sure to ask plenty of questions about his daughter's wedding. That man would talk all day about his children, and if you give him the chance, he'll remember why he's always liked you."

Gabriel sighed again and kissed her cheek. He tipped his hat to me and stepped back out into the snowy street.

Élise locked the door, then turned to face me. "What's going on, Agnes? Your telegram read like Banshee wrote it. What *is* this place? And—" She paused, sniffing. "And what on earth is that smell? That isn't *magic*?"

I wrung my hands. I wanted to be steady and unflappable, for Élise's sake, but it was difficult given that I'd spent half the night being nearly killed by impossible enchantments. I'd spent the last hour alternating between panicked ruminations about Havelock's intentions and elaborate plans for outfitting our new cat shelter, and was aware I looked more than a little manic. She listened to my story in silence, and merely narrowed her eyes at Havelock's name.

"You guessed?" I said, astonished.

"No," she said. "It wasn't a guess—the possibility occurred to me, in the same way you might wonder if you have some rare illness just from hearing it described. Apparently the mayor was briefed recently that Renard might be in the city, not New York like everyone thinks. There's been an increase in Artefact trafficking, and some of the world's most notorious magicians—including a few of Renard's associates—have been spotted in the streets. But the rumour's being kept very quiet, for obvious reasons."

"We'll have to work quickly," I said. "After Havelock moves the shelter back to Rue des Hirondelles, we'll have to fill *this* place with cats. We'll need cages, supplies, another sign—all of it."

Élise blinked. "Is *that* what you've been thinking about?"

"It's what I *have* to think about, Élise."

"Havelock Renard is our landlord," Élise said slowly. "And you're not worried about him killing you?"

"Of course he won't kill me," I said. "He wants me alive so I can continue covering for him and his abominable magic shop. Or so the shelter can."

Élise was silent for a moment. "Do we have time to operate *two* shelters? Do you?"

"We need to make time. The police are already suspicious enough—Laurent swallowed my story, but if the second shelter suddenly shuts down, that story is going to look even more like a cover for something."

Élise didn't reply, merely regarded me warily. "What?" I said.

"You're happy about this," she said.

My mouth fell open. "I'm *happy* the shelter is being used to hide the *Witch King*?"

"Maybe not that bit specifically," she said. "But you've always wanted to expand the shelter. I remember you and Robin talking about establishing a network of shelters across the city."

I flushed, looking away. "That was unrealistic. We both knew it."

"And now it's not. But this isn't the way to do it."

I couldn't understand her. "Aren't you the one who told me that it didn't matter if the shop was haunted or cursed? That anything was preferable to being out on the street?"

"I thought that was true," she said, folding her arms around herself. I realized then how frightened she was. Élise didn't show fear in the usual ways: she became still and quiet, and seemed to focus on something inside herself. She was like that after our parents died, as we sat in the hospital waiting room alongside the weeping relations of other patients. I recalled one of the nurses looking at her askance, thinking her cold, but I had known better.

"Agnes," she said, "you should leave now. Before he comes back."

I stared at her. "And go where?"

"I don't know. Anywhere. You can stay with me and Gabriel until you get yourself sorted."

"But the cats—"

"Your life is more important than the cats." She came forward and put her hands on my shoulders, pinning me in place with her grey eyes, so much like mine. "Agnes, he tried to start an *apocalypse*."

"Unsuccessfully," I said, even as another wave of nausea swept over me.

"And why was he unsuccessful?" she asked rhetorically—no one knew what had stopped Havelock's spell. The skies had darkened, the streets had filled with otherworldly shadows, and unnatural tremors had shaken the ground. Most assumed Havelock hadn't had the power to end the world, not that he'd had some change of heart.

"And will he do it again?" Élise added.

"No," I said. "I don't think it's true about him, Élise. Not everything, I mean. He claimed he was never trying to bring about the end of the world."

I said it with more conviction than I felt. Because that hadn't been what Havelock had said. What *had* he said? That it was *complicated*? Hardly a reassuring defense. Yet in my internal struggle between terror and fantasy—my fantasy about expanding the shelter, that is, and taking on more cats—it seemed that fantasy had won the day. Perhaps it was partly some form of self-defense against all I had seen, an excuse to think about something familiar, earthly. And yet—

I looked at the cats. Some slept in their nests of blankets, others watched me and Élise. I'd let a few out of their cages: those who wished to stretch their legs and were inclined to get along with one another. Clowder and her kittens were curled up in a heap by one of the radiators, and Thoreau, in one of his rare bursts of energy, was stalking a spider. I knew in that moment that I wouldn't abandon them for any reason.

I'd always known this, of course, but I suppose I'd never truly understood how far my resolve would go, that it might even stretch wide enough to accommodate villains like Havelock. The realization was both distressing and comforting.

"Oh, well, if he wasn't *trying* to," Élise said with dark amusement. "An honest mistake on his part, was it? He meant to cast the spell for ironing his shirt, but he got it mixed up with the apocalypse one he had lying around?"

"Please," I said, and something in my voice made her face soften. I knew she wasn't done arguing with me, but Élise had always followed my lead. It was a relic from our childhood, when we'd been each other's world.

"You know how I always tease you for needing to think the best of people?" she said. "That it's a compulsion, and one day you would regret it? I knew you'd prove me right, I just didn't expect it to be on this magnitude."

"Believe me, I have no desire to think the best of Havelock Renard," I said.

Élise gave me a long-suffering look.

"I *don't*," I insisted.

"I'd like to believe that," she said. "The alternative is that you've grown tired of indulging figurative monsters and now feel the need to humanize the real ones. Well, let's get to it." She looked around the shelter, her expression grim. "I assume you made a checklist?"

CHAPTER 14

I had, in fact, made a checklist while I'd been waiting for Élise, which listed all the requirements for equipping a second cat shelter. We spent much of the day securing additional cages, which required us to trudge through the snow to a farming supply store on the outskirts of the city, where we arranged to have them delivered to the shelter. Ordinarily I'd never have been able to afford so many new cages, not without scrimping and saving for months, but the recent increase in adoptions had brought with it an increase in donations, which gave us just enough to cover the cost.

On our way back to the Sainte-Sophie shelter, I convinced Élise to pass through an alley where I'd found cats sheltering before. There we met another orange tabby, who came barreling out of the cardboard box he'd been living in with an air of having expected us, then circled around me, screeching, as if I were monstrously late. He was a ragged little thing, not quite full grown, shivering in the cold.

He did not like to be picked up, evincing the contrariness that would be notable by its absence in any cat, but after I tucked him into the warmth of my coat he seemed to see the advantages, and dug his claws into my sweater. We walked the last mile back to the shelter thus, me cradling the cat with his head poking out of my coat, and him making an endless ruckus, mewling sonorously with what seemed like a combination of delight and terror. Well, I could understand *that* feeling well enough. His voice was remarkably loud and grating for such a tiny creature. Needless to say, Élise and I attracted stares the whole way home, as well as laughter and shouted remarks.

"He's Banshee's opposite," Élise remarked during a brief moment of silence while the beast caught his breath.

"It's like having an ambulance down my coat," I grumbled, and thus Ambulance we named him.

The grim reality was that, with winter setting in, the city's cat population would begin to decrease without our assistance. Soon we would be inundated with reports of cats sheltering on balconies and landings in the hopes of snatching tiny scraps of warmth, and we would not be able to help them all. But with a second shelter?

"We easily have space for another fifty here," I told Mina the following morning—I'd sent her a telegram directing her to our new location. "I'd like you to telegram all our volunteers, past and present—I want people out searching no later than tomorrow. And I'm going to speak to Havelock about paying you a salary."

The girl looked astonished. I'd told Mina the truth about our landlord's identity and the threat we were facing, for I trusted her. Her reaction had surprised me—far from being terrified, she'd merely grimaced, then nodded with a dubious sort of acceptance. More than once I'd wondered what sort of life the girl had lived before our paths crossed.

"You'll speak to—*him*?" Mina repeated.

"Of course," I said, ignoring the little shudder that coursed through me. "I daresay he owes us *some* remuneration for the danger he's put us in. And I've no doubt that horrible shop of his turns a healthy profit."

I opened the curtains, hung the *Cat Friends* sign in the window, and unlocked the shelter at nine o'clock, resigning myself to the ludicrousness of the situation. I half expected to be accosted by representatives of the bank, or perhaps the restaurant, objecting to the proximity of such an unsanitary establishment. I'd no idea what business we'd replaced, for Havelock's spell had superimposed the shelter over everything that had been here before, upstairs apartment and all, but I highly doubted it had been anything so humble as a charity. Fortunately, though, nobody took immediate offense; most of the well-heeled passersby simply did a double-take.

After barely ten minutes, the door swung open and an older man shuffled inside, stamping the snow from his boots. He was dressed in the same woolen finery as all those bound for the bank next door, and carried an expensive briefcase. Before I could even offer a greeting, he surprised me by gesturing to His Majesty, who was perched on the windowsill, surveying the street with leonine condescension.

"*Bonjour, mademoiselle,*" the man said, then added in English, "How much?"

It took me a moment to understand what he meant. "Oh! That one's not for sale. It's for the best, I promise you."

"Shame," he said, casting another look at His Majesty. "I had one just like him when I was a boy. A big black-and-white monster—half-wild and ill-tempered, but he took to me for some reason." A smile touched the corners of his eyes.

"I see." I mentally ran through our inventory, then motioned the man over to the cage belonging to Juliette, a long-haired brown tabby who came close to rivalling His Majesty in bulk. Thankfully, the cats had returned to their former colours over the course of the previous day, the enchantment draining from them like wet ink.

"She's not the colour you preferred," I said, "but she has a fiery streak. She likes to be carried from place to place like royalty, and has more than once fallen asleep in my arms."

"That sounds like my Sam," the man said with a laugh. "And that's quite a throne you've made for her. She looks positively mystical, like some magician's familiar."

I forced a laugh. Juliette's bedding, like that of the other cats, comprised one of the former tenant's cashmere scarves. Juliette's was particularly luxurious, double-layered and woven with gold thread in a houndstooth pattern, which sparkled becomingly against her fur. The scarves were undeniably useful, not only saving us money on bedding but setting the cats off to advantage, though I did feel guilty every time one of the exotic garments was the victim of a snagged claw or hair ball.

I opened the cage a little nervously, for I hadn't been lying about Juliette's temper—the beast was just as likely to claw strangers as condescend to be petted—but I need not have worried. After sniffing the man's fingers carefully, Juliette arched her neck and pushed her forehead into his hand.

"Would you like to hold her?" I enquired, trying not to sound too eager. Juliette had been at the shelter almost as long as Thoreau, owing mostly to her temperament, but she was also ten years old, and more likely to be passed over than the younger cats.

The man nodded, anticipation stealing over his expression, making his wrinkled face look years younger. I hefted Juliette and placed her carefully in his arms. The cat gave a yowl, but it seemed only an obligatory assertion of pride, for she began almost immediately to purr. The man looked her over, offering many soft-spoken compliments on her stripes, and her eyes narrowed to contented slits.

"I'm fully booked with meetings this morning," the man said, then glanced down at Juliette. "But meetings can be postponed, can't they?"

"Of course," I said, and the two of us exchanged mischievous smiles, like children.

I filled out the paperwork for him, for Juliette seemed disinclined to budge from his arms. He was Roger Fairwood, with an address in the wealthy neighbourhood at the foot of the mountain. He seemed to expect me to recognize his name, which put him in the same class as most rich men, but then seemed relieved when I did not, which made me like him better. He also insisted on paying double the adoption fee, which only increased my delight. Ten minutes later, he was out the door with Juliette—loudly protesting the affront—contained within a cardboard box, and a paper bag of food and other essentials.

"Back down to forty-five," I said to Mina, who was grinning at me from the counter. Like me, she'd long despaired of Juliette ever finding a home. "That was a stroke of luck."

"Luck," Mina repeated in a musing voice. She had one of her history textbooks propped open in front of her, for she liked to do her coursework in between clients. "Maybe. But I think this location will be good for us."

"Let's hope so," I said, my mood bolstered by Mina's confidence. Though she was a quiet person by nature, whenever Mina did voice an opinion, it tended to be proven correct.

CHAPTER 15

Élise arrived shortly thereafter, and we made our way to the Rue des Hirondelles shelter to see what had become of it, leaving Mina in charge of our new location.

"What will we do if *he's* there?" I said. Our rapid footfalls against the cobblestones echoed the pounding of my heart.

"Why would he be there?" Élise said. "He moved everything. So his workshop is on Rue Sainte-Sophie, isn't it?"

"I have no idea—I don't know how his horrid enchantment works." I hadn't gone down to the basement to check if Havelock had brought his workshop. The trapdoor was there, but there could be nothing beneath it, for all I knew. Havelock could still be in the Rivenwood.

A wisp of cold trailed down my back at the thought of that dark world, lush and foreboding. The memory was mixed with curiosity, which disturbed me almost as much as the place itself.

It was soon abundantly clear that wherever Havelock was, it was not Rue des Hirondelles. The shelter appeared unchanged from without; the green curtains, which somehow were here, too, were closed. But when I peered through the square of green glass in the door, it was as if the glass had grown thicker, more obscuring.

"What the hell," I muttered, fumbling with the key. The lock clicked and the door swung open. Because Rue des Hirondelles was on a hill, the door could only drift so far before it hit the slope of the sidewalk, which it did with a dull *clang*.

"My God," Élise said.

We were staring into—absolutely nothing. What lay beyond the threshold was a greyish void, scentless and ice cold. If that wasn't uncanny enough, the nothingness rippled slightly at the edges, as if testing its bounds. I held out a hand, wanting to see what it felt like, but Élise slapped it down.

"Have you lost your mind?" she demanded. "Don't touch it!"

"There isn't any *it* to touch," I pointed out.

"Well, then, don't touch what isn't there!" she cried, her voice rising in pitch. I stared into the absence for another moment.

"I thought there would be *something*," I murmured. But Havelock, it seemed, had been thorough in his relocation spell. I wasn't entirely certain there was even any *air* left behind. It was as if the former bakery had been torn from the fabric of the world by some god, as if I'd needed another reminder of the terrifying extent of his power.

It was fortunate that the door opened outwards—I don't know how we would have closed it again if we'd had to reach through the nothingness to grasp the doorknob. I pushed it shut.

"*Coudonc!*" I exclaimed. "This is absurd. Well, we certainly aren't opening today, are we? That will give the police another reason to suspect us of something nefarious."

"Really?" Élise gazed at the shop doubtfully. "It looks the

same from the outside. They'll probably just assume we're busy arranging the new location, if they notice at all. I don't think anyone's first thought when they see a *Closed* sign on a shop is that the owners have magically relocated to another street and left an abyss behind."

"Laurent is already suspicious of our landlord," I argued. "And he knew something was off about the cats yesterday—poor Thoreau looked like he'd been bathed in tomato juice! I don't want to put even more questions into his head."

"You mean Detective Rouzet," Élise said.

"Yes." I frowned suspiciously at the look on her face. "What?"

"You keep calling him *Laurent*," she said, knitting her brows in exaggerated confusion. "I wonder why you're on such familiar terms?"

"He asked me to call him Laurent," I said even as I felt my cheeks heat. Being a person who cried and blushed easily was enormously inconvenient, as people were always taking it to mean more than it did.

And it certainly *did not* mean anything in this case.

"I wonder if Laurent suspects that Havelock owns the place," I said, speaking half to myself. "If the mayor knows he's in the city, I'll bet the police have been warned, too."

Élise grimaced, her gaze fixed on something behind me. "Speak of the devil."

I started and whirled around, but it was only Yannick—he'd crossed the street in our direction and was now kicking his way through the snow piled against the sidewalk.

"Hello!" Yannick said, giving us one of his nervous smiles. "I trust everything is well? I'm sorry I was gone a few days—I hope those pipes didn't give you any trouble in my absence! I had some business—ah, I was visiting a sick aunt. In Gatineau.

Yes, I had business in Gatineau, in addition to the sick aunt, so—"

"Yannick," I said. "Shut up."

"We know you're a magician, you ass," Élise said, advancing on him. "And we know you were hiding Havelock Renard in the basement." She punctuated each sentence by stabbing her finger into his chest. It should have been ridiculous. Élise was a full head shorter than him, but her expression held such focused fury that Yannick blanched and fell back. "You lied to my sister, and nearly got her killed. You and that bastard you work for. If you don't start telling the truth, I'll go down to Havelock's secret little shop and find a spell that will blast you to pieces. I might not be a magician, but I promise I'll give it my all."

"I—" The colour had left Yannick's face, and he stood gawping at us. "Havelock—is he—?"

"His sister attacked us," I said. "She nearly pulled the building down on our heads. We're lucky none of the cats were injured or worse."

"Valérie," he murmured, wincing. "She found him, then. He always said she would, despite all the spells he put on the place to keep her away. Is Havelock all right?"

He looked so worried that it brought me up short. I don't know what sort of relationship I'd expected Yannick to have with Havelock—well, what kind of relationship could exist between the Witch King and his henchman?—but I'd not imagined there would be much warmth in it.

"He's alive, if that's what you mean," I said. "He had to relocate the shelter, so he's gone to the Rivenwood to collect enough magic to put it back."

Yannick looked alarmed. "The Rivenwood! But he's been trying to stay *away* from there—he promised he would. How long ago did he leave? Perhaps I can pull him back before he goes too deep."

He yanked open the door to the shelter and made to charge inside, but luckily Élise and I placed a hand on either of his shoulders and hauled him back in time.

"Oh, my." He squinted at the abyss. "That—you weren't exaggerating. He *moved* it. The whole thing! Fascinating."

He continued to stare into the nothingness as if it were some enchanting landscape. I reached out and shut the door again before the couple passing on the opposite sidewalk could get a look.

"He's been gone since yesterday," I said. "The shelter is now on Rue Sainte-Sophie. I thought you would have known he had a spare hideout in the city."

"He mentioned something about it once," Yannick admitted. "But Havelock has woven so many spells that it's difficult to keep track—some of them are beyond the capabilities of any living magician, or perhaps any magician at all, save Vortigern. I'd no idea he'd created a relocation spell of this magnitude—I didn't know this was even possible! What was it *like*? When he cast it, I mean."

"Horrid," I said succinctly. Given my recent experiences, I found the worshipful look on Yannick's face distasteful.

"Well, if Valérie is in town, that explains the business at the train station," Yannick said. "I would have been here hours ago, if I hadn't been held up."

"What business?"

"A group of magicians who came in on one of the earlier trains decided to have a bit of fun when they arrived," he said, shaking his head. "One transformed the locomotive into a team of winged horses, which levitated the cars as they pulled into the station. Another animated the benches in the station and had them lurch about, knocking people over, and made the turnstiles into hideous mouths that bit you as you went through. As you can imagine, this created some hysteria among their fellow travellers. Several people were trampled as they fled, and the northbound line had to be shut down. It sounds like the work of Valérie's followers."

"Her *followers*?" Élise repeated.

Yannick winced. "Yes—Valérie has more than a hundred of them. She calls them her apprentices, but really they're just glorified hangers-on. Wherever Valérie goes, they follow, and most have as little respect for the law, or really common decency, as Valérie herself. They live like the aristocrats of old, for pleasure and their own amusement, doing just as they please. Did you hear about the scene in Pamplona last year? Those bulls turned into minotaurs? Those were her magicians at work."

"Wonderful," I murmured. My pounding headache had returned. "Just wonderful! And now they're here. Because of Havelock."

"He isn't—" Yannick began, but as if there were some enchantment in the name itself, there came another colossal *squelch*, nearly identical to the one last night.

"*Câlisse!*" Élise swore, covering her ears. Yannick started backwards and slipped on a patch of ice.

"Why does magic have to be so *loud*?" I exclaimed. "We'll have the police at our door again."

"I doubt it," Yannick said, picking himself up. "It seemed as if all the officers in the city had been called to the train station. I'm not sure they have the time to investigate noise complaints at the moment."

Hand trembling slightly, I pulled the door open again. And there was the shelter, returned to its rightful place, flagstones and lofty ceilings and ridiculous oven and all.

The shelter, and everyone in it. The cats were yowling in outrage, and an elderly woman stood gawping by the counter. I recognized her as Thérèse, one of our regular donors and occasional volunteers, who seemed frozen in place, a blank look upon her face. I saw no sign of Mina, which meant she must have stepped out for her break.

"Oh no," I murmured, but Élise surprised me by springing immediately into action.

"Damn construction noise!" she said, taking Thérèse by the arm and gently shepherding her towards the door. "They're repairing the sewers on this street, I heard. Lovely to see you, Thérèse, but we need to close early today—it's a lot of work, opening a new location!"

On and on she chattered, until she and Thérèse reached the door. The woman spoke not one word, only stared at Élise in dull shock, then at the altered streetscape without. Bidding her a warm goodbye, Élise shut the door behind her and turned the lock.

"Well done," I said, unsure if I wanted to laugh or cry. Never have I been so grateful for Élise's gift of deception. "But you've overlooked one minor detail."

"I'm aware of that." Élise leaned against the door. Her eyes had a glazed look, but otherwise she appeared ominously calm. "If *you* can come up with a reasonable explanation for the shelter relocating itself to the other side of the city, and then moving back again, have at it. At least she's gone."

Yannick was paying us no attention. He'd gone to the rear of the shop, calling Havelock's name.

"He's not here," he said unhappily. "He must have returned

to the Rivenwood after he put the shop back—or perhaps he's at the other shop."

He made as if to depart, but Élise stepped deftly into his path. "Oh, no you don't. We've not had anywhere near enough answers from you."

"Why would Havelock be at the other shelter?" I demanded. "Isn't it a void now, like this place was?"

"*Hein?*" He gave me a puzzled look that I found more than a little absurd. "Of course not. He only moved *this* shop, not the one in Rue Sainte-Sophie. So, naturally, the Rue Sainte-Sophie shop has now assumed its former appearance."

"Naturally," I said; Yannick seemed not to notice the sarcasm.

"You should stay here," he said. "Valérie can't get in if Havelock has fixed the wards, but that won't stop her from accosting you in the street if she thinks you mean something to Havelock."

"I mean nothing to him," I said with certainty. "And Havelock claims he doesn't have the book she wants."

"Yes, and she clearly doesn't believe him," Élise said. "Surely she'll just keep attacking the shelter, if she's that desperate to get her hands on this time-travel enchantment. So how do we get rid of her?"

"I don't know," Yannick said. He looked pale and more than a little lost. "Valérie wants power. Magicians have no government, no ruling bodies, mostly because there aren't enough of us. Not that there haven't been magicians who have *tried* to set themselves up as emperor or queen or what have you, and force the rest of us to worship them. But they've all failed eventually."

"So that's it?" I said. "She wants to set herself up as a queen?"

"I don't know if she's ever said so explicitly," he said. "Valérie likes to talk about *rights*. About freedom. She believes it's wrong that magicians should have to conceal their powers, as we've always done—to 'make ourselves small,' as she says, to fit into the world. We were born with the ability to gather magic, and thus we should be free to use it as we will."

"It's clever rhetoric," Élise said thoughtfully. "Yet if I recall correctly, those minotaurs killed ten people."

"Yes," Yannick said, looking away. "I really must find Havelock. Now that Valérie has tracked him down, we must come up with—"

"You do that," I said. "I'm going down to the basement."

Yannick froze midstep. "You're— Agnes, Havelock doesn't—"

"I don't care what Havelock thinks." I turned and marched to the back of the shop, leaving Yannick to trail after me. "He's dragged me and the cats into this mess, without even so much as an apology, to hide his precious shop. It's only fair that I should see what I'm being used for."

CHAPTER 16

"Agnes, you really shouldn't— He doesn't like anyone in his workshop; he only barely tolerates me."

Yannick hovered at my elbow, looking simultaneously worried and apologetic, as I dragged the rug aside and grasped the chain on the trapdoor. Élise stepped forward to help.

"If he comes back while you're down there..." Yannick trailed off.

"He'll what?" I said. "Blast my head off? He won't. He needs me."

Élise and I lifted the trapdoor while Yannick muttered to himself and knitted his fingers together. Still, he made no move to stop me, which I suspected he could have done, if he'd really wanted to. He was a magician, after all. No—it was clear that Yannick wasn't truly afraid of Havelock. Why, I had no idea.

I wasn't about to tell him the real reason I wanted to get a look at Havelock's shop. Namely, that I'd begun to suspect he was lying to me.

Not about everything. Likely his warnings about Valérie had been true. But why was Valérie so convinced Havelock had

Vortigern's book? Wasn't it just as likely that he did and didn't want to give it up?

And if Havelock had the book, why shouldn't I take it and give it to Valérie?

I didn't doubt Valérie's malicious intentions—I'd *seen* her, after all—but I had no reason to believe she was any worse than Havelock, or would do any more damage with a dangerous Artefact than he would. After all, it hadn't been Valérie who had unleashed an apocalypse. If I gave Valérie the book, she would go away and leave the shelter alone. This felt even more important after what I'd heard about her followers.

Élise had fetched the oil lantern from the counter, and she set off down the steep wooden staircase below without another word.

"You really shouldn't," Yannick said, still wringing his hands uselessly.

"You might be right," I said. "But there are plenty of things you magicians *shouldn't* do, yet you do them anyway. So you've no place to lecture me." And I followed Élise.

The staircase was so steep that I felt safer going sideways, clinging to the railing like an old woman. It kept going down and down, much deeper than I'd expected. Consequently, I wasn't able to look about me until I stepped onto the floor, which was, to my surprise, made of creaky oak—I'd been picturing stone or earth, like the floor of a cave. Perhaps a cauldron bubbling over a fire.

My first impression was of utter disorder. The space was about the size of the shop above, I thought, and should have felt roomy, particularly given the impressive height of the ceiling. But shoved against every wall were towering glass-front cabinets filled with an assortment of the most random objects, and towers of boxes and crates filled the remaining floor space, offering only narrow passages between. Some objects had the look of archaeological finds, ceramic vessels or stone carvings, while others were more contemporary, including a gumball machine and gramophone. Near the centre of the room was a massive table where someone had clearly been writing, for by the single chair were a stack of papers and pen, in addition to the piles of books and coins and other miscellany. The place was illuminated by a warm, gentle glow, emanating from small globes of light set into the ceiling and walls, which gave it an air of an enchanted museum. It was a curious thing, for the light was uneven and flickered like starlight. I went towards one of the lights, which was surrounded by an odd, net-like lampshade.

As I leaned closer, the light darted sideways into a crevice in the wall with a quick, many-legged sort of skitter.

I recoiled. "They're spiders!"

"Yes," Yannick said, grimacing, though there was admiration mixed into his expression. "Havelock grew tired of chasing them out, so he put a spell on the entire place: any spider who strays here develops a sort of bioluminescence. Well, if we can't be rid of them, why not put them to use? And it saves on lantern oil. He called it *economical*."

Élise shook her head. "Of course he likes spiders. Proper familiars for a witch king."

The lighting no longer struck me as particularly cozy. My skin tingled as if the things were crawling on me.

Against the wall, behind the landing of the staircase we had just descended, was another set of stairs. "How deep does it go?" I said.

"I'm not sure," Yannick replied. "This is his workshop, but

below this are three more floors, mostly crammed with Artefacts, like this one. There's a trapdoor in the lowest floor, and I don't know where it leads. He keeps it locked."

"Another trapdoor," I muttered, exchanging a look with Élise.

"Maybe it leads back to the shop," she said with a mirthless smile. "Or some hellish otherworldly version."

I shuddered. "Or the Fifth Fathom of the Rivenwood."

"Not possible," Yannick said. "All doors to the Rivenwood lead to the First Fathom."

"Why?" Élise asked.

Yannick seemed to ponder. "It's difficult to explain. The Rivenwood doesn't obey our laws of nature. You can reach the other fathoms from anywhere in the forest—it doesn't matter where you start. The farther you walk, the deeper you go."

"That's clear as mud," Élise muttered.

"I always assumed the trapdoor just leads to another floor, where he keeps his rarest enchantments," Yannick said.

I'd had the same thought, which meant that was likely where I'd find Vortigern's book. I paced over to the stairs and made my careful way down to the second floor. It was similar in proportions to the first, and even more poorly organized, with boxes stacked on top of one another, some towering high above my head. It was also brighter, owing to an even larger convocation of spiders.

"This is appalling," I muttered. I didn't mean the spiders, or not *only* them; I'd never seen such a disorganized space. How did Havelock concentrate on whatever unpleasant enchantments he was concocting when he knew this horror lay below him? I wondered half seriously how I'd be able to sleep now—I, who can never retire without putting the shelter in order and writing out tomorrow's to-do list, ordered into categories. The mouldering skeletons of Havelock's victims would have been more tolerable than this.

I shuddered and went back up the stairs, almost bumping into Élise and Yannick on their way down. I was tempted to explore further, but I'd only have had Yannick breathing down my neck the entire time.

"Are these *all* enchantments?" I demanded when we returned to the first floor. "Even these?" I gestured to the closest cabinet, which was full of antique clocks, all stopped at a different hour.

"I believe so," Yannick said. "Havelock has been collecting Artefacts for years. He trades them, sometimes, for other Artefacts. Some he's enchanted himself. A few are empty of magic—he experiments, and not every enchantment turns out."

I stared at him. "You sound like you don't know what half of them do."

"Far more than half," Yannick said with a wince. "Havelock doesn't keep records. Honestly, I wouldn't be surprised if he's forgotten most of them himself, particularly those on the lower floors. It's chaos down there."

If *this* didn't already constitute chaos, I had no desire for him to elaborate. Shaking my head, I turned slowly to take it all in. What astonished me more than the Artefacts, though, were the books.

They were everywhere. A bookshelf twice my height sat to the left of Havelock's workspace—it had a ladder attached, and its shelves were disorderly, some double-stacked, others gap-toothed. I tilted my head, examining the titles. I wouldn't have been at all surprised by grimoires full of unreadable symbols, but they were novels. I spotted a few leatherbound classics—adventure tales, for the most part, including *Robin-*

son Crusoe—but most were well-thumbed paperbacks, a high percentage of which had *magic, witch, spells, dragon,* or something similar in the title. One of the shelves seemed to be devoted to mythology and folktales from various cultures. Certainly none resembled a seventeenth-century grimoire.

I went to Havelock's worktable. Buried beneath a pile of what looked like mariner's rope and cupboard handles was another novel with dog-eared pages. *Edrahil's Curse and Other Stories.*

"He likes to read," I said, a question in my voice.

"Yes," Yannick said. "Mostly when he was younger. I haven't seen him with a book in a while. Well, he doesn't have much time for it anymore."

"No?"

"The shop keeps him busy," Yannick said. "He works mostly on commission these days—someone will come to him with a specific request, and he'll take the work if it interests him. Not only magicians, some humans, those among the wealthy and powerful, have learned of him. He doesn't care about the money," he added. "Only that it allows him to purchase more rare enchantments to take apart and study."

Élise was crouched by one of the cabinets, examining a vase. "He doesn't *cast* the enchantments, then?"

"Not usually. That's not what he cares about. Magic is—it's like a puzzle to him. At least I think it is." Yannick scanned the untidy desk. "Havelock isn't much given to talking about his feelings. He isn't proud, I think he just forgets sometimes that he has them."

I couldn't connect the affectionate expression on Yannick's face to either the Havelock Renard I had met or the Witch King of his reputation. I found myself itching to examine the rest of the cabinets, to rip open the boxes and spill their contents upon the floor. It was curiosity of a morbid variety—my respect for magic was no greater than before. But mixed up with it was frustration with Havelock, somehow, though he owed me nothing of himself, as if by rifling through his collection I might also better understand the man himself, or at least dent the mystery of him.

"Havelock could return at any moment," Yannick said, half-nervous and half-despairing. I realized then what his concern was: Not fear of Havelock, but a desire to avoid—what? Disappointing him? Upsetting him?

I glanced at Élise, who appeared perfectly composed, looking about her with a moue of disapproval. But I could read the tension in her shoulders as easily as a book—she hated spiders, and there was one making its creeping way across the ceiling above her head.

"All right," I said. "I've seen enough. It looks like a load of junk to me, anyway."

This was not precisely true, but Yannick didn't argue—he looked beside himself with relief. I allowed him to lead us back up the treacherous stairs, a plan taking shape in my mind.

CHAPTER 17

It was a plan I put in motion that very night.

I made my way through the evening chores first, shadowed by Banshee. I kept stopping to inspect different corners of the building, convinced I'd find some difference, some evidence of its having been transported halfway across the city and back, but there was nothing. Even the dishes were intact.

I settled myself into one of the armchairs by the fire and waited for the hour to advance. Around me the old shop settled with its usual nighttime creaks, which had slowly grown familiar. I didn't know how long I should wait, but I wanted to ensure I was not interrupted by any uncanny visitors, who occasionally dropped by in the evening hours.

"I know," I murmured to the empty armchair across from me. It had been a habit of Robin's and mine to take a glass of wine by the fire together after a long day, and I sometimes still spoke to him then. "You don't need to tell me this is a terrible idea. But I have to attempt it—for *their* sake."

The flames rustled like paper, and I could almost see Robin frowning disapprovingly at me over his newspaper, the light catching in his auburn hair. Though there was also that familiar glint of amusement in his gaze, as if to say, *Let's see how you get on, then.*

When the fire had burned down to embers, I stood and made my way to the back room. The cats were mostly asleep in their cages, nestled into their kingly bedding, but I caught one or two tapetum flashes in the dim light. I paused above the trapdoor a moment, listening. But as far as I could tell, Havelock hadn't returned. I caught myself wondering if Valérie had come upon him somewhere and attacked him again, before reminding myself that it was none of my business what fell out between them.

And yet I was about to make it my business.

Banshee had gone to take a nap, perhaps sensing that mine was a solitary mission—her favourite sleeping spot these days was the old baker's oven, which filled me with trepidation. I had no reason to think the oven was dangerous—beyond Banshee's attraction to it, that is—but still I did not trust the thing, and wondered if I should put a grate over it.

I turned to the trapdoor. I had the lantern with me, even though it was largely unnecessary; the alternative was trusting the spiders.

Now that I knew what lay below, I was less afraid and moved more quickly down the stairs. The workshop appeared just as we'd left it, spiders glowing gently from random corners. No sign of Havelock.

Suddenly something leapt from the darkness and came stalking towards me, and I fell back with a gasp.

But it was only His Majesty, one of the luminous spiders dangling from his mouth. Judging by its frantic wriggling, it was still alive.

With a cry of disgust, I lunged forward, managing to grab

the slippery cat before he melted into the shadows. He gave a hiss of protest, which had the useful effect of forcing him to drop the spider, which scurried away. It was a curious enchantment—in a revolting way, I mean—in that only the spider's carapace was alight, not its legs, which made it appear perfectly ordinary from a distance, perhaps the flame of a small candle. Until, of course, it moved.

"How did you get down here?" I demanded. I'd shut the trapdoor behind me, I was certain. And yet wasn't it just like His Majesty? He was adept at finding narrow passages and escape routes, even by the standards of cats. Robin had once found him on the roof at the old place, though all our doors and windows had been shut. Our best guess was that he'd somehow scrambled up the chimney like a feline Saint Nicholas.

I tossed the cat over my shoulder, which he tolerated, and tried to carry him back up the stairs, which he did not—he launched himself free with his massive paws and became one with the shadows again. Sighing, I settled for leaving the trapdoor open. I'd no idea what sort of damage cats could do to enchantments, but I guessed His Majesty would make mischief somehow, and I could only hope Havelock wouldn't notice. Although, presumably, His Majesty had been exploring the basement long before me, and, with his usual feral logic, had already deemed it part of his territory.

I lifted the lantern and kept going. As Yannick had warned, the place grew progressively more disorganized the farther down one went. The third floor had crates stacked all the way to the ceiling, while I couldn't even make out a pathway through the fourth.

"Absolutely appalling," I kept muttering to myself, my

horror only growing. How did anyone live like this? It was like wandering through the nest of some mad, burrowing magpie.

Each of the steep staircases hugged the stone wall, but behind the staircase connecting floors three and four, where there should have been stairs to the fifth floor, was a trapdoor. It was more severe-looking than the one in the shop, being made of a single piece of black flagstone. It had no chain, but one edge had a groove wide enough to slide my fingers into.

I gripped the flagstone and pulled, not truly expecting anything to happen. Yannick had said that the trapdoor was locked—with a spell, I assumed. I was already thinking about how I might search the other floors for the book as the flagstone rose easily.

I dropped it as if it had bitten me. Had Havelock forgotten to lock the trapdoor? Or had Yannick meant *locked* in a more sinister sense—*effectively* locked, because continuing would bring some curse down upon me?

I drew a deep breath, then lifted the flagstone and set it to one side. Beyond was a staircase just like the others, narrow and steep, leading into an uneven rectangle of shadow. Legs trembling, I lifted my lantern and descended into the darkness.

The room at the bottom of the stairs was smaller than those above, almost cozy, with a humble ceiling, low with unconcealed joists from the floor above, and an open fire that had burned down to a few embers. Bookshelves lined every wall, and the half-open doorway in the far wall seemed to lead to a bathroom; I could just glimpse the edge of a tub. The spiders were fewer in number here—I saw only three, strung up in their webs together in a corner like old friends. Most of the uneven light came from the fire and a small lamp that burned next to a couch shoved against the only wall that wasn't occupied by bookshelves.

The hope began to form that here I might indeed find the book Valérie sought, but it went out like a snuffed flame. Because on the couch was Havelock Renard.

CHAPTER 18

I fumbled my lantern, catching it just before it struck the floor. Havelock was asleep in what looked like a highly uncomfortable slump, his shoulder leaned against the arm of the couch and his head resting on his shoulder, dark hair spilling onto his sleeve. His hand was open and dangling as if to accept something, and one leg was folded beneath him. He had clearly been reading when he fell asleep, for there was a book lying on the floor below his hand, pages folded beneath its weight.

I would have fled immediately had I not noticed that he was wounded. "Havelock!" I cried, starting forward, but he didn't wake. I was too frightened to touch him, so I picked up a book from one of the shelves and threw it at him.

I hadn't been aiming for his head but the wall beside him; still I managed to clip his glasses, knocking them askew, which was enough to waken him with a start. He blinked at me and murmured something that sounded like "Ri?"

"You're bleeding!" I cried, because I didn't know how else to describe what I was seeing—blood was the least of it.

He took no notice of the horror that was his left leg. It looked like the leg of that monstrous creature I had glimpsed twice now, Havelock's other form. It was a curve of darkness, flickering as if ember-lit from within, and yet from some angles it appeared almost normal. In addition to this, the leg *was* injured. Blood trickled from a deep gash by his knee and pooled on the floor.

Recognition came over his face, and he looked from me to the open trapdoor, his expression darkening. He touched one of his earrings and murmured a word.

I was whirling on my heel as soon as I understood, but I was too late, and the flagstone crashed shut, sealing me down there with him.

I turned back to him, holding the lantern between us as if it might ward him off. This was where my curiosity had led me: into the heart of the monster's lair. What a fool I had been to imagine I should involve myself in the affairs of magicians!

"What are you going to do to me?" I croaked.

"Do?" he repeated, his forehead wrinkling. "Turn you into a sparrow and see what your charming pets make of you. Oh, don't look at me like that. I'm not going to *do* anything. That panther was lurking up there. I'd rather he didn't make himself at home." His face went blank, and then he raised his elbow just in time to meet an explosive sneeze.

"Oh—sorry." My hand holding the lantern trembled with relief. "He must have followed me."

Havelock tried to rise, but his face contorted, and he fell back into the couch in a boneless slump. He'd passed out from the pain, or had lost too much blood.

"Look at the state of you!" I exclaimed, coming forward slowly, as I would with a wounded street cat likely to lash out at me. He was barefoot in billowy linen shirtsleeves and loose trousers—again looking like he'd raided some theatre company's costume department, though the effect was more otherworldly than ridiculous. The left trouser leg had been rolled up, as if he'd made some attempt to treat whatever ungodly thing was happening to him. His strange and disorderly appearance reminded me of the chaos of the upper floors, and my irritation overrode my fear. I removed the blush-coloured scarf—one of the former tenant's—that I'd taken to wearing around my neck and began wrapping it around his leg. It was hard to *see* that part of him—my vision swam with dizziness when I stared too hard.

I blinked and tried to focus on the scarf. I looped it around his knee, pulling each loop as taut as I could.

"What are you doing here?" he said, and I jumped. He'd awoken again and was watching me.

For some reason, I didn't even think of lying. "I was looking for Vortigern's book. I planned to give it to Valérie so that we could be rid of her."

"But I told you I don't have it." The confusion in his voice was what convinced me he wasn't lying—surely he would have been angry if he'd actually had the thing. He didn't ask why I had decided to betray him, which made me feel oddly guilty, more so than if he'd berated me.

And yet what did I owe Havelock Renard? Nothing.

"I don't know why I'm helping you," I muttered. And really, it was ludicrous—just thirty seconds before, I'd been certain he was about to blast me apart with some enchantment. Not to mention that not only did he live in a monster's lair, he looked like one.

"You seem like someone who must always be *helping*," he murmured to the ceiling, wincing as I worked. "If you aren't lecturing strangers."

This unexpected perceptiveness only made me more angry with him. "You aren't a stranger anymore," I said. "Unfortunately. And I—" I froze, the scarf slipping from my hands as I stared at him in sudden horror. "What happened to your *face?*"

He squinted at me. "What? Oh. It must be the beauty spell. What's different?"

"You—your eye. They were both brown before. Now one's green." Not only green, but it seemed a different shape than the brown one, and more heavy-lidded, so that now he looked as if he had a squint.

"Ah," he said. "That one's been flickering on and off for days. I'm not surprised. I shouldn't have tried splicing second-order magic with first."

It took me a moment to make sense of this. "You cast a spell on *yourself?*"

He blushed, then glared at me, as if to make up for it. "Why not? Is it not better to experiment on myself than subject someone else to the spells, if one should go awry?"

This display of ethics was too discrepant to be believable. "You're experimenting with beauty spells?" I said. "Is that not a frivolous use of a dark magician's time?"

"*Dark* magician?" He looked piqued. "There is only one kind of magician. The use to which some of us put our abilities could perhaps be categorized thus, but magic has only one source."

He looked about to launch into one of his pedantic speeches, so I said quickly, "I only meant that I'm surprised the great Witch King would bother beautifying himself."

"Beauty spells are of an order magicians call *phantasmic*," he said. "As opposed to *grounded* and *illusionary* enchantments. That just means that they are inherently unstable. No one has ever cast a flawless beauty spell, and indeed, they are among the most dangerous spells of all, the most likely to go awry. A magician might cast a beauty spell on Tuesday and the same spell again on Wednesday and achieve opposite results. Theorists suggest it's because beauty is inherently subjective and variable through time, unlike, say, a spell for warming one's hands. It can't be pinned down."

I would get a speech no matter what, it seemed. He had grown animated as he spoke about magic, his drawn face gaining colour, waving his hands about in a way that made me jittery, given the enchantments he wore on his fingers. "And you find this—interesting?" I said slowly.

He looked at me as if I were another species. "I'm close to perfecting the spell."

"No, you're not," I said definitively. His features had already been unusual; now he looked like he was wearing someone else's eye.

He waved a ringed hand, and again I suppressed the urge to duck. "I test each enchantment a feature at a time. It's more efficient that way—less magic."

"Right now you just look like death," I said. "Stop moving around."

He examined me. I saw none of that cold confidence now; his mistrust of me made him look younger than he was. I think because it was so ridiculous, a lion nervously eyeing a bee. Finally, he sighed and leaned his head back, his dark hair spilling across the back of the couch. I found myself studying the sharp angle of his jaw and Adam's apple, which made me annoyed with myself. The jaw probably wasn't even his, anyhow.

I returned my attention to what I was doing, tying the scarf off with a knot. I'd covered his leg, obscuring the horror lurking beneath, though not his foot, which was flickering and diaphanous. I hurriedly withdrew my hands.

"I think that worked," I said dubiously. "You're not bleeding now, anyway. Would you care to explain what the hell is happening to you?"

"I'm not sure I *can* explain," he said, still gazing up at the ceiling, his voice distant. "I only know that I've been spending too much time in the Rivenwood. Ri was right." This last was muttered.

"I don't understand the Rivenwood at all," I told him, which I meant only as a statement of fact. I had no desire to learn more about the place, which had looked, in the brief glimpse I'd had of it, like the template upon which every dark forest in every dark fairy tale had been based. I kept wishing that I could forget it.

"Most people don't," he said. "Including magicians. We only know it's a fallen world, a world of magic, and that it was corrupted, somehow, by that same magic. Nobody lives there anymore but spectres."

I looked him up and down. "And magicians?"

"The most popular theory is that modern magicians are all descended from a handful of refugees who fled from the world we now call the Rivenwood many centuries ago, as it collapsed. These refugees carried the seed of magic inside them from their world, and sometimes it surfaces in their descendants."

I swallowed. "And spectres?"

"Spectres are magicians," he said. "Or what's left of them. Those who aren't careful."

I was appalled. "Magicians, you—you turn into—*that*?"

"Not always. Many of the spectres of the Rivenwood are ancient, remnants of the people who once lived there. But the longer a magician spends in the Rivenwood, and the deeper they go, the more its magic gets inside them. Eventually, some lose their ability to take human form entirely. They remain in the woods and prey upon other magicians." He gestured at his leg. "One took me by surprise."

"Then magic is—some sort of poison?" I said.

"Not exactly. Magic is a living thing."

"So are rattlesnakes," I said, still unable to believe it. "Sensible people stay away from them."

"And devote their time to collecting city pests?"

I didn't see that there was much to joke about, given what we had been discussing. I rose and seated myself warily on the edge of the couch. Havelock's frame wasn't intimidating, at least; he was only a few inches taller than me, and was lean rather than muscular, in a way that was less suggestive of deprivation than a tendency to forget about food. "And yet you keep going back there," I said. "Despite what it's doing to you."

"You sound like Yannick. The shop had to be moved back—I couldn't very well leave a crater in the heart of the city. There wasn't time to barter for the magic I needed. You and those beasts made it essential that I act with haste, so that I could place new wards upon *both* my shops."

I frowned, not understanding. "What do the cats have to do with anything?"

"Don't you—" He pushed himself up, and his expression changed. He glanced down at his leg and moved it experimentally. "That—that feels better."

"I imagine it would. You're not bleeding out anymore."

"I wasn't going to bleed out. But wounds suffered in the Rivenwood take time to close, and—I suppose the dressing has sped the process."

He had stiffened, as if now that the pain had lessened he was aware of the intimacy of what I'd done, and of my presence there, in his private chambers, sitting on what I realized was probably his bed. He began to redden, which was unfortunate, for I've often found others' discomfort contagious, and my own face flushed.

He reached down to adjust the scarf, and I snatched his hand away with a cry, thinking he meant to remove it. He stared at me and my face heated yet again—not because I'd touched him, but because my reaction proved I cared more than I'd let on whether he bled to death, which was frankly as much of a surprise to me.

"You dropped your book," I said, desperate for a distraction. I picked it up—another novel, though the cover was too worn for me to make out anything other than the words *House of*. "Looks like you lost your page."

"No matter." He took it from me and laid it on the table. "I've read that one a dozen times."

I puzzled over this. He'd been sitting here, injured and alone, and he'd decided to read an old book?

"Well?" I said into the dreadfully awkward silence. "I asked what the cats have to do with any of this."

"The cats," he repeated. His accent made the word sound clipped, or perhaps that was just his dislike. "Well, they have the tracking spell on them too. Didn't Yannick tell you?"

"The *tracking* spell?" It came out almost as a shout.

Havelock started and drew back from me. "You didn't—?"

"Of course I didn't!" I was definitely shouting now. "You put a *tracking spell* on me?"

"Why on earth would I do that? You think I care about the whereabouts of a load of mangy ferals and their painfully earnest minder? Valérie cast it—that's why she was able to find me, and eventually undo my old wards. You led her to my shop."

"We did not!" I exclaimed. "Why would Valérie enchant a cat shelter?"

Havelock looked as if he were about to make one of his sarcastic remarks—I was beginning to learn the signs, that sardonic glint in his eye and slight head tilt. But then he seemed to deflate, as if realizing the situation was too ridiculous to be ridiculed. "I have no idea."

"Thank you!" I said. "She would have had to cast it on us when we were in the old shop, wouldn't she? How would she have known—" I froze as a thought struck me like an Arctic wave.

"It may have been accidental," Havelock said. "I'm told she started a duel with another magician a month or two ago—a man I've had dealings with in the past. When he wouldn't tell her my whereabouts, she tried to put a tracking spell on him, so she would know if he visited me. He was able to shake it off, but perhaps it rebounded on you somehow."

I forced myself to ask my next question. "Would this spell have compelled the magician to visit your shop?"

"No. That sort of magic isn't possible." He paused, his gaze growing distant. "Unless the spell was old, but that—"

"Old?"

"Old spells are unpredictable. They can warp or stretch, or take on new facets. People think that magic spells can *break*, but in fact magic is more like water. One can contain it in vessels, but it always wants to shift, to flow. I was unpicking the workings of a medieval summoning spell last week, and found it just as likely to repel as to . . ."

"Wonderful," I murmured faintly, not listening to him as he rambled on. "Just wonderful. Not only do I have a spell on me, it's a mutated spell. How comforting."

He narrowed his eyes, and I forgot for a moment how strangely easy it felt, talking to him. But he only said, "What happened?"

I explained how, in the weeks following the duel that had damaged the old shelter, I'd been drawn to Rue des Hirondelles time and again—too often, I realized now, for mere coincidence.

"Yes," he said when I'd finished. "It sounds like she enchanted you. What wonderful luck! Her spell couldn't have rebounded on a maker of ice cream or fine wines. No, it found a woman who makes my eyes itch by her proximity alone."

I realized his eyes did look red and glanced down at myself—I was wearing one of my old sweaters, which I rarely took the lint brush to.

"Sorry," I said. I couldn't work out whether I should thank him. The idea of doing so was absurd, and yet I'd endangered him by moving there—inadvertently, of course—and he hadn't thrown me out, or subjected me to some cruel form of punishment, which didn't exactly accord with his reputation. I realized I no longer believed in his reputation, though that didn't mean I understood him, or thought him good. Goodness was hardly defined by *not* being the cause of an apocalypse.

And anyhow, Havelock's quarrel with his sister had been the reason I'd lost my home. Did I really owe him any thanks, even if the quarrel wasn't of his making?

For some reason, though, the question that surfaced through all this doubt was "What does your face look like under all the spells you've put on yourself?"

"I don't have a face. I'm actually a handful of cobwebs mixed with moonlight, like all dark magicians."

I scowled, suppressing an unexpected snort. "I'm being serious."

"Are you ever anything else?" He paused. "I have only the one spell on me at present."

So he had always looked like a handful of mismatched puzzle pieces. I glanced around the room, which, now that I was able to focus on it, seemed specially designed to maximize comfort. In addition to the couch there were two wide, squashy armchairs, and lamps perched on various tables and bookshelves. Wool rugs were scattered about, a few heaped in a pile in front of the fire, as if Havelock were in the habit of curling up there when the fancy took him. On the whole, it was more like the manifestation of some librarian's fantasy than a dark magician's lair.

"Yannick thinks you store your most powerful spells down here," I said.

"Yes. He leaves me alone that way."

I gave a huff of laughter. "He said the trapdoor was locked."

"I never bothered with a locking spell. I just told him it was, and he never tested it."

So Yannick *was* afraid of Havelock, at least a little. "Why is Valérie so convinced you have this book?"

"The first thing you must understand about my sister is that she is an insufferable egotist," he said. "The surest way to stump her is to ask about the last time she was wrong about something. She claims she's been following the book's trail for years. She tracked it to a collector who sold it back in the '90s to a reclusive American magician called Walker Clem. He died without heirs, and his Artefacts were inadvertently donated to a museum. A few years ago, I was able to purchase his collection from the museum once they worked out they were magical Artefacts, not an old man's collection of antique curios—they were only too happy to be rid of them. But Vortigern's book was not among the Artefacts."

"Are you certain?"

"Of course," he said, looking offended. "I would have recognized it."

I considered this. "Where did you put Clem's collection?"

"Oh—" He waved a hand. "No particular place. I remember he had a collection of poison enchantments that mimic ordinary illnesses when cast, which I took apart and stored in one of the cabinets. They were nasty things, but fascinating in their own way, and strengthened by five-layer hexes—"

Just as I thought. "Did the collection contain any books?" I cut in, because I could see he was building up a head of steam again. "Vortigern's wouldn't necessarily look like a grimoire, yes? It could be a guidebook to mushrooms of the Acadian forest or a treatise on ridge and furrow farming. If an Artefact is just a vessel to store magic, surely there are Artefacts that don't look particularly interesting but contain powerful spells."

"I would have sensed Vortigern's enchantment," he said. "Her spells have a distinct signature."

"Are there spells for hiding other spells?"

He was fiddling with one of his rings, gazing into the distance with a slight frown between his eyes. "Yes, but—"

"And given that you didn't learn of the potential importance of Clem's collection until later, when Valérie came looking for it, you might not have examined everything closely."

He didn't reply for a moment. Absently, he removed the ring he'd been toying with and tossed it on the table. I leapt back in my seat with a muffled shriek, bringing my hands up.

He gazed at me in surprise. "What are you doing?"

"It's not going to—" The ring—studded with black opals in the shape of a crescent moon—simply lay there, and I suddenly felt foolish. "It's not going to go off?"

"It's not a gun," he said. "Anyway, I spent the enchantment it contained. Most Artefacts can be used only once—it takes a powerful magician to fold in a recursive enchantment. Even then, the magic has to be replenished regularly."

"Oh," I said, relieved.

He was eyeing me in an odd way, as if I were a character in one of his novels who'd wandered in from a different story. "Even if I *do* have Vortigern's book," he continued slowly, "I can't give it to Valérie. You don't understand the horrors she would unleash with it."

This was interesting. He no longer sounded so convinced he didn't have the thing somewhere in his rat's nest of a magic shop. Had he always known it was a possibility, despite his protestations? He struck me as the type who, given half the chance, would go out of his way to ignore truths he didn't wish to deal with.

"We could destroy it, then," I said. "And send Valérie the pieces as evidence. In any case, our first step is finding Clem's Artefacts." I stood, brushing my skirts off, as has become my habit, even when I haven't had a cat sitting on me.

"I told you," he said, "I don't know where—"

"Where you put them, yes. It's the most ridiculous thing I ever heard."

He stared at me, then opened his mouth to make some objection. I didn't let him.

"Yes, I said ridiculous. A magician who can't keep track of his spells. It's like a baker losing track of his sugar. What is the point of having a magic shop if you never do your inventory?" I paused. "Do you even know what that word means?"

"Sanctimonious *and* condescending," he said. "I wish you'd left me to bleed out; I'd be spared your tedious lectures."

I turned to leave. "I'll see you in the morning."

"Why did that sound like a threat?" he called after me. "You're going to sic those fleabags on me if I don't hand over my ledger?"

I doubted he had a ledger, or if he did, that he knew where it was in all that chaos. Perhaps I was underestimating him—I certainly hoped so. In any case, I'd frightened myself, talking to him as I had. I didn't understand why I was so confident that he wouldn't enchant me in some horrible way.

So instead of responding, I settled for a mysterious silence. He didn't aim any curses at my back, though I'd no doubt he was glaring at me, nor did he turn me into a paper clip, and the trapdoor opened easily when I pushed on it.

CHAPTER 19

Unfortunately, my plan to sort through Havelock's daunting collection of Artefacts was forestalled the following morning, as we were forced to deal with something far more important than magic: one of the cats had fallen ill. Additionally, someone had left a cardboard box on our doorstep containing three white kittens. When I opened the flaps I found them curled up together in one shivering lump of fur.

"Let's take them to the place on Rue Sainte-Sophie," I told Mina. "Just feel their fur—they're like rabbits. Mark my words, someone will want to adopt the lot, and the new cages are being delivered today. We'd best start filling them with cats."

"I'll take the tram over there now," Mina said, grabbing the key. "Then I'll check the ones in Parc Le Séraphin—some of them always survive the winter, and this could be our chance to put an end to at least one colony."

I nodded. I knew the colony she meant; there were a half dozen scattered throughout the city, but the cats in Le Séraphin were mostly friendly, likely because they were used to being hand-fed by people in the neighbouring apartments. She hefted the box, lined with three of our warmest scarves, black as ink, which I hoped would make the kittens' wintry fur all the more striking.

The ill cat was Thoreau, to my dismay. I'd found him huddled in his bed in a miserable ball that morning, and he showed no interest in his breakfast. Fortunately, the vet arrived less than an hour after I sent the telegram.

"Poor dear," she said, scratching his tufted grey ears. Dr. Noémie Para was a cheerful, unassailably calm woman in her fifties. Perhaps the most experienced veterinarian in the city, she had treated every cat we'd fostered, always at reduced rates.

"I don't hear anything wrong with his heart," she said, putting her stethoscope back in her bag, "and his temperature's normal. Has he been under any stress recently?"

I silently cursed Havelock, thinking of the relocation spell. "We had to—move his cage," I said, which likely represented the greatest understatement I would ever utter.

"That might do it," she said sympathetically. "The old-timers are often upset by change. Just don't move him again."

"I won't," I said grimly.

We didn't have any visitors for the first half of the morning, affording me plenty of time to sit with Thoreau by the oven, which was making the place smell of chocolate that day. I was hungry enough that I couldn't stop myself from poking my head in to check that there weren't actually any pastries inside it.

Ambulance ensured I would not be oppressed by the quiet, keeping up a steady stream of yowls as I tended to Thoreau. Eventually I had to let him out of his cage, though I knew His Majesty was prowling about, looking for a distraction. Sure enough, the enormous cat came stalking over and leapt on Ambulance without provocation, clawing at him viciously.

I leapt to my feet to break up the scuffle, but in the same moment, Banshee came ambling into the fray. Oblivious to danger as always, she wandered past the snarling His Majesty and seated herself beside Ambulance, who was huddled close to the floor, having managed to break free of the larger cat. His Majesty was clearly not done with him, but Banshee took no heed, and began to wash Ambulance's orange head. I could see His Majesty considering his next move. He would have to attack the oblivious Banshee to get to Ambulance, but His Majesty knew there would be no fun in this, for Banshee was as impervious to bullying as she was to common sense. She would only stare at him uncomprehendingly before trying to lick his face.

After a fraught moment, His Majesty stalked away in disgust, off to seek his amusement elsewhere.

I gave a huff of laughter. After checking that Ambulance was all right, I gave Banshee a handful of her favourite treats. There had been times—few in number, mind—when I'd wondered if the tabby wasn't quite so senseless as she appeared.

After an hour or so of being doted on, Thoreau began to show signs of improvement, and even ate a little of his breakfast. I had wondered if Havelock might make an appearance, now that he had no need to hide from me, but he did not, and I heard no noise from below—perhaps he'd bled out after all.

Serves him right, I told myself, even as another part of me debated how long I should wait before checking on him. I still couldn't work out why I was so concerned. I assumed it was because I'd seen him at his most vulnerable, and cared for him, and thus some part of me had—ridiculously—filed him into the same category as the cats. But I had also established that his irritating sarcasm was a mask for some fundamental awkwardness that was entirely incompatible with my prior impression of him. I was beginning to wonder if the apocalypse hadn't been Valérie's doing, which she'd pinned somehow on Havelock. Had that been the reason brother and sister had originally fallen out? And what about Valérie? If Havelock was not bereft of kindness, was she? Could she be made to see the error of her ways?

I was mulling all this over when a tall man bustled in, shaking snow off his coat.

"Rémy," I said, recognizing the owner of the bakery down the street, from which Élise was always buying bagels. I set down the cup of coffee I had been nursing. "How are you?"

"Agnes," he said warmly, greeting me with cheek kisses. Rémy was a well-dressed man in his fifties with close-cropped greying hair and a smattering of freckles across his brown skin. He ran the bakery with his husband, Oliver, who handled most of the day-to-day baking, while Rémy oversaw the finances.

"Well, what's all this?" he said, putting a hand playfully on his hip as he surveyed the shelter. "I hear you're selling enchanted cats. Not getting into the Artefact trade, are you? Seems a tad inhumane."

I choked on my coffee. "*Enchanted* cats?"

"That's the word on the street. One of our regulars this morning was claiming you sold him a cat that cured his insomnia. Slept like the dead last night, apparently, for the first time in years."

"Who was this?"

Rémy shrugged. "I don't actually know his name. Older fellow, expensive briefcase. Between you and me, I think he's just been listening to the rumours."

I stilled. "What rumours?"

He gave me a puzzled smile. "You haven't heard? It seems

you've been entertaining some odd characters—very, well, *magician-like* characters. And the neighbours have been hearing mysterious noises in the night. Funnily enough, there were similar rumours about Samara—she ran that scarf shop that was here before."

I let out a groan, leaning over the counter to press my hands into my face. This was just what I needed—the police would never leave us alone now! "How widespread are these rumours, Rémy?"

He laughed. "Oh, Agnes—don't worry about it. Idle gossip will not harm you or the cats—it might even bring in a few gawkers. Speaking of the cats, Oliver's won me over at last—we'd like to take her."

"Really?" My spirits lifted a little. "That's wonderful—let's get you started on the paperwork. As I said before, I think Biscuit will make an excellent shop cat; her disposition is very genial."

"Well, with that name, how could we say no? It's as if she were meant for us. And Oliver was so taken with her. I'm planning to surprise him."

As we were speaking, a boxy ambulance sped by the shop, siren blaring, nearly colliding with a horse-drawn cart plodding in the opposite direction.

"That's the second one this morning," I said.

"Yes," Rémy said, shaking his head. "It's those wretched magicians again. The ones who did a number on the train station—I heard it on the radio this morning. Absolutely no class. Imagine travelling to a foreign city just to cause chaos. Our magicians would never be so uncouth."

I made a noncommittal noise. While most feared magicians, not everyone reviled them. There were plenty who, like Rémy, appreciated living in a city with a reputation for magic.

Not in a way that implied affection, but in the manner of those who took pride in living in nonchalant proximity to dangerous animals.

He went to the window. "You can see the smoke from here."

I peered out, then gasped. I stepped outside for a better look, bracing myself against the cold. A narrow column of smoke rose in the distance above the gabled roofs and church steeples.

"What happened?" I said, shivering.

"Apparently three of the louts visited Miette last night," he said, naming one of the city's most popular cafés. "They performed a variety of tricks to entertain their table neighbours, though mostly it was to entertain themselves. They would not stop when asked, and refused to be thrown out; eventually one of their displays overturned a candle, which caught on a tablecloth. Rather than put it out, they worked the fire into their little performance, making it dance and hop about. You can imagine the rest. They lost control and the building went up. The fire department thought they'd doused it last night, but either they were in error or there was something strange about that fire, for it awoke again this morning and spread to the chocolatier's next door."

I was shivering violently at this point, and we hurried back inside, but the cold lingered on my skin. It was all too close to what I'd experienced at the old shelter. "I expect the magicians weren't caught," I said bitterly.

Rémy shook his head. "Someone snapped a photo of them, though—it was in the papers."

"Small good it will do." It was difficult enough to jail magicians who acted alone, let alone those who travelled in gangs and considered themselves apprentices of someone as powerful as Valérie.

We wrapped up the paperwork, and though I was happy to see Rémy out the door with Biscuit, I was too distracted for the pleasure to linger. The frigid morning became a cold afternoon; even the blue sky was frosted with ice crystals, and a winter wind tumbled down the street, rattling the windows and snatching up handfuls of loose snow. Several of the cages needed cleaning, so I got out the bucket and soap and rolled up my sleeves, though I found myself pausing frequently to watch as people passing the windows tugged their scarves tighter or blew into their hands. I should have been cheered by the additional shelter and the expanded capacity it gave us, but I found myself struck by a wave of pessimism, as if having my dream come to life had awakened me to its shortfalls. It was not only the danger presented by Valérie; one additional shelter was not going to solve the problem that left me sleepless on winter nights—that is, the sheer number of cats still haunting the streets, who would not be there to watch the snows retreat from the city.

I scrubbed harder, and through my gloom, a plan began to take shape in my mind, like fire slowly catching in a dark hearth.

CHAPTER 20

Élise had worked herself up into a towering fury by the time she arrived that afternoon, bringing with her a box of pizza from La Fin.

"Have you *seen* it?" she demanded, flinging the box down on the counter—I had to make a leap for it before its contents spilled onto the floor. "Our second shelter, I mean?"

"No," I said, already cramming a slice into my mouth—I hadn't eaten breakfast, and I was starving. I added with difficulty around the mouthful of steaming cheese and roasted vegetables, "I've not had a chance."

"Well, Mina's there now, trying her best not to gawp. Those white kittens have been spoken for, by the way. One of the bank tellers paid for them not one hour after Mina unlocked the door. As soon as they've had their shots and their"—Élise did her usual scissor motion with two fingers—"they'll be on their way to their new home."

"That's wonderful," I said, swallowing. "Is Mina—"

"She's coping just fine on her own," Élise said, waving her hand. "She managed to catch four cats from Le Séraphin. But oh, Agnes—it's just ludicrous. The place was a *jeweler's* before Havelock bought it. A jeweler's! It still has its display cases and everything—we've had to put the cages on top of them. The ceiling has a goddamn mural painted on it! Mina says she's had two people looking for engagement rings."

"Good," I said. "Whatever gets people in the doors. But four cats is not enough inventory. Why don't you take Clowder and her kittens over? Bring Pirate, too—he's one of His Majesty's favourite targets, and I know he'd like a break from being tormented. Mina's already sent messages to our old volunteers—we need extra hands if we're going to get our new cages filled, and I want them filled today, if possible. The paper says it will be even colder tonight."

Élise stared at me. "Are you listening? Our new shelter has a *marble floor*, Agnes. It has a *marble floor* with a *mosaic* in it!"

"That sounds like a lovely feature," I said imperturbably. "We will have to be careful about who we transfer to the new place. Mme. Minette, for instance, has difficulty remembering her manners where the litterbox is concerned."

Élise gave a groan of frustration and picked up a slice of pizza. "Sometimes I can't tell if I'm talking to you or one of your checklists."

"Élise, I would love to work myself up about this, but after the night I've had, I wonder if anything will ever surprise me again."

I recounted the whole misadventure for her. Élise listened with a furrowed brow, steadily eating her way through half the pizza. I expected her to ask questions about Havelock, or appear surprised by what I'd done, but she was not. When I had finished, she set her crust down and cut right to the point.

"I don't understand why you're bothering with this Artefact," she said. "Who cares if Havelock has it or not? Why doesn't he just—I don't know, duel Valérie? Is he not the most powerful magician in the world?"

"Valérie is determined to find Vortigern's book. From the sounds of it, she'll never give up looking. Havelock would have to kill her."

"All right," Élise said, a question in her voice.

I stared. "She's his *sister*, Élise!"

Élise continued to gaze at me in puzzlement, and it took me only a second to work out why: my perspective on Havelock might have shifted, but Élise's had not. Why would the Witch King show mercy to anyone who threatened him, even his own family?

I saw Élise examining me in turn, seeming to come to her own conclusion. "Oh, Agnes," she said finally. "You see him as one of your cats now, don't you? Because you took care of him."

"I do *not*," I said, outraged, all the more so because I'd been musing over the same thought not long before, and it was unbelievably unfair that Élise should be able to read me so well.

"You *do*. You think if you just clean him up and give him his flea treatments, you can make him respectable."

"You're ridiculous," I scoffed.

"You always have to care too much," Élise went on. "About cats. Or people. It's why you never fired Mina, though she stole half our donation money last Christmas."

"And she's barely stolen a penny since," I protested. "Don't tell me that I wasn't right—what would we have done without her these past weeks?"

Élise inclined her head in acknowledgment. "But it's dangerous to always think the best of people, love. Surely you see that now? And cats, for that matter—only you would have kept that feral bully around given all the things he's done."

"Now you're bringing His Majesty into this!" I protested.

"Agnes, that cat is a terror," Élise said. "At times I wonder if he's even a cat and not some demon in disguise. I know you say he loved Robin, but if that beast were even ten pounds bigger, he would have killed and eaten the both of you in your sleep."

"You have no idea what you're talking about. And anyway, he needs me, and there is a gentleness in him, even if it's mixed up with wickedness. How can you condemn a creature for doing what's in his nature?"

Élise folded her arms, giving me a meaningful look. My face heated, and I added hastily, "I was *only* speaking about His Majesty. Élise, you know how I feel about magicians. I haven't—"

But at that moment, the door opened, and Yannick came hurrying in.

"Hello, hello," he said, looking agitated. "What a mess! Valérie's apprentices are at it again. Did you hear about that chocolatier's? And I still can't find Havelock. He wasn't at the other place."

"He's here," I told him. "Or he *was* here, last night. I've not seen any sign of him today."

Yannick's face sagged with relief. "Thank God! I was worried something dreadful had happened to him."

"Worried?" Élise repeated. "Why, because one wicked magician isn't enough to deal with? If only those two would blast each other to bits and save us all this turmoil."

Yannick wasn't listening to her. He swept to the back of the shop, pausing only to give a pat to Banshee, oblivious to our human angst as she calmly washed her face.

"Havelock?" he called, already tromping down the stairs. Élise and I went down more carefully, and thus had not even reached the bottom step before Yannick reappeared below us.

"He's not down here," he called up.

"He's in his library," I said. "I mean, the fifth floor. It's not locked, by the way."

"No, he always answers when I call. And his worktable hasn't been touched." He charged up the stairs, forcing Élise and me to press ourselves into the wall.

"Yannick," I said, as he held the trapdoor open for us to exit, "I'm certain he's down there. I saw him just last night."

"You did?" Yannick demanded. "How did he seem? Was he—"

He was walking as he spoke, but came to an abrupt halt, leading me to collide with his back.

Havelock was sitting on the counter, scowling at the cats on the other side of the room. Banshee lay comma-shaped on her back below him, paws curled in a transparent plea for affection, which Havelock was pointedly ignoring.

"Where on earth did you come from?" I demanded, both relieved and annoyed.

"I turned myself into smoke and floated up through the heat vent, as any self-respecting dark magician would."

"Havelock!" Yannick exclaimed. And then, to my astonishment, he hurried forward and pulled Havelock into a hug.

Havelock endured this for a moment or two, then pushed Yannick away. He wore his usual array of rings, which flashed when they caught the light, and around his neck were several gold chains, their pendants tucked beneath his sweater, all of which made him look like some sort of aristocrat who'd wandered in from the Renaissance. His hair was nearly as dishevelled as it had been the night we'd met, as if he'd slept in a strange position.

"What is the matter with you?" he said. "I've disappeared

for longer than a day before. Did you really think I'd let Valérie get the better of me a second time?"

"No, I thought I'd have to find a path to the Fifth Fathom, to drag whatever you'd become out of the Rivenwood," Yannick said, sounding cross. I'd never seen Yannick remotely irritated before, and again I found myself wondering about the nature of their relationship.

Havelock shook his head slightly. "If I'd truly been taken by the Rivenwood, you'd know it."

He said it matter-of-factly, which was what made it so unnerving. I thought of that uncanny forest, and suddenly I felt as if the temperature had dropped to match that of the winter street.

If Élise noticed the tension, she didn't show it. "You didn't answer Agnes's question," she said, continuing to eye Havelock with a coldly assessing look.

Havelock blinked at her, then at me, showing the confusion most people did when they noticed how alike we were. "I was upstairs," he said. "I didn't think there was any need to lurk belowground like a minotaur any longer, so I went back to my old room."

"What!" I exclaimed. "I didn't hear you come up." But then, I remembered, I had fallen into an exhausted slumber in my clothes. When I'd arisen that morning, the door to the bedroom across the hall had been closed, but I always kept it that way, as I did with the door to the lounge, to shut myself off from as much of the apartment's intimidating opulence as possible.

"No?" he said caustically. "You didn't order that panther to chase me downstairs? It came hurtling out of your room and clawed my ankle to shreds. I only managed to chase it away by enchanting one of the rugs and rolling them both into the hallway. It will be bent on murdering me now, I suspect. Not that one," Havelock said, as Yannick glanced at Banshee. "It seems as harmless as a moth. About as witless, too."

Banshee, delighted that Havelock was at last looking in her direction, began to rub her back against the floor, baring her white stomach invitingly.

"I'll thank you not to insult my cats," I said, trying not to snort at the image of Havelock fending His Majesty off with a rug. I noted that His Majesty went out of his way to menace Havelock upstairs, but kept out of sight in the basement, though he'd clearly been exploring down there for some time—it demonstrated the malicious cunning I expected from him. "On that subject," I continued, "I have a proposition for you."

"The subject of your Behemoth? Whatever it is: no."

"Not him," I said. "The others. You're no doubt unaware of this, because you don't seem to give much thought to anything of a practical nature, but there is now a rumour going around that we are selling enchanted cats."

"I was worried something like that might happen," Yannick said, rubbing a hand over his face. "Have the police heard of it? I've had enough difficulty throwing them off the scent. We'll have to put an end to it somehow before it spreads."

"I don't want to put an end to it," I said. "I want to encourage it."

"Encourage it," Yannick repeated blankly.

"If I'm to provide cover for this ridiculous operation you two are running," I said, "and, furthermore, if my life and my cats are to be endangered by the quarrels of magicians, I deserve compensation."

"You—" Yannick looked at Havelock, seeming lost. Havelock eyed me warily, waiting.

"We'd only have to enchant two or three cats," I said, clasping my hands together in front of myself, as I often did when excited. "Just enough to add fuel to the rumours and get people through our doors. After that, the demand will drive itself."

"And when they realize most of your cats aren't *actually* magic?" Havelock said.

I waved a hand. "Some will convince themselves otherwise. For most, it won't matter in the end; it's near impossible to own a cat without falling in love with it. Don't you see? If we can get the people in this city *used* to taking care of cats, to seeing them as companions more than beasts, we could put an end to the street cat population. That means an end to cats freezing to death in winter, to suffering injury and illness alone and uncared for. To say nothing of the benefits they offer their owners!" I made myself stop, as I could feel myself beginning to tremble with excitement.

"That's a lot of sentimentality to bear in one go," Havelock said. "All right, Mme. Pangloss, you have devised a plot to foist your moggies onto more unsuspecting citizens, but why should I help you? It's my magic you're proposing to use in your experiment, and you understand by now where it comes from."

His tone didn't change in any perceptible way, but again I caught a glimpse of the flickering shadow that at times seemed to overlay him. A sliver of cold pierced my determination, but I forged on nevertheless.

"Because I've already offered to help you find Vortigern's book," I said. "Trust me when I say that my organizational skills are more than competent. I've spent the last five years as the executive director of an exceptionally demanding charity. I'll make short work of that mess down in the basement." This was perhaps overstating my confidence in dealing with Havelock's shop, but I doubted anyone could make a better attempt than I.

"If memory serves, you *offered* to ransack my workshop, steal Vortigern's book, and give it to my sister." He paused to rub the sides of his nose, then added, sounding congested, "Can you not remove that creature?"

"Here, Banshee," I said, kneeling and putting my hand out. She trotted obediently to my side, and I picked her up.

Yannick's gaze had been shifting from Havelock to me and back again, growing ever more astonished. "Then you *do* have Vortigern's Artefact? Why on earth did you keep telling me there was no way?"

"There isn't," Havelock said at the same moment I exclaimed, "Yannick believes you have it too?"

"I wouldn't go that far," Yannick said. "Only Havelock keeps such poor records that I've always thought it was possible. He refuses to organize anything. You'd think he's been hoping Valérie would simply go away."

"I didn't—" Havelock began, then stopped. When he continued, I had the sense that he'd shuttered some part of himself. "I didn't think Valérie would go this far."

"It wouldn't take much magic to enchant a cat," Yannick said, considering the problem thoughtfully. "Assuming you're thinking about a simple charm. Living things can be used as Artefacts, but they rarely are, because they can't hold much magic—no more than two-layer spells—and the magic leaches out within a few days. What were you thinking?"

"I can't believe you're entertaining this," Havelock said.

"I'm not sure," I said. "But apparently one of our clients is convinced his new cat cured his insomnia."

"A simple sleep charm would certainly be doable," Yannick said, nodding. "Or perhaps a charm for stress relief, or equanimity? Better for it to be something vague and based in subjective experience. The spell would have to be activated before the cat left the shop, and again, it would only be a temporary effect."

"I'm afraid I'm failing to understand the advantages of either end of this silly bargain," Havelock said.

"The advantage is that Valérie will leave you alone if we can find and destroy that Artefact," Yannick said. "She will leave you and this city in peace. Which is what you want, surely."

I didn't understand the question in his voice, nor the sharp look Havelock gave him. There was a storm of emotion in his gaze, too much for me to parse.

"Were you responsible for the apocalypse?" Élise said.

Havelock looked at her. He'd shuttered himself again, but imperfectly; his face was still flushed. The irritation Élise had roused, though, was easy to read. Yannick was permitted to scold him, and for some reason, so was I. Élise was not.

"Yes," he said. Clearly he thought that would be enough, that Élise would be cowed or taken aback, as any sensible person would.

Havelock, though, didn't know Élise. Her expression didn't change as she said, "Prove it."

"What are you doing?" I muttered to her. She didn't look at me.

"Prove it," Havelock repeated. He didn't look awkward anymore. He looked, I realized, like the creature of shadow and flame in all but physicality, as if his human appearance was a thin guise overlaying something else, and again I remembered what he had said about how magicians brought the Rivenwood back with them. It didn't seem like Havelock looking out from his eyes, but that other presence I had glimpsed before.

"What a thought," Yannick said with a forced sort of laugh. "I think one apocalypse was enough."

"Why?" Havelock said.

Élise gave a slight shrug. "I want to know how trustworthy you are."

"You would trust someone who nearly caused the end of the world?"

Élise gazed back with a calm that no doubt made her seem made of stone to Havelock and Yannick, but I recognized the lie—her shoulders were held in tension, her voice unnaturally flat. "I'm not a simpleton. It's a matter of relative, not absolute trust. I will place more trust in a man if I have his measure. At the moment, I can't make you out at all."

"Most prefer it that way," Havelock said.

Élise gave a huff of laughter. "You clearly wish to seem mysterious, but you don't look particularly frightening, and you dress like you are putting on a play."

Yannick seemed to smother a snort. Havelock looked down at himself. He wore antiquated leather riding boots, and his sweater had an odd cowl-like hood and oversized sleeves. "Clothes can be Artefacts too," he said. "This tunic is woven with a seventeenth-century protective charm, and each of these boots holds a separate spell for concealment. They were made nearly a century ago by a magician named Sébastien Medea, who was also a boot maker."

"Ah," I said. That explained one more mystery.

"Well?" Élise said, still gazing at Havelock. Havelock, for his part, looked as if he had been about to carry on about Sébastien Medea, and blinked as if he'd lost the thread of the conversation.

"I'm not a genie to grant wishes when commanded," he finally said.

"Just one wish," Élise said. "Think of it as one of the many favours you owe Agnes for everything you've put her through."

"What!" I interjected, my nervousness growing, because I could see Havelock beginning to yield to Élise. Most people did eventually—Élise, when she chose, could wield a disarming combination of charm and self-possession. She had a way of appearing so sure of herself that most couldn't help seeing the reasonableness of her position, even when it was fundamentally unreasonable.

"You have a peculiar appetite where wishes are concerned," Havelock said. He removed a ring from his finger—it was such an absent gesture that I didn't immediately realize the significance. Then Havelock spoke a series of foreign words, crisp with a hint of music in them, and the roof was ripped off the building.

I screamed and staggered back. Darkness poured through like fog, and a bolt of lightning struck the counter, charring the books and papers as it sent them careening through the air. Havelock lifted a hand, his lips moving—I couldn't hear the enchantment over the chaos—and the walls were torn away like sheets of paper by a violent wind. The lightning was followed by a slap of rain, then snow—this was how it had been three years ago, day turned to night and the weather thrown into chaos.

I pressed Banshee to my chest and hurled myself to the floor just as the rumbling started. It was less the sound of an earthquake than of something monstrous moaning from beneath the earth. Élise was at my side suddenly, throwing her arms over me as it began to hail, pebble-sized stones bouncing off the floor. She was yelling something, and I yelled back—hysterical demands that she stop this, somehow. I was soaked from the rain, and I could feel the hailstones tangled in my hair.

Havelock wasn't immune to the weather—he held an arm above his head as the hail pummeled him, the other hand trying to hold his hood in place as the wind buffeted it back. The ferocity of his own spell seemed to have surprised him, or perhaps he had never intended to revel in it in the first place, but he didn't argue with Yannick, who was yelling and gesticulating. He leapt down from the counter—which was still there, an improbable island amidst the nightmarish dark. The wind nearly knocked him over, but he regained his footing, and with an almost desultory gesture drew the clouds into his hand. He was left holding a single shard of hail, which he tossed onto the ground. There was something embedded in it—a ring, its jewel flashing.

Havelock spun around and began rifling through the drawers of the counter. Though the weather had calmed, the rumbling beneath the earth was only growing louder. Yannick had his hands outstretched, a pocket watch dangling from one of them, but whatever spell he was trying to unleash didn't seem to be doing anything.

Havelock excavated something from the back of a drawer and held it aloft like a magic wand. In another mood, I might have laughed—it was a pair of scissors, which I'd noticed before and had assumed belonged to the former shop owner. Havelock spoke another incantation, and the walls and ceiling abruptly returned.

In the wrong place.

I screamed again. My throat was raw by this point, but I

barely noticed. The ceiling, its beams and cobwebs and all, had become the walls, and the walls, including the windows, draperies, and shelves, had been jumbled together and plastered across the ceiling.

A wave of dizziness washed over me, and I felt certain I would be sick. The windows above me showed the streetscape outside, sunlight streaming through, perfectly ordinary and completely wrong. An old woman walked past one, pulling a shopping trolley. Havelock was cursing under his breath and shaking the scissors.

"It's old," I thought I heard him say over the tremors, which had lessened but not subsided. "Some of the magic must have leaked—if I could just—"

He gave up with another curse and flung the scissors aside. He removed one of his pendants and hurled it at the ceiling in a glittering arc, the incantation coming out sharp and angry. The pendant struck one of the windows with a noise that was more like a vibration, the clang of a tremendous gong, and the ceiling and walls sorted themselves back into place. A second later, the tremors stopped, the darkness vanished, and all was as it had been before.

CHAPTER 21

"Are you certain you should go alone?" Élise said. It was nearing nine o'clock, opening hour for the shelter, and we'd just finished the morning checklist. Our newest volunteer, a retired surgeon named Geoffrey, was completing Thoreau's grooming, combing out a mat with gentle hands.

"Quite certain," I said. We needed to find Vortigern's book, and that meant I had to start *looking* for the damn thing at some point. "Especially since, between the two of us, I'm less inclined to provoke magicians with cataclysmic powers."

She didn't look in the least apologetic. "I got what I wanted."

I didn't see how this could be the case, unless what she wanted was to be properly terrified of Havelock or to terrify *me*. Now that I considered it, it seemed entirely possible.

Élise pointed to the counter, where, as usual, she'd left a paper bag full of bagels. "Eat breakfast before you go down there."

"Why, because he'll only enchant me if I'm hungry?" But I helped myself to a bagel nevertheless—Élise had bought chocolate and orange this time, my favourite from Rémy and Oliver's menu, which I took as the apology it likely was.

After I'd eaten—and downed the rest of the coffee Élise had left out—I felt marginally more confident. I gathered my supplies and made my way to the basement, as behind me Élise flipped the sign in the shelter window from *Fermé* to *Ouvert*.

I hadn't seen Havelock since he cast his terrible enchantment two days before—we'd been too busy trapping as many cats as possible to stock the second shelter. We now had eighty-five cats and kittens in total, as well as a sizeable veterinary debt, though Dr. Para had graciously allowed us to repay her by installments.

Also, despite the lurking danger presented by Valérie, I hadn't been able to work up the nerve to see him.

For some reason, Havelock's illusion—for that was all it had been, a mere echo of what we'd lived through three years ago—hadn't touched the cats at all. After I recovered, I'd picked myself up and rushed to their cages, only to find the majority asleep as usual, and others picking at their food or grooming themselves. They had gazed at me with confusion as I stood before them, panting and overwrought. Even Banshee had been perplexed. She had endured my odd embrace—when the illusion lifted, I'd found her assiduously licking my arm—then watched me with concern as I to'd and fro'd before seeming to determine that there was nothing meaningful to worry about, just human business, and wandered off. I could only assume Havelock hadn't bothered to extend the illusion to the cats.

So I tromped down the stairs to Havelock's shop, bracing myself for another blast of hail or at least a volley of sarcasm, but the first floor was deserted. The spiders glowed gently on the walls and ceilings, and the place smelled as it always did: like a museum, wood polish and old things with a charcoal undercurrent of magic.

I checked the lower floors, shuddering at the disorder, and

even knocked on the trapdoor leading to Havelock's library. If he was there, he didn't trouble himself to reply, and I lacked the bravery to intrude.

So I simply set to work. I had decided to tackle the floors in descending order, largely because the lowest floors were such a horror that I needed time to gird myself for them. I spent an hour or so rearranging boxes and crates so that they were easily accessible—some were stacked so high I needed a ladder to reach them. Then I placed my scale, labels, and glue on Havelock's desk and started—*very* gingerly—to catalogue his Artefacts.

I'd decided I would examine the cabinets first—there were ten on the first floor—before going through the boxes and crates one by one. Some looked as if they'd never even been opened, their lids still glued shut. I had ordered a vast quantity of wood shelving, which would be delivered the next day, and which I intended to hammer into the walls whether Havelock liked it or not. What was the point in having a shop if you couldn't see half your wares?

As I worked, I heard intermittent rustling from other parts of the basement, as well as occasional thumps, which I assumed was just His Majesty, making mischief, although it *was* a magician's workshop, and perhaps some of the Artefacts were not as inanimate as they appeared.

The spiders proved themselves an utterly impractical source of illumination. Some stayed put, allowing me to see what I was doing, but others crept from place to place, so that I ended up following them around with my notebook, squinting down at the page as I tried to write. I eventually grew so fed up that I found a glass jar and trapped one of the larger spiders inside it. I felt a little guilty about this, so I took the time to poke airholes in the jar lid and toss in a few dead termites I found in one of the crates.

I had given some thought to categorization systems before largely abandoning the endeavour; I didn't know enough about magic, though I'd gleaned a little from Havelock's tedious speeches, to guess which system would be most useful. Instead I'd simply decided to number the Artefacts and divide them into portable or non-portable, which was likely to be of interest to magicians, given that they were always duelling each other. I'd noted that Havelock seemed to like wearing his enchantments in order to have them close at hand at all times. Thus the first Artefact I examined, a plain brass thimble, was labelled *1P,* while the glittering silver orrery beside it—which would attract a few stares if one hauled it down Rue du Parc—was *1N.*

I was just gluing a label to a delicate wooden music box—*12P*—when I was startled by a soft creak from the stairs behind me. I whirled and found a stranger looking back at me, who had crept down the stairs as quietly as a ghost. He had sandy hair and close-set eyes above sharp cheekbones.

I cried out, hoisting the music box to hurl it at him.

"No, no, no!" the man exclaimed, raising his arm, and it wasn't a stranger's voice, but *Havelock's.* "That's a nine-layer summoning spell so powerful it could enchant an object in Australia and pull it through the earth's core. Also, I haven't finished examining it."

My initial reaction was relief that it was only Havelock, not some thief come to murder me and steal Havelock's Artefacts; my secondary reaction was astonishment at myself that I had come to see the Witch King's company as preferable to anyone's, murderers included.

I put the music box down. "So you do know what some of your Artefacts do."

"The ones that can bore holes through the planet, yes." He narrowed his eyes at me, and I felt a spasm of disorientation, seeing one of Havelock's expressions on a stranger's face.

"What on earth have you done to yourself now?" I couldn't help demanding. His old face had been much more interesting than this new one, and I felt strangely annoyed with him for changing it.

But he only blinked at me, seeming for once at a loss for words. "Which one are you?" he said finally.

"Excuse me?"

"I don't know any sane person who would speak to me like that after the illusion I cast the other day," he said. "And given that Agnes Aubert is the most scrupulously sane person I've met, I can only assume that she has yet another twin sister, and that I am trapped in some Shakespearean comedy."

"I don't know about that last part," I said, "having never read Shakespeare. But I haven't forgotten that little display of yours, and I'd thank you not to do it again. Though I'll admit that Élise should know better than to provoke magicians who will take any excuse to show off. Also, we aren't twins."

He shook his head. "I don't understand you at all," he said in an almost despairing tone.

I laughed—it seemed the only possible response to such a hypocritical complaint.

Frowning, he brushed a hand across his face as if wiping away rain, and I stumbled backwards with another yelp and crashed into the worktable as Havelock's face appeared beneath the stranger's—he had wiped the *enchantment* away. He removed his glasses from a pocket and placed them on his nose, then he ran his hands over his hair, which darkened beneath his fingers and grew longer. He brushed his hands together with a little grimace, as if scraps of the stranger's visage might have stuck to them.

Then he was removing his boots and placing them beside the stairs with the same unhurried movements, as if there were nothing materially different about this than what he had just done.

"I do leave the shop sometimes." He doffed his coat, turning his back to me as he placed it on a hook close to a particularly well-fed spider. "Unfortunately, when you nearly bring about the end times, the authorities tend to take an interest in your whereabouts and circulate your image among themselves—hence the disguise. Were you imagining I lived like Dantès down here?"

"I don't know who that is," I said. Frustration rose within me. "I don't know what you mean half the time. I know you aren't an ordinary person, but can't you at least talk like one?"

I regretted my outburst immediately. But he only removed his gloves one finger at a time, watching me warily, which nearly made me want to laugh again. I wondered if I would always be veering back and forth between fearing him and wanting to take him by the arms and shake him.

"You claim the police will recognize you, but I don't see how anybody learns what you look like if you're always putting silly beauty spells on yourself," I said. I noted with relief that his eyes were both the same dark brown again.

"I don't change my appearance *that* often," he said, seeming to take note of the slightly ameliorated disarray of his workshop. "What have you been up to down here? It looks as if a hurricane hit the place. A fastidious, moralizing sort of hurricane."

"I'm putting things in order," I said. "Have you forgotten our agreement?"

"I have an unfortunate tendency to forget events that never took place."

I drew myself up, bracing myself to argue with him, but he only rubbed his hair and said with a sigh, "I didn't mean that. I'll enchant your silly felines, and you can continue your well-intentioned rampage through my collection, only allow me a few moments of silence. I need to rest this headache."

He sat at his worktable and lowered his head onto his hands, massaging his temples. The motion caused his dark hair to fall forward, and his enchanted rings flashed in the spiderlight. I watched him a moment, feeling a pang of sympathy. No doubt he'd been up to something wicked, but there wasn't anything I could do about *that*, was there?

I went upstairs to the kitchen. There I heated the kettle and scrounged in the cupboards until I located the familiar satchel of herbs. I went back downstairs and placed the mug in front of him, then picked up my clipboard and turned to the cabinet of Artefacts.

"What's this?" he said. I turned to find him regarding the mug with such an expression of suspicion that I couldn't help snorting.

"It's for your headache," I said. "Mugwort and dried lemon peel mixed with a strong Irish tea. It always helps Élise. She's prone to headaches when she's not sleeping well."

His gaze shifted from the mug to me. He'd drawn one leg up to his chest, and with the flush rising in his cheeks, he looked startlingly youthful.

"How old are you, anyhow?" I said.

He took a dubious sip from the mug. "Thirty-two."

"Really? You don't look it." I didn't mean that he looked

younger or older, but rather that he didn't look any particular age, a characteristic I'd noted in several of the other magicians.

"Not *all* of my face is thirty-two."

I couldn't tell if he was serious or not, and shuddered inwardly. I gestured at the mug. "I'm not going to poison you." I added, very gravely, "Wouldn't be much point, given that you're nothing but moonlight and cobwebs."

He gave a huff that might have been laughter, and I turned back to my work. I was just recording the last Artefact in the cabinet and closing the door when I caught a flash of his reflection in the glass—he'd come to stand behind me, looking over my shoulder at what I was doing.

I gave a yelp and nearly dropped my clipboard. He jumped at my surprise, and we blinked at each other. I realized that he might not be aware of how unnaturally he moved. It seemed logical that magicians simply got used to themselves, in the way that I was used to my large feet and tendency to stomp about, which Robin had loved to tease me for.

"Sorry," he said. "I just can't work out what you're doing."

"You know what I'm doing," I said, confused. "I'm organizing your collection, recording each Artefact. You can see I've added catalogue numbers—"

"Yes, but how are you recording the enchantments?"

"I'm—I'm not," I said. "Obviously I have no idea what dreadful spells are stored inside them. But I can tell that none of the Artefacts I've recorded so far are seventeenth-century books."

"Ah," he said. "But Vortigern's book might not look ancient. It might not even look like a book, as you have already pointed out. If Walker Clem knew he had one of Vortigern's spells, even if he couldn't work out what it did, he might have concealed it behind an illusion to trick would-be thieves.

Mind, it would have to be an uncommonly strong illusion to last this long. Six layers at least, with—"

"I surmised that was a possibility, yes," I interrupted, not caring to sit through another speech I couldn't understand. "The problem is that half your Artefacts are stuffed into crates or buried beneath other Artefacts. If I can get them numbered and organized, it will be much easier for you and Yannick to use your magic to examine them. I've already questioned Yannick, and he's told me that an illusion spell could change the appearance of the book, but not its weight. Thus I've made two trips to the main library to analyze the weight of books of varying sizes, and I've spoken to the woman in charge of their historical collection. From this I've calculated a weight range for a book of that age, adding an ounce on either end to be safe." I motioned to the scale before me. "I'm taking special note of Artefacts whose weights fall within that range, especially if they seem suspiciously light or heavy. Based on my initial survey, such Artefacts comprise less than ten percent of your collection. Thus, even if I do not find Vortigern's book myself, I will narrow down the number of possibilities and save you and Yannick a great deal of time."

I didn't bother mentioning that part of my motivation to organize his shop was that the thought of its disorder was driving me mad. I fully intended to organize every Artefact, even those that had nothing to do with our current predicament. The state of things was a disgrace.

Throughout my explanation, his eyebrows had drawn progressively closer together. When I finished, he regarded me in silence.

"You *are* a hurricane, aren't you?" he said. "I'm half convinced that if I get in your way, I'll find myself stuffed into a crate with a number glued to my forehead."

"Oh, no," I said. "You'd get your own shelf."

He actually laughed—I realized he enjoyed it when I taunted him, which wasn't a surprise, given that he seemed the sort of person who armoured himself in sarcasm. What surprised me was how much I enjoyed his reaction.

I returned to my work, blushing. The problem with Havelock wasn't that he was attractive, but that he was attractive in the specific way that I preferred—namely, his good looks were unconventional. A straightforward handsomeness had never caught my interest; beauty has always seemed to me to be heightened by a few jagged edges. Robin had suited this description well, with his comically large ears and deep-set eyes that sometimes seemed to disappear beneath their dark brows, which had only made his smiles seem warmer, more fundamental.

Doing my best to forget I'd thought any of this, I replaced the music box in the cabinet and took up a plain gold chain that *felt* ancient, somehow. *18P,* I wrote on a label, then attached it to the chain with a paper clip.

"Don't you know how much danger you're in?" he said. I turned to find that he'd taken several steps back, and stood behind his worktable. It felt like a closed door, a threshold I could not pass.

"From the Artefacts?" I said. "I thought you needed to speak a command to release their magic."

He didn't reply. After a moment, he said in a different tone, "Have you given any thought to how you would like your cats enchanted?" He paused. "I was going to follow that with a joke, but it feels redundant."

I pointed. "On the table."

He turned and plucked the paper I'd left for him there, a neatly typed list of possible spells that I thought likely to appeal to our clientele. I braced myself for an argument, but he only looked at me askance and said, "That's it?"

"Are they doable?" I said. "Obviously I'm not an expert—"

He waved a hand. "I have a few similar enchantments on hand," he said. "I'll need to modify them. And transfer them to your beasts, of course." He began rummaging through the notebooks piled on the table.

"You can do that?"

He gave me an amused look, but before he could reply I quickly added, "Yes, of course you can. Witch King and all that. World's most powerful dark magician."

I said it to annoy him, but he merely replied, still rummaging about, "And what should I call *you*, I wonder? Renowned mistress of moggies? Professional herder of cats?"

"You can call me Agnes," I said. "I'm nowhere near important enough for titles."

He took another sip of his tea, paused, then downed the rest. "Doctor to dark magicians? This *is* helping, thank you. That's the second time you've healed me. I'd recommend against making a habit of it—my enemies won't thank you."

He disappeared into the back of the shop and reappeared a few moments later with his hands full of an assemblage of curios: a silver dip pen, several Roman coins, a pill box dotted with tiny emeralds shaped into leaves, a ceramic figurine of a stag made from gold and lapis lazuli. He placed these on his worktable, after absently sweeping his arm across it to send a stack of papers and books tumbling to the floor (I winced), and went to one of the cabinets. From this he fetched an armillary sphere that looked as if it should occupy pride of place in a museum display, with intricate rings of silver and gold.

"Are most Artefacts beautiful?" I couldn't help asking.

"Beautiful or rare," he said. "Or ancient, or some combination. Magicians are vain; we don't like to put our enchantments into just *any* object, unless we have to—defensive spells, for example, are best hidden. The most common Artefacts are jewelry, clothes—anything that can be worn or easily carried. Many museums over the centuries have found their collections mysteriously depleted by invisible thieves."

I shook my head. It didn't surprise me that magicians felt entitled to hoard rare antiquities and works of art simply because they had the power to take them. The thought made me more weary than angry.

"What?" he said. "I can see you preparing your lecture. I didn't say I agreed with the practice."

I didn't believe him for a moment, but I also didn't see much point in arguing about it. "What are you doing in Montréal?" I said, turning back to the cabinet. "Everyone seems to think you're in New York."

"I *was* in New York. I move every few years, for obvious reasons. Before that I was in Paris."

"Paris," I echoed.

He glanced up at me, seeming to notice something in my voice. "You've seen it?"

"Naturally I haven't." In fact, I had always harboured a secret desire to visit Paris, and New York too, among a dozen other places. But it was a wistful sort of desire, not one based in anything so fertile as hope.

"Why not?"

I gave a short laugh. "It takes weeks to reach France. I haven't spent more than a day or two away from the shelter since we opened."

He turned back to his worktable. "I can't say I'm surprised."

"Where have you been, anyway?" I said, wanting to change

the subject. "Off blighting some poor farmer's crops? Enchanting small children to have nightmares about you?"

"I only blight crops on Saturdays. And children do that without my assistance. Here."

I turned to find that he was coming towards me with the silver pen. "What are you doing?" I demanded, holding up the clipboard as if it might ward him off.

He stopped. "The pen will allow you to identify the enchantments contained within each Artefact. It's quite easy: only hold it to a piece of paper, and speak the word—"

"No," I said, taking a step away from him.

He gazed at me, uncertainty clouding his expression. "It won't harm you. I've woven the enchantment carefully."

"It's a—" I remembered the coin he had offered me. "First-order enchantment?"

"Yes."

I frowned at this. "What happens if a human tries to cast a second-order one?"

"You don't want to know." He amended, "It actually depends more on the talent of the magician than the strength of the spell. Most magicians do quite shoddy work, and it's why Artefacts have gained a reputation for being dangerous to humans. On the whole, they are, but not for the reason people think. A large piece of machinery is dangerous if poorly constructed. A badly made pencil, less so. Even if you cast one of my stronger enchantments, you would likely be quite safe."

I rolled my eyes. "Hand me an Artefact meant to ward off egotistical magicians, and I'll consider it."

I made no move to take the pen, and he slowly lowered it. "I know you have good reason to fear magic," he said, "given that it cost you your home—"

"That's not it," I said. "I simply want nothing to do with it." I gave a brittle laugh, knowing how ridiculous it sounded. "Or as little as possible. I certainly don't want to playact as a magician."

He chewed his lip. "There's something else, then. You've been harmed by magicians before? Or is it because of your husband? Yannick told me he died suddenly. Is that why you despise us? You feel that one of us could have helped him?"

"No," I said, startled by this unexpected mention of Robin, but also by the fact that he'd bothered to retain such mundane information as my personal biography. "Do you really have that much trouble accepting the idea that some people might dislike magic?"

He didn't look like he believed me, and I recalled our conversation after Valérie's attack. *Magic is who I am.* Naturally he would have trouble with the concept; I might as well expect a fish to understand a fear of water.

"I have no sordid history with magic," I said. "I simply see no reason to respect the sort of people who have the power to do a great deal of good, but can't be bothered to."

"Oh, some can," he said. "Though they're few and far between. Must magic be useful? Can't it simply be beautiful, like art? If you tried it, you might find you enjoy it."

"*Enjoy* it," I repeated, thinking of the crater in the wall of the old shelter. That was art to him, was it?

"Yes," he said. "Is that a foreign concept? Enjoyment?"

"I don't take your meaning," I said coldly.

He shrugged. "Do you do anything for yourself? You spend morning to night taking care of your menagerie."

"How do you—" I groaned. "Yannick."

"He didn't have to tell me that. We've lived together for

some time now. I've heard you stomping about until midnight sometimes, cleaning, moving cages about, talking to those cats. I certainly haven't heard you throwing any parties."

I went red thinking about the silly nonsense I said to the cats when we were alone. He'd heard all that?

"They need me," I said levelly. "Someone has to care for them—nobody else is doing it. And anyway, I *like* what I do. What business is it of yours how I spend my time? Are you trying to convince me that I should see magic as some sort of—*holiday*?"

In reply, he held out the pen. He was all cold confidence again, no trace of awkwardness remaining, which I had come to interpret as the magic within him rising to the surface. I had no fear of him in that moment, though, only curiosity. After a pause, I took the pen. His hand brushed mine, and I thought of the embers of lightning I had felt on his skin after he fought Valérie.

"Now," he said, opening the cabinet and removing the gold chain I had been admiring before. The links were delicate imperfect circles. "Hold this, and speak the command. The enchantment trapped in the gold will reveal itself."

He said something then, obviously a magic word, so inhuman-sounding it might as well have been birdsong.

"I can't pronounce that!" I exclaimed. "I can barely remember it."

"It gets easier with practice." He repeated the word again.

"*Ellnose uz?*" I tried.

He winced.

"This is pointless," I said, trying to give the pen back. He put his hand around my wrist, stopping me.

"It's the language of the Rivenwood," he said. "It takes time to perfect, even for magicians. I'll say it slowly." He did.

"*Helnez althz*," I said, which sounded a little better, but still a ways off. It was a sharp-edged, hissing sort of language, and it reminded me of fire: the rustle of the flames punctuated by the snap of sparks. Somehow it was easier to say with him standing so close, enveloped in the disquieting scent of magic.

"Close enough," Havelock said. He was still holding my wrist, his thumb brushing the place where my pulse beat, and we both seemed to realize it at the same time. He released me and stepped back.

"There are actually only a handful of commands used to release spells from their vessels," he said. "That's one of the simpler ones—they increase in complexity for the more difficult spells."

"Is that why ordinary people have more trouble casting spells?" I said. "They can't get the pronunciation right?"

"That," Havelock said, pausing, "and the fact that humans have no affinity for magic, the way we do. It's part of us from the time we're born. That's why the Rivenwood calls to us."

"How unpleasant." I took up my clipboard and turned to a fresh sheet, holding the pen to it.

"Ink?" I said. He only shook his head. "You don't use ink?" I pressed.

"No, I write all my correspondence in my own blood," he said. "Agnes, it's an enchanted pen—just try it." He put the gold chain in my other hand.

I didn't know why I wasn't more nervous. I suppose it was because I didn't expect anything to happen—the idea of me casting a spell was so incongruous that the possibility barely occurred to me, even as I spoke the word he'd taught me. I liked the idea of proving him wrong, of showing him that magic and I were oil and water.

But the word didn't sound the same this time; it rose inside me, warm and almost *fizzy,* and it sounded closer to what he'd said. Afterwards my mouth tasted of charcoal and night wind.

I made a strangled sound. My hand was darting across the page—or, rather, the pen was, dragging my hand along with it. It wrote a dozen words and then skittered to a stop, a terrible sort of twitching motion that reminded me of a bird that had flown into a window. Then it was still, and it was only a pen.

I jolted to my feet, mindlessly panicking, and clipboard and pen clattered to the floor. Havelock caught me in his arms before I could flee, or faint—I'm not sure which impulse was dominant. I remembered what he'd said about magic being *alive,* and felt abruptly repulsed, as if I'd briefly given myself over to some parasite.

"Are you all right?" He settled me quickly on the table, then stepped back, all awkwardness again. "You did well. It's good that you spoke with confidence; spells always come off better that way, though your pronunciation is—well, it was an admirable first attempt for a professional cat herder."

He snatched the clipboard up, a smile spreading across his face—one of his rare genuine smiles, which chased the mordant glint from his eyes. It was in that moment that I realized two things: one, I had done magic; and two, I was beginning to have feelings for Havelock Renard. I had no idea which was more upsetting and incomprehensible.

"Oh, hell," I murmured.

"No, it's all right," he enthused obliviously. "The handwriting is hard to read because it isn't *yours,* you see. It's the writing of the magician who enchanted the necklace, an eighteenth-century magician named Sarah Thomson . . ."

He kept talking, but I wasn't listening. I blinked rapidly, but that couldn't save me this time, and my eyes began to well.

It took him a moment or two to notice, but he did, eventually. "What is it? Are you—?"

"I'm all right," I said in a broken voice. "I'm only overwhelmed. I always cry when I'm overwhelmed. It will stop soon."

To my surprise, he took me at my word. "Yes, I noticed that before. Here."

He went to his worktable and rummaged about in a drawer, excavating a handkerchief. It was a little dusty and smelled of magic, but I blew my nose on it anyway.

"Can you make it out?" he said, sitting beside me again and showing me what I'd written on the clipboard.

His unperturbed reaction to my tears was vastly more comforting than any to-do he could have made about them. I wiped my eyes and leaned forward, squinting. *"For the prevention of poisoning,"* I read. "Oh! That's what the necklace does."

He nodded. "Not all enchantments are so straightforward, but nevertheless, this will tell you what sort of magic is stored in each Artefact. As for the enchantment in the *pen*, I've woven it with a recursive spell to make it stick, so I'll only need to refill the magic every now and again."

I nodded, though I wasn't certain I understood. My head was still swimming.

"You needn't use the pen," he said, watching me. "If you don't wish to."

"It's fine," I said. "It's helpful. Thank you. I—I have to attend to the cats, but I'll return momentarily."

I tromped up the stairs, nearly tripping and falling in my haste. No doubt he assumed he'd frightened me, which was better than him guessing the truth. I could still taste charcoal on my tongue.

Élise was in the back room when I surfaced, digging through the storage cupboard.

"Don't tell me we're out of litter again," I said, trying for an ordinary tone.

She turned and fixed me with a probing, suspicious look. "You're finished already?"

I shook my head. Élise could read me well, but I could read her too, and I realized then that she knew what had upset me—she'd worked it out before I had. My eyes welled again.

"Oh, Agnes." Élise came forward and folded me into her arms. She smelled as she always did: vanilla-scented perfume woven with coffee and cat hair, familiar and comforting. "I wish you'd left him to bleed to death. It would have made everything much simpler!"

CHAPTER 22

I had little time to dwell on my predicament, however; the cats' needs were, as ever, at the forefront of my thoughts. One of our kittens found a home the following morning, which meant that we had our first opportunity to put my plan in motion.

An hour before his new owner was due to collect him, I brought the cat down to Havelock's workshop and set him on the table among the scattered notebooks and priceless Artefacts. I braced myself for—something, I'm not certain what. Perhaps a flash of light, or a shower of glittering sparks, but Havelock only placed his hand on the kitten's back and murmured a word, while the cat rubbed his face on Havelock's books.

"There," he said, rubbing at his eyes. "One feline periapt."

"Are you certain it worked?" I pressed. "Is the enchantment—"

"It's a simple charm," he said. "Activated by proximity. The more time a person spends with the beast, the more their small aches and pains will be lessened. I don't know whether it will ease other ailments—surprising as it may be, I've never enchanted a cat before."

"No, that's perfect," I said, delighted. I picked up the kitten, who yowled in dismay—all the cats seemed fascinated by Havelock's shop, and would paw at the trapdoor whenever they were allowed to roam the shelter, no doubt because it was forbidden. "How long will it last?"

"A week or two, possibly longer. Living things leak magic faster than inanimate ones."

"*Leak* magic?" I repeated.

"All Artefacts leak if they aren't taken care of, particularly if they're poorly made or ancient. Sometimes the magic is absorbed into something else. One Artefact leaked into the cardboard box it was kept in, and now I have an enchanted cardboard box."

I pictured an old wine cask, slowly dripping onto the floorboards. It was an unexpectedly mundane image to associate with magic.

"Thank you," I said.

Havelock let out a colossal sneeze. "Please don't bring them into my shop again," he said stuffily, and I hastened away, seeing no need to mention the fact that His Majesty had been skulking about down there for days.

Luck was in our favour, and two more cats were spoken for the following day: a black-and-white kitten named Chaplin and a regal tortoiseshell, Baroness. Havelock placed a spell upon Chaplin that would guarantee pleasant dreams for his owner, while Baroness got a spell for harmony—she was being adopted into a large and boisterous family.

Our foot traffic continued to increase, and even if that was not coupled with a massive rise in adoptions, we were still doing well, and had gone from eighty-five to seventy-one charges between both shelters, even accounting for several new arrivals. I was optimistic for the future; it did not hurt that Rémy and Oliver were happily spreading the story of the cat who cured his master's sleeplessness to all who stepped into their bakery.

I could not spend as much time with the cats as I wished to, though, as my priority was excavating Havelock's workshop. In this I was assisted by Yannick, who seemed delighted to be finally cataloguing Havelock's collection, even if we did not find Vortigern's book there. Most days I left the running of the shelter to Élise or one of our volunteers.

Havelock contributed little to our efforts, hunching over his worktable muttering to himself as he worked on Lord knew what manner of enchantments, sometimes disappearing for a full day or more. When he returned, I would ask if he had been off devouring maidens' hearts or cursing the firstborns of his enemies—I came up with something different each time—to which he would reply that maidens' hearts were far too bland for his taste and he preferred the seasoned hearts of elderly widows, or that his reputation would suffer if he did anything so predictable as cursing firstborns, thus he only laid curses on his enemies' youngest stepchildren or obscure cousins.

I never got the answer I sought—namely, the truth—but I did not really expect it, and anyway I enjoyed teasing him, as I enjoyed interrupting him while he hunched over his Artefacts, particularly if he was so absorbed that I made him drop what he was doing. I found myself continually drawn into his orbit, like a wayward comet pulled towards a dark star. I tried to rationalize my behaviour—yes, I felt something for Havelock, but there was nothing of substance in it. It was a troubling—though ultimately transient—infatuation.

Valérie's apprentices continued to cause an array of minor calamities, pranks, and illusions that did not set anything else on fire, but had the effect of setting the entire city on edge. I could not help wondering why she had not attacked the shop again. Yes, Havelock had strengthened his warding enchantments, but she had made it past his wards once, hadn't she? How long would it be until she succeeded again?

Because of my preoccupation with Havelock's Artefacts, it was a full two weeks before I was able to visit the second shelter in Rue Sainte-Sophie.

Yannick and I had successfully organized half of the basement's first floor, and though we hadn't come across Vortigern's book, there was a part of me that could breathe a little easier knowing that the mess had been partly tamed. From the way Havelock behaved, he might not have noticed his working environment had been so drastically altered, apart from the odd caustic complaint tossed my way about my hurricane-like tendencies, or his inability to locate a particular Artefact due to my having neatly arranged everything upon shelves, accompanied by a catalogue he refused to consult. Yannick, though, was pleased, and told me that Havelock's work would surely be much easier now, which filled me with an uneasy guilt.

But I had made my decision. I had allied myself with Havelock for the sake of the shelter. While I didn't believe in his reputation anymore, not truly, that didn't mean I understood him. And yet whatever he was, he would have continued in his chosen course without me.

So I told myself at night, when I lay awake and unable to sleep.

I felt nervous as I clambered off the tram, which stopped right outside the fortress of marble and glass that was the central bank. Business had been slow at our new shelter at first, but it had picked up dramatically as the rumours about our cats spread through the city. Two days before, Mina had even worried that they might run out, which I thought a rather optimistic concern. And one that had been almost immediately solved when a sailor arrived with a litter of six-month-old kittens he'd found aboard his ship.

Well-dressed men and women alighted beside me, then hurried purposefully up the stone stairs, and for a moment I felt like a small fish overwhelmed by a river's current. I couldn't stop or I would block the flow of those disembarking; thus I was halfway up the stairs before I extricated myself awkwardly, bumping into a scowling man in a fur coat.

I don't know what astonished me more when I stepped inside the shelter: that the place was, if anything, even more opulent than Élise had described, or the fact that it was bustling.

The ceiling was cavernous and the floors were a beautiful eggshell-coloured marble inlaid with a geometric mosaic of vines and fleur-de-lis. Three electric chandeliers provided most of the illumination, and upon the glass-topped counters that had once held costly jewelry perched several dozen cat cages. Admiring the cats were a couple with two small children, a young man with the look of a university student, two elderly women in expensive furs, and three people who I knew instinctively, from their posture and dress, to be employees of the bank. While it might not have been what most shop owners would consider an enormous crowd, it was more people than I'd ever seen in the shelter at one time.

I stood on the threshold, blinking, until Mina came to my rescue.

"I just *knew* this ritzy place would be good for us," she said, pulling me forward. "No, we haven't run out, but look—we're down to twenty-six. Twenty-six! We had forty only a few days ago."

"What!" I looked around, astonished to see that she was correct. Well over half the new cages Élise and I had purchased were now empty.

"We were thinking we might search the warehouses by the river tonight," Mina said. "I know there are still kittens down there—the ships bring them in. And I wonder if Dr. Para or one of her assistants might have time to neuter the ferals living behind city hall? That lot produces more kittens in a year than—"

I shook my head. "We can't afford that, Mina. We're already in debt to Noémie, and I can't—"

"Are we?" I realized she was giving me a sly smile.

"Are we what?"

She didn't reply, merely gestured me over to the counter, which still held the old jewelry shop's ornate bronze-and-walnut cash register with a floral design that matched the floor. She pulled the handle and the drawer slid open, and she handed me a cheque.

"What's this?" My eyes bulged as I read the number scrawled in expensive ink. "Mina! How did you—?"

"It's a donation," she said, laughing at my expression. "It came in yesterday. A nice woman who was quite taken with the shelter when she passed by on her way to the bank. It's the third we've received this week. The other two aren't anywhere near as large, but—"

She didn't finish the sentence, because I'd pulled her in for a hug. She laughed again, and when I drew back, wiping my eyes, she offered me a handkerchief.

"Thank you," I said, blowing my nose. "You're wonderful, Mina. I hope you know that."

She made a dismissive gesture, but I could tell she was pleased. "I had nothing to do with it! Shall I send a telegram to Dr. Para?"

"You had better—it seems we can pay off our debt now, with a little left over."

We spent the next quarter hour discussing our finances, during which I couldn't help noticing that Mina appeared more animated than I had ever seen her. She was still a woman of few words, but the many trials we'd faced in recent weeks had brought out the fierce determination in her that I had only glimpsed before. I wondered if it was because we'd been placing more trust in her, or if Mina, like most, simply felt her best when presented with visible evidence of her usefulness.

Afterwards, I wandered through the shelter, greeting our visitors and saying hello to the cats. Most I had not met before, including a voluminous tabby that Mina had named Champlain. At the sight of me, he began to rub his side enthusiastically against the bars, which made it impossible not to open the cage and give him a proper greeting. Champlain, though, was the sort of cat Élise and I referred to as a dine-and-dasher, possessed of a disposition so desperately affectionate that they remained at the shelter only long enough to partake in a meal or two before someone fell in love with them. As soon as the cage door swung open, he was clambering into my arms and rubbing his head against my chin, purring.

"Here, *Maman*!" one of the children exclaimed, pointing at Champlain. I gave a quiet laugh and placed the big cat in the girl's arms.

Anya, a university friend of Mina's and our newest volunteer, approached as I was petting a tuxedo named King Francis. "That man was asking for you," she said, gesturing. "He came by yesterday as well."

I turned, though I already knew who it would be—Laurent had stopped in at the other shelter a few days before, when I had been down in the basement. Sure enough, he stood by the register, chatting with Mina while his dark gaze studied me.

I felt my heart speed up—mostly from nervousness, I think, but it was also possible there was excitement there. I could hear Élise's words in my head: *That detective obviously likes you, and you like him, too. And* he *at least is an ordinary man, and quite possibly a decent one.*

She had been convinced that Laurent would invite me to dinner, and that I should say yes, because I needed to forget about Havelock. And she was correct about that, but I couldn't say if she was correct about my feelings. Certainly I found Laurent attractive, but was there more to it than that? I couldn't say.

Is it Robin? Élise had asked, watching me closely.

I had shaken my head, and she hadn't pressed the matter. No, it wasn't thoughts of Robin that kept me from entertaining thoughts of Laurent. The truth was that I had always assumed I would find someone else eventually, and this had never aroused any turmoil within me. Not because I was content to replace Robin, but because I knew he would never be replaced. Someone else might take up space in my heart, but they would never encroach upon the largest space, as quiet and cavernous as a cathedral, which would always belong to him.

I made my way towards Laurent, but before I'd taken three

steps, an older man with abundant grey eyebrows stepped in front of me, thrusting his hand out.

"Roger Fairwood," the man said, shaking my hand. "I just dropped by to thank you again. Never have I slept so well in my life. What a wonderful organization this is!"

"You adopted Juliette," I said, smiling in recognition. But my smile faded as I heard his words again. "Wait—was it you who told Rémy you had adopted an enchanted cat?"

Fairwood laughed. "I don't know that I used those words. I don't wish to get you into any trouble." He glanced over his shoulder at Laurent, grimacing slightly. "But I simply had to thank you for dear Juliette."

I forced myself to smile. From the look the man was giving me, he was convinced I was a magician and had enchanted Juliette myself. I didn't think Laurent could hear our conversation; he was still regarding me, though.

"I'm *convinced* it was her," Fairwood continued. "And of course I have additional cause now—I hear others have also benefited from your cats. Is that not so? I was chatting with one of the librarians at the main branch, and she told me her joints have never felt so spry since she took home a delightful little thing called Tapioca. I will not ask *how* you do it, but I do wonder—how do you know what each person needs?"

I hadn't the slightest idea how to respond to this, particularly as he stood there gazing at me with a kind of quiet reverence. Fortunately, when I only stuttered, he put his hand on my shoulder and squeezed gently.

"I shouldn't have asked," he said. "No doubt it's beyond my comprehension. Thank you, Agnes. I have seen many things in this life, you know. Too many, I sometimes think. I did not believe I could be surprised anymore, let alone awed."

He tipped his hat to me and departed, and I was able to make my way to Laurent, feeling more than a little discombobulated. It wasn't just that Fairwood had taken me for a magician, it had been his uncomplicated, almost childlike reaction to magic. Yes, he thought my supposed magic had benefited him, but had he forgotten all the ills magic could bring about? He had not seemed to fear me at all.

"You're a difficult woman to pin down," Laurent said, turning from the cage to smile at me. "Been busy?"

"Very." I was only too happy to tell him about the success of our new shelter—I was ever aware of his scrutinizing gaze, which seemed to perceive more than it revealed, and was eager to discuss something I could be honest about.

"I'm not surprised," he said. "You've managed to make friends in high places. Fairwood seems a great admirer of your charity."

I flushed. This implied Laurent had heard the rumours about our enchanted cats—and yet, his expression was friendly rather than suspicious. Even if he *had* heard the rumours, did I need to worry? The trafficking of Artefacts was illegal, but there was nothing illegal, to my knowledge, about placing a harmless charm upon a stray cat. It seemed the sort of item most politicians would not think to put into law, even as a footnote.

"Roger seems kind, but I admit I don't know him," I said carefully.

"No?" Laurent looked surprised. "His is one of the largest shipping companies this side of the Atlantic. Not to mention he owns a sizeable percentage of the city's warehouses, as well as the *Daily Gazette*."

"Oh! How silly of me." Of course I had seen the Fairwood

name on the side of many of the ships that roamed the St. Lawrence. "I didn't make the connection."

Something about the mention of the *Gazette* made me uneasy. That, and Roger Fairwood's influence in the city—no wonder our rumours were spreading so well, with him on our side. Yet, it was what I'd wanted, wasn't it? Gossip of magical cats, entertaining enough to draw the attention of the general public, but too vague to be widely believed?

We made small talk for a while, Laurent asking after Lynx and me gently teasing him with stories of how the cat was clearly pining for him, seeming uninterested in other suitors.

"The winter festival begins next week," Laurent said. "I don't suppose you'll have any time to spare for it?"

"Oh—I doubt it," I said. I loved the festival, which consisted of an outdoor market, tobogganing, ice castles, and other events scattered throughout the city. Robin and I had attended every year: I'd been content to tour the many food stands, eating toasted cheese and sugar pie until I felt ready to burst, while he'd been particularly fond of the masquerade in the park.

My attention drifted from Laurent as a familiar melancholy settled over me. The festival was so intertwined with memories of Robin that I'd never contemplated attending without him.

Laurent glanced away, but not before I caught the flash of disappointment in his eyes. It hadn't been a casual enquiry—he had been asking me to attend with him!

"I always make a point of seeing the snow sculptures," he went on before I could speak. "I used to compete as a boy. I won third place when I was ten."

"No!" I said, smiling. "For what?"

He looked sheepish. "A polar bear."

"Ah." I nodded gravely. "They say the classics are the trickiest to execute. The standards are so high."

"That's what I tell everyone," he said. "The truth is that the dinosaur I had in mind proved a tad overambitious. All those pointy bits."

We laughed, and he told me how the contest had been a family tradition, passed down from his grandfather, who had won a record eight years in a row. His eyes grew warm when he spoke of his family, which made me like him even better than I already did.

"Anyway," he said, "if you do have any spare time—not that it's of interest to everyone—"

"I would love to go with you," I said, realizing that it was perfectly true.

He smiled, the opacity of his demeanour dissolving, and he promised to call upon me again to arrange the details.

"Élise will be pleased," Mina said after he left, giving me an uncharacteristic wink.

I scowled. "I thought you were unloading the supplies."

"I was, but Élise made me promise to report any developments where your detective was concerned."

I gave her a mock swat and she went away laughing. I turned back to the cats, feeling more buoyant than I had in days.

CHAPTER 23

I saw nothing of Havelock over the next several days—another of his mysterious disappearances—and I missed him sitting at his worktable, muttering to himself or rubbing at his hair. I was adding another empty crate to the pile when I realized, to my astonishment, that I'd nearly tamed the entire first floor of Havelock's workshop.

There were now two tidy corridors running lengthwise from the stairs, each lined with shelves and cabinets. I'd measured and constructed the shelves myself, which was why (I noted with satisfaction) Havelock's Artefacts, which ranged awkwardly in size and shape, fit them so perfectly, not a one seeming out of place. The spent Artefacts, which had previously been mixed in haphazardly with the enchanted ones, were stored in crates against the far wall. At the centre of the middle row of cabinets was Havelock's worktable, which now seemed almost an ordinary thing in its new context, the desk of some museum curator perhaps, rather than a precarious little raft about to be capsized by the teetering waves of treasure rising around it.

"It's a new place entirely," Yannick said wonderingly when he arrived the following morning. "You can see the floor. At times I wondered if the place even *had* a floor and wasn't held up by spiderwebs."

"We still have three more levels to work through," I said with a sigh, though I was pleased by his praise. I should not have been so comforted by what I saw, for a poorly organized hoard of dangerous magic was probably preferable to one where the magician in question could find everything with ease, but such was my fondness for a well-organized space that it overrode my moral qualms. Even better than the new shelves was the fact that I'd labelled and catalogued everything in a notebook, so that any Artefact could be located within minutes.

Because of Havelock's extended absence, it came almost as a surprise when I descended the stairs one morning to find him at his worktable, taking apart a delicate music box with unhurried concentration.

"Still here, Mme. Hurricane?" he said without looking up.

"You look dreadful," I said bluntly. His eyes were darkly shadowed, and he seemed even more slender than the last time I'd seen him. "Have you had breakfast?"

"Breakfast?" he repeated, and even his voice seemed weary, with even more of a rasp in it than usual—he had a proper magician's voice, I'd always thought, as if he spent most of his time in a smoky cave. "I've had a few spiders. Dark magicians confine our nourishment to arachnids and human blood, though sometimes—"

I walked away without bothering to listen to the rest. I went upstairs and made a pot of coffee, then brought it downstairs with cups and the paper bag of sesame bagels Élise had supplied. I deposited the bagels in front of him and poured coffee for both of us.

He eyed me with a frown. "What are you doing?"

"It's in both our interests if you don't starve to death," I said. "When was the last time you ate?"

He thought about it. "Yesterday." Then, "I think."

He helped himself to a bagel and I watched, because I was, in fact, curious about whether he ate or not. He devoured the first bagel in a half-dozen bites and began to work on a second.

"Thank you," he said, all awkwardness again.

Satisfied, I went around his table, planning to return to the crate of Artefacts I'd brought up from the second floor, because I was elbow-deep in *that* mess now, then stopped. Banshee lay on the floor beside Havelock's chair, tail twitching in contentment. She opened her eyes, blinking at me, then unfolded herself in a long stretch.

"Well!" I said, crossing my arms and smiling at him. "What's this?"

"*Nothing*," Havelock said emphatically, pointing his bagel at the cat. "She's a fiend. A wraith in feline form. I can't work out how she gets in here. I've chased her out twice already."

"That was your first mistake," I said. "Cats are inherently contrary. Now that she knows your workshop is forbidden, she'll never stop breaking in."

I didn't say that I'd watched His Majesty shepherding Banshee around the workshop just the other day with the air of a tour guide. He'd shown her his secret passageway, I had no doubt.

Havelock leaned back in his chair and said plaintively, "She won't leave me in peace."

"You're her type. Dangerous and unpleasant," I said. "At least she's a quiet cat," I added, but he only snorted as if I'd made a joke.

I paused, examining him. His eyes, while shadowed, had no

redness in them, and he wasn't clutching at his handkerchief as he usually did when near one of the cats.

"Your allergy's fading," I said triumphantly. "I knew it would. You can get used to cats if you're around them enough."

Havelock swallowed another mouthful of bagel. "Is that like mithridatism?"

I made an exasperated sound and gave his shoulder a shove. I'm not sure where it came from; it was a childish gesture I had used with Robin, who was always teasing me. I drew my hand back immediately.

"You don't have to do that, you know," he said.

"What?"

His dark hair had fallen over his brow, partly shielding his eyes. "I'm not *actually* going to turn you into a sparrow."

"I know that," I said, and frowned. "I only wish I knew *why* I know that."

"So do I." He gave me a sharp look. "Even the most arrogant magicians cower in my presence. I always assumed it was your obstinate humanitarianism. You're like an altruistic bull."

"It would help if you were more forthcoming," I said.

"About what? The apocalypse incident?"

I suppressed the urge to wallop him over the head with a bagel. "Yes. That. Among other things."

"Not much to tell." His rings flashed as he fiddled with the music box. "I created the enchantment. Then it almost destroyed the world."

It took me a moment to digest the fact that he was actually answering me with something other than a deflection.

"It seems there's a great deal more to tell than that," I said cautiously, because I didn't know how long this small window of sincerity would remain open. "You created the spell. But you didn't cast it, did you?"

He didn't answer immediately. "No."

"Someone stole it from you," I said.

He gave a quiet laugh. "That's the most charitable explanation, isn't it? What was I just saying about obstinate humanitarianism?"

"Is it not the truth?" I pressed. "Was it Valérie?"

He went still, which was answer enough.

"I thought so," I said, feeling self-satisfied. "Well, it wasn't difficult to work out. I hope this doesn't offend you, but your sister is more frightening than you are."

"I created the spell when I was nineteen," he said. "I put it in one of Klinger's globes, a particularly rare specimen from the 1700s. After that it sat on a shelf for years. I kept meaning to take it apart, but the spell was so powerful, I knew doing so would be difficult and dangerous. So I put it off, then put it off again."

He set the music box aside, toying with his half-empty coffee cup. "I told Valérie about the spell. I wanted to impress her, as I often did back then. She seemed more irritated than impressed, and I assumed she was angry that I had been so irresponsible." He paused. "She seemed to forget all about it until three years ago, when she said she wanted us to destroy it together. I thought it was strange, this sudden interest of hers, but I trusted Valérie, and I thought—I still wanted to impress her. So I brought it to her in New York, where I was still pretending to live."

I shuddered—it seemed the only logical reaction. And yet there was something painfully human about the whole thing. "And she released the enchantment," I said.

"She didn't want the world to end, if that's what you're thinking," he said. "She resented my skill with magic, but at the same time, she never believed I'd really done it. That I'd been able to create something so far beyond her own abilities. She took the Artefact to the home of one of her rivals, a magician who had everything she wanted: followers, a real dragon's hoard of Artefacts. I think that she assumed the effects would be devastating but limited; she could claim credit for whatever chaos ensued, and her *other* rivals would be too terrified not to give her whatever she wanted. Above all else, Valérie is reckless. The type to jump from a precipice without knowing the depth of the water. Her luck had always held before."

"But," I murmured, when he didn't go on.

Havelock turned away from me and picked up the music box again. "You know the rest."

"Do I?" But it seemed he was finished; the window had closed. He took up one of his notebooks and scribbled something. Sweat prickled my brow, and I felt slightly ill. Nevertheless, I forced myself to ask the question I most wanted to ask. "Why did you make the spell in the first place?"

I was surprised by how easily he answered. "No one had ever created a spell to end the world before," he said. "Not even Vortigern. Most magicians thought it wasn't possible. That's the thing about magic—presumably it has limits, but we don't know what those are. Magicians are like explorers unravelling the map as they go."

Silence fell again, and I wondered if that was it. "I wanted to see if I could do it," he said at last, still looking down at his work.

CHAPTER 24

Yannick came downstairs then, and Havelock absented himself, still muttering at the music box, to barricade himself in his library, where he need not listen to us thumping about. I watched him go, frowning.

I turned to find Yannick eyeing me with a look of understanding. "What?" I demanded.

He held up his hands. "Nothing!"

"Yannick, I know what you're thinking. In case you didn't realize, I *always* know what you're thinking."

He looked away. "I— It's just—you're not the only one. That's all."

"What do you mean?" I said, though I could already guess. But I liked Yannick, and I wanted us to be honest with each other.

Yannick chewed his lip for a moment, then said in a rush, "There are at least two magicians and one collector who visit Havelock's shop on a regular basis for purposes other than perusing his wares. None have succeeded in turning his head, nor am I certain he's even aware of their feelings."

I eyed him. "And can the same be said for you?"

"Oh!" Yannick gave me a surprised smile. "That's not— I don't have an interest in romance, with Havelock or anyone. Just not my thing. And as for Havelock, I'm not sure he's capable of it."

He sighed. "I do care about Havelock, though. He took me on as an apprentice when I had nowhere else to go."

I nodded. Like many parents of magicians, Yannick's had been horrified to discover what he was. He had been handed off from relative to relative until he turned eighteen, when he'd been turned out without a penny to his name. After living on the streets for several months, struggling to find employment, he'd followed another magician to Havelock's shop, more out of desperation than anything else. And Havelock, with much sarcastic commentary and complaints, had let him stay as his apprentice, and assigned him mostly simple, useful enchantments—not spells to poison one's enemies, as Yannick had expected—and even paid him a salary.

"Havelock isn't always himself these days," Yannick said. "He's seemed—on the edge."

"Of what?"

He was quiet, thinking, and a chill seemed to settle in the air. "I don't know how to put it. I don't know precisely what happens to a magician when they're taken over by the Rivenwood, only the—aftereffects."

I suddenly didn't want to pursue the subject. "So far as I've known him, he rarely seems to fit the definition of evil villainy. Unless *evil* is defined by pettiness and snark."

"He seems almost human when you're around," Yannick said, smiling. "I've never seen anybody intimidate him like you do."

"Intimidate him!" I exclaimed.

"Well, you've been ordering him about since you got here,"

Yannick said. "Havelock pretends to be aloof. But at the core, I think he hasn't changed much since he was a boy."

"And what was he then?"

Yannick shrugged. "Quiet. He was always reading, Valérie said. He didn't make friends easily."

"*Valérie?*" I exclaimed. "You've met her?"

"Once, in the early days of my apprenticeship," Yannick said. "In New York. Havelock would send me down there periodically to run errands and keep up the pretence he still lived there. Havelock has always had enemies, even before the world nearly ended, and a need to throw them off the scent. Valérie found me in one of his old haunts—she wanted me to convince him to speak to her again."

"Really?" I was surprised. "She didn't threaten you? How polite."

"Their relationship has—deteriorated over the years," he said. "But I'm not sure Havelock was closer to anyone than Valérie in his youth. I'm not sure he had anyone *except* her. Their mother died when they were young; their father was barely present. Havelock was sickly as a child and Valérie took care of him. She came into her power much younger than Havelock did, which is unusual in twins."

"Twins!" But the truth of it was so obvious that I wondered why I hadn't guessed it before. Valérie and Havelock looked remarkably alike—the sharpness of their features, their colouring, even the timbre of their voices.

The thought made me uncomfortable. I hadn't known I was superstitious about twins, but it was difficult not to be superstitious about *magical* twins. I wondered if Havelock and Valérie could read each other's minds, or shared some sort of supernatural connection—and yet, if they did, it didn't seem to have aided Valérie in tracking him down.

"From what I can tell," Yannick said, "Valérie was fiercely protective of her brother. But as her power grew, along with her following, she had less time for him. If you ask me, I think jealousy played a part—it was clear from the day Havelock discovered he was a magician that his power was greater than hers. She began hunting for Vortigern's book not long after I took up with Havelock, and eventually grew convinced he had it and was keeping it from her out of possessiveness or spite. Now they're—this."

Yannick paused, frowning. "I don't think Havelock has ever learned to see Valérie as a rival, let alone an enemy. It's his greatest weakness."

I pondered this. There was an unsettling symmetry between Valérie and myself: I had been both mother and sister to Élise when we were orphaned shortly after my sixteenth birthday. How bitter, how fundamentally incongruous it would have been to be anything other than the dearest of friends now.

"What else did Valérie tell you?" I said.

"Not much. Havelock spent his childhood obsessed with stories about magic and adventures in other worlds. He didn't realize he was a magician until he was seventeen, which is unheard of. But then, often it's the case that the stronger the magician, the later they come into their power."

I pondered this image of Havelock in his youth, alone in his bedroom, glasses sliding down his nose as he pored over his novels. On the one hand, I couldn't picture it; on the other, I couldn't imagine him any other way. "What happened?"

Yannick frowned. "What you might expect if you suddenly granted a child like that a monumental amount of magic," he said. "He got carried away."

CHAPTER 25

By the end of the week, Yannick and I had organized most of the second floor. We had yet to find any Artefacts from Walker Clem's collection, save an enchanted portrait that hid any doors in the wall it was placed on, but we did unearth a swarm of silverfish beneath a mountain of crates against the rear wall. Horribly, the little beasts had somehow absorbed the bioluminescence spell Havelock had inflicted on the spiders, and they scattered like an army of twitchy fireflies.

I let Yannick use the pen Havelock had given me—he had an ease with it that I lacked, and never jumped when it came to life and began speeding across the page as if an impatient ghost had got hold of it.

And yet, when Yannick left to bring back lunch, I took up the pen again and used it to identify the spell in a medieval broom made from birch twigs, which turned out to be—quite logically—a spell for freshening a room. I'd found that most older spells were of a utilitarian nature and accorded with the Artefacts that bound them, whereas modern magicians tended towards unnecessary whimsy, like putting a spell for concealment in a gaudy floral parasol. I gave the floor of the basement a few sweeps, muttering the simplest of commands I'd learned from Yannick: the smell of must and cobwebs was replaced with lemon, and a breeze so pure it could have been summoned from an alpine meadow lifted the hair from my face. Once I realized what I'd done, I nearly dropped the broom.

I then used the pen to identify the spell in a gramophone (which compelled the listener to answer questions truthfully) and a stamp from the 1910s (which would deliver the letter to its recipient via teleportation). I was so absorbed in what I was doing, and in watching the looping writing emerge from my pen, that I didn't hear Yannick return. I handed the pen back to him immediately, though I couldn't ignore the pang of disappointment.

It's only because it's useful, I told myself. Yes, magic could be interesting. Beautiful, even. But that didn't negate its harms, and what use was beauty, anyhow, if it brought nothing of good into the world?

I looked around with relief. The crate Yannick was investigating held the last uncatalogued Artefacts on the second floor. It had been more of a jumble than the first, and yet it had taken us less time to catalogue each Artefact as we grew more efficient. It was now a near mirror image of the first floor, minus the worktable, with three neat rows of shelving.

Élise had to leave in the afternoon to help Gabriel with something, so I came upstairs to mind the shelter while Yannick got started on the third floor. To my delight, our visitors had only increased, and while many came simply to marvel at our supposedly enchanted cats, we saw two adoptions that day. The lucky cats were Nuit, a black cat with batlike ears, and little Lynx.

I felt a little twinge of regret, because I had always seen Lynx as Laurent's cat. And yet, I reminded myself philosophically, he couldn't expect Lynx to wait around for him forever.

By the time I had closed the shop and finished the evening checklist—feeding the cats, administering medications, cleaning cages, and so on—I was close to collapsing with weariness. I lit a fire in the oven and pulled the armchair close, sinking into the cushions with a groan of relief. Yannick had left and I was alone in the quiet shelter, most of the cats having settled down to sleep off their supper. Flakes from another snow squall pecked at the windows like the beaks of tiny birds.

"What do you think?" I murmured to the other armchair. "Have I made a dreadful mistake, making this bargain with Havelock Renard?"

The armchair sat in quiet contemplation. Banshee quickly staked a claim to my lap, lolling on her back and stretching her paws towards the fire. His Majesty skulked in the darkness against the far wall—patrolling for mice, I assumed. He liked to leave their bloody corpses lined up by my bed at night so that I could be cheered by the spectacle of his hunting prowess immediately upon awakening. I had not been treated to such a sight in some time, though, as all mice seemed to flee a place as soon as His Majesty turned up, which was perhaps why he bullied the other cats so—it was, at least in part, a product of boredom. I called to him, but he seemed absorbed in his business and vanished into some crevice.

Ambulance awoke and began his customary caterwauling. I was aware that I would not know a moment's peace until I let him out of his cage, and so I settled him on my lap, while Banshee took the other armchair.

Poor Ambulance had been adopted twice now, and twice returned to the shelter. Unfortunately, in addition to his lamentable vocal cords, the cat had the personality of a raccoon. He had proven himself a menace to both of the households who had taken him in, getting into the garbage no matter how many obstacles were placed in his way, clambering up curtains, and knocking over any item that wasn't at least twice his weight, particularly if it was easily broken.

I scratched Ambulance's cheek, and the cat leaned into me, purring thunderously. Aside from his destructive tendencies, he had an exceptional temperament, and I knew he only needed a caretaker who would be patient with him and correct his misbehaviour. I would not give up on him, even as part of me despaired at the prospect of him being returned a third time. It was not good for a cat, who could fall in love with their caretakers as easily as the reverse. After the second home failed, Ambulance had curled himself into his nest of scarves for three days, barely stirring even to nibble at his food.

At some point, I drifted off. When I awoke, the fire was down to the embers, and Ambulance and Banshee had curled up together on the rug, close to the fading warmth.

"What did I tell you about letting me doze like an old woman?" I muttered at the other armchair, though Robin had never in his life woken me from one of my fireside naps, even when I began to drool, a spectacle he had always found highly amusing.

I squinted at the fire, confused. I'd fed it only a few small pieces of kindling, and yet the embers lay as deep as the length of my thumb, and covered the bottom of the stone oven. But that was not the most peculiar thing.

Within the oven was a tray of éclairs.

Wonderingly, I scooped out two éclairs, mindful of the hot tray—they seemed a minute or two shy of perfectly baked.

Then, for reasons I could not explain, I politely shut the oven door.

I sat motionless with the éclairs on my lap, staring at them as if they would disappear. For all I knew, they would. Banshee, ever alert to the arrival of food, bestirred herself and placed her forepaws on my knee to sniff them. Finding nothing of interest in pastry, magical or not, she wandered off.

Abruptly, the light dimmed in the oven. I opened the door with a shaking hand and found what was clearly the remnants of my own smaller fire there, now lightly scented with sugar.

I pulled out my pocket watch. It was just past midnight.

I laughed. The oven was enchanted to make pastry at the stroke of midnight. But the enchantment didn't last, and the pastry vanished after a few moments. The ones I'd removed remained, however, as if my touch had broken whatever spell lay upon them.

Well, that explained the smell of baking that never left the shop even after we had filled it with cats. Perhaps it was my growing fondness for the magic pen Havelock had given me, or perhaps I was just becoming used to living in close quarters with magic, but this did not alarm me as much as it once would have.

I leaned back in my seat and bit into the first éclair. It was soft as marshmallow, and although it hadn't been iced, the pastry was sweet and buttery and delicately flavoured with lemon. The cats dozed in the flickering light, and I couldn't remember when I'd last felt so peaceful.

Naturally, that was when I caught the smoky scent of magic emanating from the rear of the shop. I turned in time to catch a fearsome glimpse of the Rivenwood yawning open behind me, a wilderness of trees cupping pools of white and pink flowers deep enough to drown in.

This time, though, the door opened onto a village, or the remnants of one. A steep hillside, dotted with an equal number of trees and houses, built upon flat shelves cut out of the mountain. They were humble in size and made of pale stone, all ruins now, and roofless, their walls enclosing small meadows of wildflowers. A flock of black birds perched atop one wall, seeming to gaze out at me, which made me shudder. Even from a distance I could tell there was something wrong about them, and I was inexplicably certain they had something to do with what had happened there.

Before I could properly take it in, something darted through—a ghost made of shadow and flame, I would have thought, if I hadn't known better. And then Havelock stood where the ghost had been, trails of lambent shadow falling about him, which vanished when they touched the floor. He turned towards the door to the Rivenwood and moved his hands as if he were *pushing* something against it, but there was nothing there. My mouth fell open in dumb astonishment as, slowly but surely, the door faded away, as if he were pushing a piece of our world into the door. The wind from that dark world buffeted at him, which made his cloak and hair billow—and then, abruptly, the door was gone, and the world was whole again.

He turned, the edges of him still sparking a little, and then, to my great amusement, he jumped like a startled cat at the sight of me. I had been cowering instinctively, but I gave a snort of laughter.

"Clearly you didn't know I was here," I said. "So I can only assume you chose a dramatic entrance for the sake of impressing the cats. Did you hope they might come to worship you as magicians do?"

He gave me a rueful smile. "More fool me if I did," he replied. "It seems clear those creatures worship no one but themselves."

"Are you certain about that?" I said, as Banshee gave one of her voiceless yowls and made her way to Havelock. She deposited herself at his feet, paws in the air and tail curled around the toe of his boot.

Havelock eyed her with the same expression I had probably worn when I saw the Rivenwood. "I can't work out what this one wants from me," he said. "Is it merely senseless, or is it plotting something?"

"She *likes* you," I said. "Banshee has never plotted anything in her life."

He opened his mouth, then stopped, turning his head aside to release a resounding sneeze. He stepped over Banshee, who watched him go with a forlorn expression.

"I thought you weren't supposed to go to the Rivenwood anymore," I said. "Yannick said so. It will make you even more wicked than you are now."

He raised his eyebrows at the half-eaten éclair in my hand. "And I thought you despised magic in all its forms. Don't tell me you're venturing off the moral high ground for the first time in your life. You'll be hopelessly lost."

"I make an exception for pastry," I said, and held the second éclair out.

After a moment's hesitation, he came towards me, bringing with him the scent of magic, and accepted it. He took a bite and sighed. "How I miss Claude."

"Oh! Are these *his*, somehow?" Yannick had told me that the baker who had rented the main shop from Havelock was a man named Claude de la Fosse, a surly sort whose unprepossessing demeanour was counterbalanced by his skill with a rolling pin.

"They're certainly a convincing imitation," he said, settling himself elegantly on the stone ledge in front of the oven. "Though I've often felt they lack a certain aftertaste Claude's had. Perhaps he seasoned his with frowns."

"How does the enchantment work?" I said, motioning at the oven. "Should I have left room for the sugar pie it will spit out at one?"

"And madeleines at two? I'm afraid not. I've no idea what enchantment is on the thing, but it fires only at midnight."

I gazed at him. In the firelight, his unearthly quality was more pronounced; the light played strangely on the planes of his face and sharp angles of his shoulders. "You don't *know*?" I said in disbelief.

He wiped crumbs from his lip. "I've sometimes used the oven to dispose of Artefacts. Those that are spent and too unsightly to repurpose. The baking began to appear after I burned a locket that held a rather unstable spell for granting one's heart's desire. Clearly the Artefact still held some magic in it, which leaked out into the oven."

I laughed, surprised. "Your heart's desire is *pastry*?"

He smiled. "Many spells from the Renaissance are vague in nature, and they never live up to their promises. A 'health and wealth' spell I came across once caused three pennies to drop from the ceiling onto my head. I was never certain about the health part, though I didn't suffer any colds that winter."

"I don't know," I said. "Those Renaissance magicians may have been on to something. Never-ending pastry seems a wiser thing to long for than the lofty ambitions many people set their hearts on, as well as far less likely to end in regret. And the absence of ailment is a blessing for which we should all be more grateful. Would not the world be better off if we contented ourselves with the small miracles of life?"

"That," Havelock said, "is exactly the response I would expect from you. If you ever tire of collecting cats, you should craft motivational cards."

I scowled, but he was gazing at me with amusement rather than rancour. He blinked, and we both looked away.

"Perhaps I *was* longing for Claude's baking when I burned the locket," Havelock said. "I don't recall. I did miss him when he left—he'd found out that I was not, in fact, some run-of-the-mill Artefact smuggler, but the man who'd nearly ended the world."

He sighed at the fire. "It would be for the best if I *did* have that book somewhere, and could unmake it—Valérie is the last person who should have that kind of power."

"Is she?"

"I may have *almost* destroyed the world," he said. "Valérie would succeed."

The way he said it, a simple statement of fact, sent a shudder through me. "You mean Vortigern's library. She wants to return to a time before it burned, and steal all that she can."

He nodded. "Vortigern is said to have constructed all manner of fantastical spells—no doubt some are merely that, pure fantasy. But others—" He paused. "Vortigern was the most powerful magician who ever lived. Some speculate she burned her own library to the ground to prevent anyone else from getting their hands on her enchantments. People say those enchantments could level mountains and armies, pull the moon from the sky, make the dead walk, create monsters hungry enough to devour cities. As well as subtler magics long thought impossible—to alter memories or the currents of the human mind. If even a fraction of the stories are true, the owner of that library could reshape the world to suit their desires. We are fortunate that Vortigern had no interest in power, only magic. It was the making of spells that she loved, the craftsmanship—she often didn't bother to cast them. Valérie is not so high-minded."

It was ghastly to think about anyone getting their hands on such a hoard, let alone Valérie. Impulsively, I leaned forward and pressed his hand. "I'm sorry."

He gave me a surprised look. "That you haven't found the thing? Why should you apologize for that?"

I shook my head. "I'm sorry you lost your sister. No matter *how* you lost her. I love Élise more than my life."

His brow furrowed as he gazed at me.

"You don't need to look at me like that," I said, amused. "I know what it's like to lose someone. And I'm not being kind to you out of some ulterior motive. Is that what most magicians are like?"

"If they aren't too terrified of me to think, yes."

"I can't imagine why anyone would be terrified of you," I said lightly.

"You only say that because you're far more terrifying than I am. I will never again underestimate the ability of a determined cat minder with a notebook and filing cabinet to wreak havoc on a place."

"Of course you would see an absence of chaos as *wreaking havoc*," I said. "And you say you aren't a dark magician."

He settled against the brick wall, gazing at me. I caught him looking at me often, in fact, and I recognized the quality of his expression—the furrow between his eyes, which could suggest either displeasure or intrigue. Since I couldn't imagine a man like Havelock taking such an interest in the likes of me, I had always assumed these looks signified the former inclination, but now I wondered. When I met his eyes, he flushed but didn't look away. I became very aware of the play of light and shadow upon his face, particularly how the darkness brushed the space below his cheekbones and pooled in the curve below his lip.

"Oh," I murmured as the realization struck me. "*That's* why you all look different. It's the light."

He raised his eyebrows. "You noticed? Most people don't."

"I'm right, aren't I?" Delighted that I'd finally solved the mystery, I seized his hand and held it up to the fire as if it contained a secret message I might read. "I thought you all looked like old paintings, but it's because of the light. It touches you differently."

"It would be more accurate to say that magicians have more darkness around us," he said. "We bring it with us from the Rivenwood."

I gazed at him, and I saw that it was true. It was as if the firelight dimmed where he sat, rendering the shadows that touched him more resonant. That accounted for the discrepancy I'd always sensed in the magicians who came into the shop—in the light of full morning, they'd worn the luminosity of dawn; in the afternoon, they'd seemed to stand at the edge of twilight.

I realized I was still holding on to him; he was sitting very still, and I guessed that it had been a long time since anyone took such liberties with him.

"You're not a very cautious person, are you," he said as I released his hand.

"Should I be afraid of you, as everyone else is?"

"No," he said. "But I'm not entirely myself. Not anymore."

I chewed on my lip. I felt a stab of impotent hatred towards the Rivenwood, that it would change him—that it already *had* changed him—sweeping away his awkwardness and prickles and replacing them with something cold and *other*. "Is there no other way to obtain magic?" I said, frustrated.

"One can repurpose it from existing Artefacts. But such magic loses some of its essence and is useful only for simple spells."

Why not content yourself with simple spells, then? I wanted to say, but it would be to no purpose. I knew him well enough by now to know that it would be like telling a hawk to stay out of the sky.

Instead I said, "What was Valérie like? Before, I mean. When you were growing up."

"She—" A moment passed before he finally shook his head. "She was *there*. It was just us, for a long time. And she was always there, whether I needed someone to tend to me when I was ill or protect me from other children at school. She came into her power much younger than I did, and I was sometimes a little frightened of her, even as I loved her. She always seemed—" He stopped again. "Like one of the heroes in my books."

We sat in silence for a moment, listening to the embers crackle. Banshee wandered back into the room with a silent yowl, no doubt hoping to cadge an early breakfast, and collapsed dramatically at Havelock's feet.

"I don't know if I should ask," he began slowly, but I didn't need to hear the rest. I recognized the tone well enough. It was how everyone sounded when they asked the question.

"What happened to Robin, you mean," I said. "I'm afraid it's not a very interesting story. He didn't die in a blaze of magic, nor was he caught up in anything scandalous."

He drew one leg up and leaned against it. "If you don't wish to discuss it, please forget I brought it up."

I shook my head. I didn't mind telling him; part of me was even relieved he'd asked. "It was his heart," I said. "He was thirty years old. Whose heart gives out at thirty? The doctors were astonished." I gave a huff of laughter. "'Exceptionally rare,' they said. 'One in a million.' His heart was too small—or too small in one spot, a bad spot; I still don't understand it exactly. I don't know how nobody noticed it. But then, they said that even if someone had, there would have been no difference. There wasn't anything—"

I was beginning to ramble, and stopped myself. I watched the embers breathe in the hearth, realizing that it had been some time since I'd spoken about Robin. It was an odd feeling, as if I were unearthing something that, in the time since I'd last checked on it, had been covered over by a layer of moss and fallen leaves. Not *gone*, but no longer as stark as it once had been.

"It was sudden," Havelock said.

I let out my breath. "He'd gone to pick up our laundry. I told him not to stop at the baker's. He was always spending too much at the baker's." My hand tightened on my knee. "That was the last thing I said to him. A lecture about bread."

I stopped, because the memory was nearly as painful as what had come after—it was something I could blame myself for, unlike Robin's death. "I've always wished I'd said something else," I finished at last.

Havelock shifted, resting his head against the stones. "Like what?"

"I don't know," I said, forcing my hand to relax. "Perhaps you and Valérie can still make amends. After she no longer has this Artefact to obsess over."

"No," he said, watching the flames. "She's often said I've

spent too much time in the Rivenwood. But in truth, it's taken more of her."

I didn't know what to say to this. I didn't know what was worse—to lose someone suddenly and without warning, or to be losing someone always, a continual process, as magic wore away at the person they were.

"Why hasn't Valérie attacked again?" I said. "You moved the shop back. She knows where you are now, and she got past your wards once."

"Because she's plotting something. Even if she *could* attack again, she would never be so uncouth as to be predictable."

I watched him. He was leaning against the fire-warmed stones, fingers woven together over his knee, looking more at ease than I'd ever seen him.

"Where *have* you been disappearing to?" I said. "Have you been spending all this time in the Rivenwood?"

"You must think I *want* to turn myself into a monster. No—I've been tracking down Valérie's apprentices and undoing their enchantments. I stopped the fire at the chocolatier's from spreading any farther than it did. It was enchanted flame, not something humans could have put out."

"I'm sorry," I said, delighted, because this was exactly what I had guessed he'd been up to. "I didn't quite catch that. Surely you didn't mean to imply you'd done anything so public-spirited, but meant to say that you stood by and gloated as the shop burned and chaos spread through the city, as a proper dark magician would."

"Even dark magicians need a place to live," he said. "This is *my* city. I won't have them burning it to the ground. You shouldn't look at me as if I've been off rescuing kittens for you. I've killed a dozen of her apprentices." He played absently with one of his rings, a frown forming between his eyes. "Most of her followers are little more than husks. Spectres wearing human skins. The weaker the magician, the more easily they're consumed."

If he had been trying to dampen my glee, he succeeded. As much as he mocked my moralizing, I didn't see much reason to condemn the deaths of those so careless about the lives of others; the whole business only seemed insoluble and terribly sad. But anyone whose line of work exposes them to the range of mistreatment inflicted upon living creatures, human or otherwise, is used to cohabitating with this feeling, and getting on with things anyway.

"There's one thing I don't understand," I said. "Why *didn't* the world end three years ago?"

He stilled for a brief moment in the act of placing another log on the fire. "Perhaps my spell failed—isn't that what most people think?" With a flick of his fingers and a murmured word, flames leapt up from the embers. "I was spectacularly obtuse at nineteen."

"I don't think that's it."

"Naturally you don't. You've come to believe the most generous explanation—that I stopped it somehow. Most likely in a display of heroic sacrifice."

"In my experience, most people *deserve* generosity," I replied. "Particularly those determined to believe they don't."

"I won't argue with you," he said. "It would be as productive as trying to convince your felines of the merits of vegetables. And in one sense, you're right. I stopped it. I was able to reverse the spell, with no small amount of difficulty. Given that no magician had ever invented an apocalypse enchantment before, nobody had ever created a spell for stopping one, so I had no templates to follow. My Artefacts weren't any better organized back then than they are now, and it took some time for me to locate the only one that could have helped—a lantern enchanted by Vortigern to absorb magic and unravel spells. The only Artefact of Vortigern's I ever owned—to my knowledge, anyhow."

"The lantern absorbs magic?" I repeated. My head was spinning a little. The woman had created a book that could turn back time, *and* a lantern that could end an apocalypse? What was next, a salt shaker that could raise the dead?

Magicians! I thought, with a familiar feeling of weariness at the power they had over the lives of ordinary people.

Havelock nodded. "I thought that if I wove it with a brightening spell, I could banish the darkness that had fallen over the world, and reverse the spell Valérie had unleashed."

"Like a sunrise," I said, unable to stop myself from smiling. It was like something out of myth, like the story of the witch who created the night by weaving it on her loom.

"I never had a chance to try my theory," he continued, turning away from me to gaze into the fire. "On the third night of the world's ending, I made my way up Mount Royal to cast the enchantment from a height, but before I could, I was accosted by a stranger, and the lantern was stolen."

"A magician?"

"I assumed so. I was being hunted by magicians from all over the world during those dark days. There's an old folk belief among magicians that enchantments can be ended by killing whoever created them. It's not true, but some people still believe it. This stranger couldn't kill me, but they managed to make off with the one thing I thought could end the darkness."

When he spoke again, he seemed to choose each word carefully, as if he'd given them a great deal of thought. "It was for the best, though. The lantern wasn't designed to undo an enchantment of that scale. I would simply have wasted Vortigern's spell—like most Artefacts, it could be cast just once. And it would have delayed me from realizing the truth."

"And that was?"

"That it was up to me," he said simply. "I had made the spell to end the world, and I had to unmake it. I couldn't rely on Vortigern or anyone else. I had to travel to the Fourth Fathom of the Rivenwood, where I could gather magic powerful enough to create a twelve-layer spell of partitioning. A spell that was strong enough to save us all."

So *that* was why he'd visited the Fourth Fathom, travelling deeper into the Rivenwood than most magicians ever ventured, and sacrificing a piece of himself—who knew how large—in the process. Yet it *had* been his responsibility in the first place, even if it hadn't been his fault, and so I did not condescend to him by praising him for it.

I looked up from the fire to find him watching me with an unreadable expression. I wondered if he expected me to lecture him, or perhaps be overcome with awe or horror at the harrowing tale. Before I could do either, though, I noticed Thoreau pawing at the bars of his cage. "Excuse me," I said, then rose and unlocked the cage door.

Havelock gave a quiet laugh. "We're talking about the apocalypse, and all you can think about is your cats."

"I didn't stop caring for them when the world was ending," I said drily. "So you can't expect me to be distracted by the memory of it."

He watched as I exchanged Thoreau's blanket for a fresh one. "I was right. You never rest, do you?"

"I suppose not," I said absently, lifting Thoreau and cradling him in my arms.

"What's wrong?"

"Oh—nothing out of the ordinary. One of our newcomers came in with a bad case of fleas. They've spread to at least three of the others, including Thoreau. It's worse for him, because they trouble his arthritis. He has difficulty sleeping."

I scratched the old cat's chin, and he leaned into me, burrowing into the warmth of my arms. "I've treated them, but it will take a day or two for every flea to die off."

"Charming creatures," Havelock said. "If they aren't clawing your leg or leaving dead things scattered about, they're spreading parasites."

I frowned. "Who clawed your leg?"

"That white-pawed demon, of course."

I resumed massaging Thoreau's scrawny back. I disliked seeing the old cat in any amount of discomfort; it made me feel I had failed him.

"Here," Havelock said. He touched one of his rings and murmured an incantation. A wind fluttered over us, and over the cat cages, smelling of something sharp and peppery.

"That should do it," he said. "It's a spell for ridding a place of pests. Pity it doesn't work on certain felines. Good night."

And then, as if what he'd done had been a mere trifle—no doubt it seemed that way to him—he disappeared into the back room.

With shaking hands, I checked Thoreau's fur. Not only had the fleas vanished, but so had the itchy red welts that had covered his skin. The cat gave a contented stretch, yawning. I returned him to his cage, and he curled up in his blanket nest.

Naturally, my response to all this was to start crying. I watched Thoreau sleeping more peacefully than he had in days, then checked the other cats. But it seemed every flea in the shelter had been blasted into dust, or perhaps Havelock had sent them off to the Rivenwood, to feast upon whatever furred things lurked among those ruins and dark forests.

I wiped my eyes. Then I marched over to the back room.

I threw back the trapdoor, not bothering to be quiet about it, and stomped down the stairs. Havelock was standing at his worktable, tidying things or fussing with one of his experiments. He looked up at me in surprise as I came towards him.

"Agnes?" he said, tilting his head. "Should I—?"

But whatever quip he was about to deliver, I didn't give him a chance. I threw my arms around him and kissed him.

At first, he might have been turned to stone. But then his lips parted slightly, and his hand came up and rested against the curve of my neck just below my ear, his rings brushing against my skin. Just as he did this, I became aware of what I was doing, and let him go.

I was still crying a little, unfortunately, and I let out an embarrassingly unbecoming sniffle into the stark silence. I dashed my hand over my eyes, then turned and marched back upstairs, leaving him standing there, knocked slightly off-balance amongst the detritus of his worktable.

CHAPTER 26

I spent the next morning determinedly trying to erase the memory of what I had done, not at all successfully. The fact that I had survived a kiss with the Witch King—which, in all honesty, I had wondered about, as Havelock often seemed to be more magic than man—did not mean it had been wise to throw myself at him.

To this end, after finishing the morning checklist, I pulled on my coat and scarf and took the tram to the Rue Sainte-Sophie shelter, leaving Élise in charge of Rue des Hirondelles. When I arrived at the bank, I found several people milling about outside the shelter, the reason for which was soon apparent: the door was locked, the sign turned to *Fermé*.

I had a key, of course, and let myself in, whereupon I was immediately accosted by Mina.

"We had to close," Mina said before I could open my mouth, shoving the door shut behind me as if the polite crowd outside might try to force their way in. She looked more frazzled than I'd ever seen her, her pale hair falling over her shoulders, half out of its braid.

"Mina, what—" I stopped and stared at the shelter.

It was empty.

"I *told* you we would run out!" Mina said, waving her hand.

I moved forward as if in a dream. I looked into each empty cage as if I might find a cat there, perhaps hiding under the water dish. But Mina was right. Every cat was gone. Several of the doors hung ajar, which gave the impression of some ailurophiliac bandit having made off with them in a hurry.

"I've sent a telegram to the shelter in Longueuil," Mina said, "to see if they can send us a few of their cats."

I nodded. I knew the man who ran the charity there. "Pierre will be happy to help. But I still don't understand how this happened."

"Here," she said, and shoved a newspaper into my hand. It was the *Daily Gazette*. For a moment I could only blink at the English words, my brain refusing to translate them. Then—

"What the hell," I muttered.

"Mystical" cat shelter under police investigation, the headline blared. Under this was the lede: *Beloved charity believed to be trafficking in enchanted cats: source.*

"What the hell" was all I could say, again.

"The reporter is quite sympathetic," Mina said. "He interviews a half dozen of our clients, who all have similar claims: their cat cured their arthritis, or their back pain, or made them unaccountably lucky. So you can understand *this.*" She gestured at the people outside, two of whom—both children—were peering through the glass, hands cupped around their eyes. "Every cat was spoken for within twenty minutes of opening. Don't worry," she added, seeing my look. "I was careful. I checked every application. They all went to good homes, as far as I could tell."

I skimmed the article. It was as Mina had said; though the story was framed as a dispassionate report, it was clear the journalist saw us as a positive paragon of a charity, while the police were implied to be overzealous pedants, and heartless to boot, in making an enemy of our humble organization, particularly given the weightier problems afflicting the city.

"This is Roger Fairwood's work," I said. "It has to be. He wants the public on our side if the police try to shut us down."

"*Are* they investigating us?" Mina said.

"I don't think so," I said honestly. "Not seriously, at any rate. Laurent has been poking around, yes—Fairwood saw him here the other day. Perhaps he wanted to scare the police off by planting a sympathetic story."

"I suppose it's good," Mina said dubiously. "Having such a powerful ally."

This was hard to argue with, as I gazed around the empty shelter. After all, was this not exactly what I'd hoped would happen when I'd asked Havelock to enchant those cats, even if I had not foreseen the rumours being so efficacious, or spreading quite so quickly? And yet I felt terribly out of my depth in the face of this sort of publicity—Les Amis des Chats had never even been mentioned in the papers before.

"What's the situation at the other shelter?" Mina said. "Do you have any cats left?"

"The other shelter," I repeated. I'd left just before Élise opened for the day, and it had taken me some time to reach Rue Sainte-Sophie—my tram had been late, then broken down, leaving me to wade through the fresh snow. I'd left Élise alone, with no idea of the stampede that was about to ensue, and no backup.

Without another word, I dropped the newspaper and dashed out the door.

CHAPTER 27

The tram came to a stop a block before Rue des Hirondelles, the way being obstructed by a crowd. The driver shouted at us to disembark, and we did so confusedly. I paused to help an elderly woman, shielding her from being jostled as we clambered out, my heartbeat thundering in my ears the whole while. I wanted to believe all this was some political demonstration, and yet I could not quite convince myself.

My fears were confirmed as I turned onto Rue des Hirondelles and saw, up ahead, the density of the crowd—two hundred strong at least—concentrate around a particular row of shops: those that included the shelter.

I let out an inarticulate moan. All these people had come for our cats? We'd had thirty-one available for adoption when I'd closed the shelter the previous night. What on earth would we do? Surely Pierre would help, but he couldn't possibly have enough cats to appease everybody. And what would happen when they found we had run out—start a riot?

Oh, how I rued asking for Havelock's help! I should have known any assistance given to us by magicians would end in disaster.

I jostled and bumped my way through the crowd, muttering apologies as I hurried up the hill, past the little square, where the benches beneath the maples and the tables outside La Fin all sat empty. A few people warned me to stop, one man even grabbing my arm. This, coupled with the frisson of fear running through the crowd, convinced me, slowly but surely, that whatever this was, it had nothing to do with the cats, nor the article in the *Gazette*.

I finally reached the fringe of the crowd, which formed a neat horseshoe around the shelter, leaving the sidewalk and road clear.

A curiously mundane scene greeted me. An elegant woman stood on the sidewalk beyond the threshold, hands stuffed casually in the pockets of her sweeping maroon cloak. She appeared to be conversing with Élise, who stood just inside. Four men and one woman, also elegantly dressed, stood in a loose knot in the street, regarding the woman in the maroon cloak. Just beyond them, a dishevelled man was slumped against the side of the shelter, a sad background detail unheeded by those around him. Otherwise, Rue des Hirondelles seemed its usual, quaint self.

And yet, upon closer inspection, the details jarred. The man slumped against the building was not a luckless panhandler, but *Yannick*, his head falling forward onto his chest so that I could not see his face, nor tell if he was alive or dead. The door to the shelter was simply gone; upon the threshold was an odd scatter of ashy sand, as if it had been consumed in a sudden, localized inferno. Élise wore an expression of furious desperation that was terrible to behold.

A generalized mutter ran through the crowd of onlookers, of which I caught only scraps. *From the sky*, I kept hearing. *They fell—the snow—from the sky.*

I knew then that the calm of the scene before me was misleading, and I was gazing into the eye of a storm.

Crumbs of snow swirled along the street, buffeted by a winter wind that numbed my mouth and cheeks. But there was something off about it; the eddies were contrary, and the snow fell heavier in some places than others, as if it were being shaken through an uneven sieve. Something had disrupted the elements, and given the smell of magic in the air, I could guess what it had been.

It was clear that Valérie could not enter the shelter, or could not enter it *yet*, or she would have been inside already. I did not like my odds of shoving my way through Valérie's apprentices to reach Élise, so I turned and fled into the crowd. I reached Oksana's bookshop and wrenched the door open.

"*You* again!" the woman began—she was at the window, looking out from between two teetering stacks of books. She yelled something after me, but I was already through her back door.

I had a brief view of the lane and the snowbound Parc Saint-Aimé beyond, where several oblivious children were building snowmen, before hastening to the rear of the shelter. No door was visible, but Havelock had told me that it was hidden by enchantment on this side.

I ran my hands over the stone wall, hoping that I could locate it by touch. But my fingers found only frost and ice that had settled between the cracks. Frustrated, I began pounding at the wall, and then I heard a sound from the other side: His Majesty, yowling as if he were enduring some dire torment.

"Your Majesty!" I called. "It's all right—it's me!"

He continued to caterwaul, which was useful; he was loudest near the centre of the wall, and after running my hands over the icy stone, I finally found the doorknob, much lower than it should have been, which became visible when I grasped it, as did the door.

The door flew open and I rushed inside, whereupon I immediately stumbled over His Majesty. He wove between my legs, making himself as much of an obstruction as possible, yowling at me with a petulant air. To my relief, he seemed unharmed.

"Hush, Your Majesty," I said soothingly, assuming that he was upset about the unfolding catastrophe outside, but he only went and stood beside his empty food bowl, then turned to look at me hopefully.

"Oh, for—" I managed to leap over the cat and reach the main shop. Élise jumped when I placed a hand on her shoulder.

"Agnes," she said, looking both relieved and disappointed. "I thought you were Havelock. Where the hell is he? She can't get in, but those horses might."

Horses? I thought, but this was not the most pertinent detail. "He isn't in his workshop?" I said.

"My brother is in the Rivenwood," Valérie said. She stood just beyond the threshold, watching us, her posture casual. She might have been a neighbour stopping by for some friendly gossip. "We had a run-in last night. I managed to trap him in that world, which is why I'm paying you a visit. I think I shall have an easier time of shattering Havelock's wards without him around to interfere."

I felt myself sway and grabbed the doorframe to steady myself. Havelock was trapped in the Rivenwood? How? And who was going to get him out? "What did you do to Yannick?" I demanded.

Valérie glanced at his slumped form absently, as if she'd forgotten he was there. While Havelock's unusual features could be considered beautiful, the version of them that Valérie wore was far from striking. Her eyes were larger and over-wide, her chin too delicate, which together put me in mind of some guileless woodland creature, and her stature was on the short side. The strength of her presence came not from beauty but the calm composure she wore like another skin, the sense that nothing was beyond her ability to solve, or ruin, depending on the direction her whims took. She was the most unnerving person I'd ever come across, and yet I could also perceive, had our goals been aligned, how desperate I would have been to befriend her. Her apprentices watched her with a mixture of amusement and admiration, not even slightly nervous about the outcome of this confrontation, as if they were only looking forward to a performance by a master.

And why would they be nervous? There were no magicians standing in the way of their goal, only Havelock's wards, which, given the meagre remnants of the door I felt underfoot, did not feel particularly secure at the moment.

My grip tightened on the doorframe.

"Poor Yannick," Valérie said. "He'll be all right—I only put him to sleep. Unlike Havelock, I try to avoid killing apprentices."

I glanced at the apprentices standing behind her. Unlike the magicians who passed through Havelock's shop, their expressions had an uncanny flatness, and I had the strange sense that their feelings, their very personhoods, were somehow rooted in shallow soil. I thought of what I knew of the Rivenwood, and of what happened to magicians who strayed too deep in search of magics they hadn't the strength to wield, and felt my stomach twist at the horror of it.

"Is obstinacy a family trait?" Valérie said, her gaze shifting from Élise to myself. "Will you also refuse to give me the Artefact, even if the alternative is the destruction of your home?"

"I didn't refuse," Élise snapped, and I felt a rush of pride at the coldness in her voice. "I told you we don't have it."

Valérie only raised her eyebrows a millimetre, as if Élise were a willful child. "You think I would be foolish enough to waste my time here if I wasn't certain that my brother has the Artefact somewhere in his magpie nest of a shop?"

She unbuttoned her coat collar and withdrew the compass I had glimpsed around her neck the last time she broke into Havelock's shop. It was a humbler thing than most Artefacts I had seen, being simply carved from dark wood, but it was no ordinary compass. For one thing, it had too many hands, some of gold or jade, others that seemed made of glass. One of these glass hands flickered into motion, darting back and forth a few times before pointing squarely at the shop.

I could only stutter and stare—I didn't have Élise's bravery, in that moment. When it was clear neither of us would reply, Valérie smiled and turned away.

"That's all right," she said. "I'd rather do it this way. I never could resist an audience."

Her apprentices were also smiling. Valérie brushed her fingers over one of the necklaces she was wearing—it had three pendants, each in the shape of a tiny, intricately painted carousel. She cupped it in her hand and shouted an enchantment at the swirling clouds.

"That's what she did before," Élise said, seizing my arm and dragging me back. "The door—"

She was too late. The clouds descended towards the street, then burst like overripe fruit, spilling a strange conglomeration of limbs, reins, and trailing hair, which eventually shaped itself into a herd of phantasmal horses. They seemed made from snow and ice, and were imperfectly formed, their limbs bearing only the suggestion of hooves, their manes fading into cloud. They looked like the carousel horses, hints of silver sparkling here and there—some even had thin poles jutting from their backs—and were of indeterminate size, ranging from overlarge to immensely large.

I had only a moment to take in the horror and beauty of them—because they were undeniably beautiful—before they flew towards the shop, dashing themselves against the windows.

I shrieked and fell backwards, off-balance from Élise's grip, landing with a thump that knocked the wind out of me. The horses exploded like the lip of a massive wave striking shore, flinging a cloud of snow into the air, and screams filled the street. The cats yowled and hissed.

I dragged myself to my feet, still struggling to find my breath. I gave a gasp of laughter, because the shop seemed intact—Havelock's wards had held.

Or almost intact. One of the windows had shattered, the glass scattered across the floorboards in a fine dust, as if it had not merely broken, but disintegrated. And upon the threshold, just inside the shop, were a handful of snowflakes and what looked revoltingly like a severed hoof, already beginning to melt.

One of the apprentices laughed, and several others applauded. "Oh, hush," Valérie said. Her hands were in her pockets again and her expression was full of mischief. One of the other magicians called something to her in a teasing tone, and she turned to smile at him. She came forward in a casual lope, stopping at the threshold and reaching a hand out to brush the empty air.

"Not yet," she murmured. "Almost there. He didn't think

I'd come at him with magics from the Fourth Fathom—poor Havelock. He likes to be the only living magician to have ventured there."

Her expression was one of barely contained ecstasy, and I understood: Valérie loved magic as much as Havelock did. No doubt she could have thrown magic at the shop in a far more utilitarian fashion, without bothering to shape horses out of snow, but she could not resist making her enchantments beautiful. Yet in Valérie, this ecstasy was paired with a hunger that was almost bestial. Like her apprentices, there was a sense of absence about her, a hollowness behind her eyes, but in Valérie, this absence seemed filled with something dark, uncanny, and insatiable.

She removed a ring from her hand. The ring was lovely, a gold-and-emerald coil of vines and roses that had stretched from her first knuckle to her second.

"Élise," I said, pulling her to her feet, for she too had fallen over backwards when the horses charged. "Find Banshee and throw her out the back door. I'll—"

I was about to say that I would open the cages and release the shelter cats, who would hopefully follow Banshee's lead and flee through the back. I didn't know what Valérie was planning, but it didn't matter—whatever it was, she was convinced she would succeed. But I had barely reached the first cage before Valérie's enchantment exploded through the remaining windows.

They were wild roses, shaped from ice and snow like the horses, and they clambered hungrily through the windows, spreading across the ceiling and burrowing into it with their thorns, unleashing a hail of plaster upon us.

I had opened the first cage, though its occupant, a grey

tabby named Brume, only spat at me and crouched in the corner, but Élise had been struck by a piece of plaster and had fallen against the counter. I dashed to her side and helped her up, brushing her dust-covered hair from her face. But she didn't even look at me.

"What is *that*?" she cried, staring through the broken windows. The view was partially obstructed by the roses, which swayed gently in the winter wind, a wind that was now funneling through the shop, heedless of Havelock's wards. Did any of the wards remain? I had only a sliver of a second to wonder about it before I saw what Élise did.

We lurched forward and gazed upon the window of darkness that had opened in the sky, through which a landscape of dark trees and forbidding mountains was dimly visible. From this, Havelock emerged in his spectral form, trailing shadows like a nightmare, and landed—far too gracefully—upon the snow, whereupon he became himself again.

Screams erupted from among the crowd—which was, remarkably, still a crowd, though the more sensible half had fled—and a cry of "The Witch King!" followed by more screaming. I wondered at that for a moment, given how few knew what Havelock looked like, before recognizing the absurdity of my confusion. Havelock's horrifying manner of making an entrance was introduction enough.

One of Valérie's apprentices raised a heavily ringed hand and shouted an enchantment. Something flew towards Havelock—a fierce wind, laced with fallen snow and shards of ice. And yet it did not blast him backwards, as I would have expected; it passed *through* him, as if he were not wholly there. Havelock's mouth moved as he touched one of his earrings, and it was as if the apprentice's human guise were wrenched from her like a cloak, revealing another monster of shadow and ember. Havelock spoke another word, and the wind pummeled her, snuffing the embers and scattering the shadow like ash.

"They're vulnerable when they're like that," I murmured.

Havelock did the same to the next apprentice, and then there were only three, in addition to Valérie—who had, bizarrely, turned away from the threat posed by her brother, and was staring down at a small, dark shape that had lunged at her leg.

"Your Majesty!" I shouted, but the cat paid me no heed. His fur stood straight up, swelling him to twice his already intimidating size, so that he seemed closer to an actual panther than a house cat, and he lunged at Valérie again, hissing and snarling. The woman fell back with a cry, and I saw that she was limping—His Majesty had clawed through her trousers below her knee, spilling her blood upon the snow. He looked entirely unhinged, but I understood his motive: the shelter was *his* territory, and he would defend that territory from anyone foolish enough to threaten it, even if that person was one of the world's most powerful magicians.

I hurled myself towards the door, desperate to grab hold of His Majesty before Valérie threw some dreadful enchantment at him, but Élise had anticipated me. She wrenched me back and pinned me against the window frame, yelling something. One of Valérie's apprentices seemed to have been inspired by her, and he unleashed a spell that ensnared Havelock in a towering thornbush of ice. But Havelock only touched another one of his earrings in an almost absent gesture, and the man was drawn up into the storm clouds, screaming. The thornbush collapsed, and for a moment Havelock stood amongst a swirl of ice crystals, as if he were caught in an overturned snow globe.

He glanced about him and then spread his arms and flung them forward again, which caused the snow lying on either side of the street in banks and valleys to rise up in a wave, growing in size until it was clear that Havelock had summoned all the snow in the street, and possibly the neighbouring streets as well. It didn't move like snow, but like some sort of creature, humping its way along the cobblestones, a crevasse opening at its forefront like a gaping mouth. This horizontal avalanche slammed itself into the remaining apprentices and swept them away, buried beneath its depths.

Havelock turned to Valérie. His face was pale and cold, and in his eyes I saw only the darkness of the Rivenwood, nothing of Havelock himself. He reached towards the sky, and churning ribbons of cloud lowered themselves towards his hand, crackling with lightning that steamed and fizzed when it touched the falling snow.

But Valérie was no longer outside the shop—she was running. Her boots pounded against the sidewalk as she fled towards the square, and she seemed to be clutching something to her chest—a large, dark shape, wriggling wildly.

"Your Majesty!" I screamed. "Put him down!"

Naturally, Valérie paid me no heed, if she even heard me. At first, I thought she was going to charge into the crowd, which had been distracted by Havelock's weather magic, mouths agape in identical looks of horror. Whatever Havelock had summoned would not be able to reach her without risking the bystanders.

That thought made me still. *Would* Havelock risk the bystanders' lives to get at Valérie? He wasn't himself. I wrestled with Élise, who was still maintaining her grip, though I was unsure if it was His Majesty or Havelock I wanted to reach.

But Valérie didn't plunge into the crowd. She shouted another incantation, and a door appeared before her, a door attached to nothing at all. It was as beautiful as any of her other enchantments, blackened mahogany with eight intricately carved panels—a story, I thought, given their arrangement, but it was there for only a heartbeat before Valérie pushed through it and vanished, the door folding itself up and trailing behind her, as if it had been turned to cloth she had tugged from a clothesline. A man standing at the forefront of the crowd gave a gasp and fell backwards into another man, clearly thinking Valérie would run through the door and into him, but she—and the door—were already gone.

For a moment, I was too stunned to comprehend it. Surely it hadn't been His Majesty in her arms—what would she want with him? But when I looked back on the memory, I could see nothing but a single detail: a long black tail curved around Valérie's side, thrashing wildly.

"Your Majesty!" I shouted, finally wrenching free of Élise and charging into the street. "Your Majesty!"

Nobody paid me any attention—everyone was focused on either the place where Valérie had vanished or where Havelock stood. Out of the corner of my eye, I saw him summon his own door and vanish through it, to another chorus of screams, but I was beyond caring about Havelock, or any other magician for that matter.

"Your Majesty!" I cried again, blundering down the sidewalk, now clear of every scrap of snow, for it had all been bundled into the avalanche Havelock had summoned. And though I called and called, there was no response, until Élise caught up with me, and I collapsed into her arms and wept.

CHAPTER 28

I slept little the next few days, and poorly. I also spent far too much of my time crying. While I kept the shelter open and my checklists up-to-date, because I would not fail the cats, no matter what calamity had befallen me, I kept having to remove myself to the back room so as not to upset our visitors with my tears. People continued to pass through our doors in large numbers, even if it was mostly to gawk at the epicentre of the greatest magical drama the city had seen in years.

Élise did what she could to comfort me. "Surely she'll return him," she said. "Once she realizes what he is, and how little Havelock cares for him. No doubt that's why she took him in the first place."

This last I believed, despite being unable to conceive of a more unlikely hostage than His Majesty, nor one less desirable for Havelock to ransom. Valérie had taken him out of desperation—her plan of breaking into Havelock's workshop having gone awry, she had stolen what she could. Perhaps she'd taken the violence of His Majesty's attack as evidence of some mutual regard with Havelock, rather than merely the manifestation of the cat's diabolical nature.

Élise's voice grew quiet, and she touched my arm. "You don't *know* that he isn't still alive."

I allowed her to pull me into her shoulder, my tears falling once more. Of course it wasn't just that keeping me from sleep. His Majesty had been Robin's cat—he'd never truly been mine. And I'd lost him.

I'd never realized before how entangled my feelings for His Majesty were with my feelings for Robin, the invisible webwork holding them together. I will not say that I felt as if I'd lost Robin all over again, because nothing could be so destructive as that, but certainly it was as if the half-healed wound had been pierced, and the pain was exquisite.

Havelock repaired the shelter within an hour of Valérie's attack, and then he vanished through another door, this one made of glittering bronze, which he summoned from the blizzard that had descended upon the city. But wherever Valérie had gone, Havelock could not track her, and he eventually returned to his workshop to sulk, or perhaps to scheme—I was too distraught to concern myself with him.

I was also disagreeably busy. Not only did we have to endure endless questions from the public, but two police officers I did not recognize turned up on our doorstep not long after Havelock completed his repairs. I would not have thought that any explanation could have appeased them, but I should have known better than to underestimate Élise.

She invited the police in with a desperate warmth, as if nothing could have come as a greater relief than their presence. Valérie's interest in our shelter—which naturally dozens of witnesses had confirmed, even if none had overheard our conversation—she blamed on the baker who had fled some months ago, who, Élise had heard, had been given to welcoming strange visitors, some of whom continued to turn up on our doorstep regularly, to much mutual confusion. Valérie had asked for the baker by name, Élise claimed, and refused to believe he was no longer in residence. Somehow—the logic escaped me, but Élise was nothing if not a consummate storyteller, and made even leaps of logic perfectly convincing—she made clear her suspicions that the baker may have been Havelock Renard in disguise. Élise furthermore insisted that the police search the shop from top to bottom to clear it of any hazardous Artefacts this supposed baker may have left behind.

Naturally I quailed at this, and made to argue with her, but Élise only shot me one of her brief, murderous looks, and I fell silent.

They marched in, their gruffness markedly reduced after listening to Élise's wide-eyed fabrication, one of them even pausing to compliment our cats. We offered them almond croissants from the batch I'd rescued from the oven the previous night, and they accepted with pleasure.

Naturally they found the trapdoor, and I watched them descend the stairs in a kind of frozen panic, certain that this was the end of everything I had worked for.

But it was gone. The workshop, the Artefacts—everything. The officers came marching back upstairs looking perfectly unperturbed, one brushing a stray cobweb from her hair. I stared through the open trapdoor, which revealed a cellar barely high enough to stand in, containing mostly empty shelves, two broken chairs, and a few half-empty bags of flour.

"How did you know?" I murmured to Élise.

She shook her head. "I didn't. It was a gamble. But given the number of ridiculous enchantments Havelock has placed on this building, I guessed he might have come up with one to pull the wool over the eyes of the police."

I hadn't expected the officers to believe us and go away, particularly given the rumours floating around about our shelter, but go away they did, though their belief did not seem absolute—they spent considerable time muttering to each other out of earshot.

Initially I had wondered why Laurent had not been part of the investigation, but as the days passed I forgot all about him—until he sent a telegram reminding me of our festival date, together with a meeting place and time.

"I can't," I said to Élise, showing her the telegram. "I can't imagine dudding up and going out, not with everything that's happened. I will have to cancel."

She grimaced. "I won't try to force you, dear. But what will he think? Can we afford to increase his suspicions even further? Also, I can't help but wonder if there isn't a way to get Laurent on our side. Would he help us, if he knew all? Yes, he's with the law, but he's also a man, and he obviously cares for you."

I had no answer to this, because the possibility hadn't occurred to me. We hadn't yet opened the shelter for the day, and Gabriel had accompanied Élise so that we could all breakfast together. Despite her admonishing him for lingering, I could see that his presence fortified her.

He shook his head slightly, looking even more dubious than I felt. "I wouldn't advise that, my love," he said. "The referendum was a strong win for the 'yes' side. And I can tell you that city council is very close to passing the bylaw—it could happen as soon as next week. When it comes to the police, I advise you to tread very, very carefully."

I put down my forkful of scrambled egg, no longer hungry. Given the tumult of my present situation, I'd paid little heed to the referendum, which had asked the city's inhabitants if we wished to approve sweeping new powers for the police to investigate the crimes of magicians, including by searching businesses and homes suspected of Artefact trafficking without warning and with the aid of magic, which would certainly reveal at least the presence of Havelock's wards, and likely his workshop too. It had been introduced in response to the disorder wrought by magicians, particularly since the arrival of Valérie and her apprentices.

"That bylaw isn't even legal," Élise said, spearing a pancake. "The courts will overturn it, referendum or no. Allowing the police to raid any business they feel like, just because they catch a whiff of magic—it's too much power, and it will be abused, mark my words. I can't believe we're even considering it."

"There's some debate about what the courts will think," Gabriel said. "Either way, the idea is popular. People want *something* to be done to stop these magicians from running amok. Yes, the legislation may be overturned eventually, but in the interim, the shelter will be at risk."

I rubbed the bridge of my nose. "You're right. I must go, mustn't I? But surely Laurent can't believe we're trafficking Artefacts, or mixed up with Havelock in any way, otherwise he wouldn't ask me to step out with him."

"I think that's precisely what he would do—it's what I'd do, if I were him," Gabriel said. Given his affability, many assumed there was an innocence to Gabriel that did not exist. He had a core of pure cunning that one only saw when his guard was down, as it was now. "To see if you'll come to trust him enough to let the truth slip out. The police are certain Renard is in the city now—and make no mistake, they're determined to catch him, dangerous as that may prove."

Élise pressed my hand, and we lapsed into a gloomy silence

until Ambulance's aggressive purring became too great to ignore, and I went to his cage to rub his head. It was his latest tactic for soliciting affection, as he'd learned at last that hysterical yowls were more likely to earn him a scolding. Only a few of our original cats remained, mostly the more difficult cases, but we'd been regularly resupplied by Pierre and by our volunteers, who had also grown in number and had been able to expand their search area to the outskirts of the city. At present, we had eighteen cats on offer between both locations, though I wouldn't have been surprised if half were snapped up by closing.

A smile pulled at my mouth. Under different circumstances, I would have been beside myself with glee—we had rescued and found good homes for more cats in a month than we had in the last two years. Our donations had more than tripled, money we'd used to have several of the most ambitious ferals at the largest cat colony neutered. And yet, if *Les Amis des Chats* was shut down, all of our hard-won gains would be erased.

I noticed that Banshee was napping in the oven yet again, and I shooed her out, ignoring her voiceless protests—since learning of the oven's enchantment, I had been trying to dissuade the cat from her new favourite bed. What if the thing decided to make pastry when she was inside?

I felt a strange urge to go and hide in the basement with Havelock, although this should have seemed the furthest thing from a place of refuge. Since I had kissed him, we had barely spoken, nor had he seemed to have any interest in addressing the matter. I hadn't the slightest idea what was going through his mind in the wake of Valérie's attack. But what else could I expect from Havelock Renard?

CHAPTER 29

Laurent and I were to meet at a park beside Lachine Canal, where the market was held. Dozens of wooden stands like tiny chalets had been erected around the central fountain, which was frozen solid, icicles draped from the tiers like the fronds of a frozen willow. I shivered and drew my scarf tighter around my neck—the wind was sharper than I'd felt all winter, the stars cold and crystalline. A bonfire had been lit, and I went towards it gratefully, removing my gloves so that I could warm my hands.

I didn't notice Laurent at first—he stood in the line for mulled wine, his red hair muted by the darkness, the bonfire picking out only a few strands of gold. When I recognized him, he was already coming towards me, a warm smile on his face, holding two paper cups.

I smiled back. I had been nervous about seeing Laurent, but nothing in his expression suggested he had changed his opinion of me, and I was reminded of how much I'd always liked him. It wasn't just that I was determined to like everyone, as Élise was often complaining; Laurent, I was certain, had a fundamental goodness in him. He was the sort of person who wanted to do the right thing.

"Good evening," he said, handing me one of the cups. His face was flushed from the cold, and in his well-tailored coat of dark wool, he looked startlingly handsome. "I'm sorry to keep you waiting—the line."

"That's all right," I said, a little nervously, because a part of me was now occupied with pondering Élise's suggestion. *Could* I trust Laurent? Not with everything that had happened, of course—he couldn't know that Havelock was my landlord. But what if I told him that Valérie was convinced that we were hiding some Artefact we'd never seen before? It was certainly the truth, or at least a part of it. Would Laurent—would the police—protect us?

Laurent took a sip of his mulled wine and winced. "I always forget that I find these too sweet," he said. "Yet every time I visit the market, I can't stop myself from ordering one. Why don't I learn?"

"Perhaps you simply enjoy tormenting yourself," I said. "Speaking of which, I have some calamitous news."

Laurent raised his brows, but at the sight of my expression, a smile tugged at his mouth. We had wandered onto one of the bridges that spanned the canal, below which several children were skating. "Shall I hold on to something?" he said.

"You'd better." I allowed a pregnant pause to elapse. "Lynx has been adopted."

"No!" he said, looking genuinely dismayed. He set his drink on the bridge's railing and leaned over it on his forearms. "That's unfortunate. My fault, of course—I should have made up my mind sooner. I confess I wasn't so set against adopting her as I implied."

"I know you weren't," I said, knocking my shoulder against his. "You expressed your affection by cruelly spurning her, just as she expresses hers by attacking whatever appendage is nearest. You would have made a perfect pair."

Laurent laughed, but then a shadow seemed to fall across his face, and he looked back at the frozen water.

"I have another potential suitor for you," I said. "She's not half as wild as Lynx, but the family who adopted her not one week ago returned her yesterday, claiming she'd deconstructed their favourite rug."

Laurent nodded. "I'm not daunted," he said. "My apartment has no carpeting at all, you see."

"You'll need to move fast. No dawdling this time. I doubt it will be long before Mairesse is spoken for."

Laurent turned to face me, still leaning one elbow upon the railing, so that we were much closer in height. "Yes, your shelter has become quite popular."

His tone was casual, but with an undercurrent that made me pause, and which disrupted our easy banter. "You've heard the rumours, I'm sure," I said, trying to summon up a little of Élise's airy guile. "The *Daily Gazette* will print anything."

Laurent looked thoughtful. His gaze drifted, and he appeared to watch the snow fort some university students were constructing in the park on the other side of the bridge. I turned to gaze at it too, and was about to remark on its size when he said, "You could tell me, Agnes."

His tone was so casual that I at first assumed it was some continuation of our banter. "Could I?" I said teasingly. "Tell you what, precisely?"

His posture was casual, his expression still thoughtful, but when I looked at him I could tell that something had shifted behind the easygoing mien he wore like a cloak, so comfortably I hadn't even noticed it before. I went still.

"About Havelock," he said in the same tone.

"Ah," I said, deciding to pretend I hadn't noticed the shift, that I was as relaxed as before, when I felt as if the breath were being squeezed from my throat. "He was in Rue des Hirondelles, outside the shelter. Élise and I saw him duel those other magicians—surely you don't need another bystander report?"

He gave a polite grimace that sent a shiver through me. "About the magic shop he operates beneath your shelter," he said.

"I— What?" I spoke with genuine confusion—I still didn't understand how abruptly the conversation had shifted. I set my cup down on the railing, for my hand was shaking.

"We've suspected he was there since before you moved in," Laurent said. "His associates have been seen coming and going at all hours. Yannick Abrams, for one—we know he's been buying and selling Artefacts on Havelock's behalf, even if we don't have enough proof for the courts. As well as Wesley Juma, Antoine Lasalle, Bette Carrington. And, of course, Valérie Renard, his sister, with whom he's had some mysterious falling out. We've been unable to confirm the particulars. I'm guessing you might know, though."

My mouth was too dry to even attempt a response to this, so I simply stood there, my mind working frantically. Élise could have found a way out of this, I was certain, but my faith in myself did not match my faith in Élise. Laurent was so self-assured that he was like a looming storm, its course impossible to alter—one could only wait to see what it would unleash.

"I'm sorry," he said, standing up straight so that his height was abruptly all that I could see. "I shouldn't have asked that. It's not germane, anyhow."

"Why did you ask me to meet you here?" I finally said.

The same shadow fell across his face then, and I knew he

regretted some part of this. Somehow that made it worse than if he'd lured me here out of pure heartlessness.

An ember of resentment kindled within me. He had used deception to bring me here, playing the role of suitor. And I had come, partly out of fear that he might do something of this nature if I *didn't*, but hoping that I could place my trust in the kindness I'd seen in him. I had come though I hadn't wanted to, though I'd wanted nothing to do with this world of illegal magics and spying and power struggles, and had, in fact, been up crying over His Majesty half the night, which had left my eyes slightly swollen. I was tired and heartsick, and yet I couldn't simply go home and curl up by the fire with the cats—no, I had to deal with yet another crisis.

"We can't go after Havelock's shop yet," Laurent said. "But soon—quite possibly tomorrow—the city council will pass their bylaw granting us special powers to search *any* place where we suspect Artefacts are being trafficked, with or without evidence, and to use our magicians in our investigations. I can assure you we will be in your shelter not one hour after the last councillor raises their hand."

This was interesting—I hadn't known there were magicians among the police rank and file. It was difficult to imagine them joining any human organization—while I knew not all magicians were as depraved as Valérie, nor as complicated as Havelock, they struck me as solitary creatures by nature.

When I showed no reaction to this, Laurent went on, his voice slightly louder, "Agnes, Havelock is a criminal. A dark magician of the worst order. He—do I truly need to explain this to you? No, I can see I don't. Then how can you—"

He stopped, and seemed to put away some part of himself. "I'm giving you a choice. If you help us, I'll do what I can for you. If you don't, I'll have to place you under arrest."

"He isn't a dark magician," I said. "There's no such thing, it's redundant. You're trying to track the world's greatest magician, yet you know nothing about magic?"

He blinked at me. "Did you—"

"I'm sorry, Laurent," I said. "I know you are attempting to be intimidating, but given the company I've been keeping lately, you'll forgive me for not finding you very frightening. Also, it's cold. Would you mind arresting me a little closer to the bonfire?"

"Agnes, I don't think you understand—"

"Oh, I see." I folded my arms, tucking my hands beneath them for the warmth. I wasn't at all nervous about Laurent anymore—it wasn't possible to be. Despite the fact that he represented the ruination of everything I had worked for, or maybe because of it, I had never felt more fed up with a person in my life, and I wanted to lash out at him—not because I thought it would get me anywhere, but for the satisfaction of it. Perhaps it was no longer Élise I was drawing inspiration from, but His Majesty.

"I'm supposed to be terribly surprised by this betrayal, am I?" I went on. "Laurent, contrary to what Élise is always saying, I don't *actually* believe that everyone is good. What I believe is that the good usually wins out over the bad, unless a person is possessed of a particularly weak nature."

He flinched as if I'd struck him. "Agnes—"

"I'm going back to the bonfire," I said. "You can arrest me there, or en route—whenever you're ready. Or you can feel free to continue standing here—you can loom over the snowman, I suppose."

I turned and walked away. As I'd expected might happen, two people who I had taken for a couple admiring the view moved to block my path.

"Would you mind—" Laurent sounded off-balance, which was some satisfaction, at least. "Agnes, if I could see your coat—"

I didn't care why he wanted it. I removed it and threw it at him, then folded my arms and pointedly shivered.

He pulled it off his head, flushing, his hair mussed. I thought one of the other two officers suppressed a smile. He rooted around in the pockets for a moment.

"That isn't Havelock's," I said. "Nor do I carry him around in my pocket."

Laurent's expression was distracted. He found the inner pocket and pulled a small object out.

It was the pen. The enchanted pen that I'd been using to catalogue Havelock's Artefacts. I'd been down there yesterday, in my coat because Havelock kept the basement too cold for my liking, claiming that the spiders preferred it that way. I must have tucked it away and forgotten about it.

I kept my expression as blank as possible, though I wasn't Élise; I no doubt evinced some reaction. But there was no reason for Laurent to recognize it as an Artefact.

And yet. He examined it closely, tapping it with a fingertip, and there was something odd about the way he gripped it between thumb and forefinger of his other hand, as if he wanted to touch it as little as possible.

"What does it do?" he asked me. He motioned to one of the other officers, who pulled what looked like a cloth bag from his coat and placed the pen inside it.

I couldn't have answered him even if I'd wanted to. I felt numb from the shock of it. For a moment I felt as if there were two Laurents before me, and I couldn't work out which was true.

"We've found that oilcloth can prevent an enchantment

from leaking from its Artefact, which has happened on rare occasions," Laurent said. "Some property of the linseed oil, we suspect."

"You're a magician," I murmured. "But you don't—you haven't got—"

I was too overwhelmed to describe it articulately, that uncanny chiaroscuro they all had, but which was absent from Laurent—who, apart from his uncommon good looks, gave every appearance of being an ordinary man. He seemed to understand, though.

"I've never been to the Rivenwood," he said. "And I never will."

He pronounced the words as if they repulsed him, which I could well understand. And yet I could not help feeling perversely sorry for him. If Havelock was correct, all magicians were drawn to the Rivenwood; it was part of them, even those who'd never been there. Even if it did make monsters of them in the end, seeing Laurent's repulsion was like seeing a cat shudder over its lust for birds.

"Come with us, Agnes," Laurent said. His composure had cracked a little, and his voice had a pleading note. "Please."

I almost wanted to force him to manhandle me, just for the guilt it would give him, but I had no interest in being wrestled to the ground in all that snow. He gave me my coat back, and I went with them.

CHAPTER 30

The police station was not as dreadful as I'd feared. It was an old brick building from the mid-nineteenth century, the lobby almost airy with lead-paned windows that went all the way up to the ceiling and wood floors polished to a shine. Things took a turn from there, however. Laurent led me past the counter and along a dingy hallway to a row of cells, only one of which was occupied by a snoring man who, judging by his black eye and the reek of alcohol, was being held for public rowdiness. Laurent put me into the cell at the other end, which had a narrow bed and a tiny sink.

Perhaps he was planning to say something to me, but I had no interest in hearing it; I turned away and proceeded to remove my coat and warm my hands at the sink. When I looked back, he was gone.

I surveyed the depressing confines of the cell. Though claustrophobic, it was tidy and smelled strongly of some sort of cleaner. After the panic and fury of the last hour, I felt comfortably empty, like a beach stripped of driftwood by a retreating tide. The fact of my arrest seemed of lesser import than my relief at being out of the cold.

I lay down upon the bed and drew the blanket over me. Slowly, the last of the shivering subsided. Then, against all odds, I fell asleep, and slept better than I had in days.

The following morning, I was presented with a breakfast of a bagel and coffee by a discomfitingly jovial woman, not unlike my usual fare, except that the bagel was stale and the coffee lukewarm, though the officer was thoughtful enough to offer cream and sugar. I almost wished for rudeness; it would have been less jarring than this casual acceptance of my captivity. I wanted to be gawped at, at least, to have the guards stare at me with confusion, never having seen such an unlikely criminal before, but perhaps that isn't an uncommon conceit among those who find themselves in a prison cell.

In my day-old clothing, and with my checklist and chores beckoning to me, unreachable, I was feeling less philosophical about my situation than I had the previous night. I wanted Élise, and the familiar smells and sounds of the shelter in Rue des Hirondelles, and Banshee's warm weight in my arms. If Laurent had shown himself, I might have been moved to plead for my release. Fortunately, he didn't, so I was able to keep my dignity intact.

At midmorning, I was escorted to a waiting room by the same jovial woman, who informed me that I was to be released on bail paid by "such a sweet young lady" with "lovely manners," at which I managed to stifle my snort. My legs had gone wobbly with relief, and I collapsed upon the bench she indicated. Then, at last, I was shepherded to the lobby, where Élise was waiting.

I fell into her arms, sobbing, and she patted me and made soothing noises. She also—too circumspectly to be noticed by the watching officer—muttered instructions in my ear. "Don't say a word. Only act confused and frightened, but not angry. If they ask you anything, just start crying again."

This last was easily accomplished, for I couldn't stop tearing up while the clerk passed the paperwork to Élise, who gave another one of her virtuoso performances. She was so visibly nervous and unfamiliar with the utilitarian environment of the police station that one might suspect she'd been innocent of their very existence. When the clerk pointed out an error in one of the forms, she gave him a look that suggested she feared he might attack her. He answered her questions condescendingly, his interest in us visibly dimming. Then, at last, we were stepping out into the blinding sunlight of a winter day.

"How did you afford it?" I demanded, for I had seen the money Élise had counted out for the clerk.

"How do you think? The Witch King has more money than he knows what to do with, the heel. Besides, the bail wasn't *that* high—they could only charge you for that illegal Artefact in your pocket. Clearly they don't have enough evidence for anything else."

"Yet," I said, and told Élise what Laurent had said. She nodded grimly.

"Yes, Gabriel thinks the legislation will pass today too," she said. "He's trying his best to raise a fuss about it. There's been plenty of criticism, after all—it's an infringement of rights, if the police can raid any business they choose without notice or evidence. But I don't think it will be enough, and I can only hope Havelock has some plan in his back pocket. We'll need to discuss it with him." She did not appear pleased by the prospect.

"How long were you at the station?" I said.

"I arrived first thing. Gabriel got a tip from a friend in the force. They made me wait over two hours, claiming they didn't have the staff to deal with me."

"Two hours?" I repeated. And it had taken nearly an hour to fill out the paperwork. And the cats had been on their own since last night! "Then who's looking after the shelter? One of the volunteers? Mina?"

Élise turned to examine a passing horse and cart as if she'd never seen one before. "Mina's far too busy supervising the other shelter; you know that."

"Not Yannick!" I exclaimed. "He doesn't know the first thing about cats."

"No, Havelock sent Yannick off to spy on Valérie's apprentices." She squeezed my hand. "Look at you—you're shivering! Let's stop at the bakery for chocolate brioche, hm? Then we'll go right home and you can have a nap. I'm sure you didn't sleep well."

A shiver of dread ran through me. "Élise, the shelter—"

"And remind me to tell Havelock to cast a proper hex on Laurent," she said. "If we're to be arrested anyway, why not first give that man what he deserves? What do you think? Boils in inconvenient places would be a good start."

"Élise," I said, grasping her arm and pulling her to a stop. "*Who* is taking care of the cats?"

CHAPTER 31

I wanted to run the distance to Rue des Hirondelles, but after slipping twice on the icy sidewalks, I was forced to slow to a brisk march. Regardless, my panicked haste must have been obvious to all I passed, for more than one person leapt out of my way, an elderly man dragging his wife from my path as if I were a speeding train. When at last the shelter came into sight, I could have cried from relief that it was still standing—Valérie had not reduced it to a crater, nor had Havelock transformed it into some gaping portal to the Rivenwood in his haste to be free of his charges.

"I'm sure it's fine," Élise said, out of breath from trying to keep up with me. "Agnes, he's not *completely* useless. He was terribly worried about you when I told him what had happened—I know because he didn't offer up a single quip about the situation."

I could not be persuaded from my fears, though, and fully expected to find the place reduced to wreckage. I hastened past the bookshop, where the face of Oksana scowled at me through the window, and wrenched open the shelter door.

Unfortunately, my expectations were met.

Immediately upon opening the door, a small shape made a

dash for the street, arrested in the nick of time by Élise. It was one of our kittens, Minuet, and she was not the only escapee; I saw at least three other roaming cats who lacked roaming privileges, all because they were notorious troublemakers. Two were making a fearful din in the corner—Patches and Genevieve—circling each other as they yowled and caterwauled, a battle that seemed not to have progressed past the posturing stage, but was alarming nevertheless. Another cat was by the oven, gnawing on something—I couldn't be certain, but I strongly suspected it was one of the midnight pastries. Papers that had been on the counter were scattered across the floor, and one of the curtains—now half torn to shreds—had been pulled entirely off its rod, while another hung askew. The empty cages—of which we had a fair few—were scattered about the shelter in odd places, as if Havelock had attempted to chase after the loose cats with them before abandoning the attempt.

There came a fell yowl from overhead. I looked up, and found myself gazing into the terrified face of Ambulance, who had somehow tucked himself into the electric sconce that hung above the door. How he had made it up there, I could not have said, but it was clear he rued his daring, and continued to yowl at me as if I'd put him there myself. I took a step forward, and my boots crunched on sand. The enormous burlap litter sack lay on its side, most of its contents spilled across the floor, while a broom and dustpan lay abandoned a foot or two away.

And in the midst of it all was Havelock, glasses askew and a bandage wrapped round one hand, looking as ridiculously elegant as he always did in his princely jewels and otherworldly clothing, but also flushed and unkempt.

"What did I tell you?" he exclaimed as soon as we entered.

"They're fiends, every last one. Hairy, flightless night-gaunts, devoted to tormenting their captors. I go to the effort of preparing their breakfast—which is the most foul slop imaginable, by the way; I don't think I will ever get the smell out of my hair—and as thanks I receive nothing but hisses and acts of violence. *Look.*" He held up his hand, which he hadn't bandaged tightly enough—a spot of blood had leaked through from his palm. "And here—" He pointed to his jaw, where there was another, more glancing scratch an inch or two from his chin. "That one was aimed at my jugular, and you won't convince me otherwise. Whose idea was it to make companions out of a species of malevolent carnivores?"

For a moment, I couldn't get a word out, I could only stare at him. "How did you get cat food in your hair?" I said at last.

"Ask this murderous little tiger," Havelock said, slamming the cage door shut on Marcel, a grey tabby who sat calmly eating his food, which was splattered across the floor of the cage in a line from the overturned bowl like the spilled entrails of a successful kill.

"*That* is the only tame one of the lot," he added, motioning to Banshee, who sat docilely by his feet with her striped tail curled around her paws, gazing up at Havelock with narrow-eyed adoration.

Élise could not have been more unperturbed about the whole thing—I believe she was suppressing laughter. "Well, they don't like magicians," she said, reaching down to right one of the scattered cages. "Though they don't seem all that bothered by Yannick, do they? Perhaps they just don't like *you*, Havelock. Cats are excellent judges of character."

I surveyed the damage—which, I decided, after mentally sorting it into a list of priorities, was not as terrible as it could have been. Now that my worst fears had been assuaged, relief filled me like water from a burst dam—relief that, I realized, was tied in no small part to Havelock. Just as I hadn't known what state the shelter would be in, I hadn't known what state *he* would be in. To see him standing there looking flushed and irritated, but himself for the most part, made me want to hug him.

I would have done so, but Havelock, to my astonishment, stepped forward first, pulling me into his arms with a sort of stiff determination, as if he'd planned it out, nervously, in advance. I leaned my face against his shoulder and breathed in the charcoal smell of magic, not minding it, nor the fact that he didn't seem entirely substantial, almost ghostly, and made the shadows shift strangely around us when I held him, as if for a brief moment I too were existing in some in-between otherworld.

"I'm sorry," he murmured, pulling back. "I didn't realize he would— They were using you to get to me. I didn't think of that. I'm not—it's only ever been me. Well, there's Yannick now, but I mean—" He broke off and rubbed his hair.

"I'm all right," I said. "As you pointed out, I needed a holiday from the cats anyway."

He laughed, and it made him seem more earthly, brightening his eyes. He leaned forward, more shy than determined now, and tilted my chin up. I was so surprised, and so accustomed to pining over him as hopelessly as Banshee did, that I didn't understand what he was doing until a second before he kissed me.

Distantly, I thought I heard Élise groan, but it wasn't something I registered until after. All I could focus on was Havelock's nearness and how gently he held me, as if *I* were the ghostly one.

Then Havelock pulled away with a start, looking flushed,

the hair at his nape mussed from where I'd put my hand in it. I would have simply reached out and pulled him to me, before I saw the object of his distraction: we'd missed one of the kittens, Mousse, who was attacking the buckle on Havelock's shoe.

"He has the right idea," Élise muttered, marching over to retrieve the kitten.

Mousse, though, did not want to relinquish his prey, particularly after Havelock gave his foot a shake, making the buckle flap about invitingly. It took the three of us to pry the ridiculous creature loose, and by the time I'd shut Mousse into his cage again, Havelock had his arms folded and was back to looking remote and disquieting. I could almost imagine it hadn't happened, if it weren't for Havelock's flush and the lingering warmth in my stomach.

"Now that *that's* taken care of," Élise said, and I didn't think she was referring to Mousse, "perhaps we can get back to discussing our problem. Namely: Laurent."

"Him!" Havelock's expression darkened. "I have several enchantments I've been saving for my enemies, and I can't think of a more deserving recipient."

"Yes, exactly," Élise said, looking pleased. "Please tell me you have a spell for boils. If you could put one—"

"Never mind the boils, Élise. Havelock, you have to move the shelter again," I said, urgency rising within me. "It's not just Laurent—they're going to try to arrest you today. Well, all of us, I suspect, and I don't know what will happen to the cats if—"

I was beginning to get worked up again, but at that moment, Ambulance gave another of his most earth-shattering yowls, which seemed to give fuel to the two locked in a brawl. Genevieve lunged forward and pinned Patches to the floor by the throat, to more dreadful caterwauling. We scattered to deal with them; I pried the brawlers apart, though they only took off towards the back room to continue their dispute, while Élise got the ladder and fetched Ambulance down from the sconce. I didn't notice what Havelock was up to until I returned with Patches, growling but immobilized by my grip on her scruff, to find that he'd scooped Banshee up and was glaring at the cat in my arms.

"That beast tried to attack her," he said defensively. "She's the only civilized one among them."

I only barely managed to stop myself from laughing. "Yes, Banshee has always been remarkably well-mannered," I said, because everyone liked their cat to be deemed an exception of some kind. And though Havelock might not have known it yet, Banshee was every inch his cat. She had nestled herself into his arms, kneading at his sleeve and looking extremely self-satisfied, as well as not at all surprised.

We managed to put the shelter in order, cleaning up the mess and finishing off the morning checklist that Havelock, to my surprise, had mostly completed, even if he'd also allowed the cats to run roughshod over him and turn the place upside down. I found myself smiling, in spite of the mess we were in. The shelter smelled of custard and raspberries—there was a plate of tarts on the counter, which Havelock must have retrieved the previous night. The chirrups of contented cats made my eyes prick with tears, and I realized how much I had come to see this place as home, and how I hated the thought of losing it.

"I'm not moving the shop again," Havelock said. He had put Banshee down and was ignoring her now, perhaps in a bid to recover his dignity, and she was letting him maintain the pretence, sprawled triumphantly in the middle of the floor with her front paws outstretched. "There's no need. The police will never find my workshop. I've put a spell on it that—"

"Turns it into a cellar when they try to get in—I know, we've seen it. But Havelock, Laurent is a magician."

"What!" Élise cried. "That hypocritical bastard."

"He—and any other magician within the police—will be able to use magic against you once the council passes this new bylaw," I said. "Could they break the enchantment you've put on the workshop?"

Havelock's expression grew thoughtful. "I don't know," he said. "I don't know how many magicians they have apart from that obsessive redhead, or the Artefacts at their disposal. The police have confiscated a large collection, including several that should belong to me; I'd bought and paid for them, but the delivery was interrupted en route."

"Stop it, Havelock," Élise said. "I don't want to feel any respect for Laurent right now."

"The lantern," I murmured.

"What lantern?" Élise said.

"Vortigern's lantern," I said. "The one that absorbs magic. You said it was stolen. Havelock—could the police have it? Could they use it against us somehow?" I didn't like the thought of an Artefact like that lurking somewhere out in the world, unaccounted for. Though I didn't much like the thought of *any* of Vortigern's Artefacts, or Vortigern herself, truth be told. Given Valérie's obsession with finding her time-travel Artefact, Vortigern felt almost like a presence, a ghost lingering in the shadows of the shop, and I wanted nothing to do with the ghost of someone with such unholy power.

"I doubt it," Havelock said, looking amused for some reason. "They wouldn't know how to wield it, anyway."

"Surely there must be some way out of this," I said, because it was ridiculous that there wouldn't be. The shop was quite literally built atop layers of magic—floors of Artefacts of incalculable power. Surely there were few problems in the world that magic couldn't solve, at least when wielded by someone like Havelock, who had ended and then *un*ended the world—how could a roomful of bickering city councillors be one of them?

I looked up to find Havelock watching me with a troubled expression. And I understood without him having to say a thing: Havelock would come through all this perfectly unscathed. Laurent had never had a chance of imprisoning the Witch King; Havelock could escape any snare either police or politicians set for him. It was me that was in danger: me, and Élise, and the shelter.

"If worse comes to worst," Havelock said quietly, "I'll create a distraction. I'm quite good at those. Perhaps a pack of elephants will parade past city hall. No, I know—I'll bring the trees down from Mount Royal to my doorstep, like the forest of Birnam, and the police can fight their way through the undergrowth. While they're occupied, I'll help you and the cats flee the city. We can go to New York."

"Élise can't leave Montréal," I protested. "She has Gabriel. What will happen to him if the shelter is engulfed in scandal, and people start pointing out the connection between Les Amis des Chats and his wife?" It was all such a tangle that I felt dizzy and sick.

We debated it for some time, interrupted periodically by the cats, some of whom seemed to be looking for reassurance that they weren't to be consigned to Havelock's care for the long term. Marcel was crying at me, while Thoreau pulled at the cage bars with his claws in a display of poor manners that was quite unlike him. I ended up allowing Thoreau to roam free—there was little danger to him with his tormentor, His Majesty, no longer in residence—and took Marcel into my arms, from which height he could more effectively glare at Havelock. For his part, Havelock kept falling out of the conversation to mutter to himself about eight-layer spells and Artefacts of manifestation, or perhaps illustration—I had little patience for his speeches just then. I understood enough, though, to grasp that he didn't have the magic at hand to move the shop to a different city, that such a spell might not even be possible, and I recalled how astonished Yannick had been when Havelock had relocated the shelter by a handful of blocks.

Élise had stopped pacing and was nibbling on a custard tart.

"These," she said, taking another bite, "are exquisite."

"Most people thought so," Havelock said. "Claude was always complaining about people stealing his wares. Well," he amended, "he was always complaining that *I* was stealing them. Which was ridiculous, I rarely touched them."

"I don't know about *ridiculous*," Élise said. "You tried to destroy the world. Yet stealing pastry is a step too far?"

Havelock was frowning irritably into the oven, his gaze distant, clearly lost in an old argument. "Not once did I steal from Claude. The man disliked me enough—you think I would encourage him to poison me? Bakers are more dangerous than magicians; if they want you dead, you won't see it coming."

The floorboards creaked behind me, and I whirled around. But no one was there—we three were alone, and I stared at the empty patch of floor as if a ghost might be hovering there.

Élise had turned in the same direction, her face tight with fear. "Is Yannick back?"

I didn't understand. But then the sound came again, and it wasn't the floorboards, as I had assumed—it came from beneath us. Someone was walking around in the basement.

Havelock had gone still. He brushed one of his rings in what might have seemed an absent gesture were it not for the expression on his face, an unnerving cross between longing and dismay. Then he turned himself into shadow and ember and sank through the floorboards.

The effect of this particular display could not have been more disturbing if he'd been trying. Élise and I both screamed and clutched at each other, because it's one thing to have Havelock in your midst, talking to you like an ordinary person, and quite another to be reminded of what he is underneath. We didn't have time to feel embarrassed at ourselves, though—we turned together and sprinted for the trapdoor, to the dismay of Thoreau, who mewled at me, as always taking my loss of composure as a personal affront.

We thundered down the stairs to Havelock's workshop, where we found two figures silhouetted against the warm light of the spiders, more of which had appeared as the winter wore on and the creatures sought refuge from the cold. The smaller figure was more difficult to see, for even though she was facing me, more of the spiders were behind her. She seemed to be holding something in her arms, the outline of which was painfully familiar.

I stepped forward as a shudder ran through me. It was Valérie, and she was facing Havelock from across his worktable. His Majesty was draped across her arms, looking equal parts indolent and disdainful. He gave Havelock a brief baleful stare.

"Your Majesty!" I surged forward, but Élise, just behind me, grabbed hold of my arm and wrenched me back. "Put him down!" I cried, writhing in Élise's grip.

"Agnes," my sister said through clenched teeth. "Look at him. Don't you see?"

No, I didn't see—I didn't want to see. His Majesty stretched and rearranged himself in Valérie's arms, looking more comfortable there than he ever had in mine, or anyone's since Robin. Ordinarily the cat would deign to be held for only a brief time, but there he was, lounging upon Valérie as if she were a throne. I didn't have the sense that he was ignoring me, particularly, as he eyed one of the spiders with the self-satisfaction of a predator that could catch anything he deemed worth his while; rather, he didn't seem to care enough about my presence to be interested. And I realized that I wasn't surprised, which somehow hurt worse than the betrayal itself.

"He showed her a way in," Havelock said unnecessarily. He held Valérie's gaze, but his focus seemed to be on something else: the string of pearls that Valérie had wrapped twice around her hand, the one she now lifted to scratch the cat's chin. I remembered those pearls, the iridescent, undersea shine of them against my own hand as I recorded them in the catalogue, but I couldn't remember what enchantment they contained. I only remembered being afraid when I found out, and replacing them hastily in the cabinet.

Panic pierced through the fog of misery that had settled over me. How long had Valérie been down here? How many of Havelock's most dangerous Artefacts had she taken into her possession?

"Where did you get in?" Havelock said. His face was cold, but it didn't seem genuine this time. I knew by now that Valérie wasn't Havelock's enemy, even if she'd declared him hers. She was only his sister.

I remembered then what the necklace did: a particularly nasty yet elegant weapon, each pearl transforming into a tiny crystalline arrowhead when the magic was unleashed, which would lodge deep beneath the skin and burrow until they reached the heart. Would Valérie truly use the enchantment on Havelock? I felt sick.

Valérie smiled. She seemed to be enjoying herself, oblivious to the turmoil in Havelock's expression. "Would it be as much fun if I told you, Lock? Never mind. It doesn't matter now, does it? I don't know if I would have ever found a gap in your wards—you wove them together so tightly, and in so many layers, after last time. But do you know who could?"

She hoisted His Majesty onto her shoulders, where he dug in his claws—probably painfully, but Valérie gave no sign of minding. "I suspect he knows more than one way in and out of your lair. But one was all I needed."

"Where," Havelock repeated.

"The basement in the shop next door has collapsed," Valérie said. "Long ago. Nothing a little magic couldn't fix, of course. And between that basement and this one is the narrowest of passages—just wide enough for a cat. Well, it was—now it's wide enough for, oh, a dozen magicians. You didn't think to extend your wards to the basement, did you? Another oversight on your part."

I had been so fixated on His Majesty that I hadn't noticed anything besides the three of them. Now I began to hear them, shuffling about among the neatly organized cabinets. They came forward, each carrying several Artefacts: there was the sword that, I remembered, could blast a hole through solid stone; the golden hourglass that would immobilize one's opponent for as long as it took the sand to fall (about four minutes); the satchel of coins that turned to molten gold, burning anything they touched; and the black-and-white umbrella that transformed into a flock of magpies when unfurled. This last had initially sounded innocuous, but Havelock had assured me that such spells created monsters bound to their master's will, and were almost always put to violent purposes.

Valérie's apprentices might have been furniture, for all Havelock reacted to their presence. His left hand, held loosely at his side, moved only slightly, his thumb sliding over his rings. Did he have upon his person any enchantments that could defeat this many magicians, bearing Artefacts from his own collection? It seemed unlikely.

"This was awfully helpful, by the way," Valérie said, adjusting her hold on His Majesty so that she could turn to pluck something off Havelock's worktable. It was my notebook, in which I'd been cataloguing the Artefacts in Havelock's collection. "It would have taken us a long time to work out which of these Artefacts would best incapacitate you. Don't you see how much easier it would have been for you if you had simply given me Vortigern's book?"

"I wanted to give it to you," Havelock said. I think he'd forgotten about all of us by that point. He never took his eyes off Valérie. "I've always wanted to. Ri—"

"Have you?" Valérie tilted her head to one side. "I don't believe you, my dear. I think the only thing you've ever wanted is to sit down here with your hoard, hidden away from the world and everyone in it, like you used to do with your silly novels. What a waste! You have so much power, and what do you do with it?" A bitter note entered her voice. "You should have let me guide you, as I did when we were young. I would have shown you how to be a proper king—all you have now is an empty title that most use only to mock you. A throne made of twigs."

"I don't care who mocks me, provided they leave me alone," Havelock said.

She made a frustrated sound. "You're so childish, Lock. Never thinking of anyone but yourself."

Havelock's hand clenched and unclenched. "Someone should, don't you think?"

"Petulant, too." She paused abruptly, and the anger faded from her face, leaving behind a glimmer of confusion, as if its presence had surprised her. "Never mind."

She removed the compass from around her neck and held it before her, then moved through the workshop, her gaze fixed upon the glass. I was trying to work out where all of Valérie's apprentices were—at least two more were on the floor below us, judging by the muttered conversation I heard. How could Havelock overpower them all?

"Ri," Havelock said quietly.

She ignored him. She came to a stop in the middle of the floor, away from the cabinets and some paces from Havelock's desk, and frowned at the compass. The glass needle, which had directed her to that spot, now spun around and around in circles, seemingly aimless—the light flashed off it in tiny sparks as it moved.

"It's below," she said to the apprentice who'd come to stand behind her, a narrow-faced man with a ragged waterfall of a beard. "Directly below us—it must be."

I went still with shock. Élise shot me a baffled look. The Artefact wasn't below us—I'd catalogued everything on the second and third floors, and most of the fourth, as meticulously as I did anything, with the exception of the boxes stacked against the north wall, which was nowhere near the place Valérie's compass was indicating. I had too much trust in my organizational skills to doubt it.

What did it mean? Was the Artefact in Havelock's library after all? How could he have failed to notice it? Was there some sixth floor Havelock had never told me about? Yes, that seemed like him. Except that Havelock's brow was furrowed in confusion.

Something brushed my ankles, and I looked down to find Banshee yowling silently up at me. She'd made her way down the stairs on quiet paws, as she often did these days, usually in search of Havelock. His Majesty's ears pricked, and he turned his imperious gaze upon her.

And as I looked at His Majesty, still settled into Valérie's arms, I took in where she was standing, and how it lined up. And I knew.

Vortigern's Artefact wasn't below us. It was above.

"Ri, I don't want to fight you again," Havelock said.

I looked from Havelock to Valérie, astonished. Didn't he understand? The number of apprentices Valérie had brought with her; the deadly Artefact she was toying with, warming the pearls in her hand as if they were something alive. Valérie hadn't come here to fight Havelock as they'd fought before, with claws sheathed. Perhaps she'd only ever held back in the hopes he'd relent and simply hand her the Artefact. But now she had the immeasurable power of it within her grasp, and there was no need to worry about anything else.

"I'm sorry, Havelock," Valérie said. "Your throne might be made of twigs, but it's still a throne."

At that, His Majesty leapt lithely to the ground, and then, in a supreme display of malice, began to wash his face, as if he could not even be bothered to look at his enemy as he was destroyed. Havelock was still gazing at Valérie, brow furrowed and lips slightly parted. I wanted to shout a warning, but before I could, Valérie flung the glimmering pearls at Havelock, the incantation falling from her lips in sharp, precise syllables.

Abruptly, there came the sound of glass shattering and wooden beams exploding, the pearls shaping themselves into daggers that flitted through the air. I screamed and covered Élise with my body, then whirled around, half expecting to see Havelock on the floor, bleeding from a dozen mortal wounds. I say *half* expecting, because there was a part of me that didn't believe he could be harmed—had I not seen him perform impossible feats of magic time and again?

I almost sobbed with relief when I looked up and found him still standing, although he was clutching his arm and staring at it as if it didn't belong to him. Blood dripped down its length and fell from his fingertips to the floor—he had deflected most of the arrows, somehow, but one had found its mark and was burrowing upwards towards his heart. I thought I caught a glimpse of it sliding beneath his skin like a parasite.

Havelock shouted an incantation—it sounded garbled, but whatever it was, it was enough, and he wrenched the arrow from beneath his skin.

"Havelock!" I cried, but I didn't see what happened next, for Élise dragged me back. I heard it, though: an explosion that shook the shop and caused a crater to appear in the rear wall—one of Valérie's apprentices must have cast the incantation in the sword. The spiders were in a panic, scattering to hide themselves in corners and crevices so that it was abruptly difficult to see, the light flickering madly before it faded away. A small voice inside me noted numbly that I would have to give up on Oksana ever taking a shine to me now that we'd blasted a hole in her cellar.

To my astonishment, the next voice I heard, rising above

the chaos, was His Majesty's. The creature had let out a yowl I'd never heard from him before, and had fallen into a crouch, hissing and spitting. Banshee loomed over him, her back arched and her fangs bared. For a heartbeat, I didn't even recognize her; I had never seen her even hiss before. His Majesty now had a tear in one ear, which was reddening with blood. I realized what had happened—His Majesty was almost at Havelock's feet, and must have darted at him in an attempt to distract him and make an easier target for Valérie, perhaps by clawing at his ankles. Banshee now stood between Havelock and His Majesty, who was gazing at the smaller cat with disbelief.

Banshee lunged forward again, nearly getting her claws into His Majesty's other ear. The big cat hissed, and then—I struggled to believe my eyes—turned tail and fled into the shadows.

"Banshee!" I shouted, but the creature ignored me completely and chased after His Majesty, her fur so fluffed she looked almost as large as the black-and-white cat.

I ran for the stairs, dragging Élise behind me. Nobody paid us any mind—no doubt they assumed I was fleeing out of terror, which was certainly part of it. I couldn't do anything to help Havelock—and yet, if my theory was correct, I could save us all.

I glimpsed a flicker of uncanny emberlight from the corner of my eye, and I knew that Havelock had shed his human form and flown at the apprentices, or perhaps at Valérie. I hoped, with a viciousness that was quite unlike me, that he tore her to pieces, but I had a terrible suspicion that she had planned this attack too carefully to be caught by surprise. After all, it was clear that she knew her brother better than he knew her.

I felt an ache for him. I didn't know if Valérie had once

loved Havelock as a sister should and the Rivenwood had destroyed that love, or if she had always been this way at her core and he simply hadn't wanted to see it—nor did I know which was worse.

Élise was shouting something, which I ignored. When at last we regained the main floor, the entire building shuddered and we fell against the wall—one of the enchantments had shaken the place to its foundations.

"Where are you going?" Élise shrieked as I dashed towards the oven. She planted her feet and tried to wrench me in the direction of the door and the relative safety of the street beyond. We tussled briefly, as if we were children again, but I had usually won our tussles, perhaps due to my broader shoulders, and managed to yank her off-balance.

"Agnes, what—"

"The oven!" I yelled, unable to be more articulate. I didn't particularly want to bring Élise with me into this new peril, and yet leaving her behind felt equally dangerous.

"Have you lost your mind!" Élise yelled back, but I dragged her up and over the lip of the stone ledge nonetheless, and never was there greater evidence of her trust in me than the fact that she let me.

"Vortigern's Artefact is in the oven," I finally managed. "It's directly above where Valérie was standing—she thought the compass was directing her to one of the lower floors, but it can't be, Élise—I've catalogued all the Artefacts down there."

I narrowed my eyes, searching. The oven was only high enough to stand in if I hunched over, and full of shadow. To my delight, one of the spiders had fallen into Élise's hair, and it retained some of its illumination, though this seemed to be fading now that it had left the basement. I plucked it from her head—Élise screamed, batting at her hair—and held it aloft, cupped between my hands.

There! Against the south wall of the oven, I could just make out the imprint of Banshee's body where she was wont to curl up in the ashes. Banshee, who was drawn to danger and loved the smell of magic, had claimed this, of all places, as her personal nest.

I couldn't say it was my deductive skill that had enabled me to work it out, and it certainly wasn't my knowledge of magic. No, it was Banshee. She'd led me to it—her quirks and habits, which I knew as well as my own, as I did those of all my cats.

I babbled all this to Élise, who was still yanking at her hair and moaning about spiders—neither of us was truly listening to the other.

"Havelock must have tried to burn it," I said, setting the poor spider down—it staggered off as if drunk—so that I could feel along the edge of the oven, turning my hands black from the soot almost instantly. "If Vortigern enchanted it to make it appear useless—if her magic was greater than his—"

I broke off—my hand had snagged on something. I gave a cry of triumph as I pulled the book free.

It was a small thing, perhaps half the size of an ordinary book, clearly an antiquity but too well-preserved, at first glance, to be as old as any Artefact of Vortigern's. The cover was badly singed but the rest was mostly intact. I flipped through it, but the pages were empty. No *Property of the great magician Alice Vortigern* written on the inside cover, nor any diary entries recounting eventful days of strolling through the Rivenwood or crafting any number of appallingly dangerous spells.

"The pastry," I said wonderingly as another piece slid into place. "Havelock thought it was because of a Renaissance

Artefact, but it was *this* all along. The magic has leaked into the oven, and every night it turns back time to when the baker was here. It's ridiculous that it should do so every midnight, but old magic often behaves strangely, Havelock said. The rules warp. Then he *is* stealing Claude's wares, just as Claude complained about—he's doing it from the future!"

I tried to imagine how it might have happened. Had Havelock been thinking about Claude while he sat by the fire with the book in his hands? Was that how the spell worked? One had to think about the moment in time they wanted to return to?

I didn't have to wonder which moment in time I should return to. I already knew, because Havelock had told me.

I spoke the incantation Havelock had taught me for releasing magic from its vessel, thinking hard about the date. Was that how it was supposed to work? When nothing happened, I spoke the date out loud.

Nothing.

"Agnes," Élise said, tugging on my arm. "Just leave it—it was a good theory, but the spell probably doesn't work anymore. It can bring us pastry, but that's it. Let's gather the cats and get as far away from here as possible."

Despair overwhelmed me. I needed to save Havelock, as well as the cats—I needed to save *all* of us. I had thought for one glorious moment that I'd found the solution, and yet here I was, crouched ridiculously in an oven, covered in ash, all my courage and determination just an impotent thing inside me, of no use to anyone.

And yet, wasn't I used to the feeling by now? How many times had I told myself that I could make things better, only to have the world remind me how small I was, a leaf in a vast river whose currents were governed by forces I could barely understand? Perhaps magicians like Havelock or Valérie could shape those currents, but I could not. I could barely even keep the shelter going before Havelock came along, barely protect the cats in my care from meeting a variety of unhappy ends. And every year the cycle began again: more cats, more suffering, and me flailing about with my checklists, trying to rescue them all, not realizing that I was being drowned by the current we were all caught in.

Tears trickled down my cheeks, and I let Élise pull me out of the oven and into the shop, where I realized that the world had fallen silent.

CHAPTER 32

I knew as soon as I staggered out of the baker's oven that the spell had worked. The cats in their cages and the filing cabinets were gone, replaced by a long counter topped with glass display cases.

Despite everything, I found myself briefly spellbound by the craftsmanship of the baking itself. About half the cases were empty—I assumed to be filled by the labours of the morning. But those that were stocked held cakes and pâtisserie of all shapes and colours, from delicate custard tarts to cakes piled with fruit and bonbons to madeleines with bright strawberry icing. Small wonder Havelock had been upset by Claude's departure!

The baker had been active before bedding down—several pies were cooling on the counter closest to me, each with latticework as intricate as weaving. I hovered a shaking hand above one—rhubarb, I thought—and felt the steam warm my palm. There were lemon éclairs, like the ones Havelock and I had stolen from the future, and I shivered. The oven was half blocked by a proofing cabinet, open shelves that held a dozen or so mounds of dough rising in their pans.

I wasn't surprised that the baker had continued his work,

though the world was ending; I knew others who had done the same, opening their shops or maintaining social engagements through the storms and the darkness, either refusing to believe that the world wouldn't be saved, or because it was simply how they wished to spend their last days. The bakery smelled of fresh bread and roasted apples in a way that was painfully familiar, because an echo of it remained in my time, preserved by magic.

A tremor rumbled deep beneath the earth. I went to the window and found the view an almost incomprehensible contrast to the homey atmosphere of the bakery. The elements were in chaos—a storm pelted the cobblestones with pebble-sized raindrops, forming deep puddles, but even as I watched, the rain pittered to a stop and strands of fog drifted down the street.

The most unnerving thing, though, was the darkness. Not only had Havelock's enchantment made the sun wink out like a snuffed flame, but every electric light had flickered and died. Candles had been the only option, and I saw a few gleaming now from behind the windows. The result was a sky full of more stars than I had ever seen before or since, as well as dancing ribbons of blue and green, though Montréal was too far south for the aurora in ordinary times. It would have been beautiful if it hadn't been so disturbing.

I had known Havelock had done this, and yet knowing was different from witnessing it again, and being forced to connect the two: the Havelock I knew and *this*. How could one person, magician or not, have so much power?

"It's so quiet," Élise murmured. "I'd forgotten that."

I nodded. The apocalypse had been peaceful, less like an ending and more like the world was falling asleep. After the first day, at any rate. The first day had been filled with the sort of noise and panic one would expect—people fleeing the city, clambering into cars and carriages and trying to get as far away as they could, before they realized that nowhere was far enough, that this darkest of magics had enveloped the entire world.

"Have we really—" I felt ridiculous saying it, because the evidence was there in front of me, and yet the larger part of me still refused to believe it. It was partly that there had been no shift, nothing to mark the change. Time had run backwards in an invisible arc, as unseen as its passage always was in the other direction. *I* felt strange, though, as if I were trapped in a dream—voices swirled around me, echoes too distant to be made out, and the light flickered in a way that reminded me of sunlight reflecting on the windows of a fast-moving train. Yet as the moments passed, these sensations faded, and I felt no different than I did in my own time.

"Are you all right?" I asked Élise.

She was rubbing her temples. "Dizzy," she said. "It's fading, though. Why have you brought us *here*?"

"To steal a lantern," I said. "Vortigern's lantern—Havelock said it can pull enchantments into itself. It's powerful enough that he was going to use it to stop the world from ending, so it should be able to make short work of Valérie and her apprentices, if we can only get it to him."

Élise's face was pale, her eyes a little glazed, but still it was only a second or two before she nodded and said, "Good. That sounds promising. But I still don't understand—why this moment?"

"Because I think this is when I stole the lantern," I said, and I told Élise what Havelock had told me about the stranger who had taken the lantern from him, forcing him to travel to the Fourth Fathom of the Rivenwood and invent a new spell to stop the end of the world, sacrificing a piece of himself in the process, perhaps the largest part.

"And you think that person was you?" Élise said dubiously.

"I'm certain of it," I said, though I struggled to explain why. Being here, in this time, felt like turning myself into a ghost, the sort who retraced the same lonely path night after night, floorboards creaking under her insubstantial weight. My feet wanted to pull me into the street and to Havelock. Yet how did I put any of that into words? It didn't even make sense to me.

"Why not go back to when Vortigern made the thing, and take it from *her*?" Élise said. "It seems safer than trying to wrestle it away from Havelock—pretty much anything does. Hell, Agnes, why don't we just stop Valérie from taking His Majesty? That goddamn cat is the reason she was able to get in."

"We can't change the past," I said. "At least, Havelock didn't think we could. Either that or we *can*, but the world will come apart."

Élise pressed her hands to her eyes and moaned. "*Coudonc*, how did I get mixed up in all this? We're not magicians, Agnes! Maybe *they* can make sense of travelling to other worlds and fiddling with time like the hands of a clock, but this whole business gives me a raging headache."

We argued about it for a while longer before I finally said, "You're thinking about it too much. This *feels* right, Élise. I feel as if I've been here before."

She threw her hands up. "Of course you've been here before! You're here right now, probably back at your apartment on Rue Sainte-Roseline with Robin."

Neither of us spoke for a moment after that. I saw the old shelter in my mind's eye, before it had been damaged by magicians, the fire flickering in the hearth and His Majesty lounging on his favourite chair. Robin sitting across from him with the newspaper, occasionally reading aloud to the cat and asking his opinion—we'd always chuckled at how His Majesty would stare at Robin as if enraptured.

Élise came to my side and pulled me into her arms. "I'm sorry," she said. "I shouldn't have—"

"It's all right," I said, even though it wasn't. The pull towards Robin felt like starvation, all-consuming. I hadn't thought about this part when I made my decision to return to this moment. If I had, I would have realized that I wasn't strong enough. I'd lost Robin more than two years ago, but here, in this time, I still had another year to spend at his side, and I would have sacrificed ten lifetimes to live it over again.

The only way to stop myself from falling apart was to focus on Havelock and the cats, back at the shelter three years from now. They needed me. Banshee and Thoreau and the others *needed* me. So did Havelock, who needed no one, or pretended to. Valérie had come to kill him, and with his Artefacts in her possession, how could she fail?

"You want to rescue him," Élise said. She'd been eyeing me with knitted brows as I thought. "Don't you?"

"I want to rescue them all," I said, half in exasperation— partly at myself, I think.

She shook her head. "I *knew* it. I knew you saw him as one of your cats."

She was scowling but there was amusement in her gaze, and I couldn't hold back a laugh. "You're going to say he doesn't deserve it."

She gave a resigned shrug. "Well, *they* don't either, really. Is there anything more contrary and self-centred than a cat? Yet I'd risk my life for them." She gestured at the floor. No, not the floor—the basement. "Is he down there now, do you think?"

The question made me feel like even more of a ghost than I already did. I pictured Havelock, three years younger and brokenhearted from Valérie's betrayal, hunched over his worktable only a few yards from where I stood.

"I don't know," I said. "Even if he is, though, this isn't where he lost the lantern, so we can't go down there."

Élise made another inarticulate noise and rubbed the bridge of her nose.

I released the breath trapped in my chest and said, "Trust me, Élise. Please."

She looked up, glaring at me. "All right. But if this doesn't work, we're going back in time to when you agreed to move into his goddamn shop, and I'm going to beat you over the head with one of your file folders."

I gave a shaky laugh, and then we both froze. We'd been keeping our voices down, to avoid waking the baker sleeping upstairs in what was *my* room but also wasn't yet. But now the floorboards were creaking overhead in a pattern that I recognized: someone had walked to the window, as if to identify the source of a disturbance, and was now moving down the hallway towards the stairs.

I seized Élise's hand and we fled into the street.

CHAPTER 33

To step into that dark city was to enter another world. Without human-made light, the stone buildings rising to either side looked like walls of trees, watchful and quiet. It didn't help that the wind carried with it the charcoal tang of magic. A man hurried past on the opposite side of the street, bundled into his cloak. Some people had moved through the city like that in those dark days, with a furtive haste, trying to evade the weather. Others had thrown parties. Some musicians had set up on street corners. A few businesses had been looted, but only a few; overall, the city's reaction to the end of the world had been as varied as the people living in it. I had been too worried about the cats to leave the shelter, so I'd huddled indoors, watching the storms come and go through the window.

Which was a relief—I didn't like to think what would happen if I saw myself in the street.

"Where are we going?" Élise said, when at last we paused for breath beneath the awning of a library. The city's libraries had remained open during the apocalypse, and I could see several people inside, clustered around a table where a single candlestick was burning.

"Mount Royal," I said.

"Yes, but *where*?" Élise pressed. "The park is too large—we need specifics. And *when* did Havelock lose the lantern?"

"I'm not certain of that either," I admitted. "Havelock told me it happened on the second night. It's only about an hour till midnight"—we had just come into view of the clock tower—"so we should go to the park and wait, I guess."

"You *guess*," Élise repeated in a despairing sort of voice. "Please tell me that you know how to get us back to our time after all this is over."

"Of course," I said, trying to project confidence. "The enchantment leaked into the oven, so we will simply return to the oven and speak the incantation again."

"I wish you were a more convincing liar," Élise said with a groan. "I would very much like to believe that you know what you're doing right now."

We hurried on. On the next block, I noticed a small shape moving inside an overturned garbage can. As it heard our footsteps, it limped out, mewling.

I was moving before I was even conscious of it. The black cat was so scrawny that her age was difficult to guess—six months, perhaps? One of her front legs was shorter than the other three, which made her walk with a curious shuffle, her back end trying to get ahead of her slower front half.

"Agnes!" Élise cried. "Are you mad? Just leave her."

But I had already scooped the kitten up and tucked her into my coat. "She's not heavy," I said, as if this were the primary concern.

"What were you just saying?" Élise said in a scolding voice. "About changing the past? That it would throw the world into chaos?"

"I can't leave her," I said. Given her deformity, this creature was even more defenseless than most. I added a little desperately, "Perhaps cats are an exception to all this."

"Perhaps," Élise said. "If any beast were an exception to the laws of space or time, it would be cats. Well, I should have known you'd find someone to rescue, even at the end of the world."

I excavated from my pocket a few bits of dried meat, which I always carry with me, and the cat devoured them with gusto. She seemed content to nestle into the warmth of my inner coat pocket, alternating between licking my neck and sticking her head out occasionally to gawp at the ominous scenery with interest. Cats are rarely troubled by the things humans fret over, which apparently included the apocalypse, and I found myself comforted by her insouciance.

We passed through the university grounds and came to a corner where a dense row of hedges and maples provided a shield against the tempestuous weather. Several vendors had set up food stands painted in gaudy colours. Here there was the most activity I'd seen—at least a dozen people milled about or huddled under umbrellas on the benches, and on the whole the place had a defiant, festive atmosphere. The crêperie was advertising a twenty-five percent "end of the world" discount.

Élise insisted that we stop, despite my objections, arguing that she could not be expected to save the world when she was fainting from hunger.

"We're not saving the world," I said. "Havelock is—mostly we're just getting in his way."

But as usual, Élise won the argument, and we purchased a paper bag of chocolatines from a blithe, red-faced woman before hurrying on. The towering cross at the top of the mountain was stark against the glittering sky, until abruptly it was shrouded in cloud. It began pouring when at last we reached the stairs that would take us to the summit.

"This is ridiculous," Élise said as we huffed and puffed our way up. "How are we supposed to find Havelock, particularly in the dark?"

I didn't reply. My instincts had brought us to this time, but it was harder to trust them now. The trees lining the stairs were wet with rain, and as they closed around us, the world grew so dark that I could hardly see where I was going. Black birds flitted through the trees, and I started every time I heard them rustling. They couldn't be the same birds I'd glimpsed in the Rivenwood—could they? Why did they give me the same impression of something uncanny?

As we neared the top of the stairs, the rain stopped, chased away by a blast of icy wind that brought the stars out again. The stairs turned into a path that rambled up the final slope of Mount Royal, which would bring us to the observation terrace. I pulled Élise to a stop.

"Here," I said, surprised I hadn't thought of it before.

"What?" Élise huffed.

"Well, Havelock will come this way, won't he?"

Élise bent over, holding her side and breathing hard. We visited the park from time to time, but we rarely scaled the stairs so fast. "So what do we do? Talk to him? You'll have to take the lead—I never learned the knack for it."

"No," I said. "He can't recognize us—we'll keep our hoods drawn. I'm not going to be responsible for time coming apart."

Élise groaned again. "These magicians! Do they ever think to themselves that perhaps they have *too* much power? That nobody should be able to make an enchantment that unravels time or ends the world?"

"I doubt it," I said. "People with too much power aren't usually the ones harmed by their mistakes, are they?"

"So how do we get the lantern? We hide behind a tree and—trip him?"

We gazed at each other glumly. There was nothing more to be said—it was a ridiculous plan, of course, and we could only wait for it to unfold. I could see the city through a window in the trees. Its unnatural darkness made its cobbled streets and church spires, as familiar as my own name, look like the hills and valleys of an otherworldly landscape.

I ate one of the chocolatines, which only added to my sense of the ridiculous. Somehow it did not seem appropriate for a quest of this magnitude—we had travelled through time itself to accost the world's greatest living magician, and here we stood, huddled awkwardly in the park, eating pastry. It felt amateurish, a sure portent of failure, but what did I know? Perhaps magicians did this sort of thing all the time.

Élise, of course, seemed perfectly unperturbed by such reflections, rifling noisily through the bag to tear pieces off the chocolatines and licking her fingers clean. A part of me wanted to throttle her; the larger part wanted to throw my arms around her and sob with relief that she was there. I was remembering to be afraid again. We were about to confront the man who had caused all this, and even if that man was Havelock, we weren't friends here. To him I would be a thief, and an enemy.

An hour passed, and still Havelock did not appear. The black kitten kept us somewhat occupied as she awoke from her slumber. She demanded to be put down; then, after giving her surroundings a desultory sniff, to be picked up again. These deliberations she repeated two minutes later.

"What if we've missed him?" I fretted.

"Then we'll know we were supposed to miss him," Élise replied, irritatingly logical. "As this has all happened already, hasn't it?"

I couldn't be so calm about it—though I could tell that Élise wasn't as calm as she seemed, but was making herself pretend, for my sake. Thunder boomed and lightning flickered, before the clouds were swept away to reveal the dazzling sky with its overwhelming palette of colour.

"Aren't you glad we ate?" Élise said.

I gave the ghost of a laugh. I was. My stomach was in knots, but the sugar had blessed me with a nervy wakefulness, and I felt as ready as I could be to confront Havelock.

Suddenly, Élise gripped my arm. Far below us, in the street that curved around the base of the mountain, a light had bloomed. It shot down the street and went out.

"What was that?" Élise said.

Almost as soon as she spoke the words, there came an echoing crash that shook the ground. It sounded as if one of the lantern-posts had been toppled onto the cobblestones. This was followed by another, and another, and then a second light flared and went out.

"Someone's coming," Élise said, and dragged me off the path and into the forest.

A heartbeat later, a man came charging up the path. I knew he was a magician instantly, not only because a small globe of light darted ahead of him, illuminating his path, but because he was moving too quickly. It was as if he'd placed an enchantment on his shoes that gave a bounce to his stride, making the steep path easy going.

It wasn't Havelock—the man's frame was too bulky, and even with the enchantment I could tell he didn't move like Havelock, who had an eerie grace. The man didn't notice us hiding among the trees, and within seconds he and his light were gone.

"Who do you think he was running away from?" Élise murmured.

"*Was* he running away?" I said. The man's furtiveness had put me in mind of someone preparing an ambush. "Havelock said he was hunted by other magicians after Valérie cast his spell. They thought if they killed him, the spell would break."

Élise cursed under her breath. "What are we getting in the middle of?"

We moved deeper into the trees. The black kitten, which I'd tucked into my sweater, leaving only her head showing, gave a discontented mewl. It was an uncomfortable position—the earth was damp from the rain and roots poked at my ankles. But we didn't have to wait long this time.

Something was brewing in the trees below us. A wind, fierce and cold and smelling of magic, rose unnaturally from the ground, dashing dead leaves in our faces. An orb of light was careening up the path, and behind it ran a figure, moving as swiftly as the wind.

It was Havelock.

I recognized him from the way he moved more than anything else. He was running *with* the wind; he must have summoned it and it was sweeping him along. He travelled at a much quicker pace than the other magician, but it came at a cost: the stairs switched back and forth, and the wind didn't always give him time to correct his course. A branch slapped him in the face and he gave a curse, and then, just below us, he tried to veer left to avoid a tree, but ran right into it.

The wind carried on up the mountain without him, sweeping the orb of light along with it like a will-o'-the-wisp. Havelock gave a groan. In the darkness, he looked like a pile of shadows against the tree, his tangle of dark hair only dimly visible. I moved towards him—this was my chance. If I could grab the lantern from him before he recovered—

The tree he had collided with gave a horrible *crack* and began to plunge towards him.

I shrieked. The tree had been wrenched up by the roots, and soil sprayed across my face. It was a moment before I could see anything else, but once I'd finally wiped the grit from my eyes, I saw that Havelock had somehow evaded the tree, which had fallen over the path, and was duelling two magicians.

The first, a woman with a long black braid, had a bow pointed at him, an arrow nocked. It must have been an Artefact, and one of the more straightforward ones I'd encountered, for when she loosed the arrow, it sailed directly towards Havelock's heart, adjusting course as he moved. Havelock had his cloak half-off and held in front of him like a shield, which it seemed to be. The arrow struck the fabric and bounced off it like stone.

The second magician, a tall, elderly man, had a globe of fire cupped in his hand; he tore pieces off and flung them in Havelock's direction. One hit his cloak and caught at the hem, forcing Havelock to wrench it off and stamp the fire out. Clearly he hadn't thought to make it fireproof.

Havelock tugged a pendant from beneath his shirt and spoke an incantation. The woman with the bow and arrow screamed as the earth beneath her feet exploded, sending her sailing into the forest darkness. Undaunted, the other magician threw another handful of fire at Havelock, forcing him to dive to one side.

"Give up, Witch King," the elderly man spat in such a

mocking tone that I guessed they'd known each other, before. "We'll keep coming until you're dead, or until you end this darkness you've wrought upon the world."

"Not that anyone bothered to ask, but that's what I'm *trying* to do." Havelock seemed to be rummaging in his pockets, and I caught a flash of light as several coins tumbled free. He made a frustrated sound and wrenched one of the rings off his hand, letting loose another enchantment.

The other man's flame went out and he began making a peculiar sound, as if he were trying to scream but had lost his voice. When the breeze touched him, I realized that he'd become two-dimensional, or near to it. In width he was perhaps the thickness of a crêpe. The breeze lifted him off his feet, still making that tiny screaming sound, and sent him drifting through the forest in an almost peaceful way. He ended up wrapped around the trunk of a tree like a loose flyer.

Havelock looked displeased by the effects of his enchantment, which to my eyes had been horrifically effective. "Shoddy, second-order knickknack," he said, hurling the ring into the forest. I realized that he must be running out of defensive spells. I didn't know how many enchantments a magician could carry on their person, but if Havelock had been battling magicians all night, no doubt he'd already cast the more useful ones in his possession and was now forced to make do with whatever was left. I wondered what the original purpose of the spell had been, or if it was some half-baked experiment of his.

Élise was suddenly at my side, shaking me, and I turned to see the magician who had run past us earlier hurtling down the mountain path like a boulder. He was astride a horse that looked as if it had been summoned from the underworld, huge and misshapen, with fire-bright eyes.

"Havelock, behind you!" I shouted.

Havelock whipped around. The other magician was bearing down on him impossibly fast. Too fast for evasion. Havelock began to shout an incantation, and it wasn't clear if he'd finished before the horse knocked him down, trampling him underfoot.

"Havelock!" I cried.

Élise was screaming, too. Havelock might have been a ragdoll beneath the horse's bulk, and the snow where he had fallen was ominously dark in a way that made me grateful there was so little light to see by. The thunder of hooves mingled with the snap of bone was a sound I doubted I would ever forget.

I dashed out from the tree cover, heading for Havelock's mangled form, a sob in my throat. But when I reached his side, the bloodied face staring sightlessly up at the sky wasn't Havelock's.

It was the other magician.

"Agnes!" Élise was gesticulating. Havelock had turned the horse around, so that its head was facing us. Somehow, he'd switched places with its rider and taken control of his spell. The horse didn't seem to appreciate the swap, however, and shied first one way and then the other. It turned its head, teeth gnashing.

"Leave off, you brainless monster," Havelock said, sounding winded as he tried to keep his hold on the reins, and then he wrenched a button from his cloak, sputtering out another spell. The hellish horse went still with a sort of *urk* and then, abruptly, it was gone. In its place was an enormous box covered in gaudy wrapping paper and tied with a green bow.

For a moment, I could only stand there, blinking. The black kitten, which through all this had stayed in my sweater, gave a long, heartfelt hiss. The horse was clearly still inside the parcel, for I could hear it gnashing its teeth, and it seemed to be banging its head against the walls, but this only had the effect of making the box shuffle forward a few inches.

Unfortunately, my hesitation cost me dearly. I stood in full view on the path, and so when Havelock leapt off the box and came towards me, there was no possibility of hiding myself. Nor was there any possibility of convincing him that I was a friend, not yet another magician who had come with the others to end him.

He didn't look like Havelock at all. He looked like a nightmare—or, rather, he looked like the all-powerful Witch King of his reputation. His feet didn't stir the forest leaves as he came forward, as if he were entirely spectral. His hair was slightly longer than it would be in three years, but just as dishevelled, giving him the look of some wild creature. I felt as if I were meeting him for the first time—which, I realized with a shudder, I was.

He held up a coin, speaking an enchantment before I was fully conscious of what was happening, but suddenly Élise was there, shoving me back. I *felt* the spell hit her, a sort of dull *whump* like a bird hitting a window.

"Élise!" I screamed as she sagged to the ground. She'd shoved me so hard I had no hope of catching her; I staggered backwards, arms windmilling. Havelock stepped over Élise and advanced on me. Likely he would have already enchanted me, but he seemed unable to locate a useful spell, and was sifting through the inner pockets of his cloak.

I'm not proud of what I did next. But I had to keep Havelock from enchanting me, though I had no power over him, no spells I could throw his way.

So, I threw the cat.

The black kitten gave a yowl as I launched her at Havelock. He began to yowl, too, flailing his arms as the cat's claws made contact with his face, before his shouts became a strangled sort of sneezing fit. He tripped over a root and landed hard on his back.

I was at Élise's side in an instant. To my immense relief, she was still breathing, and her eyelids flickered. "Élise," I said, shaking her. "Élise!"

"So tired," she mumbled. "Agnes, run . . . That bastard . . ."

The rest was half-intelligible cursing. Élise tried to push herself up, but she only fell back, head lolling. Had Havelock placed a sleep spell on her, as he'd once threatened to do to me?

Behind me, Havelock let out a groan. He'd shoved himself up on one hand and had the other pressed to his cheek, which seemed to be bleeding. I couldn't see where the cat had gone.

"Havelock, it's me," I pleaded. It was nonsensical; Havelock didn't know me yet. But I couldn't stop myself.

He looked at me—we were only a few feet from each other. A flicker of recognition passed over his face, and he stilled. He said, very quietly, "Vortigern?"

I stared at him. He stared back at me.

Then I burst out laughing.

I laughed so long my throat ached and I began to cough. When I finally caught my breath, Havelock was glaring at me. He didn't look otherworldly anymore—he looked like his familiar, awkward self.

"I don't see why that's a ridiculous question," he said, and even in the dark, I could see his face was red. "You're cloaked in Vortigern's magic. Not every magician could sense it, but *I* can. And she was said to be half mad, which would explain why you were wandering around in the woods with a cat down your sweater."

"I'm Agnes," I said. "Sorry to disappoint you."

"Agnes," he repeated doubtfully. "Not Alice?"

I could see he still thought I could be the great Vortigern, and it threatened to send me over the edge again. I wondered why he couldn't tell that I wasn't a magician—but then, I realized, given the darkness, it was no longer obvious that *he* was, now that he wasn't being swept along by impossible winds or hurling spells at people. I'd been able to defeat him, even if it *had* been with a cat rather than an enchantment, which no other living magician should have been capable of, and if Vortigern's magic still clung to me from the time-travel spell, it wasn't an illogical conclusion for him to draw, I supposed.

I suppressed another half-hysterical snort.

Havelock was examining my face as if trying to read an antiquated book. "I *do* know you, don't I? Have we met before?"

A shiver ran through me. Did time not work the same way for magicians as it did for humans? Did Havelock possess some gift of foresight beyond my ability to comprehend? Or was it the spell I'd used, Vortigern's Artefact, that had made this moment echo through time like a carillon?

And then, fast on the heels of that thought: *Havelock* knew *me. Not now, in this moment—three years from now.*

I saw our first meeting unfold again before me—what I had thought was our first meeting, back in the shelter on Rue des Hirondelles. Valérie's attack, which had only happened because I was there; Havelock in his nightclothes, casting her out. How he'd come towards me, the strange look on his face.

Agnes, he'd said. *You're here.*

I hadn't understood, at the time, the look of recognition in his eyes. He'd known me, because he'd met me before—here, on the second night of the world's ending.

And then, I supposed, he'd spent the next three years wondering if he'd met the great Alice Vortigern. How disappointed he must have been when we met again on Rue des Hirondelles, to find I was not the greatest magician who ever lived, but the exceptionally ordinary proprietress of a cat shelter.

"Yes, you know me," I told him. How much could I say, I wondered, without opening some vast fissure in time? "Though it seems impossible that you would remember. That shouldn't be how memory works."

"This is precisely what I was hoping for," he said. "A mysterious stranger to burden me with riddles. As if I don't have enough to do tonight." His voice had an undercurrent of laughter that bordered on unhinged and he looked wearier than I'd ever seen him, the hollows under his eyes even more heavily shadowed than usual. He seemed relieved to rest there on the forest floor, dabbing at the scratch on his face.

"I don't see that you have any right to complain about *that*, given that you talk in riddles fully half the time," I said.

"And you would know, would you?" Havelock said. "Very well, you ridiculous person. What is it you want?"

"The lantern," I said. "You must give it to me, Havelock. If you don't, a great many people will die."

I was thinking of the cats when I said this—the cats and Havelock, *my* Havelock. Perhaps a loose definition of *people*, but I will make no apologies for that. And who knew how many other lives would be at risk if Valérie wasn't stopped?

"I can't *give* it to you," Havelock said, with another disbelieving laugh. "Whatever your errand is, it can't possibly be more important than mine. Vortigern's lantern can—"

I shook my head. "It won't work. You will only waste the enchantment in the lantern. You can stop the world from ending, but you must travel to the Fourth Fathom of the Rivenwood, and you must gather enough magic for a twelve-layer spell of partitioning."

He stared at me in complete befuddlement. In fact, I shared some of his surprise; I hadn't realized I had ever listened to him closely when he went on and on about magic.

"You aren't a person at all, are you," he said. "Just an enigma wearing a human face. I'll admit, partitioning magic is an interesting idea, but there's no such thing as a twelve-layer partition spell. No one's ever managed more than nine."

"You will," I told him. "You'll invent one. You *can*, Havelock. You've done *this*, haven't you?" I made an incoherent gesture—at the unnatural dark of the city below us, the sky full of tempests, the crumbling edifice of the world.

He stood there, gazing at me in a way that made him look very young. He was also trembling lightly, as if he'd not slept or eaten in days. Had Havelock been alone during all this?

Yes, of course he had. Havelock had no friends among magicians, who feared and distrusted him—apart from Yannick, whom he hadn't met yet. He had only ever had his twin sister.

He reached into an inner pocket of his cloak and withdrew a small object that glowed only faintly. The lantern was a beautiful thing, though smaller than I'd expected, about the height of my hand. It was made of silver and stained glass, and though its light was like fire, I saw no candle within it.

"Very well, Mme. Pythia," he said, handing it to me. "I've not the slightest idea why I'm so certain I can trust you."

This was belied by the almost hopeful way he was gazing at me, and I realized he was giving me the lantern because he still thought I might be Vortigern. No doubt my telling him about the twelve-layer spell had only encouraged him in this. The deception made me prickle with guilt—but, I reasoned, surely he would forgive me if I used the lantern to save his life.

"I have a trustworthy face," I said. "Now, undo whatever it is you have done to Élise."

Élise gave a grunt. She was still slumped upon the cobblestones, supporting the weight of her upper body with her hands. "Undo," she slurred, "it. Bastard. What my sister sees . . ." The rest was lost in an incoherent mumble.

Havelock frowned. "I'm afraid I can't. It's a sleep enchantment, and I never bothered to work out a counterspell. It will wear off in a few hours."

"A few hours!" I exclaimed. Élise gave an outraged grunt.

"It's remarkable that she's conscious at all," Havelock said, examining Élise with interest.

"My sister is quite single-minded," I said. Then, before I could question the wisdom of it, I threw my arms around him, pulling him close enough to feel the brush of his hair against my cheek, and smell the magic on his rain-dampened skin. He still felt like Havelock, still seemed more magic than flesh and blood, but there was more substance to him than there would be in three years. The thought made me sad.

Havelock had gone stiff. He lifted his arms as if to embrace me, then lowered them, then lifted them again and let them rest awkwardly at my waist.

"Will you be all right?" I said when I drew away.

He gave a quiet laugh. "That remains to be seen."

He helped me to my feet, then lifted a hand. A seam opened in the world, through which I saw trees waving, smelled the overrich scent of unfamiliar flowers. He turned back to me, a frown between his eyes.

"You shouldn't be here when I return," he said at last. "I don't know what state I'll be in, given how deep I must go."

I nodded, my heart thundering in my throat. I didn't want him to leave. "Havelock," I said, but stopped myself there—it would only unsettle him further. "We'll see each other again," I finished.

He gave me one last frown. Then he stepped through the door and was gone.

CHAPTER 34

I had thought that retrieving the lantern from Havelock would be the most difficult part of our ridiculous quest. And yet the true test turned out to be a much more practical challenge: that of hauling my sister from one end of the city to the other.

"I'm," Élise slurred. "Lighter. Than you."

"You keep saying that," I said, leaning against a lamppost as I tried to catch my breath. Élise had one arm slung around my shoulder, and though she was capable of moving her feet, I needed to support her to keep her upright.

"It's beside the point who's lighter," I added. "Havelock hit *you* with the sleep spell, not me. Anyway, do you hear me complaining?"

"I hear," she said. "You. Thinking it. And you're. Grunting. Like. A bear."

We had to stop again so that I could lean against a building, laughing until I couldn't breathe. Élise was laughing too, which in her present somnambulatory state came out wheezier with a great deal of snorting mixed in, which only made us laugh harder. This was the third time we'd had to pause for this reason—likely a product of stress, or perhaps mild hysteria given the events of the evening. Either way, it was like being children again, unable to stop ourselves from giggling at the most inappropriate times. Sometimes curtains would twitch and people would gaze out at us from their windows, frowning and perplexed, but some laughed at the picture we presented.

Fortunately, the black kitten hadn't needed much encouragement to follow us down from the mountain. I would have preferred to carry her, given her disability, but I couldn't manage both her and Élise. A remarkably obliging cat, she trotted along at our heels like a dog, pausing only to sniff at the occasional trash can before limping to catch up.

"Telling you," Élise said. "I'm. Lighter."

"Oh, why don't we take turns, then?" I said. "You can carry me for a bit. Let's test who's been eating the most chocolatines."

Élise gave an especially noisy snort, and we were lost again.

At last we came to Rue de Violette, which was only a block from the shelter—or, in its current iteration, bakery.

"The magic must be attached to the oven after it leaked out of the book," I said. I was repeating myself, seeking reassurance from my own words. "We can go back there, and I'll say the enchantment again, and we'll return to our time."

Élise's disbelieving grunt did not require clarification. It seemed a plausible enough theory, but what did I know? I didn't want to think about the very real possibility that we would be trapped here, potentially unravelling our own histories in the process.

I settled Élise on a bench. It had begun to snow again, but there was no help for that. "I'll go make sure the baker went back to bed," I said, setting the lantern beside her. "Then I'll return for you. Wait here."

Élise said something that sounded like *What else do you expect me to do*, but that was a guess. It seemed more difficult for her to fight Havelock's enchantment when she wasn't standing. I bunched up my scarf and put it beneath her head, and she began to snore lightly. I motioned to the cat, and she hopped onto Élise's chest and burrowed beneath her coat, until all that was visible was a small wriggling lump and a tuft of tail.

I made my way to the bakery, and was relieved to find that the lights were off. Unfortunately, the baker had locked the door we'd left open, which meant we'd have to break in—but how?

I was just rounding the corner to return to Élise, full of anxious thoughts, when I heard a familiar voice. "Agnes!"

My instinctive reaction was relief. It was a voice I associated with safety—the voice of someone who would make all of this easier, because he made everything easier. Then I felt as if I had been turned to stone.

Robin was strolling towards me, hands shoved in his pockets and an umbrella tucked under his arm. He looked a little dishevelled by the weather, but otherwise exactly as I remembered him, only more handsome. He could not have always been this handsome, and I didn't remember his smile being so bright. If it had been, surely I would have appreciated it more.

"What are you doing out here?" he said, his smile growing as he approached me. I was overwhelmed by his presence—it was too much, and for a moment I wanted to run. I knew I could not survive this.

Then he leaned forward and kissed me, and the world righted itself. Some fundamental pattern had been askew, but now it had been corrected. I was no longer a ghost in this time, but myself, as if I'd stepped back into my body.

"I—I thought I'd walk out to meet you," I replied, smiling back at him. I was astonished at how easy it was to talk to him, as if we'd never stopped. "I guessed you'd take Rue des Hirondelles—it's such a pretty street. How is your aunt?"

Because of course I knew where he'd been—in *this* time, his aunt lived only a few blocks to the east; he'd gone to visit her daily after Havelock's enchantment had been unleashed upon the world. A shudder ran through me, remembering that the old woman would die only a few months from now. And with that, I was a ghost again.

"Better, I think," he said. "I brought her groceries and helped her with the washing up—it's why I'm so late."

I nodded distantly. I wasn't listening to the words at all, but the timbre of his voice.

"Something's the matter," he said, frowning as he examined me closely. A lock of hair had fallen onto his forehead. Robin had dark hair—about as dark as Havelock's, but with more red in it. His face was paler, his eyes hooded in a way that made him look attractively languid, I'd always thought, as well as slightly amused, from the permanent creases at the corners. "What is it? You don't normally come looking for me."

"I—" I shook myself, then said simply, "Nothing is normal these days. I couldn't sleep."

"Go home," he said, kissing me again. "Go to bed. I promised Thérèse I would look for those kittens she saw under the bridge—knowing her eyesight, it's equally likely they were raccoons."

"They were opossums the last time," I said. I found I couldn't stop smiling at him, even as I felt as if I were drowning, cold pressing in on me on all sides.

He nodded mock-seriously. "And as I said then, there's no reason we can't expand the charity. I quite like opossums."

"You like everything," I said. "*You* go home. I'll look for kittens." If he got home and found me in bed—where no doubt a version of me was, at this moment—he would only assume I'd changed my mind, and taken a shortcut. I couldn't remember him ever mentioning this meeting of ours by Rue des Hirondelles—but then, why would he? He would have had no need to remind me of something he assumed I'd experienced myself.

I kissed him again. I wished I could never stop kissing him. "Give Ariel my love."

"Of course," he said, seeing nothing strange about this, because he knew I hated to be away from Ariel, an elderly shelter resident who had been with us for several months before passing away, never having found a home, but having found much love with us.

"I'm sure he's curled up by the woodstove now," Robin continued, "dreaming of his mouse, not even aware we're gone."

I gave a quiet laugh. That mouse had been the only one Ariel ever caught while he lived at the shelter, his final triumph. Whenever the old cat twitched his paws in his sleep, Robin and I would joke that he was dreaming of his mouse, and when I admonished the cat for sharpening his claws on the floorboards, Robin would say he was only keeping himself in fighting form should the mouse return. The joke was as familiar as a groove worn in a stair by my own feet.

"I missed you," I said, gripping his arms with a sudden, painful desperation, because it was impossible to think of letting him go. It didn't matter if the world ended before my eyes or time came apart.

But I didn't want to frighten him. So I forced myself to smile, as if I'd meant it half in jest. "I always miss you."

He smiled and brushed a curl from my forehead. "I missed you too. Don't worry about all this, love. It's like I keep saying—the magicians will sort it out. I'll see you soon."

I nodded, caught up in his eyes—so familiar, down to the tiny line that ran between them. There was so much more I wanted to say, and yet nothing was equal to the moment itself: Robin standing before me, warm and whole and smiling. I wished I could pluck it out of time and press it between paper. I felt the familiar presence of countless unspoken things, and yet they were not a weight upon me now; I saw in his eyes that he knew them all already.

I kissed his cheek, and then—looking back, I don't know how I did it—I was pulling my hands away.

He turned, without any ceremony or sense that the moment had been of any significance, not even looking back. I did not think I was strong enough to watch him vanish around the corner, so I squeezed my eyes shut, as around me the weather shifted again, a gust of wind blowing the snow sideways, mixed now with rain.

But when I opened my eyes, he was still there, on the other side of the street. He *had* looked back, and was gazing at me with concern.

I put a smile on my face, and then I walked away, the scuff of my boots against the cobblestones the loudest sound I had ever heard.

CHAPTER 35

Even in her half-asleep state, Élise noticed something was wrong. I couldn't speak, for one thing, only shake my head when she mumbled questions at me. I was able to support her weight all the way to the bakery, and then I found a loose brick and smashed the glass in the door—I wondered why I'd been so worried about the problem before. Now I barely thought about it, even as the broken glass jabbed my arm, sending a trickle of blood down my sleeve.

Élise and I clambered into the oven—one at a time, for its cavernous entrance was half blocked by the proofing cabinet of sourdough—and I spoke the incantation again. But when I poked my head back into the bakery, there were the pies on their racks and the storm pelting the windows with hail. Worse, from the floor above came a groan followed by a thumping sound, as of a large and ungainly person rising from their bed.

"It has to work," I said frantically. The black kitten sniffed at a pile of ashes, within which was a half-disintegrated roll, and gave a worried chirp.

"Is it one way?" Élise mumbled. She was leaning against the stone wall of the oven, oblivious to the ash staining her dress.

"Havelock said *there and back*." I pressed my sooty hands into my hair, increasingly desperate. "There and back. I'm certain of it."

"Agnes, it's old," Élise said. "Maybe it—maybe the spell isn't strong enough to take us back."

"He said there and back," I murmured. Some part of me recognized the logic in Élise's words, but the larger part refused to believe that Havelock—Havelock!—could be wrong about anything related to magic. I said the incantation again, and again. Nothing changed—the hail pounded, the shop remained a bakery. I needed to return to the cats, and to Havelock, whom we had abandoned just as Valérie and her apprentices blasted him with every dark enchantment he'd ever hoarded in his damn shop.

And then a different longing hit me, the need to abandon the entire ridiculous quest and run into the street, to catch Robin and tell him—what? There was nothing I could say that would save him. But I could hold him again, and abruptly there was nothing I wanted but that.

The competing desires buffeted me like waves, threatening to drown me.

The kitten, meanwhile, was washing her paw. When she'd finished, she shook the paw and set it down gingerly, seeming to dislike the soot of the oven. She sniffed at the proofing cabinet—the sourdough had risen since we'd left, warmed by the heat retained in the brickwork—and then vanished.

I stared dumbly, shock erasing the panicked ruminations. It had looked as if the cat had stepped *into* one of the loaves, and I started forward as if to rescue her from being drowned in sourdough. But then I realized.

"It's the way home," I cried. "Élise—the spell worked, but

it's *smaller* than it was before. The way back to our time, I mean. But the kitten found it—she found a gap!"

"A gap?" Élise repeated. "Agnes, that makes even less sense than—"

I wasn't listening. "I should have known," I murmured. "She's a cat, and cats always find a gap."

I gave a laugh that was far too loud, and went on, and on—I leaned against the wall of the oven, unable to stop. Rather than being astonished by my discovery, Élise only let out a low groan and said, "Goddamn you, Havelock, this whole thing just gets madder and—"

Before she could finish, I was dragging her forward, still giggling in sharp bursts, and into the proofing cabinet. At the last second, I squeezed my eyes shut, certain I would end up on the floor of the bakery covered in sourdough, but the cabinet vanished, and Élise and I spilled out of the oven and onto the floor, Élise landing on her rear and I flat on my back.

Yet even as I stared up into the worried face of the kitten, who looked appalled by my gracelessness, as if there were nothing difficult at all about stepping through a gap in time, I thought that it still hadn't worked, and we were truly stuck in the old bakery. It seemed for a moment as if the counter were still filled with pies, the air laced with sugar, but then I blinked, and the cages were back, as were the yowls of their occupants. I was dizzy, and I saw flickering lights again, which faded as I focused on the flagstones beneath my feet and the ashy smell of magic.

I left Élise on the floor by the oven—not as unkind as it sounds; I could not bring her into danger in her current state—and sprinted towards the trapdoor with the lantern clutched in my hand. The air was filled with dust from the fallen plaster, but I could also smell smoke. Had I come back too late? I'd wished to return to the very moment I'd left, but maybe the enchantment hadn't understood.

The smoke was worse in Havelock's workshop, which meant I caught only glimpses of the chaos that had descended upon the place. Regular tremors shook the building, and flames crackled somewhere, the smell of magic and burning wood thick in the air. I could make out at least two bodies lying motionless amidst the rubble and overturned furniture, and another magician who looked, horrifically, as if she'd been entombed in an enormous spider's nest on the ceiling, but I could not identify if any were Valérie. As I paused on the landing, a magician hiding behind one of the cabinets threw a lion at me—this was more puzzling in retrospect than it was in the moment, when my only thought was getting out of the way of the thing—but fortunately the beast seemed more illusion than substance, or perhaps the magician had cast the enchantment poorly. It came racing across the floor, snarling and far too swift, but then merely scrabbled at the lowest stair before flickering in and out of existence.

Havelock had been backed up against the stairs leading to the lower floors, and somehow he'd dragged one of the cabinets in front of him, which had been sliced through diagonally as if by the talons of some enormous raptor.

"Havelock!" I cried, tears running down my face. *He's alive*, was all I could think for a moment, before I remembered I had a role to play in all this, absurdly, and could not simply cower there, waiting for it to end.

I would have liked to have thrown the lantern at him, but

I didn't trust my aim, so instead I ran up the stairs, dodging some uncanny bird that swooped at me and leaping over a hole that had been blasted in a stair. When I was parallel to where he stood, I jumped, landing gracelessly at his side.

He turned towards me, pale and verklempt, and then his eyes widened in astonishment. I tripped, coughing on the smoke, and a tremor shook the floor, sending me crashing into him—probably a good thing, for the wall behind us abruptly exploded, hit by some enchantment. I thrust the lantern into his hand.

He actually began to laugh, even as dust rained down upon us and one of the floor beams above cracked and splintered. I had to shake him to return him to his senses.

"I will never again complain of the uncanniness of your cats," he said, his voice hoarse from the smoke. "For they are only taking after their minder."

"Havelock!" I cried.

"Yes, yes." He lifted the lantern almost reverently and stood, then murmured the spell to unleash the magic. Somehow, his quiet words cut through the chaos and noise like the reverberation of a gong.

A wave erupted from the lantern. At least, that is the closest I can come to describing it. It was cold, but pleasantly so, and had the soft, spongey texture of wool. It was as dark and glimmering as the ocean under a sky of stars. It washed over the workshop and then withdrew, and as it did, it carried things away with it: the lion, wisps of flame shaped into beads of light, the outlines of the glowing spiders, though not the spiders themselves. I did not understand it all, for what I glimpsed was exceedingly strange—I also saw windows to other places, landscapes of looming mountains and coppery desert, as well as the ghostly outlines of people, dancing or talking or weeping, as if they'd been cast there by a film projector. All swept away by the enchantment like a tide retreating with a miscellany of small treasures, shells, and driftwood. And while it was strange, it was also impossibly beautiful. Havelock stood at the centre, the lantern light against his face, his hand slightly extended and his brow furrowed as he guided the magic he had unleashed.

When the wave finally receded back into the lantern, all of it fitting neatly inside the tiny dimensions, I drew in a gasping breath, but the feeling of being plunged into cold water was already fading, leaving only gooseflesh behind. Valérie lay at Havelock's feet, her eyes closed and her face turned to one side, like a sailor washed ashore after a shipwreck. She breathed but she also seemed strangely grey, as if the colour had been drawn out of her.

"There," Havelock said quietly. He added, "I'm sorry, Ri."

I didn't know what he was apologizing for, because I did not fully comprehend what the spell had done. All I knew was that the fighting had stopped and Valérie was defeated. Just as important, the place no longer seemed to be on fire. The shop gave a groan, followed by a deafening grinding noise, and then it seemed to settle into an equilibrium, emitting only occasional creaks like exasperated grunts. Perhaps these events had not been the strangest it had endured in its long lifespan.

Havelock didn't go to Valérie, though. He set the lantern down upon his worktable—it continued to glow gently, seemingly unchanged from before—and came to my side, pulling me firmly if a little stiffly into his arms, as if he weren't entirely clear on the mechanics. He could not have known why I was crying, and so hard that my body shook, or possibly he'd guessed, but he held me without speaking. We sat there in the sudden dark of his shop—the spiderlight had gone out—until concern for Élise, as well as the outraged yowling of the cats, forced me to my feet with the tears still wet on my face, and back up into the light of the shelter.

CHAPTER 36

"How long do you think we'll have?" Yannick said, folding his arms and squinting nervously at the door, through which the winter light filtered wanly.

"I don't know." I was pacing by the cat cages and made myself stop. "I'm amazed the police have waited this long. Even with the distraction of Valérie's apprentices."

I'd slept little the previous night. Havelock and I had been awake until the small hours of the morning, putting the shelter back in order—him with enchantment, I with a mop, broom, and conciliatory rations of cat food. Despite the late hour, several neighbours had visited, including Rémy, unsurprisingly concerned by the peculiar noises that had shaken the shelter. From them I learned that the police were occupied on the other side of town, chasing magicians as they dashed from street to street, lighting fires and setting off minor explosions. Eventually, Yannick had arrived and confirmed our suspicions: before coming to the shelter, Valérie had ordered several dozen of her apprentices to draw the police's attention, so that she could make her final assault upon Havelock's lair without petty interruptions from the law.

Someone knocked at the door and we all jumped. We stood motionless, eyeing it nervously, but the knock wasn't repeated.

Yannick scrubbed a hand over his face. "I wish we knew where Valérie went," he said.

"She takes after His Majesty, it seems," I said drily. After Havelock had cast Vortigern's enchantment, we'd been required to turn our attention to the shop, ensuring all the fires had been put out and the foundations were secure and in no danger of crumbling from the sheer volume of magic unleashed within the building's walls. Amidst the chaos, Valérie had slipped away with two of her apprentices, perhaps using the same escape route as His Majesty.

"It doesn't matter," Havelock said. He was frowning at nothing in particular, his gaze abstracted. "She isn't a danger anymore."

"We're not certain of that," Yannick said. "I like certainty where your sister is concerned. I would prefer not to be magically blasted into unconsciousness again. I still have a headache."

Havelock had examined Valérie's apprentices, those she had left behind like spent matches, sprawled unconscious on the floor of Havelock's workshop. They were no longer magicians. Or, at least, they no longer possessed the innate power to reach the Rivenwood. Their gift had been drawn out of them by the lantern, just as it had pulled the magic out of every Artefact and spider on the first floor. Not even Havelock understood how Vortigern had woven it—he kept declaring, in increasingly plaintive tones, that such a thing should be impossible—but even I could see that it was true. The apprentices now lacked the characteristic look of a magician—when one held a light to them, it played over their features in a way that was utterly ordinary, not seeking to avoid touching them.

Havelock eventually sent them away, either by magic or by simply dragging them outside and leaving them on a park bench; I didn't see, as I had been too occupied with Élise and the cats.

"That headache is your own fault," Havelock said. "Do you think I gave you that ring with the shield enchantment as a token of my regard? Come here."

Yannick, who had been rubbing his temples, gave a sigh of relief. When he reached Havelock's side, Havelock removed one of his earrings and placed his fingertips against Yannick's head with surprising tenderness and murmured a spell. Yannick's expression was one of relief.

"There," Havelock said. "And the next time one of my enemies tries to fight you, run the other way. You're too new to magic to win any duels."

"No, I'm just too used to duelling *you*," Yannick said, regarding him with exasperation. "You always let me win."

"Shouldn't you stay below?" I said to Havelock. He was perched on the counter again, looking as conspicuous as ever. Havelock's presence had always been like a shout in a quiet room, but now, in addition to his usual otherworldly attire and the shadows he carried everywhere, he flickered slightly when he moved, like firelight, as if he'd absorbed some of the magic from the lantern. I kept worrying he would set something on fire.

He shrugged moodily. "I'm not going to let you get arrested."

"What does that mean?" Yannick said nervously. "I thought we were trying to avoid entanglements with the police."

"It seems a bit late to worry about that," I said. "What *are* you planning?" I didn't want Havelock harming anyone, not even Laurent—whom I was no longer angry with, as he had only been doing his job, as I'd told Élise the previous night. (Élise had expressed her disagreement in colourful terms.)

Havelock scrubbed his hands through his hair and scowled at both of us. "Everyone always expects me to have plans and plots," he said. "All I've ever wanted is to be left alone with my experiments."

Thoreau hopped up beside Havelock, making him start. "What does this one want?" he said, then looked astonished as the old cat unceremoniously laid himself down upon Havelock's lap, as if it were his usual habit at that time of the morning.

"Is this supposed to be part of the charm?" Havelock said. "Being treated like a piece of furniture?"

"It is," I said, trying to suppress my amusement. "You're lucky Banshee has never grasped the concept of jealousy."

Banshee, indeed, was lying on her side against the counter, having followed Havelock there, absorbed in bathing herself, and would only look up if Havelock shifted position, as if having made a resolution to shadow his every move.

"They all seem to take to him," Yannick said to me. "Have you noticed?"

"They're kindred spirits," I said, pretending to be nonchalant, when in fact something about the sight of Havelock grudgingly scratching Thoreau's head filled me with a sparkling sort of pride. "Solitary and cantankerous."

"I take exception to *cantankerous*," Havelock said. "And I see no evidence these creatures are not motivated by a simple desire to torment me as they do the poor spiders."

"Did you truly spend the last three years thinking I was Vortigern?" I asked.

He seemed for a moment like he did not wish to respond, tapping his heel against the counter and pretending to be absorbed by Thoreau. "In truth," he said at last, "I continued to wonder about it for a few days after we met in the shelter. I thought perhaps she was playing some prank on me."

"What!" I cried through my laughter. "A curious prank, to come into your life with a lot of cats."

"Vortigern was at least half mad," Havelock said. "And had a fondness for mischief in her youth. She was a recluse for most of her adult life—she kept to her hovel in the Breton woods, scaring away anyone foolish enough to visit with nasty enchantments, or possibly just her personality, depending on which story you believe. And she kept cats."

"Ah," I said. "Until that last, I was about to ask if *you* are secretly Vortigern."

Yannick let out a snort.

"I eventually assured myself that you were *not* her," Havelock said, "and thus you must have used Vortigern's book to visit me in the past. Which meant, most likely, that I *did* have Vortigern's book somewhere in the shop, proving Valérie correct, which I did not much appreciate. But it was clear you had no memory of having met me before, which meant your need for the lantern, and your visit to the past, had not occurred yet. After I worked that out, I didn't really know what to do. I couldn't fathom why an unassuming cat herder would have need of Vortigern's lantern. I also lack Vortigern's intuition regarding time-walking—the whole thing makes little sense to me. But I have no particular desire to end the world again by unravelling time itself, so it seemed safest not to say anything to you about it. When you were mucking around in my shop, rearranging my Artefacts, I kept expecting you to unearth the book at any moment."

"Mucking around!" I exclaimed. "In order for me to *re-arrange* your Artefacts, they would have needed some particular arrangement before, which they did not have, any more than does a squirrel's acorn hoard."

Yannick was shaking his head. "I should have paid more attention to the oven. The enchantment always felt peculiar. But, well—" His gaze strayed to Havelock. "This is a peculiar place."

Another knock came at the door, hesitant and too quiet, as if the visitor half hoped to be ignored. I realized that it was past nine, and thus past opening, and also that what I had taken for the murmur of the wind was actually the murmur of human voices, which had been gradually growing in volume.

"What now?" I said despairingly. I found it hard to believe the police would bother knocking if they had what they needed to bring the full weight of the law down upon us, but that didn't mean we were not about to be beset by some new peril. I cracked the door, and then let it swing open, too astonished to do anything but stare.

A crowd had gathered on the sidewalk beyond the shelter. Not only the sidewalk; there were enough of them to spill out into the street, requiring the carriages to pass single file to get through. When the people standing nearest saw me, they cheered. Others turned at that, and suddenly the entire crowd was cheering and applauding. An older man bundled into several layers of scarves came up to me and shook my hand. "There she is!" he said warmly. "Don't you worry, Agnes—we won't let them through!"

"I—thank you," I said, not having the slightest idea what I was thanking him for, nor how he'd come to know my name. Was there another story in the *Gazette*? Some fawning biography of me or the shelter? A few in the crowd called out to me—"How are the cats?" and "Any left? I have a bad knee," which was followed by general laughter.

Many of the people milling about were carrying signs. *Les Amis des Amis des Chats*, some read. Others seemed to be opposing the bylaw—the one I was expecting to have brought down upon me at any moment in the form of the police slapping me and Élise in handcuffs and dragging us back to prison.

That brought about a shiver of trepidation. Surely these people wouldn't try to stand in the way when the police came. What if they were hurt?

"Agnes!" Élise was pushing her way through the crowd.

"Let her through! It's her sister!" a woman called—my mind boggled even more—and the crowd parted obligingly.

"Élise," I said, dragging her inside as soon as she reached me, then closing the door firmly behind her. "What the hell is all this?"

She waved a hand, pausing to lean over and rest her hands on her knees. She was breathing hard, as if she'd run all the way, and laughter tugged at the edge of each breath. She'd been gone only a few hours—after Havelock's spell wore off, she'd gone home to Gabriel, who would have worried about her absence. She seemed to have changed her clothes, but a little smudge of soot remained on her cheek.

"They're protesting at city hall, too," she said unevenly. "An even bigger crowd than this. People know the shelter's a target of the new bylaw—Roger Fairwood keeps running stories about it, but even if he didn't, the rumours about our enchanted cats have spread too well."

"But why?" I demanded. "Not that I don't appreciate all this, but what's the point? Didn't the new law pass yesterday?

Laurent seemed certain it would." I'd been far too occupied to check any of the papers.

Élise shook her head. "Laurent clearly has an overly optimistic understanding of municipal politics. The council spent too long arguing about some construction project, and then they couldn't get enough votes in favour of continuing past six o'clock—" She waved her hand, looking equally pleased and exasperated. "You know how these meetings go. They put the vote on the bylaw off until this morning. But now, given that public opinion has shifted, Gabriel thinks they're going to defer it."

"Defer it!" I exclaimed, because I was familiar enough with the workings of city hall, through Gabriel, to understand what *that* meant.

Élise smiled, seeming to read my thoughts. "Exactly. 'For further study and consultation.' It will be six months before it's even brought up again, but with the election coming up—Agnes, they're just going to bury it."

I felt my knees weaken and I caught hold of the windowsill as Élise went on excitedly. "Most of the councillors don't want to touch the issue now that it's become a hot potato, especially since the French papers have started covering our 'mystical' cat shelter—I saw an article on the front page of *La Ville* on my way over here. And Gabriel says the councillor who proposed the bylaw is almost sure to lose his seat—some scandal about accepting free theatre tickets."

"Then—then we're safe," I said. I was finding it hard to believe. Though the quiet murmur of conversation in the street outside paired with occasional cheers of support were comforting beyond words, it was difficult to accept that Laurent would not at any moment come knocking on the door with half the police department in tow.

"I think we are. So you can stop shaking, dear." Élise pulled me into her arms. When she drew back, she shot Havelock a glare. "Provided *this* one doesn't start any more magical wars."

Havelock looked exasperated. "As I keep saying, not that anyone is listening to me, I have no interest in wars, intrigues, plots, machinations, et cetera. If only people would leave me alone, none of this would have happened."

Élise gave a snort of laughter, though I could see she was too exultant to make more than a half-hearted attempt at her usual antagonism towards Havelock. "And I'm going to believe you are the innocent victim in all this?"

"No, you're going to believe I feast upon the hearts of infants and sleep beneath a blanket of kitten hides, like you always have."

"I almost wish you did," Élise said. "Agnes would have stabbed you to death a long time ago. Also, you look like you're about to spontaneously combust. Agnes, should he be so close to the filing cabinets when he's like that?"

Yannick, who had been quiet through all this, his hands pressed into his hair as if attempting to physically contain his astonishment, said, "I don't understand. Didn't everyone see Havelock fighting Valérie outside this very shop? Surely the public knows there's some connection—why are they supporting us?"

Élise rolled her eyes. "I was hoping you weren't going to mention that. Didn't you read the signs?"

She drew one of the curtains back, and we crowded around the window. I had not been paying the signs too much attention before, but now I examined them more carefully, my mouth falling open.

Havelock Renard is not the enemy, read one. Another: *Have-*

lock saved my daughter's life. And: *Magicians are part of our community, too.*

My initial impression hadn't been wrong—most of the signs were about the cat shelter or opposing the bylaw. But there were far more signs expressing favourable sentiments towards Havelock than I would have anticipated, that number being zero.

"Havelock," I called faintly, but he had already come to stand behind me at the window. He made an inarticulate sound of dismay and turned away to begin pacing from one end of the shelter to another.

"How did this happen?" Yannick said. He looked nearly as disturbed as Havelock did. "Did Roger Fairwood—"

"It wasn't the *Gazette*," Élise said. "Or not *only* them. Haven't you noticed that the papers have spent the past week talking about that battle between Havelock and Valérie's apprentices? Initially the reports said that Havelock was equally to blame, that it was another irresponsible street duel that got out of hand. No one was even mentioning the shelter. But more eyewitnesses have come forward, all saying that Havelock wasn't trying to duel Valérie, he was trying to stop her from tearing the shelter apart—and not only that, but he also used his magic to protect the crowd from Valérie's apprentices."

I gave a short laugh. "I don't recall that part. Though I suppose—" I thought it over. "I suppose you could interpret things that way. Those magicians were causing chaos, with no thought to bystanders, and Havelock *did* stop them."

"Do they know this is his shop?" Yannick demanded.

Élise shook her head. "I don't think so, though some may suspect it. The story I saw this morning in *La Ville* speculated that he lives in the neighbourhood and stepped in to stop

Valérie out of samaritanism. The paper ventured no explanation for *why* Valérie attacked us, but seemed to imply we are not only trading in enchanted cats, but Artefacts too."

I groaned. "Naturally. That's what their police sources would have told them."

Havelock hadn't been listening to us. "No," he said. "I—no. I refuse to be part of a *neighbourhood*. I will never be left alone. There will be people demanding not just charmed cats, but horses and umbrellas and all sorts of silly things. This is not some magical tinker's shop."

Élise looked up, her jubilation becoming a malicious sort of glee. "That's right, they *won't* leave you alone if they find out you are not the fearsome variety of villain at all, merely the crabby, antisocial sort, like some old witch who lives alone in the woods, cackling to herself. I would say you owe the world a great deal of enchanted umbrellas, Havelock Renard."

He only rolled his eyes at her characterization, but then the import of her words seemed to sink in, and he looked ill. "It won't be hard to make them afraid of me again," he said. "I'll just unleash a few illusions on the city. Dragons, wolves, perhaps a chimera or two—"

"You will not!" I cried. "This is all so ridiculous—Havelock, what you *should* do is shut yourself away in your workshop again and never come out. Pretend you aren't here, like you did before. Let these people think the rumours of you are just that—rumours."

He looked so relieved I briefly wondered if he would kiss me again, and an unexpected warmth climbed up my neck. "That's a much better idea," he said.

I had my eye on the clock. "Given that I'm not, at present, in danger of being arrested, we might as well open the shop for the day."

Yannick pressed his hands to his head again, his expression so transparently despairing that I almost laughed. I felt a great deal like laughing all of a sudden. "Agnes, we can't *open*," he said. "What are we going to say to these people if they ask about Havelock? What about the rest of Valérie's apprentices? They weren't all blasted by that lantern. We have to resolve all this before—"

"We can resolve it later," I said, holding my hands up. "Right now, we have cats needing homes, and donations to collect." I found my relief giving way to a jittery, triumphant sort of determination. "Something tells me we won't fall short of donations today."

CHAPTER 37

I paused to give Séraphine one final pet before lifting her into the cardboard box. Her paws windmilled but she gave only a token cry of protest before settling into the scarf-blanket. I once again wondered if cats couldn't sense when their fortunes had changed for the better, even if they resented the accompanying disruption. Poor Séraphine, a remarkably quiet Siamese, had lost her guardian the previous week and been left in our care by the old woman's daughter, who could not keep her.

"There you are," I said, handing her off to her new caretaker, a soft-spoken conductor with greying hair and a grim look. "I would recommend indulging her at first, even if she misbehaves. She's suffered a loss, which cats do not forget as easily as people think."

"I know a bit about that," the man said, then fell silent. I pressed his hand briefly, and finished up the paperwork for him. We had already completed our interview and I was confident that Séraphine would be happy in her new home.

After the man left with the box tucked under his large arm, looking less nervous than when he'd come in, I flipped the sign and locked the door.

The shop was warmly lit by both fire and lamps, and the faintest scent of baking still hung in the air—the enchantment seemed to have sunk deep into the stones of the oven, and still reliably turned back time each midnight. Only two pairs of eyes gazed at me: those of Simone, a small grey tabby, and Mme. Annette, a matronly calico, both only a few days in our care. We had restocked both shelters twice in the fortnight since Valérie's attack, and had even accumulated a waiting list. Our donations had also shown no sign of decreasing, and we were making plans with Dr. Para and half a dozen other vets to have as many feral cats trapped and neutered as possible over the next several months. I was optimistic that we could halve the city's stray cat population within the next two years, and if things continued as they were, that would be only the beginning.

"I'll head out, then," Mina said, emerging from the back room, where she'd been writing up a supply order. "Unless you need anything?"

"We'll be fine. Enjoy your evening," I told her. "Studying?"

"Studying," she agreed with a sigh, though she returned my smile. We'd been able to increase Mina's wages and she was no longer behind on her tuition payments. She'd also moved to a new apartment, one closer to school and the shelter, and far more comfortable than her previous cramped accommodations.

She pulled on her coat and headed out. I paused to pet Thoreau, who was napping by the fire. Banshee, I assumed, was downstairs with Havelock. This had become her habit whenever Havelock was in his workshop, which hadn't been often these past two weeks; he had been occupied with tracking down Valérie's remaining followers. Whether it was to destroy their Artefacts and discourage future attacks upon himself or simply to seek revenge, I wasn't clear—given the charity's newfound popularity, I'd had little time for the intrigues of magicians.

Ambulance, meanwhile, had found a home—with Laurent.

He'd come to apologize the day after Valérie's attack, and though Élise had been disinclined to let him through the door, I had been pleased to have the opportunity to officially forgive him, and had accepted his apology warmly, ignoring Élise's ferocious glare from across the room. She would say later that Laurent had taken advantage of my generosity, as others had done before, but as I was often reminding her, I would rather be taken advantage of now and again than go through life seeing monsters everywhere.

Laurent had seemed relieved by my reaction, and I could tell that his conscience had not been easy since our last encounter. It was only when he had asked if he could do anything else to make amends that I had felt my gaze slide to little Ambulance.

Did it give me some fleeting satisfaction to contemplate the broken cups and vases, not to mention hours of lost sleep, that Laurent would have to contend with in the coming weeks? I will not deny it. However, I would not have given Ambulance over to Laurent if I did not think the match a good one. Laurent's guilty conscience, I suspected, would be a strong motivator for him to make a proper house cat out of Ambulance, who had seemed intimidated by Laurent's cool confidence in handling him. The cat needed boundaries.

We'd spent the past few days in peace, more or less; the newspapers had at last stopped reporting on our doings and printing endless speculation about Havelock's whereabouts, and had moved on to the next story. It helped that Havelock had made himself scarce, as I'd asked, admitting not even magician visitors to his workshop. Our foot traffic had yet to lessen, and I was beginning to make plans to open another shelter on the north side of the city. Élise joked that we would soon run out of cats to house, which was not a fantasy I would allow myself to entertain yet, though as the days passed with cats being adopted almost as soon as they arrived and donations pouring in, it seemed less and less improbable.

As for Havelock, on the few occasions I'd seen him, I'd had the sense that he was on the verge of saying something to me—something meaningful, not another wry remark—but each time I'd given him the chance, usually with a warm, encouraging look, he'd made some excuse and disappeared, once literally. I was beginning to think I'd imagined that there was anything connecting us beyond the banality of landlord and tenant.

I went to the back room and lifted the trapdoor. "Havelock?" I called. I wasn't certain what exactly I wanted him for, only I preferred to know where he was, out of some desire to fix him to the tangible world, I think. He still ate and slept but rarely, and vanished mysteriously with such frequency that he often seemed to exist merely as a lurking presence, or perhaps a sentient shadow, and I wished to change that.

I went down to the first floor, where I found his worktable cluttered and abandoned. I wondered if he'd gone to speak to Yannick, who was over at the other shelter, filling in for one of our volunteers. Yannick had taken a shine to our charges and had even worked out how to embed a wellness spell in a cat's claws, which was longer-lasting than spells attached to the cats themselves. We didn't enchant the cats often these days—just one or two, here and there, to ensure the rumours kept circulating.

"Havelock?" I called again. My voice seemed to dissolve

against the cabinets full of Artefacts, gleaming in the spiderlight—for of course Havelock had recast the enchantment on the poor spiders. The first floor of the basement was still filled with cabinets of beautiful antiquities, but it was a desert from a magical perspective; not one Artefact had retained its enchantment after Havelock had unleashed the magic in Vortigern's lantern. As much as Havelock had moaned about it, he still had plenty of Artefacts to continue his experiments, as the other floors had been unaffected.

There came a low rumbling sound I knew well, and I followed it around the side of Havelock's worktable to find Banshee curled up on his chair, blinking sleepily at me.

"Well!" I said, giving her nose a teasing tap. "And what would the Witch King think of this? Don't tell me—he scowled, and insulted you in some witty fashion, then pretended that he didn't need the chair after all?"

Banshee gave a contented stretch. She looked about, then gave a huff and hopped to the floor.

"He's downstairs, is he?" I said, and could not help smiling as Banshee continued to stalk forward as if determined to give Havelock a dreadful lecture for sneaking off without her knowledge. But then Banshee had often seemed to view Robin and me as if we were troublemaking wards she must watch over, rather than the reverse, which she seemed now to have extended to Havelock.

Banshee's reaction to His Majesty's departure had been difficult to gauge—I had assumed she would appreciate it; His Majesty might have excepted Banshee from his bullying, but he had rarely been kind to her. Yet at times I had the sense that she was looking over her shoulder for someone, and she seemed small and forlorn resting on the armchair she had been wont to share with the larger cat. She had taken to Cataclysm instantly—that was what we had named the black kitten, whom I hadn't put up for adoption, given Banshee's affection for her. I wondered if the other cat, having been plucked from her own time by enchantment, bore some lingering scent of magic enticing to Banshee's danger-loving nose. They now spent much of their time curled up together by the oven.

There had been one clear beneficiary of His Majesty's departure: Thoreau.

With the old cat now safe from His Majesty's vicious brand of bullying, I had officially adopted him. Not that he didn't have other suitors; given the newfound popularity of Les Amis des Chats, even our older or more difficult cases were often spoken for within days, but I'd found that, once the prospect was actually before me, it was too difficult to contemplate parting with him.

I had seen His Majesty—and Valerie—again, purely by chance. Valérie had been emerging from a hotel only a few blocks away, her hood drawn up to hide her face. I would have thought she would flee Montréal as soon as possible, but according to Yannick, she'd been lurking around the shelter for days, clearly hoping to cross paths with Havelock without having to actually beg him for an audience, either out of fear or pride. Yannick thought she would try to convince Havelock to undo Vortigern's enchantment, but I wondered if it wasn't a guilty conscience where her brother was concerned, or *some* sentiment at least, that had kept her in the city.

His Majesty had been sprawled over Valérie's shoulder, her hand supporting his rear end and his front paws dangling, looking as happy as if he had been presented with a dish of raw sparrows. What he saw in Valérie, I doubt I will ever know, or perhaps he simply enjoyed her habit of carrying him about with her like an emperor on a litter. But I had known, in that moment, that I could not take him from her.

I would have gone home that instant and cried myself sick, but the wind had blown Valérie's hood back a little, and I caught a glimpse of her face. She was looking at His Majesty, perhaps to check his balance, and in her eyes I saw exasperation mixed with affection, characteristic of every cat owner I knew. The warmth in it made me start, and even if it lasted only a heartbeat before she turned to the waiting car, her usual marble serenity settling over her once more, I could not stop thinking about it.

I followed Banshee down to the fourth floor of the basement, where the greatest convocation of spiders always gathered, making the place feel almost like full day, and there I found Havelock on his knees, rummaging through a chest, having swept the hem of his cloak around him to use as a kneepad. It was one of his odder ones, shabby and grey but with unexpected flounces, exactly the style I pictured on a travelling magician in the Renaissance.

"Did you not hear me calling you?" I demanded. "Have you been down here with the spiders all day?"

Havelock blinked at me, then glanced around at the spiders as if noticing them for the first time. "I must hold court with my subjects sometimes, mustn't I?"

"Come upstairs," I said. "I already know you haven't eaten. Rémy brought us a quiche."

"One moment." He held up one ringed hand and stood, seeming to forget all about whatever he had been looking for in the chest. "I finished work on them today. I was going to wait until you went out, so as to surprise you when you returned. But knowing you, you'll be here till midnight cleaning cages, then up at dawn to do your accounts over again, and not give me another opportunity."

"Finished work on what?" I said. "Also, my accounts never need doing over, as I do them correctly the first time."

He only held up his hand again, then he sifted through his pocket, unearthing a piece of string, then a crystal, then a compass, a pinecone, and a handful of pearls. These he picked through until he found the largest one, then rummaged about in his other pocket until he came out with a beautiful yellow feather that looked distinctly tropical. He held them in either hand and muttered incantations over them, and the air filled with the smell of magic. Then the building gave a gentle rumble.

"What was *that*?" I cried, grabbing at the nearest cabinet. "Please tell me you haven't moved the shop again."

"Not exactly," he said, looking infuriatingly pleased with himself. He seized my hand and dragged me towards the stairs with an almost boyish enthusiasm.

"Not *exactly*," I said with a sigh, though I allowed myself to be dragged. His hand was warm against mine, and more solid than it often felt, and Banshee trotted happily alongside us, as if approving of this turn of events. "It's the sort of thing you can only be exact about. Either the shop is in one place, or it's in another."

He did not enlighten me, only turned to give me one of his mysterious half-smiles, which didn't fool me for one moment—he was evidently nervous, which only made *me* more nervous in turn. Halfway up the main staircase to the shelter was when I began to hear it: a melodious cacophony that could only be one thing.

"Birds!" I exclaimed. "Havelock, what have you done?"

But he would make no reply, not even a sarcastic one, and I let go of his hand and hurried into the front room of the shelter ahead of him.

Immediately I let out a shriek as something skimmed past above me—I heard the whir of small wings, and turned to find myself face-to-face with a hummingbird as vivid as a fistful of jewels, who hovered for a moment before darting up into the cavern of the ceiling. There, several dozen perches had sprouted, atop which rested birds of all description, but mainly of a bright-feathered, tropical variety, nothing like what might be found in our northerly latitude. They darted to and fro, squawking and calling to one another, sometimes even descending to the shelter to alight upon a windowsill or piece of furniture.

The shelter cats gazed upwards in awestruck silence, as if receiving a vision from the heavens, while Cataclysm darted back and forth, seeming to believe herself in hot pursuit of any bird who strayed within twenty feet of the ground. Even Thoreau had deemed the event more interesting than his fireside nap, and had hopped up onto the counter to gain the advantage of height, looking more spry than he had in years. Banshee, meanwhile, crouched low to the ground and let out the first sound I had ever heard her emit apart from purrs: an eerie chitter like the mechanical stutter of a sewing machine.

"What do you think?" Havelock said. "I thought they might appreciate some variety in their days, particularly the shelter cats, even if it is only an illusion. Everyone needs a purpose in life, and why should they be any different?"

I couldn't begin to think of a suitable response. One of the birds passed low over my head, and I ducked again, though I felt no breeze from its wings. There came another burst of song from above, and several yellow and green feathers drifted towards the floor. We might have been standing in some lord's aviary.

"But," I began, half laughing as I spoke. I felt eight years old again, all astonished delight at some circus act or clever street performer. "But people will—"

"The enchantment will only take hold at dawn and twilight," Havelock said. "I took inspiration from the oven. But you can send it away with a word."

He spoke the incantation. *Oro liada* is what it sounded like to me, which Havelock deemed "close enough."

"What will you do with yourself," Havelock said in a musing tone, gazing at the rows of empty cages, "if you run out of cats to rescue?"

I pretended to think it over. "I might try my hand at taming dark magicians. I understand there's quite a need for it, and it's not as if anyone else wants the job."

"If I meet any, I'll warn them. They would need a strong tolerance for cat hair and didactic speeches. You wouldn't want to waste your time with the truly wicked ones, anyway."

"I don't think you're wicked," I said.

"Only because you don't think anyone is."

In fact, my opinion of Havelock's character was no longer a minority one, at least locally. Since he'd defeated Valérie in the street that snowy day, a wild rumour had spread through the city—not believed by all, but enough that it was difficult to imagine it not travelling to other places. Specifically, that Havelock had not, in fact, been the magician who caused the apocalypse—it had been Valérie, and Havelock had stopped her.

Local pride, it seemed, had something to do with the rumour's rapid spread. The fact that the world's most powerful magician had been living in the city for some time, not Paris or New York, as previously supposed—a detail revealed by the *Daily Gazette,* citing anonymous police sources—was the subject of much chatter. While some were surprised by his choice of residence, they hid it well, expressing instead their astonishment that they had not guessed it before. Given the city's character, not to mention antiquity—which must, everyone agreed, provide an ideal ambience for the practice of magic—it was likely that many notorious magicians had made it their home in secret, and overall, the revelation was an opportunity for taking stock of the city's advantages, and the wisdom of those who dwelt there. The fact that Havelock had lived unobtrusively, without bothering anyone in the neighbourhood, was taken as a sign of his respect for the citizenry, and another mark in his favour. In general, there was a great appetite for rumours of the hidden beneficence of Havelock Renard.

"I have something else to show you," he said.

"But you have given me a gift already," I protested.

"That's for *them,*" he said. "I wondered if you would accept a gift for yourself if I didn't think of them first, as you are always doing."

"I didn't mean the birds—" I couldn't continue. I had told him about Robin, or at least started to; I could never get out more than a sentence or two before coming apart.

"It's *I* who should be thanking *you,*" I finally finished, gazing at him earnestly.

"For being dragged into my quarrels and nearly killed—yes, I've been expecting flowers for days," he said, looking away with a hint of desperation and pretending not to understand my meaning. Despite my emotion, I felt a laugh rise within me. Havelock seemed to have no more idea of what to do with gratitude than he did with cats.

"Let me show you what I came up with," he said. "Though you may despise it or deem it morally objectionable in some way, in which case I've no doubt you'll educate me at length."

He led me towards the stairs—not the ones leading to his workshop, but to the upper floor. I followed as if in a dream, still rather overwhelmed—and, if I'm honest, on the edge of tears from the look of delight on Banshee's face.

He paused in the hallway and reached for the attic cord. The narrow staircase descended and he took my hand again—this time for balance; the attic stairs were rickety.

I grew nervous, wondering what strange magics he might have stored up here. But I let my breath out when I reached the top.

"It's still our attic," I said, suppressing a sneeze as I looked around. I'd only ventured up here once or twice to store extra boxes of cat supplies, and it looked as it had on my last visit: a jumble of boxes, mostly of scarves—the former shop owner had stored her damaged or inferior product up here.

"Yes," he said, motioning me over to the window. "Only it isn't above the shelter anymore."

I was beginning to feel dizzy. "Havelock."

"Agnes," he said, and I couldn't help smiling at the excitement in his eyes. I went to stand by his side. The window was unchanged, but beyond it—

My hand squeezed the windowsill as the breath went out of me.

The familiar skyline of Montréal was gone, its innumerable church steeples and stained glass, as was the violet twilight and drifts of snow. In its place was a starlit night and a sprawling city, laid out before me like a child's model. I recognized it instantly, though I'd seen it only in artists' sketches: the narrow, winding streets of the medieval understory; the wider boulevards and squares lined with trees, their dark branches like jumbled scrawls of ink; the Seine carving its way through the streets, black splashed with gold from the streetlamps; and in the distance, the proud domes of the Sacré-Cœur.

"Another illusion," I murmured.

"No," Havelock said, looking slightly offended. He turned the handle on the window and pushed it open, and the wind brought it to me: the smell of another world. To me, anyhow.

"You said you hadn't moved the shop," I said plaintively. The dizziness was intensifying.

"I didn't," Havelock said, his expression growing animated. "Just the attic. Which proved nearly as tricky as moving the entire shop—you wouldn't think so, but it's a matter of lining things up. The six-layer portal spell turned out to be the easy part; I then had to stitch it with two seven-layer binding spells, one to hold the shop in place in Montréal, the other to affix the attic to its new location in the 17th arrondissement. If I hadn't done that, one or the other would have fallen apart or wandered off somewhere, and *that* isn't an easy fix, even for me. I needed magic from deep in the Third Fathom—"

I let his speech wash over me as I gazed out the window; it didn't last as long as I'd expected. I looked back to find him regarding me with an inscrutable expression, seeming more in shadow than he had a moment ago, his otherworldly self settling over him like a veil.

"The attic is in Paris. But how—" I stared at the open trapdoor, with the Montréal apartment clearly visible below. "How does one *get* there?"

He gestured to the window overlooking the glittering city. "There's a fire escape. I've tried it already; it's quite safe."

"Where did you get the idea for this?" I said. "One of your novels?"

A crack appeared in his veneer of confidence, and I realized how thin it was. He said, a little sheepishly, "Most of my ideas for spells come from my novels."

I began to smile. "That must make the work more engaging," I said. "And how convenient, to have a ready supply of inspiration in the form of your library."

"It is," he said, and told me about the book he'd taken this idea from, growing more animated as he spoke of this impossible unravelling of the rules that shaped the world. I wanted to ask if he could put my bedroom in the Alps, to give me fresh air and a fine view each morning, but stopped myself—he might actually do it.

"But what is all this about?" I said when he was finished, folding my arms. "These extravagant gifts. Do they mark some occasion?"

It was as if all the magic in him went out, and he just stood there, gazing at me uncertainly. "I felt the need to apologize," he began, then floundered.

"You know," I said, "you could have simply asked me to coffee. It would have spared you a great deal of effort."

He flushed. "The attic was merely— I wouldn't presume, given everything—"

I decided to take pity on him. Havelock Renard might have created a spell to end the world, roamed the deepest fathoms of a fearsome otherworld, and defeated a dark magician in a blaze of magic, but I had seen no evidence that, in all his life, he'd asked a single person to coffee, or anything else for that matter.

"You're right," I said, suppressing a smile; of course I'd not intuited any meaning from his confused spluttering. "Paris has its share of cafés, doesn't it? Restaurants too, I hear. The question is: Can you show your face in any of them?"

My dry tone seemed to steady him. "I can certainly show *a* face."

"No," I said, holding my hands up. "No disguises. Please."

"Why?"

"Because it's *horrible*," I said. "I will never get used to you changing your features the way normal people change clothes. I'm sure you can come up with something else." Besides, I quite liked his face the way it was, but I wasn't about to say that; he might disappear again.

He seemed to consider. "One of the cafés in Montmartre is owned by a magician. We're not the best of friends, but she owes me a favour. We can visit after closing."

"That sounds lovely," I said.

A genuine smile flashed across his face, chasing the sardonic glint from his eye, and for a moment I hardly recognized him. "I'll speak with her now. You can follow in a few minutes, or I can return for you."

Now it was my turn to splutter. "I— *Now?* I didn't—"

But he was already pushing the window back and clambering onto the narrow balcony beyond, and then he was gone, the sound of his boots stomping down the ladder rungs fading into the night.

I looked at the stairs leading to the shelter. I hadn't finished my evening checklist—the cats had been fed, yes, but Havelock's joke had hit the mark—I wanted to clean several of the empty cages in preparation for new arrivals from Longueuil's shelter, and also put the monthly receipts in order. We had volunteers who could do both tasks, it was true—in fact, there had been days recently when Élise and I had more volunteers than we knew what to do with. It would have been more sensible to remain than to follow Havelock, whose spell no doubt carried with it significant danger, not to mention that it was simply irresponsible to be transporting attics halfway around the world.

But perhaps I was tired of being sensible.

Banshee had followed me into the attic, trailed by Cataclysm. I put my hand out, but both were too occupied with cat business, sniffing every shadowy nook for threats or delicacies, ideally in the form of mice, and neither attended to me at all.

I turned back to the window, squaring my shoulders and trying to calm the thundering of my heart. I stepped over the window ledge, and then I lowered myself onto the uppermost rung of the ladder, taking my first step into a new city.

ABOUT THE AUTHOR

Heather Fawcett is the *New York Times* bestselling author of the Emily Wilde series, as well as a number of books for children and young adults, including *Ember and the Ice Dragons, The Grace of Wild Things,* and *A Galaxy of Whales.* She has a master's degree in English literature and a bachelor's in archaeology. She lives on Vancouver Island.

Heatherfawcett.com
Instagram: @heather_fawcett
Substack: heatherfawcett.substack.com

Find out more about Heather Fawcett and other Orbit authors by registering for the free monthly newsletter at orbit-books.co.uk.

RAISING READERS
Books Build Bright Futures

Dear Reader,

We'd love your attention for one more page to tell you about the crisis in children's reading, and what we can all do.

Studies have shown that reading for fun is the **single biggest predictor of a child's future life chances** – more than family circumstance, parents' educational background or income. It improves academic results, mental health, wealth, communication skills, ambition and happiness.[1]

The number of children reading for fun is in rapid decline. Young people have a lot of competition for their time. In 2024, 1 in 10 children and young people in the UK aged 5 to 18 did not own a single book at home.[2]

Hachette works extensively with schools, libraries and literacy charities, but here are some ways we can all raise more readers:

- Reading to children for just 10 minutes a day makes a difference
- Don't give up if children aren't regular readers – there will be books for them!
- Visit bookshops and libraries to get recommendations
- Encourage them to listen to audiobooks
- Support school libraries
- Give books as gifts

There's a lot more information about how to encourage children to read on our website: **www.RaisingReaders.co.uk**

Thank you for reading.

---

[1] OECD, '21st-Century Readers: Developing Literacy Skills in a Digital World', 2021, https://www.oecd.org/en/publications/21st-century-readers_a83d84cb-en.html

[2] National Literacy Trust, 'Book Ownership in 2024', November 2024, https://literacytrust.org.uk/research-services/research-reports/book-ownership-in-2024